UGLY AF

by
Phil M. Williams

Printed in the United States of America.
First Printing, 2024.
Phil W Books.
www.PhilWBooks.com

ISBN: 978-1-962396-07-3
Print Edition

A Note from Phil

Dear Reader,

If you're interested in receiving two of my popular thriller novels for free and/or reading many of my other titles for free or discounted, go to the following link: http://www.PhilWBooks.com.

You're probably thinking, *What's the catch?* There is no catch.

Sincerely,
Phil M. Williams

PART I

The Early Years

Sixty percent of poor children in the US live in families headed by single mothers.

—National Women's Law Center, 2020

CHAPTER 1

The Golden Arches

Curtis sat on the leather couch, gaping at the big-screen television. He imagined himself in Bikini Bottom with SpongeBob SquarePants. His new front teeth jutted forward, making it difficult to close his mouth.

The baldheaded stranger had said, "That boy got some buck teeth."

Audible moans and mattress squeaks came from his mother's bedroom, despite the loud television.

Curtis pretended he was best friends with SpongeBob. He imagined catching jellyfish and eating burgers and fries at the Krusty Krab. His stomach rumbled, remembering his mother's promise to take him to McDonald's for dinner. He padded to the kitchen, stood on the step stool, and accessed the treat cabinet. It was filled with Tastykakes, Pop-Tarts, Oreo cookies, Doritos, Pringles, and various sugary cereals. He grabbed three Oreo cookies and returned to the couch.

The bedroom door opened, and the old man exited, his bald head shiny from perspiration. The man grinned at Curtis's mother and handed her cash. "Damn, baby. You know what you're doin'."

Sara took the cash. "I aim to please."

Curtis hugged his knees to his chest and stared at the pair.

The old man smacked Sara on the butt. "I love that ass."

She giggled.

The old man winked at Sara, then left the apartment.

Sara slipped the cash into the front pocket of her cutoff jean shorts and addressed her eight-year-old. "Are you spoiling your dinner with cookies?"

"No," Curtis replied with his mouthful.

★★★

They descended two flights of stairs and left their three-story apartment building. Curtis wore shorts and his Washington Redskins jersey. The jersey was too big, hanging low like a dress, but it was a real jersey, just like the NFL players wore. He wore number 26, Portis written on the back.

On the way out of their apartment building, a man held the door for them and said, "Lookin' good, Sara."

"Thanks, Lionel," she replied.

Lionel turned his attention to Curtis. "You gonna play for the 'Skins, big man?"

Curtis grinned. "Yeah."

Lionel held out his hand. "My man. Gimme five."

Curtis slapped Lionel's hand with all his might.

The sun was orange and low on the horizon. It was humid, the air sticky, but Sara held Curtis's hand as they walked away from the apartment building toward McDonald's. Curtis wondered what it would be like to play for the 'Skins. He imagined running on green grass, a football tucked into the crook of his arm, his teammates congratulating him after scoring a touchdown. He figured if he became a Washington Redskin, all his teammates would automatically become his friends.

Curtis and his mother hiked on a dilapidated sidewalk, past other apartment buildings in Alexandria, Virginia. Cars and trucks tooled past, their motors buzzing in the background, leaving the acrid smell of exhaust. A street performer played the acoustic guitar, singing a Bob Marley tune. His drum case was open, seeded with dollar bills to encourage donations. Curtis tugged at his mother's arm, wanting to run in his new Air Jordans, but Sara held him back.

"No running, baby. I don't want you to get hit by a car."

Beyond the street performer, three smoking men leered at them as they approached. Sara switched sides with Curtis, shielding him from the men.

One of the men said, "*Damn, girl.* Holla at your boy."

One of the other men flicked the butt of his cigarette and said, "I'd hit that."

Sara gripped Curtis's hand and gazed straight ahead, as they trod past.

Beyond the apartments, Sara pressed the button for the crosswalk. They waited for the cars and trucks. They continued past the check-cashing place, the pawn shop, the liquor store, and the gas station.

Curtis salivated when he saw the golden arches. He grinned at his mother. "Can I get a cheeseburger and fries?"

She smiled back. "Of course, baby."

"I want a double quarter-pounder with cheese. I bet I could eat the whole thing."

"Whatever you want, baby."

They entered McDonald's, and the smell of fries and burgers made Curtis's stomach growl. Sara ordered two value meals—quarter-pounders, fries, and sodas. Sara paid with a one-hundred-dollar bill. She grabbed a large handful of ketchup packets, then carried the tray to a lonely corner, strategically away from the loud teenagers. Curtis practically inhaled his burger and fries. He was always hungry, despite the plethora of food available at home.

A group of teen boys crowded into a nearby table. They joked and ate and tossed fries at each other. Sara watched them from the corner of her eye.

One of the boys said, "She fine."

Another boy asked, "What the fuck is that?"

The first boy replied, "What the fuck are you talkin' about?"

The boy pointed at Curtis. "Little man over there. Next to that fine white bitch. I can't tell what he is."

One of the other boys said, "That boy's so ugly, when his mama breastfed him, she closed her eyes and thought about other babies."

The entire table burst into laughter.

Sara stood from the table and began packing the food into the brown McDonald's bag.

Curtis furrowed his brow. "I'm not done."

"We'll finish eating at home," she replied, wrapping the remnants of Curtis's burger in the wax paper.

The teens laughed, as Sara led Curtis outside, while he sipped his Coke. Walking back toward their apartment, Curtis thought about the teens in McDonald's. He knew they had been talking about him. Ironically, Curtis had many of the same traits as his beautiful mother, but people had never viewed him as handsome or even cute, which every little kid could achieve.

The spattering of freckles under Sara's eyes made her appear youthful, but Curtis's freckles dotted his face like dirt. He even had freckles on his lips. Her blue eyes were big and bright. His were small and beady. Her red hair was wavy and hung to the middle of her back. His was in tight curls and cut short. Her facial features were small and cute, whereas Curtis had a wide nose, wide-set eyes, and big lips. Sara had big lips too, but hers were somehow pretty, and his weren't. Sara had milky-white skin that appeared ethereal. Curtis often thought of his mother as an angel. His skin was just as white, but somehow it was wrong.

One of his mother's *friends* had once asked, "Is your boy black or white?"

Curtis knew the answer. He was neither.

Back in their apartment building, they trudged upstairs to their top-floor apartment. Curtis slurped the icy remnants of his Coke through his straw, as his mother turned the dead bolt with her key.

They entered their apartment. Derek lounged on their couch, watching a college football game. He didn't live with them but had a key to their apartment and slept over sometimes. Derek stood from the couch and eyed the McDonald's bag.

Sara let go of Curtis's hand and sauntered to Derek. "Hey, baby."

Derek smacked the McDonald's bag from her hand, tearing the bag in one swipe and spilling fries and ketchup on the dingy carpet. "Where's my fuckin' money?"

Curtis gaped at them, his eyes wide open.

"I got it right here." Sara reached into her pocket and handed the bills to him.

Derek towered over Sara. The dark-skinned man was built like the men playing football on their television. His baggy clothes made him appear bulkier than he was. He wore several thick gold chains and diamond stud earrings. Derek grabbed Sara by the upper arms and pulled her in close. "The money comes to me first. Then I'll give you what you need. You got me?"

Sara nodded, her eyes bulging. "I'm sorry, baby. I forgot."

Derek let go and leered at Sara. "We're gonna do real good together." He reached into his pocket and produced a clear baggie with three small white rocks inside. He placed the bag in Sara's palm. "If you need a pick-me-up."

CHAPTER 2

It's Not All Scooby-Doo and Strawberry Jelly

Curtis sat on the couch, watching Scooby-Doo and Shaggy hide from the ghost in trash cans. He imagined being best friends with Scooby-Doo, feeding him a Scooby snack, and the talking dog licking Curtis in the face.

Angry voices came from his mother's bedroom. The door flung open, smacking against the wall. A muscle-bound man appeared, buckling his belt, followed by Sara.

"I need my money," she said, holding out her hand.

"I don't fuck with rubbers," he replied.

"I have to be safe."

"Not my problem."

"You still have to pay." Her voice was desperate. "You booked the hour."

He smacked her across the face, knocking her to the carpet. "I ain't payin', bitch."

Curtis ran to the man, his hands balled into little fists. The man smacked Curtis, sending him flying backward.

"Don't touch him," Sara shrieked from the floor.

Curtis stood and rushed the man again, his little face beet red and scrunched.

The man palmed Curtis's head and tossed him aside like a rag doll.

"Leave him alone." Sara went to Curtis and wrapped him up in an embrace.

The man pointed at Sara. "You need to get *yo* ugly ass kid under control." He pivoted and left the apartment, slamming the door behind him.

Curtis bawled, while Sara held him and rubbed his back. Eventually Curtis calmed, and Sara led him to the couch. They sat together, Curtis escaping into the Scooby-Doo marathon, Sara touching the cut on her lip with her tongue.

"First day of school tomorrow. Are you excited?" Sara asked.

Curtis kept his gaze on Scooby and Shaggy. "I don't wanna go. The kids are mean."

Sara put her arm around her son and pulled him close. "It'll be better this year. Just be nice."

"That doesn't work." Curtis scooched away from his mother, sitting on the opposite end of the couch.

Sara sighed and stood. "Are you hungry? How about a peanut butter and jelly sandwich?"

Curtis turned to his mother. "Can you put chips inside?"

Sara stepped to Curtis and pecked him on the cheek. "Of course, baby." She padded to the kitchen. "Grape or strawberry jelly?" she called out.

"Strawberry," Curtis called back from the living room.

The dead bolt turned, and Derek entered the apartment. He sauntered to Sara. "How was it?"

Sara chewed on her bottom lip. "He wouldn't pay. He wanted it raw."

Derek grabbed Sara by the throat, squeezing like a python. Her face turned scarlet. She pawed at his muscular arms to no avail.

Curtis raced to the kitchen. "Let go of my mom."

Derek scowled at Curtis, still squeezing Sara's neck. "What you gonna do about it, nigga?"

Curtis ran to Derek and pounded on his lower back with his little fists, but it had no effect.

Derek sneered at Sara. "How many times do I have to tell you to get the money up front?" He let go, and Sara fell to the linoleum in a heap, wheezing for breath.

Curtis rushed to his mother's side, wrapping his arms around her.

Sara sat up and caught her breath, while Curtis latched on to her like an appendage. "I tried to get the money up front. He hit me. You're supposed to protect me."

"I'll get his ass, but I can't be with you all the fuckin' time," Derek said. "Stop bein' so fuckin' stupid."

CHAPTER 3

The Half-Breed

Curtis walked home from school alone, yet surrounded by other walkers from his elementary school. It had been his first day of third grade. He had made it through the entire day without being teased or bullied. He hadn't made any friends and had eaten lunch by himself, but he hadn't been ridiculed either.

"Are you an albino?" a fifth-grade boy asked, as they hiked past an apartment complex, headed for a busy crosswalk.

Curtis kept walking, his gaze straight ahead, emulating his mother.

"Are you deaf?" asked the fifth grader.

"He's a freak," said another fifth grader.

Several kids snickered.

"He got some nice Jordans," said the fifth-grade boy.

Someone shoved Curtis in the back, sending him sprawling onto the sidewalk, his hands breaking his fall. Several boys tugged on his shoes.

"Get the shoes," said one of them.

Curtis turned on his side and kicked at the boys, striking one in the chin. The boy yelped in pain, and Curtis scrambled to his feet and ran. Despite the big orange hand on the crosswalk sign, he sprinted across the street. An SUV slammed on its brakes and honked, but Curtis kept running. He kept running until he made it to his apartment building. Curtis caught his breath, as he climbed the stairs. He removed the key around his neck that was tied to a shoelace, opened the dead bolt, and pushed inside.

His mother's distressed voice came from her bedroom. He shut the door and locked the dead bolt. He removed his Jordans at the door, stepped into the kitchen, and dumped his backpack on the table. Curtis crept to his mother's bedroom and placed his ear to the thin wooden door. It sounded like she was on her cell phone, as Curtis only heard her voice.

"Please, Mom. Curtis needs a stable home. This isn't a good place for him." Sara listened for a few seconds. "I know, Mom. I need to figure things out. Maybe I could go back to school." Sara listened again. "I know I made adult decisions, but none of that is his fault. Curtis shouldn't suffer for my mistakes." She paused for a beat. "He's a sweet little boy. If you got to know him, I'm sure—" She listened for a moment. "That's not very Christian of you at all. I can't imagine Jesus—" She paused for a second. "I'm not trying to manipulate you. I'm stating a fact." She listened again. "*Don't* call him that. He's not a half-breed. He's a beautiful boy. I can't believe you'd say that." She paused. "Now I remember why I left. Curtis will never know someone so hateful. I hope you rot in Hell."

Sara smacked the bedroom door and screamed, startling Curtis. Then she opened the door, holding her cell phone, her face beet red, and her eyes glassy. She forced a smile when she saw Curtis. "Hi, baby. I didn't know you were home. How was your day?"

"It was okay."

She bent down and hugged him tight. She sniffled. "I love you so much."

"I love you too, Mom."

When she let go, she stood, wiped the corners of her eyes, and forced another smile. "How about an after-school snack? I could make ants on a log."

CHAPTER 4

Two Years Later ...

On the first day of fifth grade, Curtis followed the familiar route home from his elementary school, his classmates surrounding him on the sidewalk. Heat reverberated off the nearby street in a haze.

"Hey, Curtis," said one of his male classmates.

Curtis stared straight ahead and walked faster, leaving the crowd of his classmates. A few boys and one popular girl jogged to catch up.

"Where are you goin'?" asked the tall boy.

"Yeah. Where are you goin'?" the sidekick asked.

"Why are you wearin' an old shirt with holes on the first day of school?" the girl asked. "Are you poor?"

They all stopped at the crosswalk. The orange hand was lit, instructing them to wait.

"Those shorts are dirty too," the sidekick said.

"You're so poor that the tooth fairy gave you food stamps," the tall boy said.

They all laughed.

"Look at his teeth. *Eww.*" The girl scrunched her face in disgust. "And you're so skinny."

"Do you even have food?" asked the tall boy.

Curtis saw a break in the traffic, so he bolted across the street.

"Run, Forrest. *Run,*" the girl said in a Southern accent.

Everyone laughed again.

Curtis ran home as he did when he was bothered or sensed danger. He cut through the warm air, pumping his arms and legs, his toes hurting from his too small secondhand shoes. His mother had sold his Jordans last year while he was sleeping. Ironically, classmates and neighborhood kids had tried to steal his shoes many times, but ultimately his mother took them.

He entered his apartment with the key attached to the shoelace around his neck. He locked the door behind him. His mother sat on the couch, slack-jawed, drool coming from the corner of her mouth. The shades were drawn, the sunlight coming in small slivers.

Curtis went to the kitchen, opened the fridge, and removed the only contents—a half loaf of Wonder bread and several ketchup packets. Curtis had stolen the ketchup packets from McDonald's, and he'd purchased the bread for one dollar from the day-old Wonder Bread store. He'd stolen five dollars from his mother while she had been passed out, on the rare occasion she had money.

He grabbed a plastic plate from the cupboard and sat at the metal table. Apart from the dingy couch and the mattress in the bedroom, it was the only furniture left in the apartment. The couch doubled as Curtis's bed. Everything else had been sold for drugs. Curtis squeezed the ketchup out of each packet on to the bread. He was careful to force every bit of ketchup from the packets. He slapped a piece of white bread on top, completing his sandwich. He took a bite, savoring the sugar and carbohydrates.

As much as he hated school, he was ecstatic about the free breakfast and lunch offered to qualified children, like him. It had been a very lean summer, sometimes going days without food. Now he was at least guaranteed ten meals per week. He had spent most of the past summer at the public library, reading, which was the only place he rarely saw kids from the neighborhood. He had also scored food from Dumpsters behind fast-food restaurants and convenience stores, although he eventually had to stop, as that became dangerous. Several managers had threatened to call the police if they saw him again.

After eating his snack, Curtis checked his mother. She was comatose, sitting on the couch, her shoulders slumped, and her chin touching her chest. He placed his hand near her mouth and nose, feeling her breath. A crack pipe and a lighter sat on the carpet near her feet.

Her complexion was blotchy, and her bony body was marred with sores. Her red hair was matted, the ends split, her bangs cut haphazardly, giving her an eighties' style mullet. Her lips were cracked and chapped. He sat next to her and put his arm around her, feeling her protruding spine.

"It was the first day of school. I had a great day. Everyone was really nice to me. I already have a bunch of friends. I think it's gonna be different this year. You don't have to worry about me. You can worry about yourself. You can get better." Tears welled in his eyes. "I love you, Mom."

Her barely audible breathing was her only response.

CHAPTER 5

Worthless

Curtis walked to the public library after school. He read *The Lion, the Witch and the Wardrobe* by C. S. Lewis, until closing time. Then he ran home, like he was Forrest Gump. Curtis climbed the final steps to his apartment. A notice was taped to the door. He felt sick to his stomach as he read it.

EVICTION NOTICE
Date: 9-7-2007
Tenant: Sara Duffy
Address: 1200 Washington Avenue Apartment 302 Alexandria, VA

You are hereby notified that you currently owe $1,121.00 in past-due rent and late charges.

This is a demand for payment. You must pay the full amount owed that is stated in this notice within the next seven days. If you fail to make full payment of the amount due, your right of possession to the apartment will be terminated, and eviction proceedings will begin immediately.

He grabbed the notice, put his key in the dead bolt, and turned the lock.

"Nobody wants to fuck a crack ho," Derek said.

"Please, baby. I can still be sexy," Sara replied.

Curtis entered the apartment. Derek and Sara stood in the spartan living room. No lights were on. *The electricity must be off again.* The blinds beyond them were askew, allowing crooked beams of sunlight inside.

"*Naw.* You're fuckin' worthless. I'm done with you," Derek said.

"*Please.* Give me a chance. I'll do anything," Sara replied.

Curtis stepped to them.

Derek stared at Sara, with one side of his mouth raised in disgust. "You ain't got nothin' I want." He pivoted to walk away.

Sara went to her knees and wrapped her arms around his leg. "Please, Derek. I'm hurting bad. I really need a fix. *Please.* I'll do anything."

Derek let out a heavy breath. He reached into his pocket and removed a plastic bag with a single off-white rock inside. He tossed the baggie toward the corner of the room, and Sara scrambled after it, like a dog chasing after a bone. Derek addressed Curtis. "She's all yours, little man." He walked away.

Sara sat in the corner, heating the rock in her crack pipe with her lighter.

CHAPTER 6

Bastard

Curtis paced in the living room, while his mother still slept on the couch. He thought about what Derek had said. *She's all yours, little man.* But he didn't know what to do with her. He had thought, if he took care of himself and didn't ask her for anything, she'd take care of *herself.* But it didn't seem to matter that he wasn't a burden.

Sara's eyes fluttered and opened. Her blue eyes were sunken and hollow. She moved like she was one hundred years old. She rolled her neck and skinny shoulders. She moved her mouth, as if she tasted something foul. Her teeth were covered in a yellow film.

Curtis stared at his mother, with his hands on his hips.

"What do you want?" Sara snapped.

Curtis removed the eviction notice from his back pocket, unfolded it, and handed it to his mother. She scanned the notice.

"Does this mean they're gonna kick us out?" Curtis asked, thinking of the many times he'd seen neighbors with their belongings in the parking lot.

She crumpled the notice and tossed it on the floor. "It's fine."

"I don't think it is."

"Don't start with me, Curtis. I have a splitting headache."

"You always have a headache."

She staggered to her feet. "I need to get out of here." She took three steps toward the front door, but Curtis blocked her way.

"Don't go. We need help. We can't keep living like this."

Sara glanced around the nearly empty apartment. "You want to go someplace else?"

"Yes."

"Fine. You tell me where to take you."

"I … I don't know. Anywhere but here."

Sara placed her hands on her hips. "Anywhere, *huh?*"

Curtis held out his hands like a beggar. "What about your parents? You said they were rich. Maybe they could help us."

Sara laughed, but she didn't sound happy. "My parents, *huh?* Your grandparents, who you've never met?"

"I wanna meet them."

"Fine." Sara grabbed Curtis by the wrist and dragged him to her bedroom.

Curtis twisted his arm. "Let go."

She let go when they reached her mattress. "We'll ask them together." Sara snatched the prepaid cell phone from the bed, pressed the numbers, and then hit the Speakerphone button. Sara held up the phone between them, the ringing audible.

"Hello?" a woman asked, her voice husky.

"Mom, it's Sara."

The woman sighed. "What do you want?"

"Curtis needs a place to live. Can he come live with you and Dad?" Sara spoke in a monotone, as if she cared little about her mother's answer.

The woman huffed. "I haven't heard from you in two years, and you want me to take care of your half-breed bastard? You made your bed a long time ago. I suggest you lie in it." Sara's mother, Curtis's grandmother, disconnected the call.

Tears slipped down Curtis's cheeks.

Sara glared at her son. "You still want to meet them?"

CHAPTER 7

Baby Mama Drama

Sara fast-walked on the cracked sidewalk, Curtis right behind her. The collective hum of the city played in the background. Clouds shaded them from the afternoon sun. The corner store clerk leaned on his broom, eyeballing them as they passed, and guarding his doorway from the riffraff.

"I don't wanna live with him," Curtis said. "I wanna live with you."

"Too late for that. You said, *Anywhere but here,*" Sara replied.

"I didn't mean without you. *Please*, Mom."

"You said, *We can't keep living like this.* You're right. We need a change."

"That's not what I meant. I wanna be with you."

Sara stopped and pivoted to her son. She poked his chest with her bony finger. "Shut up. I'm not discussing this anymore." She pivoted and continued walking.

Curtis followed several steps behind, sniffling and crying quietly. They hiked to the nearest Metro station. They needed a Metro card to ride the subway, which cost money they didn't have. So they stood by the entrance to the subway platform, which featured several turnstiles, where passengers inserted their Metro cards. Then the turnstile opened briefly, long enough for the passenger to slip through.

"We need cards," Curtis said.

"No we don't," Sara replied, watching the turnstiles. "Just get close behind someone and go through. It's easy."

Curtis watched his mother follow close behind an older man, slipping past the turnstile without paying. Sara pivoted and beckoned Curtis. With a thumping heart and sweaty palms, he followed close behind a woman, slipping through the turnstile without paying.

They rode the metro from Alexandria, Virginia, to L'Enfant Plaza, where they switched trains to the Green Line, then took that train to Anacostia, which was in Washington, D.C. Curtis stared out the window of the subway car at the tunnel walls, the rhythmic *click-clack* of the train tracks taking him to another place and time. He remembered his mother making him after-school snacks—ants on a log or apples and cinnamon sugar—and telling him how much she loved him. His stomach rumbled at the thought of food.

The subway jolted to a stop, and the man in the speaker announced their stop—Anacostia. They hiked several miles from the subway station, through a neighborhood of brick rowhomes. A man with baggy pants and a baggy black T-shirt leaned against a chain-link fence.

Sara noticed the man, then stepped away from Curtis, sidling up to the stranger with a wry smile. "You holding?"

The man squinted at Sara. "You got money?"

"I can pay you back."

The man sneered at Sara. "Get the fuck outta here. Busted-ass crack ho."

"Please. I'm good for it."

The man shoved Sara with one hand. "Get the fuck off my corner."

Sara stumbled backward. Curtis caught his mother, saving her from falling on the sidewalk.

"Let's just go back," Curtis said.

"*No.*" Sara grabbed Curtis by the wrist and pulled him down the sidewalk.

As they walked, Curtis thought about what his mother had said about his father over the years. She rarely talked about him, the subject always making her angry. Nevertheless, Curtis had pieced together what he could from several conversations. He knew his father's name was Rodney Tyson. His friends called him Hot Rod. He was once the most popular boy at T.C. Williams High School. Hot Rod was the handsome football, basketball, and track star. With Hot Rod by her side, Sara had been the envy of her classmates.

Sara had gotten pregnant as a sixteen-year-old junior. Rodney had just graduated and had promised to care for Sara and their child. He had been there for the first six months of Curtis's life, but Sara had thrown him out, after she'd found out he had gotten another woman pregnant. Rodney had fathered several children over the years, with several different women. Curtis didn't know if Rodney had a relationship with his other children, but Curtis hadn't seen his father since he was a newborn. Curtis had always imagined that Rodney loved his other children. He had figured they were athletic and handsome or pretty.

Rodney always had a scheme—or a *business opportunity*, as he liked to call it. He had worked odd jobs and on various construction sites but never anything stable. He had been arrested for grand theft auto a few years ago. He had been recently released. At least that's what Sara had heard from one of his friends.

They climbed the stairs to the front door of a redbrick rowhouse. Iron bars covered the first-floor windows. Sara double-checked the address on the folded piece of paper.

"I wanna go home," Curtis said.

Sara blew out a tired breath. "What home? The one with the eviction notice?"

"I don't know."

She squeezed his hand. "Don't worry. We'll figure it out."

Curtis nodded.

"You nervous about meeting your dad?"

"A little."

"You don't have to say anything." She reached for the doorbell. "You ready?"

Curtis nodded again.

Sara pressed the doorbell.

A little girl opened the door. She stared at them.

Sara smiled. "Is Rodney home?"

A tall, muscular man appeared behind the girl. Curtis gaped at the man. He had beady eyes, a wide nose, and large lips just like Curtis, but he was handsome. He had smooth dark skin, instead of the freckled mess that covered Curtis's face.

The man nudged the little girl. "Go on back inside." Then he shut the door, and stepped on the stoop, causing Sara and Curtis to step back.

The man scowled. "Sara?"

Sara smiled. "Hi, Rodney."

Rodney raised one side of his mouth in disgust. "What the fuck happened to you?"

Sara's smile evaporated. "Life, I guess."

He glanced at Curtis, still wearing that same look of disgust. "Is that Curtis?"

Sara nodded. "He's a good boy. So smart. He can run so fast. Just like you."

He crossed his arms over his chest, peering down at them from his six-foot-two frame. "What do you want?"

"We're in a bad way. I was hoping for some help."

"You want money?"

"It doesn't have to be money. Maybe you could take Curtis for a few months, while I try to get my life together."

Rodney shook his head. "I can't do that." He gestured to the row-house. "This is Charise's place. I can't be bringing more kids up in here."

"Can you help us with money then?"

"So you can blow it on drugs?"

"I'm not on drugs."

Rodney sneered at Sara. "You think I'm stupid? Look at you. You look like a fucking crack whore."

Curtis flinched and dipped his head.

Sara flushed beet red. "Fuck you, *Rodney*. I've made some mistakes, but at least I'm trying. What about you? What kind of man abandons his son?"

The front door opened, and a curvy black woman stepped onto the stoop next to Rodney. Curtis figured she was Charise.

"What the hell's going on?" Charise asked.

Rodney swallowed hard.

Charise snapped her tongue off the roof of her mouth. "Lemme guess. Baby mama drama?"

Rodney turned to Charise. "They were just leaving."

Charise glowered at Sara and Curtis. "This ain't Rodney's place. This is *mine*. I don't want this craziness at my house. Y'all ain't gotta go home, but you need to get on up outta here."

Sara addressed Rodney. "*Please.* This isn't about me. Your *son* needs your help."

Rodney didn't make eye contact. "You need to leave. *Now.*"

Sara took Curtis's hand. "Come on, baby. Let's go."

They walked away from the rowhouse, back the way they had come. Once they were around the corner, Sara burst into tears.

CHAPTER 8

Guardianship

Curtis came home from school, the apartment sweltering and dim without air conditioning or lights. His mother was in the living room, dumping his clothes from the cardboard boxes he used as a makeshift dresser into a plastic garbage bag.

Curtis rushed to his mother. "What are you doing?"

Sara continued to pack the garbage bag. "I think it's time we bought you some new clothes."

"If you sell my clothes, I won't have anything to wear."

Sara frowned at her son. "I'm not selling your clothes. Nobody would give us any money for these old rags anyway."

Curtis placed his hands on his hips. "What are you doing then?"

"I told you. I'm going to buy you some new clothes. We'll donate these."

"With what money?"

"Don't worry about that."

Curtis narrowed his eyes.

She took his hand. "Come on. I need to see a friend in Mount Vernon. He'll help us. I've already set it up. We'll get you some new clothes afterward."

"What *friend*?"

"I told you. He's a friend from Mount Vernon. I think you'll like him."

They hiked to the Metro and snuck their way onto the subway

platform. Curtis wondered why they were sneaking into the subway if they had money, but his mother was seemingly in a good mood, so he didn't question her.

Curtis stared out the window of the Metro train, as they traveled to the end of the yellow line. The sky was bright blue, with cotton-candy clouds. Sara sat next to her son, a manila folder in her lap and Curtis's clothes at her feet. They exited with everyone else at the last stop—Huntington. It was crowded with men and women traveling home from work. It was easy to slip behind a commuter to thwart the turnstile, their theft covered by the hustle and bustle of the Metro station.

They exited the Metro station and scanned the parking lot. Some commuters walked to their cars, briefcases and laptop bags in hand. Others were picked up in temporary parking by loved ones. A large black man standing next to a van waved at them. Sara waved back. She led Curtis to the man.

"Sara?" the man asked.

"Yes. You must be Mr. Henderson," Sara said.

Mr. Henderson shook hands with Sara. "The kids call me Mr. H. You can call me Russel." Mr. H. turned his attention to Curtis. "And you must be Curtis."

Curtis gaped at the big muscular man. He was even bigger than his father, with a square jaw, shiny bald head, big ears, and a long horselike face.

"Say hello to Mr. H.," Sara prompted.

"Hello," Curtis said, wondering if this was his mother's friend, and, if so, why were they just meeting. "Are you gonna help us?"

"Yes," Mr. H. replied.

Curtis relaxed during the short ride in his van, reassured by Mr. H.'s confident *yes*. Mr. H. drove them to a two-story house in a middle-class neighborhood. An errant kickball sat in the front yard. A pickup truck and an SUV were parked in the driveway. A middle-aged Latino sat on the pickup's tailgate, eating a sandwich.

They exited the van. Voices came from the backyard. Mr. H. took Curtis's clothes, helping Sara. Curtis figured they were donating the clothes to him. Mr. H. introduced them to the middle-aged man.

"This is Mr. Vasquez," Mr. H. said. "He takes care of the maintenance and grounds for several of our homes in the area. He'll give you a ride back to the Metro."

They exchanged greetings. Sara shook hands with the short and wiry man.

As Mr. H. led them to the side door, Curtis saw boys his age playing football in the backyard. Mr. H. led them into the house, through the large kitchen, down a hallway, and into an office.

He gestured to two seats in front of a metal desk. "Have a seat." Mr. H. sat behind the desk, while Curtis and Sara sat in front. "Did you bring his paperwork?"

Sara handed Mr. H. the manila folder. "That should be everything. His birth certificate is on top. My license is in there too."

Mr. H. flipped through the papers. He checked her license, glanced at Sara, and said, "Looks good." He handed Sara some papers to sign, along with her license. "Read them carefully. These give the state guardianship." He paused for a moment. "You can still change your mind."

Sara nodded and read the papers. After a few minutes, she took a deep breath and signed the papers. Sara stood from the chair, her eyes glassy. Curtis stood too, thinking they were leaving together. Sara hugged her son for several seconds, pulling him tightly to her bony body. She stifled a sob.

When they separated, Curtis asked, "What's wrong?"

Sara bent her knees, so they were eye to eye. "You need to stay here for a while."

Curtis's eyes bulged. "What are you talking about?"

"They have food here. Other kids to play with—"

"I don't wanna stay here. I wanna be with you."

Mr. H. stood from his seat.

"I need you to be strong," Sara said, her voice quivering. "I need you to understand that, no matter what, I love you with all my heart. I have to do this. It's for the best."

"How long are you leaving me here?"

"I don't know."

Curtis dissolved into tears. "Don't go. Please don't go. I won't complain anymore. I promise."

Tears slipped down Sara's cheeks. "I'm so sorry." She pivoted and left the office.

Curtis ran after her and wrapped his arms around her waist, bawling. "No, Mom. Don't leave me. Don't go."

Mr. H. removed Curtis from his mother gently but with enough force to be in total control. Sara ran outside. Curtis struggled like a feral cat in Mr. H.'s grasp. The pickup truck roared. Mr. H. finally relented, releasing his new ward. Curtis ran outside. He sprinted after the truck, stopping at the end of the driveway, as it disappeared around the corner.

Curtis collapsed on the asphalt and curled into the fetal position, bawling like a baby.

Mr. H. lifted him off the ground with one arm. "Stand up."

Curtis placed his feet on the asphalt and stood, his body still convulsing with sobs.

"It'll be okay. I promise."

CHAPTER 9

House Rules

Curtis sat in the office, his knees pulled to his chest, still crying. Mr. H. sat in the chair next to him.

He placed his hand on Curtis's back. "You need to pull it together."

Curtis sniffled, rubbed his eyes, and sat up in his chair. "I want my mom."

"I know you do, but she's not here, and she won't be here. This is your life now. The sooner you accept the circumstances, the better off you'll be. Do you understand?"

Curtis sniffled again and nodded.

"Good." Mr. H. leaned back in his chair, retracting his hand from Curtis's back as he did so. "Now. This is a group home for boys like you, without a guardian. Eight other boys near your age live here. I live here too. If you run into any problems, you come to me. I'm the supreme being in this house. Do you understand?"

Curtis nodded.

"Sit up straight and answer like you mean it."

Curtis sat up straight. "Yes, Mr. H."

"Better. You need to follow a few rules." Mr. H. went to the filing cabinet and retrieved two sheets of paper. He sat behind his desk and handed one paper to Curtis. "Read along with me. Let me know if you have any questions."

Curtis read the rules silently, as Mr. H. read them aloud.

HOUSE RULES

1. Treat each other with respect. Say **please** and **thank you** and **excuse me**.
2. Obey Mr. H. without backtalk. Address him as Mr. H. or sir.
3. Tell the truth, no matter what.
4. Be kind and be helpful to your foster brothers.
5. Never take food outside the kitchen and dining room.
6. Homework must be done before any gaming or TV watching.
7. Clean up after yourself.
8. No whining or complaining.
9. No hitting, punching, or kicking. Definitely NO violence of any kind.
10. Always wash your hands after using the bathroom. Always wash your hands before eating.
11. Always brush your teeth in the morning and again before bed. Floss at least once per day.
12. Shower once per day. Use soap on your body and shampoo in your hair. Showers to be limited to five minutes or less.
13. Never use any curse words.
14. Dinner is at 6:00 p.m. sharp. Breakfast is at 7:00 a.m. sharp. If you're late, you don't eat. Lunch, whether eaten here or at school, will consist of sandwiches prepared by the boys themselves.
15. Never enter Mr. H.'s bedroom or bathroom.

Curtis looked up from the paper.

"Any questions?" Mr. H. asked.

"No, sir," Curtis replied.

"You're a smart boy, Curtis. I can see that. If you follow the rules and do your best, things will get better."

"Yes, sir."

"Good." Mr. H. stood from his seat. "Let's meet your foster brothers. Then I'll show you to your room and get you settled."

Mr. H. carried Curtis's trash bag full of clothes out of the office. He led Curtis out the sliding glass door to the back patio. Mr. H. called out to the kids playing football in the backyard. "Come over here and meet your new brother."

The boys grumbled but dropped the football and trudged to the house. The ragtag group of boys were sweaty, with grass and dirt stains on their clothes.

"This is Curtis," Mr. H. said. "He's from Alexandria city. I expect each and every one of you to treat him like family because he *is* family. Got me?"

"Yes, Mr. H.," the boys said in unison.

"Good." Mr. H. then introduced each boy to Curtis, punctuated by eight handshakes. One boy, a bigger boy named Jimmy, squeezed Curtis's hand extra hard.

After the introductions, the boys went back to football, and Mr. H. led Curtis upstairs. Four bedrooms and three bathrooms were upstairs. The master bedroom and bathroom were for Mr. H. The other three bedrooms varied in size from big, medium, and small. The small bedroom had one bunk bed. The medium-size bedroom had one bunk bed and one single bed. The biggest bedroom had two bunk beds.

Mr. H. led Curtis into one of the hall bathrooms. "You can use either of the hall bathrooms to shower and to do your business. There's another toilet downstairs that you can use too, but no shower. I'll get you everything you need from the storeroom. Toothbrush, towel, soap. The toothpaste, shampoo, and floss are communal, so take what you need but only what you need. We don't waste in this house."

"Yes, sir," Curtis replied.

Mr. H. showed Curtis to the biggest room. His bed was the top bunk along the north wall. Mr. H. set Curtis's trash bag full of clothes atop a nearby dresser. "This is yours. You can put all your clothes in here. I'll get you some more clothes from the storeroom." Mr. H. glanced at Curtis's ratty sneakers. "And some new shoes. What size are you?"

"I don't know." Curtis gestured to his feet. "These are too small."

"Probably a three or four. I'll bring both, and you can try them on."

"Thank you, Mr. H."

Mr. H. put his heavy hand on Curtis's shoulder and squeezed. "You're welcome, Curtis. Go ahead and put away your clothes." Mr. H. checked his watch. "Dinner is in forty-five minutes. Don't be late."

Mr. H. left Curtis alone in the large room. Curtis folded his clothes and stocked the wooden dresser that had been assigned to him. He cried quietly as he worked. A cacophony of quick steps climbed the stairs and pounded the hallway to the large bedroom. Curtis sniffed and wiped his face with his T-shirt. His foster brothers surrounded him against the wall in a half circle. They smelled like sweat and grass. One of the boys cracked his knuckles. Several had crooked smiles that didn't feel friendly.

Curtis forced a close-lipped smile, careful not to show his teeth, and said, "Hi."

Jimmy broke from the half circle and stepped closer to Curtis, his blue eyes narrowed. "Were you cryin'?"

"No," Curtis replied.

Jimmy towered over Curtis and most of the other boys. He had pale skin and a dirty blond buzz cut. "Don't lie. Don't you know the rules yet?"

"He's lying," said one of the other boys.

"His eyes are all red," said another boy.

"Why were you cryin'? You miss your *mommy*?" Jimmy said *mommy* in a mocking voice.

Curtis reddened. "No."

"What's wrong with your teeth?"

Curtis shut his mouth tight.

"Show us your teeth."

Curtis shook his head.

"Come on. Show us," said one of the other boys.

"Come on," another boy said.

Curtis shook his head again, his eyes on the floor.

Jimmy grabbed Curtis's T-shirt, crumpling it in his hand, and pulling Curtis close. "Show us your *fuckin'* teeth."

Curtis opened his mouth, showing his crooked buck teeth.

The boys laughed.

"His grill's jacked," said one of the boys.

"That's why his mom left him," Jimmy said. "She couldn't stand to look at his ugly ass."

The boys laughed. Tears welled in Curtis's eyes.

"He's crying," one of the boys said.

"What a punk," said another boy.

Jimmy let go, and Curtis slumped to the floor, bawling. Curtis rocked back and forth, his arms covering his face and head.

"What do you think you're doing?" Mr. H.'s booming voice came from the doorway.

The boys moved away from Curtis, like he was infected with the plague.

"We didn't do nothin'," Jimmy said.

Mr. H. went to Curtis and helped him to his feet. He took Curtis's hands and knelt before him. "Take a deep breath. Relax. Breathe. In and out."

Curtis took several deep breaths, his sobs dissipating.

"Good." Mr. H. stood and glared at the boys. "I'm disappointed with all of you. I remember your first day. You were all scared and sad. Yet you were treated with kindness. But you can't pay that forward? You all think you're a man because you can bully someone? I have news for you." Mr. H. pointed at the boys. "You're all cowardly little boys." He shook his head. "No gaming or television for a week.

And I'll be assigning extra chores too."

The boys let out a collective groan.

"Aww, come on, Mr. H.," Jimmy said. "We didn't do nothin'."

"*Anything*. We didn't do *anything*. And, if you tell me another lie, I'll make it *two* weeks."

CHAPTER 10

Punch Party

Curtis dreamed he was falling. He woke on the floor next to his bunk bed, surrounded by the boys in their pajamas, with clenched fists and bared teeth. Dim light from the moon filtered through the windows. Jimmy forced a rag into Curtis's mouth, then yanked him to his feet and pinned his arms behind his back.

"Take it like a man," Jimmy said in a hushed voice.

The boys lined up in a single-file line.

"Don't hit the face," Jimmy ordered.

The first boy punched Curtis in the arm, not hard.

"That was weak."

The next boy punched Curtis in the chest, a little harder.

The boy after that punched Curtis in the stomach, causing him to cry out in pain, his cries muffled by the rag.

Every boy took his shot; then Jimmy turned Curtis to face him. Jimmy wound up and punched Curtis in the stomach. Curtis dropped like a stone, coughing into the rag and writhing on the carpet.

Jimmy bent down. "If you tell, next time it'll be worse."

CHAPTER 11

Muddling Through

Curtis woke to his roommates getting dressed and talking with each other. He groaned as he sat up in bed. His entire body was sore. He checked the clock on the wall. It was 6:58 a.m. Curtis glanced at his roommates, but they didn't acknowledge his existence.

"Hurry up. We're gonna be late," one said.

The three boys ran from the room, headed for breakfast.

Curtis climbed out of bed, every movement giving him a shot of pain. He dressed in shorts and a T-shirt. He padded down the hall to the bathroom, taking his toiletries with him. He used the bathroom and brushed his teeth. Before leaving the bathroom, he stood before the mirror and lifted his shirt, revealing a cluster of dark bruises.

He returned to his room and went to the window overlooking the front lawn. He stared at the road, mentally willing his mother to appear. Curtis stood in front of the window for thirty minutes, hoping and imagining his mother would come for him. She ran down the street, calling for him, looking healthy and beautiful. In his imagination, he ran outside to meet her. She hugged him tight, telling him over and over again how much she loved him and how sorry she was for leaving him. It was all just a bad dream. She had a nice apartment for them and a good job. They could be a family again.

Curtis was jolted from his daydream by the group-home boys leaving for school, wearing their backpacks, joking and laughing.

"You missed breakfast," Mr. H. said.

Curtis turned from the window. "Sorry. I wasn't hungry."

"That's good because you're not getting anything to eat. You need to be on time for meals. Rules are rules."

"I know."

"You ready to go to school?"

Curtis shrugged. "I guess."

Mr. H. nodded. "We're not always ready for life's challenges. Sometimes we have to muddle through."

"What does *muddle* mean?"

"It means to struggle through a confusing mess."

Curtis nodded.

"I'll take you to school today. Get you registered. You can take the bus home with the boys."

Curtis put on his new shoes. They weren't Jordan's, but the generic running shoes were comfortable and clean. Curtis followed Mr. H. downstairs to the kitchen.

Mr. H. handed Curtis a backpack. "I put your lunch and school supplies inside."

Curtis inspected the green backpack. "Thank you."

"Let's go."

Curtis followed Mr. H. outside. Curtis sat in the front passenger seat of the van.

"Put on your seat belt," Mr. H. said.

Curtis did as he was told, and Mr. H. drove them toward Curtis's new elementary school.

"When is my mom coming back?" Curtis asked.

Mr. H. exhaled. "I don't think she's coming back."

Curtis stared out the passenger window, fighting his tears. They drove past West Potomac High School and its football stadium on the way. Banners hung from their press box, paying homage to their many state championships.

Mr. H. parked in a visitor space at Bucknell Elementary School. Curtis followed Mr. H. inside, wearing his new backpack. Curtis sat in the office waiting area, while Mr. H. spoke with someone behind closed doors.

Mr. H. eventually appeared from the back office, followed by a middle-aged woman wearing a skirt suit. Mr. H. introduced the counselor as Mrs. Taylor. Mr. H. bent down to Curtis's level. "Work hard and listen to your teacher. Okay?"

"Yes, sir," Curtis replied.

Mr. H. said, "Good."

Mrs. Taylor escorted Curtis down the hall of the single-story school. Muffled voices of teachers and children came from the shut doors.

As they walked, Mrs. Taylor asked, "Are you excited to meet your teacher?"

Curtis didn't reply.

"It's okay to be nervous, but I think you'll love Mrs. Little. She's one of the best teachers in the whole school."

Curtis nodded, still not looking at the counselor.

The counselor stopped in front of a door decorated with construction paper flowers. A sign over the door window read, Mrs. Little, Fifth Grade. The counselor tapped on the window, then opened the door and led them inside.

Colorful posters adorned the walls. About thirty students sat at their desks in perfect rows and columns. There were white and black students, but none resembled Curtis. A reading area was along the back of the classroom, with bookshelves, shag carpet, and purple beanbag chairs. Curtis's eyes bulged at the smirking boys in the back—Jimmy and two other boys from the group home. Jimmy's presence was shocking, as Curtis had figured Jimmy was a seventh grader.

Mrs. Little approached with a smile. "You must be Curtis."

Curtis nodded again.

The counselor left the classroom.

Mrs. Little wore a turtleneck and a jean jumper. Her brown hair was straight and streaked with white. Her teeth were crooked with a slight overbite. Her easy smile, despite her imperfection, surprised him.

She held out her hand, like they were equals. "I'm Mrs. Little."

Curtis shook her hand.

Mrs. Little leaned in close and said in a hushed voice so the kids couldn't hear, "You're handsome, smart, and such a good boy. I'm an expert. I can tell." She winked, then stood and faced the class. "Everyone. This is our new friend Curtis. Everybody say, *Good morning, Curtis. We're so happy to meet you.*"

The class repeated in unison, "Good morning, Curtis. We're so happy to meet you."

Curtis watched the boys in the back, giggling, the only kids who didn't repeat the mantra.

★★★

During recess, Curtis punched the tetherball by himself, seeing how many times he could get the tethered ball to wrap around the pole with a single punch. His classmates played in several groups, separated by gender and activity. Boys climbed on the jungle gym. Several girls monopolized the swings. Other girls played double Dutch. Other boys played tag. Another group of girls huddled nearby, talking. One of the girls broke from the huddle and skipped toward the tetherball pole. Curtis continued to punch the ball, pretending not to notice the little brunette.

The brunette placed her hands on her hips. "What are you?"

Curtis watched the tetherball wrap around the pole.

"What are you?" she repeated.

Curtis faced the girl. "What do you mean?"

"Like what are you? You look really weird."

Curtis dipped his head and spoke barely above a whisper. "I'm just a boy."

She cocked her head and replied, "You're not like any boy I've ever seen."

"Leave me alone."

"You're the ugliest boy in the whole school." She pivoted and ran back to her friends.

Through glassy eyes, Curtis watched the brunette tell her story about the ugliest boy in school. The girls giggled at the conclusion. Curtis swallowed the lump in his throat and punched the tetherball, imagining the ball was the girl's face.

Another girl broke from the huddle and approached Curtis.

"Leave me alone," Curtis said, still punching at the tetherball, tears in his eyes.

"Courtney's stupid. Don't listen to her." The girl paused for a beat. "I'm Amanda."

Curtis glanced at Amanda. She was taller than Curtis, with wavy blond hair past her shoulders, the ends tinged with red. Her face was cute, with a button nose and small blue eyes. She reminded Curtis of an angel in her white dress. Curtis turned away, not wanting to be humiliated further. He said again, "Leave me alone."

Amanda walked away.

Curtis punched the ball with all his might.

CHAPTER 12

Dogpile

Curtis sat on the school bus, peering from the window, noticing the puffy clouds. One in particular resembled a teddy bear. He sat alone on the seat large enough for two. A cacophony of voices and laughter surrounded him. Something hit and stuck to his cheek. It didn't hurt. He removed the spitball and turned to the source of the projectile. Another spitball connected with his forehead.

"Bull's-eye," Jimmy said, holding a straw.

The boys around him snickered, holding their straws.

More spitballs came, aimed at Curtis's face. More laughter came, aimed at Curtis's psyche. Curtis pulled his knees to his chest and covered his face with his arms. He held back the tears by imagining himself as a high school football star at West Potomac High School. In his mind, he transported himself to the future. He imagined himself streaking down the football field for a game-winning touchdown, like Clinton Portis.

The boys continued to shoot spitballs for a few more minutes, until they were bored from Curtis's lack of response.

The school bus stopped at the bus stop near the group home. Curtis tried to enter the aisle from his seat, but the boys from the group home pushed him back, making him exit after them. Curtis exited the bus, wearing his backpack. The school bus drove away. Curtis trudged toward the group home, walking on the sidewalk past suburban homes.

The group home was situated on a cul-de-sac, along with three other homes. A small stretch of woods separated the cul-de-sac from the rest of the neighborhood. This was where the sidewalk ended, and the boys walked beside the woods, mostly out of view. Here, the group-home boys waited and watched for Curtis. As Curtis neared them, they nudged each other, giggled, and spoke in hushed whispers.

Curtis took a wide berth, trying to avoid them, but Jimmy pushed him down on the weedy roadside. "Where do you think you're goin'?" Curtis stood and tried to move past them, but Jimmy pushed him down again. "Your mom's never comin' back."

Curtis sat up but didn't try to stand.

Jimmy and the other boys surrounded Curtis. Jimmy said, "Why are you so fuckin' ugly?"

Curtis looked away.

"He got beat with the ugly stick," said one of the boys.

"You're gonna be a lifer. You know what a *lifer* is?" Jimmy waited for a response that never came. "It means nobody's gonna adopt your ugly ass. It means you're stuck here forever."

Curtis hung his head, tears welling in his eyes.

"He's crying again," said one of the boys.

"What a little bitch," Jimmy said.

The boys cackled. Once the laughter subsided, tired of tormenting Curtis, the boys walked away. Meanwhile, Curtis cried in the shade of an oak tree, thinking about his mother. He eventually stood and trudged to the group home.

The boys were already in the backyard, playing football. Jimmy was the quarterback, throwing tight spirals and long arching bombs. Curtis watched until Jimmy spotted him. Curtis entered the group home and went upstairs to his bedroom. He set his backpack on his dresser and climbed into his top bunk.

He shut his eyes, and, at first, he imagined living in a new apartment, with his mother. She was like she was before the drugs, but he couldn't get her to tell him that she loved him. How could he when she obviously didn't love him?

His mind shifted to Jimmy and the boys taking their shots last night and again on the way home from school. He imagined being big, tough, and strong. He imagined he knew how to fight, and, when the group-home boys tried to hurt him, he blocked their punches and knocked them out with one punch. Curtis was so big and so strong that nobody could ever hurt him again. He was unbreakable.

"Curtis?" Mr. H. asked.

Curtis sat upright in his bunk. "Yes, sir?"

Mr. H. faced Curtis. "How was school?"

"It was okay."

"The boys are out back, playing football. You like football?"

Curtis nodded.

"Why don't you go play with them?"

"I don't think …" Curtis trailed off.

Mr. H. stepped closer, lowering his voice. "I know it's hard to make friends, but you won't make friends isolating yourself up here. It's important to try."

"I don't … know how."

"You can start by getting your butt out of bed."

Curtis forced a smile and hopped down from his bunk bed. "They won't let me play."

Mr. H. rested his hands on Curtis's shoulders. "If you go outside and ask to play, I guarantee they'll let you."

Curtis nodded again. "Okay."

"Good."

They both walked downstairs. Mr. H. went to his office, and Curtis went outside to the backyard. Mr. Vasquez sprayed weeds growing in the cracks of the back patio, seemingly uninterested and oblivious to the football game. Curtis inched closer to the action.

"What the hell do you want?" Jimmy asked.

"Can I play?" Curtis asked.

"No way," one of the boys said.

Another boy said, "Not on my team."

"Do you know how to play?" Jimmy asked.

"Yes," Curtis replied.

"You can be on my team then."

"The teams are uneven now," a boy complained.

"I'll be all-time QB," Jimmy said, tossing the football to himself.

Curtis huddled with four boys, including the all-time QB. Jimmy told the three boys to go long. He said to Curtis, "Just do a little button hook right in front of me, like five yards. On two." He whispered something to one of the bigger boys, before breaking the huddle.

The boys lined up across the imaginary line of scrimmage. Jimmy held the ball out. "Ready, set. Hut, … hut." Jimmy dropped back to pass.

Curtis sprinted forward five yards and turned around. Jimmy passed the ball. Curtis caught it, turned, and sprinted up field, the other team giving chase. One of his teammates ran toward him. Curtis expected him to block one of the boys on the other team. Instead, he slammed into Curtis, driving Curtis into the ground.

"Dogpile," Jimmy called out.

Then everyone jumped on Curtis, pinning him to the turf, the weight of the boys making it impossible to move and difficult to breathe. Their weight pressed against Curtis's tender bruises.

"Get off me," Curtis shouted. "Get off me."

Jimmy jumped on top of the pile, causing a bunch of boys to groan. Then he got off and did it again, cackling as he did so. Eventually, the boys stood one by one from the pile, leaving only Curtis on the ground, stained with grass and dirt.

Curtis scrambled to his feet, dropped the football, and ran. He sprinted from the backyard into the woods. Under the tree canopy, sunlight filtered to the forest floor in ethereal rays. He ran through the woods, brushing by saplings, until the boys' voices were nearly silent. Then he hid behind the thick trunk of an old oak tree. He sat at the foot of the tree, his back against the rough bark. He felt like crying again, but nothing came out. He thought about what Jimmy had said. *You're gonna be a lifer.*

Slow footsteps approached, crunching the leaves. Mr. Vasquez appeared. "*Joo* okay?"

Curtis stood. "I'm fine."

Mr. Vasquez raised his eyebrows. "*Joo* need me get Mr. H.?"

Curtis shook his head. "No. I'm fine."

Mr. Vasquez peered up at the darkening sky. "Rain coming."

CHAPTER 13

Smear the ...

The next day the boys didn't shoot spitballs at Curtis on the bus. They didn't harass him on the walk home from the bus stop either.

Curtis went to his bedroom and set his backpack on his dresser.

Jimmy entered the bedroom. "You wanna play football?"

Curtis pivoted to Jimmy and replied, "No."

Jimmy tossed the football to himself. "We were just messin' around yesterday. We weren't tryin' to hurt you."

Curtis crossed his arms over his chest.

"Come on. We need another player. It'll be fun." He tossed the ball to Curtis.

Curtis caught it.

"Nice hands," Jimmy said. "Come on. Let's play."

Curtis tossed the ball back to Jimmy. "Okay."

Curtis followed Jimmy to the backyard. The other boys were already there, clustered together. Jimmy joined the others. Curtis kept his distance, maybe five yards away.

Jimmy smirked at the group of seven boys. He tossed the football to Curtis and shouted, "Smear the queer!"

Curtis caught the ball, just as Jimmy and the boys rushed him. Curtis planted right, then cut left and sprinted around the boys, leaving them in the dust. Curtis ran to the end of the lawn area, imagining he had just scored a touchdown. He turned to face the group. Jimmy and several boys still chased him. Curtis ran toward them, juking left and right, zigzagging around the slower boys again.

Curtis ran to the other side of the yard, imagining he'd scored another touchdown. This time he did a little dance in celebration. Most of the boys laughed, but Jimmy sprinted toward Curtis, red-faced, his hands balled into fists. Curtis waited until he got close, then sidestepped Jimmy, causing Jimmy to slip and fall into a muddy puddle at the edge of the lawn.

The other boys ran to the scene, not to tackle Curtis but to praise him. Several boys patted Curtis on the back and marveled at his speed.

Jimmy stood from the mud, his sweatpants and shoes caked with Virginia clay. He stomped toward the group.

The boys laughed at Jimmy.

"He juked you," said one boy.

"He broke your ankles," said another boy.

"Shut up," Jimmy said, through gritted teeth.

Curtis tossed the ball to Jimmy, but he batted it down. He grabbed Curtis by the collar of his T-shirt. Curtis wiggled from his grasp, but Jimmy latched on to Curtis's arm and dragged him to the puddle. Jimmy tossed Curtis into the mud, then pounced on him, forcing Curtis's face into the muddy water.

"Let him go," said one of the boys.

"Yeah. Let him go," said another boy.

Curtis held his breath, flailed and bucked, trying to turn his head, but Jimmy was too strong.

"Get off him," Mr. Vasquez shouted.

Jimmy let go.

Curtis lifted his face from the muddy water and sucked in a sharp breath. His shorts and T-shirt were caked in orange clay, not to mention his knees, face, and hands. Mr. Vasquez helped Curtis to his feet and out of the mud. "*Joo* okay?"

Curtis nodded.

The middle-aged man pointed at Jimmy. "*Joo* are bad boy. Me tell Mr. H."

Jimmy mimicked Mr. Vasquez, with a mocking tone. "*Joo* are bad boy. Me tell Mr. H. You sound fuckin' retarded." Jimmy surveyed the other boys, expecting laughter, but they were silent.

"*Joo* in trouble."

Jimmy snickered, mocking him again. "No. *Joo* in trouble. I should call immigration on you. Do you even have papers?"

"Me tell Mr. H." Mr. Vasquez escorted Curtis to the back patio and the hose.

"Go ahead," Jimmy called out to their backs. "I ain't afraid of Mr. Potato Head."

Some of the group-home boys called Mr. H. *Mr. Potato Head* behind his back because of his big bald head and big ears.

Mr. Vasquez turned on the water, then handed the nozzle to Curtis. "*Joo* clean."

"Thank you," Curtis replied.

Mr. Vasquez patted his back. "*De nada. Joo* welcome."

Curtis sprayed his legs and shoes, cleaning off the mud.

Mr. Vasquez went inside.

The boys played football, as if nothing had happened—although Jimmy was nervous, throwing errant passes and constantly checking the back door for Mr. Potato Head.

Once he was clean, Curtis turned off the water and set down the nozzle. Mr. H. exited the sliding glass door to the patio.

He inspected Curtis. "You all right?"

Curtis nodded.

"Good. Go inside and get cleaned up. I'll take care of this." He glanced at Curtis's wet shoes. "Take off your shoes before you go in."

"Yes, sir." While Curtis took off his shoes, he watched Mr. H. make a beeline for Jimmy.

Mr. H. pulled him aside from the other boys, yanking him by the collar. His words were inaudible but sharp. Jimmy bowed his head, his face beet red. Curtis wasn't certain, but he thought he saw tears in Jimmy's eyes.

CHAPTER 14

Sweet Dreams

That night Curtis lay in his top bunk, unable to sleep. He thought of the threat he'd received while taking his dinner plate to the kitchen sink. Jimmy had been at the sink, sentenced to two weeks of dishwasher duty.

Under his breath, Jimmy had said, "You're dead."

Curtis imagined Jimmy and the boys taking him from his bed in the middle of the night, like last time. Curtis listened on high alert. Every creak, the whistle of the wind, the tapping of a branch on the window, every sound caused Curtis to stiffen and to scan the room for potential danger.

Exhaustion finally won, and he drifted off to sleep.

Curtis dreamed of Derek straddling him in his bunk, his big hands around his neck, squeezing like a vise. Curtis stared into Derek's dark eyes, flailing at his muscular arms in vain, remembering the beatings Derek had given his mother. Derek smirked, and his face transformed into Jimmy, but the smirk remained, exactly the same.

Curtis thrashed and cried out. He woke to his roommates gawking at him, the morning sunlight shining through the windows.

"What's wrong with you?" asked one of the boys.

Curtis sat up, his breath regulating. "Nothing."

CHAPTER 15

Wake Up

Sara said, "Curtis. Curtis. Wake up."

Curtis's mother blurred, blackened, and disappeared.

His eyes fluttered and opened. Curtis raised his head from his desk.

His classmates giggled.

Mrs. Little stood next to him in the aisle. "Settle down, class. Let's have some DEAR time, while I take care of Curtis."

DEAR stood for drop everything and read, so the class retrieved their novels and sports biographies.

Mrs. Little bent down next to Curtis. "Are you okay, honey?"

"I'm just tired," Curtis replied, barely above a whisper.

"You look tired. I would like for you to go to the nurse. I'll write you a pass." Mrs. Little scribbled on the pass and handed it to him.

Curtis walked to the nurse's office. Nurse Easton was a plump woman with curly gray hair. The nurse ushered Curtis to a table covered by a paper sheet.

The nurse checked his vitals. "Did you sleep last night?"

"A little," Curtis replied, sitting on the table.

"You look exhausted. Did you stay up too late playing video games?"

"No. I don't play video games."

Nurse Easton arched her eyebrows. "That's a first."

Curtis shrugged.

"What kept you up?"

Curtis shrugged again.

"Well, you can't sleep in class." She gestured to a cot in the corner. "I'll let you sleep on the cot, while I call your parents."

Curtis stared at his hands. "I don't have any parents."

"You have a guardian, don't you?"

"Mr. H."

Nurse Easton patted his knee. "Okay, sweet pea. I'll call Mr. H."

★★★

Mr. H. drove Curtis home from school in his SUV. He flipped down the visor, blocking the sun, as he turned onto Route 1. "You can't sleep in school."

"I know," Curtis replied, sitting in the front passenger seat.

Mr. H. glanced from the road to Curtis and back again. "Why didn't you sleep last night?"

"I don't know."

"When we get home, finish your schoolwork. Then I want you to eat dinner and go right to bed."

"Yes, sir."

For the rest of the ride home, Curtis stared out the window, thinking about his mother. Mr. H. parked his SUV in the driveway next to the group home van.

"Can I call my mom?" Curtis asked.

Mr. H. turned in his seat to Curtis. "Do you know her phone number?"

Curtis shook his head. "We didn't always have a phone."

"I don't think it's a good idea."

"Why not?" Curtis's tone was desperate.

"I know it's been hard for you without your mother, but contacting her will only open that wound again."

"Please, Mr. H."

Mr. H. pursed his lips, then let out a heavy breath and said, "Okay."

Curtis followed Mr. H. to his office. Mr. H. searched through a filing cabinet and removed a manila folder. He opened the folder and scanned the paperwork. He wrote a phone number on a Post-it note, turned around his desktop phone, and placed both items in front of Curtis.

"This is the number she left with me." Mr. H. stepped to the office door. "I'll give you some privacy." He exited his office and shut the door behind him.

Curtis stared at the phone number for a few seconds. Then, with a trembling hand, he removed the phone from the cradle and placed it to his ear, listening to the dial tone. He dialed the number.

A robotic voice answered. "This number is no longer in service. Goodbye."

Curtis worked on a long division worksheet in his room at the group home, showing his work in pencil, as Mrs. Little had requested. Halfway through his homework, his mind drifted to his mother. *Maybe she's in trouble. She might be hurt. What if she needs me, but I'm not there?*

Curtis stood from the desk in his bedroom and stepped to the window, overlooking the backyard. The boys didn't play football on that Friday afternoon. Instead, they weeded and spread mulch in the rear flower beds. It was their punishment for teasing Curtis on his first day at the group home. It was hard to believe he had only been at the group home for four days. It felt like a lifetime.

Jimmy spotted Curtis in the window. The bully made a finger gun and shot Curtis. Curtis moved to the window overlooking the front yard. The flower beds were freshly mulched. Birds chirped in the oak trees. Nobody was out front.

Curtis crept down the hall and down the stairs. He snuck past Mr. H.'s office and out the front door.

He ran like the wind.

CHAPTER 16

Home

Curtis ran to the end of the block, the sun warming his skin. He ran to the end of the neighborhood. Like a magnet drawing him home, he turned right on Route 1 and ran several miles to the Huntington Metro station.

Like his mother had taught him, he snuck onto the subway platform, walking close behind a paying customer, passing through the turnstile together. He rode on the Metro to the King Street station.

He snuck through the turnstile again, then ran several more miles to his apartment complex. As he approached his apartment building, his heart pounded more from nervousness than from running. He stopped at the front door to their apartment building, his chest heaving, as he sucked in air. The main door was locked, and he no longer had a key.

Curtis waited for an older man to exit the building, and he slipped inside before the door shut. He sprinted up two flights of stairs to his apartment, grinning from ear to ear. He knocked on the door, expecting his mother to be home in the afternoon, but nobody answered.

★★★

Almost two hours later, Sara climbed the stairs, arm in arm with an older man. She wore a red tube top, a tight skirt, and high boots.

Curtis spotted her before she spotted him.

The old man said, "You better be as good as you say you are."

"I'm the best. You know what they say. Once you go red ..."

They both laughed.

Sara's giggles ceased when she saw Curtis. "What the hell are you doing here?"

"I wanna come home," Curtis replied, stepping closer to his mother, hoping for a hug.

Sara glowered at Curtis, her eyes dilated. "You need to go back."

Curtis held out his hands, his tone desperate. "But I wanna be with you."

"This your kid?" the old man asked.

"Give me a minute." Sara opened the apartment with her key and said to the old man, "Go in and make yourself comfortable. I'll be right there." The old man entered the apartment, and Sara shut the door behind him.

"I can't stay in that place," Curtis said. "I wanna be with you."

She shook her head. "You can't stay with me. You're better off in the group home. I can't take care of you."

Tears filled Curtis's eyes. "Please, Mom. I won't ask for anything. You won't have to take care of me. I can't live there."

Sara crossed her bony arms over her chest. Her face was rigid. "I was sixteen when I had you. My parents wanted me to abort you. Did you know that?"

Curtis knew what *abortion* was. "You never told me that."

"I could've gone to college." She gestured to her slutty outfit. "You think I like doing this?"

Tears wet his cheeks. "I don't understand."

Her eyes were glassy. "It's simple. My life would've been so much better if I never had you."

Her words cut like a knife. Curtis gaped at her, stunned. When he recovered from the shock, he bolted down the stairs, out of the apartment building, and into the night. He sprinted back to the King

Street Metro station, tears streaming down his face. Curtis slumped on a bench, just outside the station, his knees pulled to his chest, rocking back and forth. His throat was raw, and his eyes itched from bawling.

He considered his options. None of them were good. He never wanted to see his mother again. He didn't want to go back to the group home. He thought about living on the streets and stealing to survive, but that didn't sound appealing either. Sara had once told him that young homeless people often sell their bodies.

"Curtis?"

Curtis raised his gaze.

Mr. Vasquez stood before him. "People looking for *Joo*."

"I wanted to see my mom," Curtis replied.

Mr. Vasquez removed a cell phone from his pocket and sat next to Curtis. "Mr. H. say that. *Joo* see her?"

Curtis nodded. "She doesn't want me."

Mr. Vasquez blew out a ragged breath. "Me very sorry."

"Am I in trouble?"

"*Joo* no worry." Mr. Vasquez opened the flip phone, selected a Contact, and pressed the green button. He pressed the phone to his ear. "Me find him. At Metro." He listened for a moment. "Me bring him." Mr. Vasquez disconnected the call.

"Was that Mr. H.?" Curtis asked.

"*Jes.*"

"Is he mad at me?"

Mr. Vasquez shook his head. "He happy you okay."

Curtis swallowed the lump in his throat.

"Me happy too. *Joo* good boy. Me no like ..." Mr. Vasquez frowned. "Sorry. Me English no good." Mr. Vasquez hesitated. "*Joo* no deserve."

CHAPTER 17

Puta

After breakfast on Saturday, Curtis lay in his top bunk, staring at the ceiling, replaying what his mother had said to him. *My life would've been so much better if I never had you.*

Jimmy entered the bedroom and said, "Hey, Curtis."

Curtis turned his head away from the bully.

Jimmy approached Curtis's bedside. "Hey, man. I'm sorry for pickin' on you so much. That's just what we do to the new guy."

"Whatever," Curtis replied.

"We're playin' war in the woods. You wanna play?"

"No."

"Come on. Everybody's cool now. They all want you to play. They asked me to come get you."

Another boy appeared in the doorway. "Is he coming?"

"I don't know." Jimmy turned from the boy back to Curtis. "Are you?"

Curtis hopped down from the bunk bed. "Okay."

Curtis followed Jimmy and the other boy to the woods. They hiked to a makeshift fort in the middle of the woods, about two hundred yards from the group home. The fort leaned against two large maple trees and was made from scrap wood and old tarps. Four boys worked on an addition to the dwelling.

Jimmy and three other boys surrounded Curtis. The other four boys stood by the fort.

"What are you doing?" Curtis asked.

"We're sick of you gettin' us in trouble," Jimmy said.

"Leave him alone," said one of the boys by the fort.

"It's not funny anymore," another one said.

Jimmy mean-mugged the dissenters. "Shut up."

One of the boys surrounding Curtis shoved him into Jimmy, who shoved Curtis back the way he came. The boys shoved Curtis back and forth, like a pinball. On the way back to Jimmy, the bully wound up and punched Curtis in the stomach, dropping him like a sack of potatoes.

Curtis lay on the ground, wheezing, trying to catch his breath.

Jimmy and his buddies cackled.

Heavy steps came from the woods, like an animal barreling through the brush. Mr. Vasquez appeared, his wiry muscles tense and his face like stone. He knelt next to Curtis. "*Joo* okay?"

Curtis nodded, his breath regulating.

Mr. Vasquez helped Curtis to his feet. He glowered at Jimmy and the other boys. "*Joo* bad boys. Why *joo* do this?"

Jimmy cackled and mocked Mr. Vasquez. "*Joo* bad boys. Learn some fuckin' English."

Mr. Vasquez stalked closer to Jimmy. He pointed a craggy finger in Jimmy's face. "*Joo* weak. *Joo* no strong."

Jimmy was several inches taller than Mr. Vasquez. He lifted his chin to Mr. Vasquez. "I bet I could kick your old ass."

Two boys laughed, but most of them were dead silent.

Mr. Vasquez took a step back. "*Joo* can try. *Puta.*"

"Oh, shit. He just called you a bitch," said one of boys.

"I think *puta* means motherfucker," said another boy.

Jimmy reddened and raised his fists. "You're dead, old man."

Mr. Vasquez raised his fists.

The boys surrounded the two fighters, forming a human ring.

"Get him, Jimmy," said one of the boys.

"Yeah. Fuck him up," another boy said.

Jimmy threw a wild right hook, which Mr. Vasquez ducked with ease, then countered with a lightning-quick smack to Jimmy's face.

"He got you, Jimmy," said someone from the peanut gallery.

Jimmy threw another wild right hook. Mr. Vasquez ducked and countered again, smacking Jimmy across the face. Jimmy's cheek was beet red now. He rushed Mr. Vasquez, but the old man sidestepped him and tripped the boy. Jimmy fell flat on his face. When Jimmy stood, Mr. Vasquez hit him with those lightning-quick hands, slapping him multiple times, knocking Jimmy backward. Jimmy rubbed his face, tears welling in his eyes.

"He fucked you up, Jimmy, and he's not even trying," said one of the boys.

"He made you his bitch," said another boy.

"No, his *puta*."

The boys laughed.

Jimmy ran toward the group home.

Mr. Vasquez gestured to the boys surrounding him. "*Joo* hit Curtis, *joo* get this." Mr. Vasquez shook his fist.

A few boys ran back to the group home.

Mr. Vasquez motioned to the rest of the boys. "Go home."

They all ran home, except Curtis.

Curtis approached Mr. Vasquez. "They don't like me."

"*Like* no matter. *Joo* need *respect*. *Joo* need learn fight." Mr. Vasquez held up his fists to illustrate his point.

"I don't know how."

"Me help *joo*."

That morning in the woods, Mr. Vasquez taught Curtis the basics of boxing. He showed him the proper stance for a right-handed fighter. He taught Curtis how to move and to avoid crossing his feet. He taught Curtis the jab, the cross, and the left hook. Then he taught Curtis how to throw the punches in combination. After the boxing lesson, Curtis and Mr. Vasquez hiked back to the group home together.

"Are you gonna tell Mr. H. about what they did?" Curtis asked.

"*Joo* want?" Mr. Vasquez asked.

"No. I don't."

CHAPTER 18

Night Terrors

Curtis brushed his teeth and spat in the sink. He rinsed his mouth and forced a toothy grin in the mirror. His bottom teeth were crowded and crooked. His upper front teeth grew outward at an angle, giving him an extreme overbite. He pushed on his front teeth, trying to push them back, but they didn't budge. He shut his mouth, which wasn't comfortable because of his overbite. When he wasn't paying attention, his mouth always hung open, for everyone to see.

He exited the bathroom, his towel around his neck. Jimmy marched down the hall toward the bathroom, his towel over his shoulder. Curtis dipped his head and walked close to the wall, giving Jimmy a wide berth. Despite this, Jimmy grabbed Curtis and slammed him against the wall.

Jimmy pulled Curtis close by the collar of his T-shirt. Jimmy spoke in a hushed whisper, close enough to smell the spaghetti they'd had for dinner. "You're lucky you didn't snitch. Ugly motherfucker." Jimmy slammed Curtis against the wall again, then let go, and continued to the bathroom, as if nothing had happened.

Curtis stood paralyzed for an instant. His heartbeat returned to normal, and his fear retreated. He went back to his bedroom, hung his towel on the bedpost, and crawled into his top bunk. His three roommates joked among themselves, as if Curtis didn't exist.

Mr. H. appeared in the doorway. He glanced at his watch. "Time for bed."

Curtis thought about Derek's flashy gold watch. By comparison, Mr. H. wore a simple black watch with a leather band. Probably cost $9.99.

The roommates groaned but went to their respective beds. Mr. H. turned off the overhead light, plunging them into darkness. Curtis wrapped his blanket around him, like a cocoon, and drifted off to sleep.

He ran on a sidewalk, bathed in the yellow glow of the streetlights. Curtis glanced over his shoulder. Jimmy chased him, and he was gaining ground. Curtis faced forward again. A light in the distance beckoned him. The light grew larger. It was an open door. Sara appeared in the doorway. Curtis ran for his mother but didn't seem to get closer, like he was running on a treadmill.

Sara beckoned him with her hand. "Hurry, Curtis. Hurry."

Curtis sprinted faster. His legs and lungs burned. He wheezed for air. He was gaining ground now, getting closer to his mother. The pounding of Jimmy's sneakers on the concrete sidewalk grew louder. Curtis dared to glance over his shoulder again. Jimmy was only a few feet behind, sneering at Curtis.

Just before Curtis reached his mother, she slammed the door in his face. Curtis banged on the door, begging her to open it. He felt Jimmy's hot breath on the back of his neck. Curtis turned around, and Jimmy was gone, replaced by a far scarier foe. Derek grabbed Curtis by the neck, lifted him off the ground, and squeezed. Curtis choked and flailed his legs, like he was riding an imaginary bicycle. Curtis hit Derek's arms, but his blows were ineffective.

The door opened, and Sara appeared before them.

Curtis croaked, "Help me."

Derek looked at Sara and asked, "What do you want me to do with him?"

Sara shrugged. "I don't care."

She disappeared, and Derek squeezed Curtis's neck with the force of a boa constrictor. Curtis tried to scream, but nothing came out.

Curtis stared into Derek's empty black eyes. The blackness of Derek's eyes grew, until there was nothing.

Curtis screamed into the darkness.

The light flicked on, with Curtis midscream. Mr. H.'s face appeared over him. His large hands shook Curtis.

"Wake up, Curtis. You're having a nightmare," Mr. H. said.

Curtis scanned the bedroom, his breathing labored. His three roommates stood nearby, bleary-eyed, scowls on their faces.

"Breathe. You're okay," Mr. H. said.

Tears filled Curtis's eyes. "I'm scared," he whispered.

"I know. Relax. I'm not going anywhere."

"What's wrong with him?" asked one of the roommates.

"Nothing," Mr. H. replied, his gaze still on Curtis.

"It's so annoying," said one of the roommates.

"I know," agreed another.

Mr. H. glowered at them. "*Enough.*" Mr. H. had Curtis and his bunkmate switch beds, so Curtis was now on the bottom bunk. Mr. H. moved a chair next to Curtis's bed. "I'll stay with you until you fall asleep."

Curtis nodded.

Mr. H. turned off the light and told the other boys, "Go back to sleep." Mr. H. sat next to Curtis and held his hand, until he fell asleep again.

CHAPTER 19

Fugly

At lunch on Monday, Curtis sat at his desk, eating the lunch he had prepared for himself—a bologna and cheese sandwich, crackers, a banana, and two juice boxes. Mr. H. had made his lunch during his first week of school, but now, like the other boys in the group home, it was his responsibility.

The desks had been moved and clustered together to accommodate the various cliques in Mrs. Little's fifth-grade classroom. Everyone ate, talked, and laughed. Except for Curtis. His desk seemed to contain a force field that prevented anyone from coming within ten feet of him. Curtis didn't mind the solitude. Nothing good ever came from consorting with his classmates. Curtis ate his bologna sandwich and tried to do his math homework, but he couldn't concentrate with the gossip circulating around him.

Of the three boys in his class from the group home, one was Curtis's roommate. That boy told Jimmy and several other fifth graders about Curtis screaming in the middle of the night.

"What a freak," Jimmy said.

"He looks so weird," a girl said. "What do you think he is?"

"I don't know, but I bet his parents are *fugly*."

The kids giggled.

"Don't be mean," Amanda said.

The kids moved on to another topic, making fun of the boy who was in love with Amanda.

"I am not," the boy said.

"You all need to grow up," Amanda said. She picked up her lunch and stepped toward Curtis. She touched the empty desk next to him. "Do you mind if I sit with you?"

Curtis gaped at Amanda, then he shut his mouth, suddenly aware of his hideous teeth. Curtis shrugged.

Amanda set her lunch on the desktop and sat at the nearby desk.

Curtis tried to ignore her, but his entire body buzzed from her proximity.

She flipped her blond hair off her shoulders and gestured to Jimmy, holding court with a group of kids. "Don't worry about them. They're immature."

Curtis nodded.

Amanda ate a few potato chips from her lunch and then held out the bag to Curtis. "You want some?"

Curtis stared at her beautiful face for a beat, then shook his head.

"You don't talk much."

Curtis looked at his half-eaten lunch.

"That's okay. People talk too much anyway. What do you like to do?"

Curtis shrugged.

She tilted her head. "You don't know what you like to do?"

He cleared his throat. "I like cartoons."

Amanda grinned. "Me too. What's your favorite cartoon?"

"SpongeBob."

"I *love* SpongeBob." She held up her hand for a high five.

Curtis hesitated, then gave her a high five. He smiled, covering his teeth with his other hand.

Curtis sat at the desk in his bedroom, working on his math homework. Jimmy and two other boys sauntered into the bedroom. They surrounded Curtis at the desk.

"You think you're friends with Amanda?" Jimmy asked.

"I don't know," Curtis replied.

"She would never be friends with an ugly ass weirdo like you."

The other boys laughed.

"Leave me alone," Curtis said.

"I would, if there was something else to do. You got us banned from TV and gaming, remember?"

Curtis returned to his homework, hoping they'd leave him alone if he ignored them.

Jimmy smacked Curtis on the back of the head. "Remember?"

Curtis tried to concentrate on his math homework through glassy eyes.

"He's crying *again*," said one of the boys.

"What a pussy." Jimmy snatched Curtis's math homework. Then he smacked the back of Curtis's head one more time before they left, taking Curtis's mostly completed assignment with him.

CHAPTER 20

Freak

"Everyone, get out your math homework," Mrs. Little said, holding a copy of the homework with the correct answers. "Let's go over the answers."

The fifth graders dug into their backpacks and retrieved their homework.

Mrs. Little scanned her students. "Did everyone complete the assignment?"

"I didn't finish the last three," said one boy.

"I finished mine," Jimmy said, holding up his homework, likely copied from the one he'd stolen from Curtis.

Mrs. Little stared at Curtis, the only student without a paper on his desk. She marched down the aisle to Curtis. "Do you have your homework?"

Curtis shook his bowed head.

A few students giggled.

"*Quiet.*" Mrs. Little addressed Curtis again. "I'll get you a blank worksheet. Try to follow along. In the future, I expect you to come to school prepared. Do you understand?"

Curtis nodded.

Mrs. Little brought Curtis a blank worksheet. He worked on the long division worksheet, zipping through the familiar problems almost as fast as Mrs. Little gave the answers.

Curtis still worked on his homework sheet as the students queued up for recess.

Mrs. Little put her hand on Curtis's shoulder. "Time for recess, honey."

"I'm still trying to finish," Curtis replied.

Mrs. Little took his paper. "That's good enough. Line up with your classmates."

The fifth graders burst into the playground, enjoying the perfect weather—warm enough for shorts but cool enough for pants. Boys climbed on the jungle gym and played kickball on the baseball diamond. Girls sat on the swings, talked, and played double Dutch.

Curtis sat in the grass, as far from the others as was allowed. He would've preferred to stay in the classroom, doing math problems. Amanda left the girls playing double Dutch and stepped to Curtis.

She smiled as she approached, her teeth perfect. "You wanna play double Dutch with us?"

Curtis shook his head, sensing a pity invitation.

Amanda sat next to him in the grass, cross-legged. "What are you doing way over here?"

Curtis ripped blades of grass in two. "Didn't feel like being around ... some people."

"Like Jimmy?"

Curtis nodded.

"Jimmy can be a jerk."

"Yeah."

"You just moved here, *huh*?"

Curtis still focused on the grass, ripping the blades. "Yeah."

"Where did you come from?"

"Alexandria city."

"That's not too far. I heard you live at the group home with Jimmy and them."

Curtis nodded again.

"How is it?"

Curtis turned his head, meeting Amanda's gaze. "How do you think?"

Amanda frowned. "Sorry."

"Are you asking me stuff so you can make fun of me?"

"*No.* I wouldn't do that."

Curtis shrugged.

"You don't believe me?"

"I don't know."

"Then I'll tell you something about me that's embarrassing."

Curtis turned his body to face Amanda. She did the same.

"My stepdad left a few months ago," Amanda said. "I never liked him, but he at least had money."

Curtis nodded.

Amanda held out her hands. "Your turn. Where's your dad?"

"My dad doesn't want me."

She leaned in. "What about your mom?"

Curtis looked away and said, "She doesn't want me either."

Amanda hugged Curtis. He inhaled her flowery perfume, his entire body melting in her embrace.

★★★

Curtis sat tight to the bus window, watching the world go by, trying to ignore the cacophony of high voices. A strong voice silenced the others.

"I heard you kissed the freak," Jimmy said.

"I did *not*," Amanda replied.

Curtis gritted his teeth, pretending not to hear.

"I saw you hug him at recess," Jimmy said. "Put your body all over him. *Nasty.*"

A few girls said, "*Eww.*"

"It wasn't like that," Amanda said. "I was trying to be nice."

"Tell the truth," Jimmy said. "You think he's ugly."

"Don't say that."

"Then you *do* like him."

"I *don't*."

"Do you think he's ugly then?"

Amanda hesitated. "Yes."

Curtis swallowed the lump in his throat, fighting the tears.

Jimmy strutted several rows down and sat next to Curtis. "You hear that, freak? Amanda thinks you're ugly."

Curtis stared out the window, ignoring Jimmy.

"Everybody thinks you're ugly as fuck."

Curtis clenched his fists.

"You're a little bitch." Jimmy shoved Curtis, hard enough that the side of Curtis's head hit the window.

Curtis rubbed the side of his head, as Jimmy sauntered back to his seat in the rear of the bus.

The bus stopped. A dozen kids exited, including Amanda. She didn't look his way. The bus driver shut the door and continued. At the final stop, Curtis waited for everyone to move past his seat, before entering the aisle. Otherwise, he was likely to be pushed.

When Curtis exited the bus, Jimmy and the group-home boys waited for him. Curtis trudged toward the group home, ignoring the boys. Jimmy walked alongside Curtis, the other boys surrounding them.

"You like Amanda, don't you?" Jimmy asked, nudging Curtis with his elbow.

Curtis walked faster.

"Leave him alone," said one of the other boys.

"Shut up." Jimmy walked faster, getting in front of Curtis and blocking his path. Jimmy poked Curtis's bony chest. Jimmy stood about six inches taller than Curtis and was more muscular. "She would never like your ugly ass. You're so ugly, you make her sick."

Curtis threw a right cross, using his hips to generate power, just like Mr. Vasquez had taught him. Jimmy's head jerked backward. He stumbled and regained his balance.

Several boys cheered the punch.

"*Damn*," said one boy.

"He got you good, Jimmy," another boy said.

Jimmy touched his lip, checked the blood on his finger, and glared at Curtis. "You're fuckin' dead."

"Get him, Jimmy," said one boy.

"Fuck him up," said another boy.

Jimmy stalked to Curtis, his fists cocked and ready. Curtis was ready too. He gave Jimmy a quick one-two—left jab and right cross— connecting with Jimmy's face again. Jimmy howled in a rage and ran at Curtis, slamming him to the ground. Jimmy straddled Curtis on the ground, punching Curtis in a wild fury. Curtis tried to block his blows, but several punches landed on his cheeks and head.

The boys surrounded the fight, whooping and hollering at the violence.

A large shadow of a man appeared behind Jimmy. The man yanked Jimmy by the collar, easily pulling him off Curtis.

"Get off him," Mr. H. said.

CHAPTER 21

Punishment

"What the hell's going on?" Mr. H. asked, sitting behind his desk, wearing a scowl.

"It wasn't my fault," Jimmy replied, sitting in one of the chairs opposite Mr. H.

"It wasn't? You're older and bigger than Curtis. You think you're tough picking on a smaller kid?"

"He punched me first." Jimmy touched his fat lip. "Look what he did."

Mr. H. addressed Curtis, who sat in the chair next to Jimmy. "That true?"

Curtis nodded. His cheeks were bruised, and his left eye was already starting to swell.

Mr. H. shook his head. "I'm disappointed with both of you. You're both on dish duty for the next month."

"This is bullshit," Jimmy said, his face beet red. "It wasn't my fault."

Mr. H. slammed the side of his fist on the desktop, causing Jimmy and Curtis to flinch. He glowered at Jimmy. "What's *bullshit* is your attitude. If you don't figure it out real soon, you're headed for a life of misery. Prison and poverty. I can see your future as clear as day."

Jimmy dipped his head.

"And since you two wanna fight so much, I'm taking you both to the gym on Saturday. You're gonna fight so much that you won't wanna fight anymore."

CHAPTER 22

Respect

Early on Saturday morning Mr. H. escorted Curtis and Jimmy into an old boxing gym. It was packed with wiry men, punching heavy bags, speed bags, and each other. Several shadowboxed, practiced their footwork, and jumped rope. The smell of body odor and sweat hung in the air.

Two men sparred in the elevated ring, each wearing gloves and headgear. Their hands were lightning quick as they glided across the mat. They fought back and forth. One fighter was clearly dominant, although he didn't take any unnecessary shots. When the bell rang, the two men hugged, then went to their corners.

Mr. Vasquez spoke to the dominant fighter in Spanish, the muscular man listening intently. When they were done talking, Mr. Vasquez turned to Mr. H. and grinned.

Mr. H. and Mr. Vasquez shook hands.

"Thank you for doing this," Mr. H. said.

"*De nada*," Mr. Vasquez replied.

Mr. Vasquez wrapped their hands and fitted them with used boxing gloves. Once Curtis and Jimmy were ready, Mr. Vasquez taught them the basics of boxing, similar to what he'd already taught Curtis in the woods last Saturday. Curtis retained more of the lesson the second time around.

They started without the gloves, jumping rope for several one-minute intervals. Neither Curtis nor Jimmy were particularly good at jumping rope, often getting whipped in the legs with the speed rope. They were exhausted after jumping rope, and that was just the warmup. Curtis had a new respect for his double-Dutching class-mates.

After the warmup, Mr. Vasquez had them do a few stretches to loosen their muscles. Then they laced up their gloves and punched Mr. Vasquez's padded hands, working on their punching form and accuracy. Mr. Vasquez encouraged them when they did something right and instructed them when they did something wrong.

After the instruction period, Curtis and Jimmy were fitted for headgear and sent to separate corners. Mr. H. was in Jimmy's corner, and Mr. Vasquez was in Curtis's. It all happened so fast that Curtis didn't have a chance to be nervous or scared.

Just before the buzzer, Mr. Vasquez said, "*Joo* fast. *Joo* make him move."

The buzzer sounded, and they were sparring.

A few boxers surrounded the ring, cheering for the boys.

Curtis was quicker than Jimmy, tiring him out by avoiding his punches, just as Mr. Vasquez had coached. Once Jimmy tired, Curtis took his shots: One-two, jab and cross combinations. A few *jab-cross-left hook* combinations too, although Curtis mostly missed with his left hooks.

Jimmy was tough though. He took Curtis's punches and kept coming. Midway through the third round, with both of them gassed and barely able to lift their arms, Jimmy landed a hard right, knocking Curtis to the mat. Curtis lay on the mat for a few seconds, more thankful for the rest than hurt.

"Get up," Mr. Vasquez said.

Curtis staggered to his feet, his legs rubbery and his arms like jelly.

Jimmy and Curtis ran out the final round with a few punches, but neither of them had enough energy to do much damage.

At the end of the three-round fight, Curtis and Jimmy hugged.

Jimmy patted Curtis's headgear. "Good job, man."

CHAPTER 23

The Open House

Curtis's roommates dressed in their Sunday best, but they weren't attending church.

One of his roommates peered out the front window. "These people have a Beamer. I'm gonna live with them."

"I don't understand," Curtis said. "What happens at an open house?"

Mr. H. had briefly explained to Curtis that some people were coming over to meet him and the other boys, but then Mr. H. had gotten a phone call, and they never finished the conversation.

Jimmy stepped into the room, looking tough with his shiner. "It's bullshit. People come and look at us to see if they wanna take us home, like we're dogs at the pound. But they never do. We're too old."

"That's not true," said one of the roommates, as he buttoned his shirt. "Everyone goes to a foster home eventually."

"That's not a real home. A foster home's worse than here."

"What about Alan and Jalen? They're getting adopted."

Jimmy shrugged. "Every dog has its day."

"Do we have to go with them if they want us?" Curtis asked, his eyes like saucers. "My mom's gonna come back for me."

Jimmy put his arm around Curtis. "You don't have to go with nobody. You can be a lifer like me. Fuck these people."

The roommates ran from the room, excited for the barbecue and the prospect of a new family. Jimmy and Curtis followed, moving much slower.

As they descended the stairs, Jimmy said to Curtis, "It's gonna be a shitload of dishes."

Mr. Vasquez worked the grill, while Mr. H. greeted the guests and ordered the boys around, telling them to do various chores for their guests, such as getting them drinks and food.

"They're not here for a dog. They're here for a slave," Jimmy said, under his breath.

They had six guests, a rich married couple—the one with the Beamer—another married couple who drove a station wagon, and two middle-aged women who had come separately in minivans. According to Jimmy, the minivan women were foster moms, so they weren't long-term options.

Jimmy glanced at the station wagon couple and whispered to Curtis, "They're Jesus freaks."

"How do you know?" Curtis asked.

"Look at the guy. What a dork with his shirt buttoned up like that. And the wife has one of those old-timey dresses."

"What about the rich people?"

"Forget it. They could do way better than us. No way they adopt anyone here."

After the guests had drinks and appetizers, they all sat around several foldable tables on the back patio and ate barbecue chicken, cheeseburgers, baked beans, and salad. They had watermelon for dessert. The adults declined the watermelon, while the boys spat their seeds and stained their shirts with the juicy goodness.

As they digested their food, the orphans and the adults mingled, getting to know each other. It wasn't exactly like the pound. Nobody immediately took a child home. Several steps were involved, but this was the first one.

Curtis sat on a lawn chair, watching his fellow orphans jockey for attention from the prospective parents. They made jokes. They bragged. They even hugged. But Curtis wanted no part of it.

Mr. H. approached with a soda in hand. "How are you, champ?"

"I'm okay."

"Want a drink?"

Curtis shook his head.

Mr. H. sat in the lawn chair next to Curtis. Mr. H. wore a short-sleeve button-down shirt and slacks that looked like they came from Goodwill. "You wanna talk to any of these people? They're all nice folks. They'd be lucky to have a kid like you."

"No thanks."

Mr. H. nodded. "Okay."

Curtis watched Jimmy play catch with the rich guy for a moment. Then he turned in his seat to Mr. H. "How come you don't have a family?" Curtis had never seen or heard of Mr. H. having a girlfriend, wife, or children.

"I have you knuckleheads."

"No, I mean, like your *own* family."

Mr. H. didn't answer for a long time. "I had a wife and a little boy once."

"What happened?"

Mr. H. stared into the bright blue sky. "It didn't work out."

"Why not?" Curtis asked.

Mr. H. opened the soda and held it out to Curtis. "You sure you don't want it?"

Curtis took the soda. "Thank you."

They sat in silence for a minute, Curtis sipping his soda. Mr. H.'s expression was blank, like he was there but not there.

Curtis broke the silence. "I had fun yesterday at the gym."

Mr. H. came to life and raised his eyebrows. "You liked boxing?"

Curtis nodded. "Jimmy's been cool, ever since we boxed."

Mr. H. grinned. "I'm glad to hear it."

Jimmy threw the football like a frozen rope to the rich guy, as if he was trying to break the guy's hands.

But the rich guy caught the ball with soft hands, smiled at Jimmy, and said, "You've got a great arm."

★★★

A pile of plates and silverware were stacked precariously on the counter to his right. Curtis took plates from the top, rinsed them, then set them on the counter to his left. Jimmy took the rinsed plates and arranged them inside the dishwasher.

"Did you like that guy?" Curtis asked.

"Mr. Marshall?" Jimmy replied.

That was the rich guy.

"Yeah, him," Curtis said.

"He was all right," Jimmy replied, setting a plate inside the dishwasher.

Curtis rinsed another dish. "I think he liked you."

Jimmy shrugged and loaded another dish.

"You think the Marshalls will try to adopt you?"

Jimmy chuckled. "No way, man. I'm a lifer. Remember?"

"Yeah. Me too."

CHAPTER 24

Accepted

At recess on Monday, Curtis took his usual place on the grass, far from the other kids.

Jimmy found Curtis and said, "Come on, man. We're playin' kickball."

Curtis stood and followed his former nemesis to the baseball diamond. Ten boys milled around home plate. They picked teams, with Jimmy the captain of one team and another tall boy the captain of the other. Curtis's stomach flipped, worried he would be the last person picked.

But, with the first pick, Jimmy pointed and said, "I got my man, Curtis."

Curtis was worthy of a first-round pick too. He was impossible to get out. Curtis usually kicked the ball out of the infield, and, even when he didn't, he was too fast to throw out at first. He ran down pop flies in the outfield, again using his speed. By the end of recess, Curtis was sweaty, smiling, and disappointed that they had to return to class.

★★★

After school, Curtis boarded the bus and sat in his usual seat. Jimmy and Amanda boarded the bus together and walked down the aisle.

Jimmy stopped at Curtis's seat. "Get up. You're sittin' in back with us."

Curtis followed Jimmy and Amanda to the back, where the cool kids sat.

Jimmy lifted his chin to one of the other group-home boys. "Move. Curtis is sittin' there."

The boy went to the second row from the back and said to another boy, "Move. I'm sitting there."

Jimmy and Amanda sat together in one of the back seats. Curtis and another group-home boy sat in the other.

As the bus drove away from the school, Jimmy told Amanda, "Me and Curtis can beat up anybody in the whole school." Jimmy turned to Curtis. "Isn't that right, Curtis?"

"I don't know," Curtis replied.

Jimmy frowned. "What do you mean, you don't know? We're the only boys who know how to fight. Everyone else is a pussy." Jimmy turned back to Amanda. "We got a real trainer too. He trains professional boxers."

"That's cool," Amanda said.

"Me and Curtis are gonna be professional fighters."

"That's so badass."

Jimmy turned to Curtis. "Right, Curtis?"

Curtis smiled. "Yeah."

Jimmy turned back to Amanda and took her hand in his. She blushed.

Curtis's smile receded.

CHAPTER 25

Twix are the Best

"Hey, Curtis. Wake up. Wake up."

Curtis's eyes fluttered and opened. Jimmy stood next to his bed, shaking him.

"What?" Curtis asked, his voice raspy with sleep.

"Get up. We're goin' to Walmart," Jimmy whispered.

Snoring and rhythmic breathing came from his roommates.

Curtis sat up in bed. "Walmart? For what?"

"Come on. It'll be fun."

Curtis climbed down from his bed. He dressed in a pair of jeans and a hoodie. They crept down the hall and tiptoed downstairs. They exited through the side door, careful to leave the door unlocked for their return. They walked away from the group home, the moon shining above them.

Curtis sucked in the cool night air. "Why are we going to Walmart?"

"I want some candy," Jimmy replied.

"I don't have any money."

Jimmy chuckled. "Me neither."

"If we get caught—"

"Relax. Leave it all to me."

They hiked out of their neighborhood to Route 1. As soon as they saw a break in traffic, they sprinted across the six-lane highway. They hiked another mile or so to Walmart. The well-lit parking lot was nearly empty, except for the cluster of cars huddled near the entrance.

Before they entered Walmart, Jimmy put his hand on Curtis's shoulder and said, "Just be cool. Act like you belong here, like we're here to buy somethin'."

Curtis nodded.

They entered the automatic doors. Thankfully, there wasn't an elderly person stationed there, greeting the public. They walked into the big box store and turned right, away from the cash registers.

"They have candy back there," Curtis said, gesturing to the registers.

Jimmy whispered, "You can't steal from there. The cashiers will see us."

Jimmy led Curtis to the Halloween section. It was five weeks until Halloween, but Walmart was always supplied early for holidays. Jimmy found a bag of mini-Twix bars, the packaging decorated with little bats. Jimmy sucked in his stomach, lifted his oversize T-shirt, and shoved the bag of candy halfway down his pants. He covered his bulge with his shirt.

"Let's go," Jimmy whispered.

They made a beeline for the exit.

Curtis's heart pounded. His palms and underarms were sweaty. He glanced about, worried that an employee would stop them. As they approached the exit, an older male employee stared at them. Curtis fought every instinct to run.

Jimmy smiled at the guy and said, "Have a nice evenin', sir."

"Thank you for shopping at Walmart," the man replied.

Curtis grinned when they exited the store. Jimmy grinned back.

On the walk back, they ate mini-Twix candy bars.

Jimmy opened a Twix, shoved the candy bar in his mouth, and tossed the wrapper on the roadside. He said with his mouth full, "I fuckin' love Twix."

"Me too," Curtis replied, also with his mouth full.

Jimmy held out the bag to Curtis. "Have some more."

"Thanks." Curtis took a big handful of Twix bars and shoved them into the front pocket of his hoodie.

They ate several more mini-Twix bars, walking in silence, enjoying the sugar rush.

Curtis swallowed. "Do you really think we could be professional fighters?"

"Yeah. Why not?" Jimmy replied. "Or maybe professional football players. I could be the quarterback of the Redskins, and you can be my top wide receiver. You're fast enough." Jimmy popped another mini-Twix into his mouth.

Curtis beamed, thinking about being a professional athlete.

They ran back across Route 1. A car honked at them, not that they were in danger, but the driver was likely startled by kids running across the highway at midnight. Jimmy and Curtis laughed, enjoying the adrenaline rush in addition to their sugar high.

They entered their neighborhood. Jimmy held out the mostly empty bag of mini-Twix.

Curtis shook his head. "I'm so full."

Jimmy patted his belly. "Me too."

They hiked in silence for a minute.

"What if Mr. H. finds out that we snuck out?" Curtis asked.

"He won't. He's a heavy sleeper," Jimmy replied.

Curtis wasn't sure about that, since Mr. H. had come to Curtis's aid when he had that nightmare. "Do you like Mr. H.?"

"He's all right. Too strict, but he's all right."

"Did you know that he was married with a son?"

"I heard that before," Jimmy said. "You know what happened to them?"

"No. Do you?" Curtis asked.

Jimmy nodded. "This one time, I was gonna sneak out, but I heard Mr. H. in his office talkin' on the phone. He said his wife went out with her friends or some shit, so he stayed home to watch the baby, and the baby died for no reason. Just died in the crib. Mr. H.'s wife was so mad at him that she married some other dude."

"*Damn.* That's messed up."

"Yeah."

They hiked in silence, until the group home was visible in the distance, the white siding glowing in the moonlight.

"How old were you when you came here?" Curtis asked.

"Ten. Like you," Jimmy replied.

"How come ..." Curtis trailed off. He had almost asked how come Jimmy was in the same class as Curtis, but he had realized that might embarrass his new friend. Curtis knew Jimmy was older than him because Mr. H. had said so, but he didn't know exactly how much older. Curtis guessed he was twelve.

"How come what? How come I'm only in the fifth-grade?"

"It doesn't matter how old you are."

Jimmy kicked a nearby rock. "It's not my fault. I didn't go to school for a whole year."

"Why not?"

Jimmy kicked another rock. "Because my mom's a stupid bitch. Cares more about meth than me."

Curtis thought, *My mom's coming back for me.*

CHAPTER 26

The Lucky One

"You're lucky," said one of the group-home boys, sitting on a lower bunk in their bedroom.

Jimmy shrugged and grabbed a black hoodie from his dresser. Fall weather was forecasted for that first Sunday in October.

"You wanna wear my Clinton Portis jersey?" Curtis asked.

"*Nah.* I'm good." Jimmy slipped the hoodie over his head.

"Where are your seats?"

Jimmy tried to contain his smile, but it bloomed. "Mr. Marshall's company has box seats."

"Damn. You are lucky," said the group-home boy, standing from the bunk bed. "If you get adopted, you can go to every game."

Curtis's face was taut. "You think you'll be adopted?"

"No way," Jimmy replied. "They're just slummin' it. Tryin' to prove that they're good or some shit."

The doorbell chimed.

Jimmy, Curtis, and the other boy all looked out the window, spotting the Marshalls' BMW in the driveway.

"Check you later." Jimmy left the bedroom.

"He's gonna get adopted," said the group-home boy, once Jimmy was out of earshot.

"No, he won't," Curtis replied.

Curtis left the bedroom, following Jimmy. He stopped at the top of the stairs, watching Jimmy with the Marshalls and Mr. H. downstairs.

Mrs. Marshall hugged Jimmy, and he hugged her back. Mr. Marshall handed him a folded burgundy garment. Jimmy unfolded the garment to reveal an official number 8 Washington Redskins jersey, with *Brunell* stitched across the back.

"Look at that," Mr. H. said. "Mark Brunell."

Mr. H. was referring to the quarterback of the Washington Redskins.

Jimmy grinned from ear to ear and put the jersey on over his sweatshirt. "Thank you so much."

Mr. Marshall shook Jimmy's hand, and Mrs. Marshall gave him another hug.

The group-home boy sidled up to Curtis. "Sure looks like he's gonna get adopted."

"Shut up," Curtis replied.

CHAPTER 27

Trick or Treat

Curtis jockeyed for position in the bathroom mirror with the other group-home boys, checking his eye black. He looked like a badass with the thick lines of eye black underneath his eyes and his Clinton Portis jersey.

All the boys wore football jerseys and eye black. Some of them wore elbow pads and knee pads. A few crumpled papers and taped the balled-up masses of notebook paper under their jerseys to create makeshift shoulder pads.

Satisfied with his Halloween costume, Curtis left the bathroom for Jimmy's room. Jimmy stood by the window, watching the front yard and the driveway.

"It's almost five," Curtis said, addressing the designated start time for trick or treating.

Jimmy turned from the window, wearing his Mark Brunell jersey. He had a pained expression on his face. "I'm, uh, … I'm going to the Marshalls' neighborhood."

Curtis drew his eyebrows together. "You just saw them."

Jimmy hesitated for a beat. "Rich neighborhoods have the best candy. They give like full-size candy bars."

Curtis clenched his fists. "But you have to walk really far."

"Mr. Marshall has a golf cart. He said I could drive—"

"That's stupid."

Jimmy tilted his head, his eyes narrowed. "No, it's not."

Curtis bowed his head. "I thought we were gonna go together."

"You have the whole group home to go with."

"So?"

The rumble of an engine came from outside.

Jimmy checked the driveway. "Gotta go." Jimmy started for the door, but stopped and patted Curtis's shoulder. "Don't go to that yellow house on the corner. The old bag gave us fuckin' carrots last year. I'll bring you some rich-people candy."

"Yeah," Curtis replied.

Jimmy left.

Curtis watched through the window, as his best friend left with Mr. Marshall. He imagined being Jimmy, being a handsome kid, being a kid who someone wanted.

CHAPTER 28

Never Too Old

Curtis and Jimmy sat on chairs in front of the television, playing Madden Football on the PlayStation. Several other boys sat on the couch in the living room, cheering and jeering the matchup between the pixelated Dallas Cowboys and the pixelated Washington Redskins. The winner of the matchup would play the next boy in line. The loser would go back to the couch and the back of the line.

A decorated Christmas tree stood in the corner, its little lights shining. It was eleven days until the big day. The boys had decorated it a few weeks ago, the day after Thanksgiving.

The doorbell chimed.

One of the boys stood from the couch. "I'll get it."

On the PlayStation, Jimmy threw a long bomb to Santana Moss. He stood from the chair, his hands in the air, mimicking the referee on the screen, signaling the touchdown. "That's game." He turned to Curtis. "You're my boy, but you suck at video games."

Curtis grinned, showing his buck teeth. "Shut up."

The boy who had answered the front door, returned to the living room and said to Jimmy, "Mr. and Mrs. Marshall are here to see you."

Jimmy set his controller on the chair. "Curtis can take my place. He needs the practice." Jimmy left the living room.

In a trance, Curtis watched Jimmy leave.

One of the boys nudged Curtis. "You playing?"

Curtis shook his head. "You can take my spot."

"*Yes.*" That boy and another filled the seats in front of the television.

Curtis crept from the living room toward the front door. Partially hidden by the stairwell, Curtis peeked at Jimmy and the Marshalls standing in the foyer.

"We think you're a great kid," Mr. Marshall said. "We've enjoyed getting to know you over these past few months."

Curtis figured they were gonna make some excuse as to why they couldn't adopt Jimmy. Over the past few months, Jimmy had visited with the Marshalls often, but he'd always maintained they would never adopt him, that he was too old. Jimmy was happy to take their gifts and play the game though.

"We want you to be a part of our family," Mrs. Marshall said, with glassy eyes. "We love you, and we want to adopt you, if that's something you want."

Jimmy was speechless for several seconds. He hung his head. His body convulsed. Curtis couldn't see his face from his vantage point, but he was pretty sure Jimmy was crying. Jimmy hugged Mrs. Marshall. Mr. Marshall joined the hug, hugging them both at the same time.

CHAPTER 29

Jimmy's Last Sparring Session

Curtis watched Jimmy spar with another boy from their group home. Jimmy toyed with the boy, not wanting to hurt him, but working on the skills he had acquired over the past three months of working with Mr. Vasquez.

Last night, while hanging out in Jimmy's room, Curtis had asked, "They're adopting you?"

Jimmy had taken a deep breath. "Yeah."

"But it takes a long time, doesn't it?"

"For the adoption?"

"Yeah. Until you go to live with them."

Jimmy had been quiet for a moment. "The Marshalls are already foster parents. I'll live with them, while we wait for the adoption."

Curtis's stomach had lurched. "When are you leaving?"

"Before Christmas."

The buzzer sounded, and Jimmy hugged the other boy, patted him on the back, and said, "Great job. You're gettin' better."

Mr. Vasquez motioned to Curtis. "*Joo* ready?"

Curtis nodded and climbed into the ring, his headgear and gloves already on. His opponent was another group-home boy. Artie was bigger and slower than Curtis and had only been boxing for two weeks.

The buzzer sounded, and Curtis went after him, stunning the boy with quick combinations. One-two. One-two-three. Artie recovered and swung wildly. Curtis ducked and pounded the boy's flabby midsection. Artie let out a groan. Curtis continued to pound the boy with jabs, crosses, and hooks. Artie covered his head with his gloves, but it wasn't enough to stop the barrage. Curtis caught Artie on his chin with a perfect left hook, dropping the boy for the count. Curtis stood over Artie and flexed his skinny muscles. The buzzer sounded.

Mr. Vasquez hurried onto the mat to check Artie. Once Artie was upright and seemingly okay, Mr. Vasquez ended the sparring session. Mr. Vasquez stalked to Curtis and pulled him to the far corner of the ring by his arm. Mr. Vasquez scowled at Curtis. "No. *Joo* no do that."

"What did I do?" Curtis asked, his voice going up an octave.

Mr. Vasquez wagged his finger. "*Joo* know. It's bullshit. *Joo* no respect him."

Curtis bowed his head.

Mr. Vasquez gestured to Artie in the opposite corner. "*Joo* tell him *joo* sorry."

Curtis trudged to the boy. "Hey, man. I'm sorry about that."

Artie held out his gloves. "It's cool."

Curtis tapped Artie's gloves with his.

At the end of the workout, Mr. Vasquez called all the boys together. He grabbed a cardboard box from under the ring, handed it to Jimmy, and said, "For *joo*. I know *joo* leaving soon."

Jimmy grinned from ear to ear as he opened the present. Inside the box was a new pair of boxing gloves. "Thank you, Mr. Vasquez. Thank you for everything." Jimmy hugged the old man.

CHAPTER 30

Missing Jimmy

Curtis stared at Jimmy's empty desk on the last day of school before Christmas break. His classmates worked on the Christmas word searches provided by Mrs. Little. They'd done little work that day, instead playing various Christmas-themed games, but it hadn't been fun without Jimmy.

"Lunchtime, everybody," Mrs. Little said.

Everyone grabbed their lunches, switched seats, and sat with their friends. Many of Curtis's classmates still worked on the word searches. Curtis didn't move, electing to sit by himself. He ate his bologna sandwich, even though he wasn't hungry. He watched Amanda eat lunch with the biggest boy in class, Chad, who only held that title because Jimmy was gone. Amanda noticed Curtis staring. She waved at Curtis and offered a somber smile. Curtis pretended to work on his word search.

As he ate his lunch, he thought about what Jimmy had said about his own mom. *My mom's a stupid bitch. Cares more about meth than me.* When he'd said that, Curtis didn't see the similarity to his own mother. At the time, he had felt sorry for Jimmy, and Curtis was thankful *his* mom would eventually come back for him. But now Curtis wondered if that was wrong.

Maybe my mom cares more about crack than me. Curtis tried to think of something else, anything else.

Mrs. Little diverted Curtis's attention when she said, "I have a little holiday gift for you all."

She handed out little baggies full of holiday-themed candy. Inside were various chocolates and hard candies. The fifth graders thanked their teacher and ate candy for dessert or, in some case, in place of their lunches.

Curtis fished out the sugar cookie mini-Twix. He stared at the shiny gold package, remembering his friend.

CHAPTER 31

Must Be Nice

On a Sunday in the middle of March, Curtis sat at his desk, working on his homework—a book report on any book of his choice. He had read the first book of the Harry Potter series and was summarizing the story for the report. Curtis had identified with Harry's lack of parents, although he hadn't mentioned that in his report.

A blue BMW pulled into the driveway of the group home. Curtis stood from his desk and watched the driveway from his bedroom window. Mr. and Mrs. Marshall exited the vehicle, along with Jimmy. Jimmy wore a stylish black jacket and brand-new Timberland boots. He had a fresh haircut and a big smile.

The Marshalls and the future Marshall son rang the doorbell. One of the boys answered the door. Excited voices came from downstairs. Mr. H.'s booming voice mixed with the high-pitched voices of the boys. Curtis crept down the hallway to the top of the stairs. He listened to the boys catch up with Jimmy. He listened to Jimmy tell them about his great life. All the places they visited. The things they did together as a family.

Curtis went back to his room, back to his homework. He stared at his book report for several minutes, unable to concentrate.

"Hey, man," Jimmy said.

Curtis turned from his homework to Jimmy in the doorway. "Hey."

Jimmy approached Curtis. "What's up?"

Curtis stood from his desk and shrugged. "Nothing. What about you?"

Jimmy struggled to hide his smile. "I'm not gonna lie. It's pretty great to be a Marshall."

"I thought it would take like six months for them to adopt you."

"That's just paperwork. I'm already a Marshall."

Curtis nodded. "Must be nice."

Jimmy smacked Curtis on the shoulder, not hard. "What about you? I bet you're whoopin' everyone's ass at the gym."

Curtis shrugged again. "Not really. Mr. Vasquez doesn't want me doin' that."

"Yeah. But you *could* whoop their asses."

Curtis forced a smile. "Yeah. I guess. What about you? Are you boxing?"

"*Nah.* Not really. I'm goin' to a bunch of quarterback camps this summer though. Dad—I mean, Mr. Marshall—thinks, with some good coachin', I could play college football."

"That's cool."

"Yeah. It's pretty cool."

"Where are the camps?"

Jimmy hesitated for a second. "California."

"That's a long way to go."

"We're movin' out there."

Curtis dipped his head. "You're never coming back here again, are you?"

"I don't know."

Curtis slumped into his desk chair and spoke barely above a whisper. "I thought we were gonna be lifers."

"You're gonna find a family too. If I can do it, anyone can."

"You're not ugly."

CHAPTER 32

Good Friday

On the Friday before Easter, Curtis ran a slant pattern, using his quickness to shake the defender. The quarterback threw a strike. Curtis caught the ball, juked two defenders, and raced for the end zone, leaving everyone in the dust. His teammates and fellow orphans joined him in the end zone, celebrating their backyard football victory.

Mr. H. appeared in the backyard, with two uniformed police officers. Mr. H. called out, "Curtis. Come over here."

The group home boys looked from the police officers to Curtis with concern.

Curtis shrugged. "I didn't do anything." He tossed the football to one of the boys and trotted to Mr. H. and the police officers. Their faces were somber. The officers held their hats in hand. A sick feeling came from the pit of Curtis's stomach. "What is it?"

"Let's go inside," Mr. H. replied.

Curtis followed the men inside. They went into Mr. H.'s office. Mr. H. insisted that Curtis sit, but nobody else did.

"What's going on?" Curtis asked, searching the faces of the three men for answers.

"Sara Duffy died yesterday of an overdose," a police officer said, his voice monotone. "I'm very sorry for your loss."

Curtis was stunned, as he processed the information. Tears welled in his eyes. His throat tightened. He stood from the chair. His voice quivered, as he asked, "Can I go now?"

Mr. H. put his hand on Curtis's shoulder and squeezed. "Hang tight for a minute. I need to talk to you." Mr. H. left Curtis in his office, as he escorted the police officers outside.

Curtis slumped in his seat. The dam burst, and the tears flowed, while Mr. H. was gone.

Mr. H. returned shortly. Curtis stood from the chair and wiped his face with the sleeve of his sweatshirt. He tried to push past Mr. H., but Mr. H. blocked his path and hugged him tight. Curtis's body convulsed with sobs.

Mr. H. held him. "I know, son. I know."

PART II
High School

Victory has a thousand fathers, but defeat is an orphan.

—Count Galeazzo Ciano,
Italian Foreign Minister

CHAPTER 33

Friday Night Lights

Curtis stood on the sidelines, under the Friday night lights of West Potomac High School. His uniform was sparkling clean, his silver helmet tucked under his arm.

Their quarterback threw a deep post to Terrel Sanders, which appeared to be overthrown. Terrel sprinted under the floating football, reached forward at the last second, and caught the ball with his fingertips. He cradled the football and sprinted the rest of the way to the end zone. The blue-and-silver-clad crowd cheered.

"Touchdown. Terrel Sanders. His third of the night," said the announcer.

Curtis still dreamed of being the superstar football player, like Terrel Sanders, but it was hard to believe in something so unrealistic.

With a comfortable lead late in the fourth quarter, Coach Giles called out to the sideline, "Second team, get ready."

That meant Curtis would be in the next time the offense took the field. Curtis began to sweat. His stomach churned. Bile crept up his throat. He swallowed the hot sickness. He rubbed his palms together. They felt slick with sweat. He rubbed them on his silver pants.

Curtis watched the second-team defense struggle to stop Yorktown High School's first-team offense. Yorktown made several first downs, reaching West Potomac's twelve-yard line. But, on fourth and two, the second-team defense stuffed their inside run, ending Yorktown's drive and likely their last chance at points.

Curtis trotted onto the field, with the rest of the second-team offense.

In the huddle, the quarterback called the play. "Twins right, twenty-eight lead toss. On two."

Curtis lined up near the right-hand sideline. On the second *hut*, Curtis blocked the defensive back in front of him. The quarterback tossed the ball to the running back, and he ran toward the sideline, but the lead blocker missed the defensive end and the running back was smothered for a two-yard loss.

Curtis jogged back to the huddle.

The quarterback glanced at the signal from the sideline. He checked his wristband and the play that corresponded to the signal. He frowned. "Twins left, twenty-nine lead toss. On one."

It was the same play to the opposite side and the same result. Another two-yard loss.

On third down, the quarterback called, "Pro left, swing left, go. On two."

This was a play designed for the wide receivers to run down the field to draw the defensive backs. The quarterback could then throw a swing pass to the running back, and theoretically, he should have running room. This play worked especially well against man coverage.

Before Curtis jogged to his spot, he said to the quarterback, "I'll be open."

On the second *hut*, Curtis sprinted past the cornerback. He was open by five yards and gaining distance on the defender. The quarterback launched a bomb to Curtis. It was a tight spiral, a perfect pass that hit Curtis in the hands ... but he dropped it.

A collective gasp came from the crowd.

Curtis jogged back to the sideline, his head down.

"Damn. Catch the fuckin' ball," said one of his teammates.

This wasn't the first time he'd had problems catching the football. Last year, as a sophomore, he'd been so good in training camp that he'd earned a starting receiver spot, along with Terrel Sanders, who was a junior at the time. However, Curtis got nervous under the lights and in front of the crowd. Consequently, he'd dropped nearly every ball thrown his way. After two games, he had been demoted to junior varsity.

Curtis had taken the demotion maturely, working hard and being a star on junior varsity. Of course, nobody cared about JV, and the stands were empty for JV games. This year, he'd had another stellar camp, but the coaches were hesitant to play him, after the disaster of the year before. The pass he'd just dropped had been the first of the season thrown his way. Curtis figured it would likely be his last too.

After the game ended, Curtis walked toward the bleachers to talk to Mr. H., even though he wanted to hide somewhere. Mr. H. was easy to spot, since he accompanied eight kids, ages nine to eleven. The boys at the group home when Curtis had arrived six years ago were all gone—adopted or placed in foster care. Curtis was a lifer, just like Jimmy had said.

The group-home kids ran toward Curtis, one of them cradling a football in his arms.

"Good game, Curtis," said one of the boys.

Two of them gave Curtis a hug, before running onto the football field with the others.

Curtis met Mr. H. on the rubber track that surrounded the football field. Curtis had thought Mr. H. was indestructible when he'd arrived at the group home, but he was starting to show his sixty-one years of age. Deep grooves had emerged around his mouth, along with flecks of gray in his eyebrows.

"Thanks for coming. Sorry. ... I was nervous. I can't seem to ..." Curtis trailed off.

"You got nothing to apologize for," Mr. H. said.

Curtis hung his head. "I think I have a problem with stage fright. I get nervous when it really matters."

"It's normal to be nervous in high-pressure situations. It shows that you care. I used to get so nervous that I would throw up before big games."

Once upon a time, Mr. H. had played linebacker at Central Virginia University.

Curtis raised his gaze. "What did you do about it?"

"I worked my tail off. If you practice enough, your body will simply react. You won't need to think about it. Relaxing yourself in the moment helps too. Focus on taking deep breaths. Visualize success. Shake your legs and arms. Loosen your body."

Curtis nodded. "Thanks. I'll try that."

Mr. H. clapped Curtis on the shoulder pads. "We'll wait for you in the van."

Curtis walked across the football field toward the locker room. He passed Amanda in her cheerleader outfit, flirting with Terrel Sanders. She gave Curtis a discreet wave.

CHAPTER 34

Boxing or Football?

Curtis punched the heavy bag, sweat spraying from his skin with each snap of his punches. Several boxers worked nearby, their humming-bird-fast punches and perfect timing causing the speed bags to respond with rhythmic rattles. His stopwatch buzzed, signaling the end of the round. Curtis dropped his hands, feeling the burn in his shoulders.

Mr. Vasquez approached Curtis. "Why are you here? No practice today?" His English had improved after training dozens of group-home boys over the past six years.

"We have films, but that's only for the starters," Curtis replied.

"You don't wanna be a starter?"

Curtis loved football and wanted to play, but maybe that was the problem. Maybe he wanted it too much. "Yes, but—"

"Then you need to go to practice."

"I wanna be a professional fighter, like you."

Mr. Vasquez scowled, showing the deep grooves in his weathered face. "No, you don't. I fought twenty fights. No money. Football is better *oportunidad*. You get good grades. You go to college, get good job. No need to fight."

Curtis had had this conversation with Mr. H. too. West Potomac had a stellar football program, and roughly ten seniors earned scholarships each year. Curtis had the physical tools to earn a scholarship. Mr. H. had assured Curtis they could find the financial aid, if a scholarship didn't materialize. But Curtis couldn't imagine going to college without playing football. His backup plan was becoming a professional fighter.

"I think I'm a better fighter than a football player," Curtis said.

"I don't know about that." Mr. Vasquez tapped Curtis's chest with his craggy finger. "You need to believe in yourself. I know you can do it, but *you* need to know you can do it."

Mr. Vasquez was right of course. If Curtis couldn't catch a pass under the Friday night lights, how could he fight in a packed arena with all eyes on him?

"I could make a lot of money. I could be a champion." Curtis said the words, but they sounded hollow.

"For every champion, there's a thousand fighters like me. You need to go to college. You can fight later if you want."

Curtis bowed his head and nodded.

Mr. Vasquez held out his hands, and Curtis tapped them with his gloves. Mr. Vasquez went to the center ring and worked with an up-and-coming Mexican middleweight named Jose Alvarez, who had five professional fights under his belt, all wins by knockout. Mr. Vasquez wore mitts on his hands, and Jose snapped combinations with laser-like accuracy.

Curtis stood by the ring, mesmerized by Jose's skill. When the round was over, Mr. Vasquez appeared agitated and said something in Spanish to Jose. They both looked disappointed. Curtis figured his sparring partner hadn't shown.

"I'll spar with him," Curtis said.

Mr. Vasquez shook his head at Curtis. "It's not a good idea."

Jose stared at Curtis with interest.

"I can do it," Curtis said.

Jose said something to Mr. Vasquez in rapid Spanish. Mr. Vasquez said something back.

Mr. Vasquez beckoned Curtis to the ring. "Okay."

Curtis climbed into the ring.

As Mr. Vasquez fastened the headgear to Curtis's head, he said, "*Cuidado*. He's very fast."

"I know," Curtis replied.

The buzzer sounded, and Curtis and Jose converged in the center of the ring. Jose jabbed several times, landing all of them. Curtis tried a combination, landing his right, but paying for it with Jose's left hook. The blow caused Curtis to stumble. If it had been a real fight, Jose would've finished off Curtis with a flurry of punches. Instead, he let Curtis recover, so they could continue to spar.

They sparred for three rounds. Jose was the superior fighter, never going for the kill when he could've. Yet Curtis had been an adequate sparring partner, lasting all three rounds and landing some good shots.

Jose hugged Curtis at the end of the sparring session and thanked him for the work. Jose was the best fighter Curtis had ever sparred. Curtis was used to sparring with amateurs and kids from the group home, so he was confident in his boxing skills, but now he wasn't so sure.

He wondered if Mr. Vasquez was reluctant to endorse Curtis's desire to become a professional fighter because he knew Curtis didn't have what it took to be a champion.

CHAPTER 35

Two Steps Back, One Step Forward

Curtis sat in front of his locker, tying his shoes. His teammates bantered back and forth in various stages of dress. The smell of sweat, soap, and mold hung in the air.

Coach Giles stuck his head in the locker room. "Curtis, I need to talk to you in my office."

Curtis followed the head coach into his office.

"Shut the door," Coach Giles said.

Curtis shut the door behind him. The walls were covered in plaques and framed photos of past championships. Curtis sat across from Coach Giles at his desk.

Giles was tall, dark, and intimidating. It didn't stop Curtis's black teammates from joking about his dark skin behind his back. Despite being biracial, Curtis didn't think he was black enough to join in the jokes. Some of their recurring favorites were:

> *Coach Giles is so black, he was riding a motorcycle and got a ticket for tinted windows.*
> *Coach Giles is so black, when he went to night school, he got marked absent.*
> *Coach Giles is so mean and so black, he's the reason kids are afraid of the dark.*

Coach Giles cleared his throat. "I'm moving you back to JV."

Curtis slumped his shoulders and nodded.

"You have all the talent in the world, but I can't put you out there if you can't catch the football."

"What if I moved to defense? I'm not afraid to hit."

Coach Giles rubbed the stubble on his chin for a moment. "It's not a bad idea. I think you'd make a helluva strong safety, but you still need to go down to JV. You need to learn the defense. You need to learn the position. Means you probably won't play on varsity until next year."

"I know. I didn't think I was gonna play anyway."

"Probably not."

Curtis left the coach's office, grabbed his backpack from his locker, and exited the building. The waning sun and the brick building cast a shadow over the parking lot. Amanda argued with Terrel Sanders, next to his new Ford Mustang. Her arms were crossed over her chest. Her face was beet red. Her blond hair was tied in a tight ponytail, enhancing her angry expression.

Curtis watched the scene. Amanda still had the cutest button nose, which was the opposite of Curtis's wide monstrosity. Her short shorts and tight T-shirt suited her athletic build.

Terrel pivoted to Curtis. "What the fuck you lookin' at?"

Curtis clenched his jaw and narrowed his eyes.

"Keep it movin'."

Amanda gave Curtis a subtle nod.

Curtis walked away. As he left, he thought he heard Terrel say, "Ugly ass motherfucker."

CHAPTER 36

Learning Experience

Curtis took his demotion to JV as a learning experience. He learned the defense and how to play strong safety, becoming the best defender on the junior varsity. His JV coaches lobbied Coach Giles to give him a shot as a varsity defender, but the West Potomac Wolverines were undefeated. Coach Giles couldn't justify benching anyone on an undefeated team. His attitude was, if it ain't broke, don't fix it.

Curtis did play special teams on varsity, specializing in punt and kickoff coverage. He was, by far, the team leader in special teams tackles. He was hopeful that next season, his senior season, would be his year to shine and to earn a scholarship.

Curtis put on his jacket, slung his backpack over his shoulder, and left the football locker room. Outside, a cool breeze bit at his ears. The sun was low and orange on the horizon. Terrel Sanders chirped the rear tires of his Mustang and sped away from school. Amanda was left in his wake, sitting on the curb, her face in her hands.

Curtis approached Amanda. "You okay?"

Amanda nodded, but she didn't lift her face.

Curtis stepped close enough to see she was crying. "You sure?"

She sniffed and wiped her face with a balled-up tissue. She pocketed the tissue, stood from the curb, and said, "Terrel broke up with me."

"He's an asshole anyway."

"I don't know what I'm gonna do."

"You're gonna move on and find someone better."

She shook her head. Then she stared at Curtis with glassy eyes and said, "I'm late."

Curtis sucked air through his teeth. "*Shit*."

"Exactly. I'm fucked. Literally and figuratively."

"Not necessarily. How do you know you're pregnant? Did you take a test, or is it just because you're late?"

"I'm rarely late."

"You need to take a test to find out for sure."

Amanda nodded again. "Would you go with me to Walmart?"

"Right now?"

"*Please?*"

Curtis and Amanda hiked a few miles from school to Walmart. The conversation was stilted, with Amanda distracted by the situation. They weren't really friends anymore. They hadn't been for a long time. After Jimmy had left at Christmas in the fifth grade, they still talked occasionally, but they were more acquaintances than friends, without Jimmy to act as the glue between them.

They found the pregnancy tests in the family planning section. Amanda picked a test that promised easy, instant, and accurate results. As they waited in line, Amanda fidgeted more and more, as they neared the register.

With only one customer in front of them, Amanda faced Curtis and whispered, "I can't do it."

"Do what?" Curtis asked.

"It's too embarrassing. I can't buy it." She reached into her purse, retrieved a twenty-dollar bill, and thrust the bill at Curtis. "Will you buy it?"

Curtis frowned but took the money. "Okay."

When the customer in front of them finished, Amanda slipped past the cashier, and waited on the bench near the bathrooms. The middle-aged cashier glared at Curtis, as he handed her the pregnancy test. Curtis imagined her thinking, *Who the hell would have sex with this ugly motherfucker?* Curtis knew the answer to that question. *Nobody.*

After paying for the pregnancy test, Curtis went to Amanda and sat beside her on the bench. He handed her the plastic bag with the pregnancy test inside and said, "Your change is in the bag."

She took the test. "Thank you for doing that. I felt like that woman was gonna judge me."

"She probably would've," Curtis replied.

Amanda stood from the bench. "I'm gonna go to the bathroom and take this. Will you wait for me?"

Curtis leaned back on the bench. "I'm not going anywhere."

"Thanks, Curtis." Amanda went to the bathroom.

Curtis went back to the checkout area and waited in line again, but with a different cashier. He grabbed a full-size Twix bar, paid for it, and returned to the bench.

Fifteen minutes later, Amanda returned from the bathroom, beaming.

Curtis stood from the bench. "All good?"

Amanda nodded. "I'm *not*. Thank God."

"Yeah. Thank God."

"Let's get out of here. My brothers are probably wondering where I am."

On the way out, Curtis handed her the Twix. "I figured this could be a celebration Twix or a consolation prize."

She took the candy bar. "Definitely a celebration Twix. I love Twix, by the way."

"Me too," Curtis replied.

They stepped through the automatic doors, into the parking lot. It was almost dark.

"You should have half." She stopped, opened the candy bar, and handed Curtis one of the skinny bars.

He smiled. "Thanks."

They walked toward home and ate their candy bars in just a few bites.

Curtis swallowed and said, "Jimmy and I stole a huge bag of Twix from that Walmart once."

"*Really*? He never told me that."

"We snuck out of the group home at like midnight. Walked to Walmart, and Jimmy went to the Halloween section, grabbed a big bag of mini-Twix, and shoved it down his pants."

Amanda laughed. "Sounds like Jimmy."

"An old guy was watching us when we were leaving. I thought for sure he was gonna bust us. Then Jimmy said, *Have a nice evening, sir*. And we just walked out."

Amanda laughed again. "I miss Jimmy. Do you ever talk to him?"

"We used to talk on the phone sometimes, but I haven't talked to him in like four years."

"That sucks."

They hiked beyond the Walmart parking lot, alongside a road with heavy rush-hour traffic.

"Yeah. He's different," Curtis said. "Last I heard, he doesn't even play football anymore. Plays lacrosse and goes to private school."

"Must be nice," Amanda replied.

"Yeah. Must be."

Curtis walked Amanda home, not that it was a chore. He enjoyed her company, and her house was on the way to the group home. She lived in a little brick rambler with her mother and two younger half brothers. Toys were scattered in the weedy lawn. No car was in the driveway. Curtis wondered if Amanda's mom still waited tables at Denny's at night.

They stopped at the end of her driveway.

"Are you supposed to be watching your brothers?" Curtis asked.

"They're old enough to take care of themselves for a few hours," Amanda replied.

Curtis nodded. "I guess I'll see you later."

"Thank you for helping me."

"It's no big deal."

Amanda took his hand. "It was a big deal." She pecked Curtis on the lips, pivoted, and walked toward her house.

Curtis's heart pounded, as he watched her walk away. He still felt her lips on his. It had been the first time a girl, other than his mother, had kissed him.

CHAPTER 37

She's Not for You

The football team drank water and enjoyed a brief respite from practice. With the cool weather, Curtis wasn't thirsty. Instead, he watched the cheerleaders practicing in the distance. He watched Amanda doing handsprings, splits, kicks, and various cheers. Despite the weather, her perfectly athletic legs were bare, although she wore her warmup jacket. Her movements were graceful and precise, her smile infectious.

His stomach fluttered at the memory of the kiss they'd shared. He imagined walking Amanda home after practice. Terrel used to give her a ride, but that was over now. Of course, she might get a ride from one of the other cheerleaders.

Terrel Sanders sidled up to Curtis, his helmet in hand. He watched Amanda with Curtis for several seconds. "She's not for you."

Curtis returned to the practice field.

After practice, Curtis shouldered his backpack and left the locker room. He had hoped to find Amanda waiting for him outside the locker room, as cheer practice ended before football practice. But he didn't see her. Curtis thought he took too long, so she had already caught a ride with a fellow cheerleader. As he walked through the parking lot, he spotted Terrel's Ford Mustang. Amanda contorted herself in the front seat, in Terrel's lap, making out with the star receiver.

Curtis faced forward, zipped up his jacket, and walked toward the group home. A haze of despair covered him like a blanket. As he hiked the two miles to home, he thought about Amanda. *She would never like someone as ugly as me. What the fuck was I thinking?* He wondered if his mother thought he was ugly, like everyone else. *Of course she did. She wasn't blind.* Curtis tried to picture his mother's face, but the picture in his mind was blurry. He didn't have a single picture of her. He never did.

CHAPTER 38

We're Not Even That

Curtis opened his school locker and hung his jacket inside. A few classmates also accessed their lockers but not many, as it was still twenty-five minutes until the first bell. Most of his classmates arrived later, likely savoring a few extra minutes of sleep. Curtis preferred to be early, using the extra time to study. Curtis grabbed the textbooks for his first three classes of the day—English, Algebra II, Driver's Ed— and shoved them into his backpack. He wouldn't be near his locker until fourth period.

He shut his locker to reveal Amanda's smiling face.

"Hey," she said.

Curtis scowled and slung his backpack over his shoulder.

"What's wrong with you?"

He exhaled. "Why are you still with him?"

Amanda flushed. "It's none of your business."

"It's not? Then why was I buying you a pregnancy test less than twenty-four hours ago?"

"*Shh.*" Amanda glanced over her shoulder, making sure nobody heard. She whispered, "I love him, okay?"

Curtis whispered back, "If he loved you, he wouldn't have thrown you away like trash when he thought you were pregnant."

"He was scared."

"I would never do that to you if …"

"If what?"

Curtis hesitated for a second. "If we were together."

She cringed at the idea.

Curtis bowed his head. "I'm not stupid. I know you would never be with someone who looks like me."

"It's not that. I just don't think of you that way. We're just friends," Amanda whispered.

Curtis raised his gaze. "I don't even think we're that." He walked away.

CHAPTER 39

Gone

Curtis ran home from practice, concerned about the darkening clouds and the charge in the air. The rain finally came, just as he entered the side door of the group home. He stepped into the kitchen, still breathing hard, his backpack slung over his shoulders. The smell of peperoni pizza came from the oven, the timer still with six minutes to go. He walked beyond the kitchen to the living room. The younger boys played Madden Football on the PlayStation.

"You wanna play with us?" asked one of the boys.

"Lemme put my stuff down," Curtis replied. "Who's winning?"

One of the boys holding a controller raised his arm with a cheesy grin. "I am."

"You're the man to beat, *huh*?"

"I bet I can beat you too."

Curtis chuckled. "All right, little man. We'll see. I'll be back." Curtis left the living room. On the way to the stairs, he waved at Mr. H. in his office but had no intention of stopping, as Mr. H. was on the phone.

He heard Mr. H. say, "If you need anything, please let me know."

Curtis climbed the stairs to his bedroom, dropped off his backpack, and went downstairs to play Madden with the boys. But Mr. H. called Curtis into his office, before he made it to the living room.

"Shut the door," Mr. H. said.

Curtis shut the door behind him.

"Sit down."

Curtis sat across from Mr. H. at his desk.

Mr. H. rubbed his eyes. He appeared exhausted.

"Are you all right?" Curtis asked.

Mr. H. let out a heavy breath, his shoulders sagging, like a deflating balloon.

Curtis's stomach turned. "What's wrong?"

"Mr. Vasquez had a heart attack."

Curtis sat on the edge of his seat, his eyes bulging. "Is he okay?"

Mr. H. shook his head slowly. "He's gone."

The alarm on the oven sounded. The pizzas were done.

CHAPTER 40

Scout Team Hero

Thursday practices were always light, given it was the day before the game, and the coaches didn't want to tire out the team or to suffer any injuries. This Thursday practice was especially light, given that tomorrow was the last game of the regular season against the winless Thomas Jefferson Colonials. Despite lip service from the coaching staff about not taking Jefferson lightly, the West Potomac Wolverines were already looking ahead to the playoffs.

They wore shoulder pads and helmets, with sweatpants but no leg pads. During half-padded practices, hitting was minimal, and tackling to the ground was prohibited.

Curtis was in a fog, as he lined up as the slot safety, mimicking Thomas Jefferson's 3-3-5 defense. Terrel Sanders sprinted toward Curtis on the snap, faked inside, then cut outside. Curtis fell for the fake and sprinted after Terrel, several yards behind. Terrel caught the perfect pass and sprinted for the touchdown. Curtis had been close enough to dive and make the tackle, but it was Thursday.

As Terrel jogged back to the huddle, he said to Curtis, "That shit was too easy."

Curtis had been off his game all day. In fact, he had been sleepwalking through life since yesterday, when he'd heard about Mr. Vasquez. Curtis was pretty certain he had bombed his Algebra II test, and his English teacher had reprimanded him for not paying attention. Some of the group-home boys had stayed home from school to grieve, but Curtis didn't see the point. It wouldn't bring back Mr. Vasquez.

After the touchdown, Coach Giles reset the ball on the fifty-yard line. "First and ten on the fifty, with forty-five seconds left. One time-out."

The first-team offense ran another pass play. This one a screen to Terrel. Curtis had been in a perfect position to make the tackle. If they had been in full pads, Curtis would've drilled him, but again it was Thursday. Terrel didn't seem to care, as he lowered his shoulder and knocked Curtis on his butt. Then he ran for another touchdown. Curtis stood from the wet ground, the moisture cold on his rear end. His teammates oohed and aahed and heckled Curtis.

As Terrel jogged back to the huddle again, he called Curtis a *punk-ass bitch*.

Curtis tensed and clenched his fists.

After the touchdown, Coach Giles reset the offense again, setting the ball on their thirty-five-yard line. "First and ten, with one minute and twenty seconds left in the game. No time-outs left."

On the next play, they ran a draw play. The running back ran for five yards, lowered his head, and ran through the linebacker, but another linebacker wrapped him up, and Coach Giles blew the whistle, stopping the play.

"Second and five," Coach Giles said. "Clock's running. Hurry up."

The offense hurried for another play. The defense hurried to line up too. Curtis covered Terrel Sanders again. The center snapped the football, and the quarterback dropped back to pass. Terrel ran a quick slant pattern. Curtis read the pattern perfectly, seeing Terrel and the quarterback at the same time. As the quarterback cocked his arm, Curtis planted and sprinted forward. Terrel tracked the football spinning in his direction in a full sprint, his hands up, ready for the easy catch.

As the football hit his hands, Curtis slammed his shoulder into Terrel's chest, both young men sprinting at full speed. The crack of shoulder pads gave way to an audible gasp from players and coaches. Terrel's feet nearly went over his head, as his back and skull slammed into the ground with a *thud*. Curtis stood over the star receiver, as Terrel lay motionless on the ground.

Curtis's teammates didn't ooh and aah like they had when Terrel had run him over. Instead, several members of the first-team offensive line attacked Curtis. The center threw a punch. Instinctually, Curtis dodged the punch, then countered to the center's pudgy midsection, dropping the boy like a stone.

The coaches rushed the melee, shouting, "That's *enough*."

The linemen backed away.

The trainers tended to Terrel and the center, both of whom were now moving.

Coach Giles grabbed Curtis by his facemask, shaking him like a bobblehead. "What the hell's wrong with you, boy?"

Curtis shoved his coach. "Fuck you. I didn't do anything."

Coach Giles sneered at Curtis. "Get off my field. You're done."

Curtis removed his helmet and dropped it on the ground.

"Take your equipment to the locker room," Coach Giles said.

Curtis undid his shoulder pad straps, removed his shoulder pads and jersey together, and dropped them on the ground.

Spittle came from Coach's mouth as he shouted, "I said, take your equipment to the locker room."

Curtis brushed past his coach on the way to the locker room, leaving his equipment on the ground. His teammates and the assistant coaches stared, dumbfounded.

CHAPTER 41

What Now?

While his former teammates finished practice, Curtis changed, grabbed his backpack, and left the locker room. As he walked home, his breath condensed into the air, and his rage turned to sadness. *What am I gonna do now?* He dreaded telling Mr. H. what he'd done. *I should've stayed home today.*

With the group home in view, he took a detour into the woods, not ready to face the music. He went to the old fort. Moss grew on the weathered boards. The roof on one side of the fort had collapsed from rot.

Curtis crawled into the makeshift fort, sat on the wood floor, and leaned against the wall. His throat tightened, and his eyes welled with tears. He thought about Mr. Vasquez and how he had taught Curtis to respect his opponent.

But what if they don't respect me? What am I supposed to do? Just take it?

Curtis hugged himself and brought his knees to his chest. He shut his eyes, letting his mind meander to his mother, his father, Jimmy. Mr. Vasquez. *Why do they all leave?*

Curtis dried his eyes with the sleeve of his sweatshirt.

The sun disappeared, replaced by a full moon.

Mr. H. called out, "Curtis. Are you out here?"

Curtis emerged from the fort and stood.

"What are you doing out here?" Mr. H. asked.

Curtis slumped on a large tree stump. "I got kicked off the team."

Mr. H. sat next to him, while Curtis recounted the events at practice.

When Curtis finished, he said, "I don't know what to do."

"I'm not gonna blow smoke up your ass. You messed up, and you're paying the consequences," Mr. H. replied.

Curtis nodded. "I know."

"Do you still wanna play college football?"

Curtis laughed, but he wasn't happy. "What difference does it make? I'm off the team. A scholarship is impossible now."

"That's not what I asked. Do you still wanna play college football?"

"Yes."

"My roommate from CVU is the defensive backs' coach now. If I ask him to give you a fair shot as a walk-on, he'll give you a fair shot."

Curtis sat up straight, his eyes wide open. "Just like that? You ask him to give me a shot, and he will?"

Mr. H. stood from the stump and faced Curtis. "No. Not just like that. It comes with one condition."

Curtis stood. "What condition?"

"You need to get bigger, faster, stronger, and more skilled. I won't recommend you if you're not ready."

"Will you help me train?"

Mr. H. put his arm around Curtis. "I hope you're ready to work."

CHAPTER 42

Senior Year

The Denny's busboy added more dirty dishes to the stainless-steel counter. Curtis sorted the dishes on various plastic racks, depending on the type. Curtis set the plastic dish rack over the sink, filled with plates. He grabbed the hanging hose and sprayed the dinner plates, washing food scraps down the industrial garbage disposal. He fed the rack into the automated dishwasher, the machine pulling the rack inside on a track.

As Curtis washed the dishes, he listened to the radio. His former team played in the state championship again. Last year, Terrel Sanders had scored two touchdowns in the state championship game. He was a freshman at the University of Maryland on a football scholarship. Curtis was a high school senior now. He should've replaced Terrel Sanders. He couldn't help but think it should've been his time to shine, to earn a scholarship.

But he had a different path to college. A path that involved washing dishes three nights per week. Mr. H. had insisted Curtis work because he'll likely need money as a walk-on. It sometimes took several years for walk-ons to earn a scholarship. In the interim, he'd have to pay for his tuition, room, and board. He'd have loans and grants, but he'd need some savings too, not to mention spending money.

On the radio, the announcer said, "Eight seconds left. West Potomac is down by seven to Hampton. It's first and ten. West Potomac has the ball on the Hampton twenty-six-yard line. West Potomac comes out in an empty formation. Five receivers. Ethan Dobbs drops back to pass. He launches an arching spiral to the corner of the end zone. Freddie Harrison makes a leaping grab. Touchdown. No flags. What a pass. What a catch."

Curtis stopped washing dishes and stared at the radio, not sure whether to be happy or sad.

"Coach Giles of West Potomac needs to decide whether to kick the extra point to send this game into overtime or to try the two-point conversion to win it right here. It looks like they're going for two, as the offense takes the field. The crowd is at a fever pitch. West Potomac lines up in a goal line set, with two running backs and three tight ends. It's a toss right. He's not gonna get there. Oh, no, it's a throwback to the quarterback. Ethan Dobbs runs under the floating pass. The two-point conversion is good! It's pandemonium on the West Potomac sideline. West Potomac wins the 2014 Virginia 5A State Championship. West Potomac wins."

Curtis turned off the radio and went back to the dishes. He was sure now. He *wasn't* happy.

CHAPTER 43

Work Is the Way Out

His alarm clock chimed. Curtis was already awake, imagining his former teammates and their moment of glory. He reached to his bedside table and turned off his alarm, quick enough not to wake his foster brothers. The time read 5:00 a.m.

Curtis dressed in his sweats and running shoes. He grabbed his knit hat and gloves and exited his bedroom. He crept downstairs to the kitchen, drank a protein shake, and left the house.

A cold breeze nipped his nose. It was still dark. He started slow, jogging until his sore muscles loosened. His breath condensed in the air. Once loose, he picked up the pace, running as fast as he could to West Potomac High School. The gate to enter the track and football stadium was chained and locked. Curtis scaled the chain-link fence and entered the stadium. Empty bleachers and a press box surrounded the track and football field. He jogged to the far corner of the track and stretched in the dark, using the fence as support.

The early morning sun rose and provided dim light.

After stretching, he did a few speed and strength drills that Mr. H. had taught him. High knees, butt-kicks, bounding, shuffling, lunges, and side-squats.

He completed ten forty-yard sprints with only ten seconds rest in between. Mr. H. said, to be in football shape, Curtis must be able to run his sprints with little to no degradation in speed from the first to the last. Curtis wasn't there yet, but he was close. He supplemented the forty-yard dashes with two-hundred-meter sprints to build his anaerobic endurance.

After the sprints, Curtis worked on football-specific footwork. He backpedaled until his thighs and hip flexors burned. He worked on transitioning from a backpedal to a full sprint, simulating turning and running with a receiver. He planted and changed directions, simulating driving on a running play or covering a short passing route.

Curtis put his hands on his knees, catching his breath, his legs like Jell-O.

"Hey, you," an authoritative voice said.

Curtis turned his head to the school security guard marching his way, his flashlight beam bobbing in the early morning light.

When the security guard made it to Curtis, he said, "You can't be here. I've told you twice already."

Curtis stood upright and placed his hands on his hips. "I'm just running. I'm not hurting anyone."

"You're trespassing."

"I go to school here."

"Doesn't matter. The gate was locked for a reason."

"I doubt it's to keep out runners."

"Just get out of here, before I call the police."

Curtis showed his palms. "I'm leaving." Curtis jogged for the exit, leaving the security guard behind.

He ran back to the group home and finished his football drills in the cul-de-sac.

Mr. H. exited the group home, walked down the driveway, and watched Curtis do the W drill. Curtis backpedaled, planted, and sprinted forward, stopped, backpedaled again, then planted and sprinted forward again, making an imaginary W. Then he did it three more times without a break.

After the drill, Curtis put his hands behind his head, sucking in the cold air.

Mr. H. sidled up to Curtis. "Looking good. Your feet look faster. Explosive."

Curtis dropped his hands and shrugged. "I don't know."

Mr. H. clapped Curtis on the back. "*I* know. You're making progress. Consistency. That's the name of the game."

Curtis nodded, his head bowed.

"What's wrong?"

"You're not gonna mention the game?"

"I don't care about any game unless one of my boys are playing."

Curtis smiled. Sporadic raindrops fell from the sky.

Mr. H. glanced up at the dark clouds. Then he put his thick arm around Curtis. "Come on. I'll make you breakfast."

Curtis stood in his bedroom, watching the rain. It was a cold rain, just warm enough not to freeze. He dreaded walking to Denny's. It was a thirty-minute walk or a ten-minute jog. Mr. H. rarely gave rides anywhere within walking distance of the group home. With nine boys to look after, it wasn't practical, not to mention Mr. H. thought healthy hardship built character.

Mr. H. entered his bedroom. "What time's your shift?"

Curtis turned from the window. "Two. I need to get moving. I'm gonna be late."

Mr. H. stepped closer, jingled his key ring, and handed it to Curtis. "Here."

Curtis took the keys with arched eyebrows. "You're gonna let me borrow your car?"

"No. It's yours."

"You're *giving* me your car?"

"It's getting cold. It'll be tough to walk to work all winter."

"I can't take your car." Curtis handed the keys back to Mr. H.

But Mr. H. wouldn't take them. "It's a gift. For your birthday."

"My birthday's in August."

"I'm not planning to give you another birthday present in August, if that's what you're angling for."

Curtis smiled. "Thank you." He hugged Mr. H.

When they separated, Mr. H. said, "I'm proud of you. son."

PART III
University

The gut-check message is, do we have the right balance in our culture? Or are we in a position where hero worship and winning at all costs has subordinated our core values?

—Mark Emmert

CHAPTER 44

Do or Die

All his worldly possessions fit in one suitcase, two trash bags, and a laptop case. Curtis shut the hatch to his old Nissan Pathfinder, a gift from Mr. H., and squinted into the sun. His foster brothers engulfed him in a group hug on the driveway, the boys jockeying and pushing for a better position in the huddle. They broke the huddle, and Curtis hugged Mr. H. The former linebacker wasn't quite as imposing as he had been when Curtis had arrived at the group home nearly eight years ago. Mr. H.'s muscles had softened some, and his face was a little droopier.

When they separated, Mr. H. said, "You belong."

Curtis tilted his head, confused.

"You belong as a student and as an athlete." Mr. H. pointed at Curtis, his face stern. "No matter what happens, don't let anyone convince you otherwise. You understand me?"

"Yes, sir."

"Good."

Curtis stepped to the driver's side door and climbed inside his SUV. Curtis backed out of the driveway of the group home, a place he'd called home for almost half his life. As he drove away, his foster brothers waved and yelled his name, a few running behind the SUV. He glanced in the sideview mirror, catching a glimpse of Mr. H. He stood in the sun, his arms crossed over his barrel chest, a grin on his face, the grin of a proud papa.

Curtis's throat tightened, as the group home disappeared in his rearview mirror. His mother had dropped him off with Mr. H. as a child. Now he was leaving as a man. Curtis had barely slept the night before, excited and afraid at the same time. The group home was exactly that—his home.

Mr. H. had done more for Curtis than many fathers would for their own flesh and blood. He had helped Curtis apply for every grant and educational scholarship possible. Curtis's tuition and room and board at Central Virginia University were nearly covered. Curtis had loans and a part-time job to cover the rest. He did have some economic flexibility, given that he'd saved most of his money from working at Denny's.

Mr. H.'s plan to send Curtis to a four-year university with the opportunity to play football had worked perfectly. Curtis had kept up his grades, graduating high school with a 3.2 average. His SAT scores had been below average the first time Curtis had taken the test, but Mr. H. knew a tutor. With a few months of SAT prep, Curtis had improved greatly.

Curtis had been religious about the workouts Mr. H. had prescribed, often going above and beyond. Consequently, Curtis was a preferred walk-on to the Central Virginia University football team, courtesy of Coach Marvin Williams, Mr. H.'s old friend and roommate.

Curtis drove on Route 1, headed for 95 South, one hand out the window, surfing the wind. He thought about what Jimmy had said long ago. *You're gonna be a lifer.* Jimmy had been right, but now that was over. He had turned eighteen last week, on August 4. His life as a ward of the state was officially over. There was no going back. It was do or die.

CHAPTER 45

The Forty

Curtis stood in line with around two hundred other fit young men, wearing shorts and T-shirts, with numbers for name tags. The line was at the edge of the indoor practice facility. It was 90 degrees and humid outside but comfortable inside. At the front of the line, Curtis took off his cleats and stood on the scale. An assistant coach checked his height and weight.

The coach said, "Six feet even. One hundred ninety-one pounds."

A student volunteer held a clipboard and wrote Curtis's stats on the paper.

After they were measured and weighed, they did active stretching to get loose. They queued behind the goal line, along the hash marks. At the forty-yard line, coaches stood on either side of the hash marks, their stopwatches in hand.

Curtis watched his fellow walk-ons approach the line, bend down in a sprinter's stance, and explode toward the finish line. His stomach churned, worried that he'd screw up the start, run a slow time, and fail to make the team. At the finish, several coaches called out the times they had on their stopwatches, so the student volunteer could record the information.

"Four point eight three," one coach said.

"Four point seven nine," said another coach.

"Four point eight six," the third coach said.

Curtis had yet to see Coach Williams, Mr. H.'s friend and contact, which added to his anxiety.

Four scholarship football players stood on the sideline, watching the tryouts. Three of them were boisterous, joking and pointing at various walk-on candidates. One of them stood alone, watching in silence. Curtis didn't know them, but he'd overheard the other walk-ons talking about them. The quiet loner was senior cornerback Felix Gamble. He'd been a second-team All-American last season.

The tall white boy with the beard was a redshirt freshman. His name was Justin Love, and he was likely to be the starting quarterback for Central Virginia. He had an older brother, Brandon, who had played wide receiver for the Tennessee Titans and a father who had been a backup quarterback for the New York Giants. The two scholarship athletes with Justin were the two starting wide receivers—Kavon Drake and Andre Willis. Apparently, they'd both been All-ACC last season.

As Curtis neared the front of the line, his throat was dry and tight, and his hands trembled. He had practiced this sprint thousands of times but never with these stakes. This was the most important of all the exercises they were scheduled to perform that day. He hadn't felt stage fright since he'd dropped that pass during his junior year. Of course, this was his first time on a stage since then.

He thought back to Mr. H.'s advice to combat stage fright. *If you practice enough, your body will simply react. You won't need to think about it. Relaxing yourself in the moment helps too. Focus on taking deep breaths. Visualize success. Shake your legs and arms. Loosen your body.*

Curtis closed his eyes, visualizing exploding down the field and running a 4.4 forty. He took a deep breath, the nerves dissipating. He shook his arms and legs, loosening his body, the nerves further dissipating. By the time he got to the front of the line, his mind was clear.

He bent down, his feet staggered, his left hand on the turf, his right arm cocked back, high in the air. He exploded out of his stance, his right arm swinging down like a hammer for the first step. He sprinted toward the cones, the adrenaline coursing through his veins. He ran past the cones, not slowing until he was ten yards beyond.

Curtis walked back to the finish line, his hands on his hips.

One coach read from his stopwatch. "Four point four eight."

Another coach said, "Four point four six."

The final coach said, "Four point four nine."

Curtis smiled wide, forgetting about his teeth.

Justin Love said from the sideline, "God *damn*. That is one ugly ass dude."

"That's some snaggletooth shit," Andre added.

The scholarship athletes doubled over with laughter.

Curtis closed his mouth and jogged back to the line. He didn't think they meant for him to hear, as they weren't particularly loud, so Curtis pretended like he hadn't.

"I don't even know what the fuck he is," Justin said.

"Looks like he's got shit all over his face," Kavon added, referring to the black freckles covering Curtis's face.

They laughed again.

CHAPTER 46

Making the Team

After the tryout, Curtis went to a convenience store and bought a prepaid cell phone. He didn't like the idea of spending $100, but he wanted to tell Mr. H. about the tryout.

Curtis sat on a bench near the store and called Mr. H.

"Groveton Group Home," Mr. H. said.

"It's me," Curtis replied.

"Curtis, my boy. How was your tryout?"

"I ran a 4.4 forty."

"That's *outstanding.*"

"I was nervous, you know? But I remembered what you told me about breathing and visualization and staying loose."

Mr. H. chuckled. "I'm glad to know you've been listening. How did the rest of it go?"

"Good. I benched 290. Squatted 405. I was one of the fastest in the three-cone."

"I'm proud of you, son."

Curtis beamed. "I never would've been able to do this without you."

"You did it on your own. All I did was push you in the right direction. When do you hear if you made the team?"

"They're supposed to email us tomorrow by five at the latest. Whoever made it will have to practice the next day."

"Did you meet Coach Williams?"

"He wasn't there."

Mr. H. grunted. "I figured he would've been there."

"Is it bad that he wasn't?"

"Not necessarily, but they only take ten to twenty new walk-ons, depending on how many they lost to graduation and attrition. If the defensive back coach is there, and you're a defensive back, you're more likely to make it."

Curtis frowned. "That's not good."

"You're fine. Sounds like you killed it. I doubt it'll matter." Rowdy voices came from Mr. H.'s phone. He covered the receiver, his booming voice muffled. "What's going on out there?" He uncovered the receiver. "I have a situation here. Can I call you back?"

"It's okay. I was just calling to tell you about the tryout. I'll call you later."

"All right. We'll talk then." Mr. H. disconnected the call.

Curtis walked back to the dorm, carrying his backpack, comfortable in the summer heat. He had been acclimated to the heat, purposely running at the hottest times of the day during his training.

His dorm was a five-story apartment-style building with an elevator, although he always took the stairs to the fourth floor. The elevator was notoriously slow. He walked down the hall to his room, the dorm dead quiet, as most students didn't report for nearly three weeks. He unlocked his dorm room and entered.

The room resembled a cell, with empty cinderblock walls, painted beige, a laminate floor, and generic furniture. He had already packed away his clothes in one of the dressers. The other dresser was for his roommate, Ben. He had never met Ben, but that's who had been assigned to him as his roommate. Curtis expected Ben with the rest of the student body in a few weeks.

Curtis sat at his desk and opened his laptop. It had been his first big purchase from the money he'd earned washing dishes. He opened his email to see if he'd gotten a message about the tryout. He wasn't surprised they hadn't responded yet.

★★★

The next day, Curtis checked his email every hour on the hour, in anticipation of the email about the tryout. In the late afternoon, it finally came. His heart pounded, and his eyes bulged, as he clicked on the email.

From: CVUFootball@CentralVirginiaUniversity.edu
To: CurtisDuffy2323@gmail.com
Date: 8-11-2015
Subject: Football Tryout

Dear Prospective Football Player:
Thank you for trying out for the 2015 football season. We had over 200 prospective student athletes at the tryout. Our decisions were incredibly difficult, as we only have space for 12 new walk-ons this year.

Unfortunately, you did not make the football roster for the 2015 season, but I encourage you to try out again in the spring.

CHAPTER 47

The Roommate

Curtis's new roommate, Ben Davidson, brought a lot to their room. The couch was his. The little fridge. The big screen TV, complete with a DVD player, and a PlayStation. The posters were his. Even the one with Bob Marley smoking a joint.

Curtis helped Ben set his television on the entertainment center.

"Thanks, man." Ben gestured to all his stuff. "You can use any of this whenever you want."

"Thanks," Curtis replied.

Ben was about Curtis's height but skinnier. He had straight brown hair, with a cowlick in the front and the back, some acne on his face, and patchy facial hair.

Ben stepped to his suitcase, which was on his bed. "You smoke?"

"No. You?"

Ben opened his suitcase, retrieved a massive bong, held it up to Curtis, and said, "What do you think?"

Curtis frowned. "If we get caught with drugs or even a bong, we could get kicked out of school."

Ben showed his palms. "Dude. Relax. Both my brothers went here. They smoked a shit load of weed. They told me that they never check. If they did, they'd have to get rid of almost everybody."

"I'm still not into it. If something happens, it's your responsibility, not mine."

"Yeah, man. Of course." Ben tossed his bong on the bed. "You should loosen up though. We're in college. We only have four years to get fucked up and to fuck college chicks." Ben smirked. "Maybe five years for me."

CHAPTER 48

Tips for Tania

With an hour to kill before Psychology 101, Curtis sat in the library, reading his *Intro to Social Work* textbook. If he didn't make it as a professional football player, which was likely, he wanted to help orphans. He wanted to be like Mr. H. The reading was his first assignment from his first class on his first day.

Curtis glanced at the analog clock on the wall—*10:51*. He stood from his chair, collected his books, and packed his backpack. He left the library, descended the steps, and surveyed the quad or central courtyard. The center of the quad was paved, with raised brick flower beds and benches. Beyond the center were lawn areas, with sporadic shade trees. Surrounding it all were gothic stone buildings. Students dotted the quad, some sitting on benches, some standing and laughing in cliques, some kicking a soccer ball in the grass. A young woman played the acoustic guitar and sang a soft song.

Curtis reached into his back pocket and retrieved his campus map. He found the building for the School of Psychology and oriented himself on the map. It was almost directly across the quad. So Curtis strolled through the quad, enjoying the sun on his face.

He was drawn to the angelic voice of the young singer. She sang alone at the far corner of the paved area, away from the hustle and bustle. Her guitar case was open, without a single dollar. She was a waif, with straight dark hair parted down the middle and hanging to the center of her back. Her face was perfectly symmetrical, with plump pink lips and a petite nose. Her brown eyes closed as she hit the high notes of her haunting melody:

>You stole the air from my lungs.
>You told me I was the one.
>But I'm nothin', nothin' without you.
>I'm nothin', nothin' without you.
>Nothin' without you.

When she finished, Curtis clapped.

She blushed. "Thank you."

"You have a beautiful voice," Curtis replied.

She shrugged and strummed her guitar. "I don't know." She motioned to the quad and the bustling students. "You're the first person to stop."

"It might help to move to a better spot."

"I tried that, but campus security didn't want me blocking people."

Curtis furrowed his brow. "That's bullshit. How long have you been playing over here?"

"About two hours."

"I'm no expert, but I think, if you keep playing, you'll have tons of people listening." Curtis reached into his pocket, removed his wallet, and retrieved a five-dollar bill. He dropped the cash into her guitar case.

"You don't have to …"

Curtis tilted his head. "You don't want people to give you tips?"

"No, I do. It's just you're so nice. I didn't want to take your money."

Curtis smiled, being careful to keep his mouth closed. "You didn't take my money. I gave it to you."

She smiled back.

He held out his hand. "I'm Curtis Duffy, by the way. I'm a freshman."

She shook his hand. "Tania Berry. I'm a freshman too."

"It's nice to meet you, Tania. I'd love to hear more, but I have psychology at eleven."

"It was nice to meet you too, Curtis."

He smiled again and walked away. He had only taken a few steps, when he pivoted back to Tania. "Hey, Tania?"

"Yeah?" she asked.

"It might help if you put a few dollars in your guitar case. I think it encourages people to give money. I used to live in the city. That's what the street performers did."

"Thanks for the tip."

CHAPTER 49

Finish What You Start

Curtis loaded glasses on the plastic rack. Then he fed the rack through the dishwasher. The dishwashing system at the campus dining hall was similar to the one at Denny's, although the pay was fifty cents less per hour. Plates, bowls, glasses, and utensils were piled on the stainless-steel counter to his right. Curtis sorted the various dishes into the appropriate plastic racks, rinsed food down the garbage disposal, then fed the racks into the dishwasher. The assembly line halted, signifying the counter beyond the dishwasher was full. Curtis washed his hands and went to the opposite side of the dishwasher. He put away the clean dishes and restacked the plastic racks to be reused. He did this a dozen times, working quickly, worried he wouldn't finish by the time his shift was over.

Curtis glanced at the clock, noticing his shift *was* over, but he still had a small pile of dirty dishes. So, he continued to work, stacking the plates in the appropriate plastic rack.

His supervisor, a pudgy middle-aged woman, entered the dishwashing area. "What are you still doin' here?"

"I wasn't quite finished," Curtis replied.

"Your shift is over. You know we can't pay you for the extra time."

"I understand, but I'd like to finish, if that's okay."

She scrunched her face, as if she'd eaten a lemon. "You like washin' dishes or somethin'?"

"I like to finish what I start."

After his shift, Curtis lifted weights at the athletic center. He lay back on the bench and spaced his hands equally. He pressed 225 pounds off the rack. He controlled the weight down, until it touched his chest, then he pressed upward, nearly locking his arms. He did ten repetitions. The last two were a struggle, but he'd managed. In retrospect, he probably should've asked someone for a spot, but the gym was mostly empty, with most of the student body at the football game.

Between sets he watched one of the flat screens, hanging from the ceiling. The Central Virginia University Lions were leading the University of North Carolina Tarheels, 28–3. Justin Love dropped back to pass. The pocket collapsed, pressure coming up the middle from two North Carolina defensive tackles. Justin spun away from the defenders and raced to his left. It looked like he might run out of bounds, but Justin threw a laser across his body just before the boundary, a perfect pass to Andre Willis on the crossing pattern. Andre caught the ball and sprinted up the sideline for a sixty-one-yard touchdown.

The announcer gushed. "Justin Love has been sensational this afternoon. I've covered CVU football for twenty-four years, and I've never seen a more talented thrower of the football."

CHAPTER 50

The Republic

Curtis was at the athletic center for four hours. His lifting workout was nearly two hours long, followed by a grueling sprint and agility workout on the indoor track. He showered in the locker room, changed, and walked back to the dining hall. He ate dinner by himself, while reading Plato's *The Republic*, the assigned reading for his Philosophy 101 course.

After dinner, he returned to his dorm, his legs like Jell-O from the sprints and his upper body still tender from lifting. He climbed the steps of his dormitory. Three drunk guys raced down the stairs, giggling and jumping halfway down each flight. One fell and nearly hit his head on the concrete landing. The other two laughed. Then the one on the ground laughed too.

Curtis continued upward to the fourth floor. He walked to his dorm room, fished his key from his pocket, and turned the lock. When he opened the door, Ben blocked the doorway. He guided Curtis back into the hallway, shutting the door behind him. Before he shut the door, Curtis saw a young woman sitting on the edge of Ben's bed, next to his bong.

Curtis held out his hands. "What's going on?"

Ben glanced back at their shut door. "I met a girl. She's DTF."

Curtis frowned.

"Can you crash somewhere else tonight?"

"Where the fuck am I supposed to go?"

150

"There's a shit load of parties on fraternity row. You might meet someone."

Curtis let out a heavy breath. "Don't expect me to do this every weekend."

Ben grinned. "Thanks, man. I owe you."

Curtis lifted his chin to the door. "I need to get my stuff."

Curtis grabbed his toiletries, his pillow, and blanket. On the way out of the dorm, he stopped in the communal bathroom, peed, washed his hands, and brushed his teeth. He went outside to the parking lot. Curtis leaned the back seat of his SUV forward, increasing the size of the back area. He took off his shoes and climbed into the back with his pillow, blanket, and *The Republic*. He lay in the back, covered by his blanket, his head propped by his pillow, reading his book by the ambient light of the nearby light post. He read one passage over and over again.

> You know that the beginning is the most important part of any work, especially in the case of a young and tender thing; for that is the time at which the character is being formed and the desired impression is more readily taken. Shall we just carelessly allow children to hear any casual tales which may be devised by casual persons, and to receive into their minds ideas for the most part the very opposite of those which we should wish them to have when they are grown up?
>
> We cannot. Anything received into the mind at that age is likely to become indelible and unalterable; and therefore, it is most important that the tales which the young first hear should be models of virtuous thoughts.

Curtis thought about what he'd heard when he was young. *Freak. Albino. Ugly ass motherfucker. Half-breed.* That was what his grandmother had called him. Curtis remembered being so excited about going to McDonald's with his mother. He had been so hungry. Then those teenagers had said, *That boy's so ugly, when his mama breastfed him, she closed her eyes and thought about other babies.* Curtis knew it was hyperbole, that it was meant to be a joke. *Maybe it was the truth. Maybe she was disgusted by me. Maybe she was embarrassed by me. Why else would she take me to a group home, drop me off, and never talk to me again?*

CHAPTER 51

Is it a Date?

After lunch at the dining hall, Curtis returned to his dorm room to grab his Spanish textbook for his afternoon class. Ben sat by the window, on the couch, his bong gurgling. He inhaled marijuana vapor, held it for a few seconds, then turned his head to the open window and exhaled.

Ben set his bong on the coffee table and grinned. "Curtis, my man. How's it hanging?"

Curtis packed his Spanish textbook into his backpack. "I'm doing all right."

"You wanna go to a party tonight at Sigma Chi?"

Curtis shouldered his backpack. "I don't think so. I'm not much of a partier."

"Come on, man. I'm trying to rush. A lot of football players are in Sigma Chi. You might like it."

"I doubt bringing me is gonna help you."

"My boys are rushing another frat. They'll be at another party."

Curtis frowned. "So, I'm your last choice."

"No, dude. Mallory's going too. I just wanted a friend there."

Mallory was the girl Ben had hooked up with last weekend.

"Why not rush the same frat as your boys?" Curtis asked.

Ben stood from the couch and stepped closer to Curtis. "I'm a legacy. My dad and my brothers were in it."

Curtis nodded. "What's the cover?"

"No cover, but we have to bring a girl to the party. Don't worry. I got a girl for you. Mallory's roommate wants to go."

"All right," Curtis said.

Ben clapped Curtis on the shoulder. "Thanks, man."

"I'll go, but I'd like to ask someone else."

Ben raised his eyebrows. "You dog. You met a chick?"

Curtis restrained his smile. "Sort of."

Curtis left his dorm early, intent on checking the quad for Tania before his Spanish class. Even though they'd had a friendly exchange almost two weeks ago, Curtis hadn't talked to Tania since. He'd seen her from afar and had noticed that she'd developed a small crowd of fans, just as Curtis had predicted.

He'd tried to talk to her on two occasions. On the first occasion, she'd been talking and laughing with three handsome guys. On the second occasion, he'd waited to talk to her, but she'd been mobbed by a dozen students, telling her how much they loved her music. He had felt awkward and stalkerish, standing by himself, waiting to talk to this beautiful singer.

But now he had a purpose to talk to her.

He heard her angelic voice before he saw her. She was obscured by about fifteen students, bobbing their heads and tapping their feet. She wore a long bohemian dress, with a flower behind her ear. Despite the lyrics, this song was more upbeat than the last one Curtis had heard.

I don't blame you. We got carried away.

I try to laugh about it, like it's okay.

I lie awake and think about it sometimes.

What could've been. What would've been.

But I don't blame you. We got carried away.

When she finished, the students clapped. Several left one-dollar bills. Her guitar case was littered with crumpled cash.

"Thank you so much," Tania said. "I'll be back at two, if you'd like to hear more."

Curtis waited for the crowd to leave, but one young man lingered, a guy wearing flip-flops, khaki shorts, and a pink polo.

Mr. Preppy was dangerously close to Tania. "You're fucking awesome, you know that?"

Tania had a pained expression on her face. "Thanks."

"When are we gonna hook up?"

Curtis stepped around the young man and dropped a five-dollar bill in the case.

"Curtis," Tania said, turning away from Mr. Preppy.

Curtis smiled with his mouth closed. "Hey, Tania."

Tania set her guitar in the case and embraced Curtis like they were old friends. Curtis was stunned initially, then wrapped his arms around her petite body. Her hair smelled like flowers and the sun. His heart thumped in his chest. It was only the second time in his life that a woman, other than his mother, had hugged him.

When Mr. Preppy walked away, she let go. She showed Curtis her palms. "I'm so sorry to do that to you."

Curtis struggled to find the words. "It's, uh, ... it's okay."

"That guy tries to hang around me after I play. It's creepy. He's been asking me to hook up with him like every day."

Curtis cringed. "I'm sorry to hear that."

"I know. It's cringey."

"Your last song was ... really great. Do you write your own songs?"

"I do some covers, but I like to write."

"That's cool."

She reached out and touched his forearm for a beat. "I was wondering when I'd see you again. I've been looking for you for like two weeks."

Curtis still felt her touch, like a beautiful brand. "Sorry. I saw you a couple times, but you were with your fans. I didn't wanna bother you."

She mock-frowned. "Didn't wanna bother me? That's silly. I wanted to thank you." She gestured to her guitar case. "I've been getting so much money since you told me about putting some money in first."

"That's *great*. You have a big crowd now too."

Tania grinned. "But you were the first."

"I have good taste in music."

Tania giggled.

Curtis cleared his dry throat. He felt the familiar pangs of stage fright—stomach fluttering, heart rate increasing, sweaty palms. "I wanted to ask you if you would, um, … like to go to a fraternity party tomorrow night?"

"A fraternity party?" She pointed to Curtis's CVU Football T-shirt. "Do you play football?"

"No. I tried out, but all I got was this crappy T-shirt."

"Oh, sorry."

Curtis shrugged. "It's no big deal." That was a lie. "So, do you wanna go?"

"I'm kinda surprised. You don't look like a frat guy."

"Why? Too ugly?" Curtis chuckled, but his eyes were dead.

"*No.* You just don't seem like the type."

"I'm not. My roommate asked me to go with him. I can't get in without a date."

Tania narrowed her eyes.

Curtis showed his palms. "I wasn't thinking this was a date though." That was another lie. "I thought you might be able to sing there. From what my roommate said, there's gonna be a ton of people."

CHAPTER 52

Sigma Chi

"Where are you from?" Tania asked.

Tania and Curtis followed several paces behind Ben and Mallory, strolling along fraternity row. The grand southern mansions displayed their Greek letters on their facades. Music and a cacophony of voices came from the frats.

"Alexandria, Virginia," Curtis replied, carrying Tania's guitar. "It's in northern Virginia, about twenty minutes from DC. What about you?"

"I'm from here," Tania replied. "Well, like forty minutes from here, in Troy."

"That's cool," Curtis said. "Do you commute? I guess I assumed you were in the dorms."

"I'm in Franklin Hall. I actually wanted to commute, but my parents wanted me to have the college experience. My dad's a huge CVU football fan."

Curtis nodded. "Nice. I'm gonna tryout again in the spring. I've been working out, trying to get bigger, faster, and stronger. Hopefully, ... you know." Curtis trailed off.

Tania tilted her head up to Curtis, as they walked side by side. "You're braver than me. Those guys are *huge*."

Curtis chuckled. "Yeah. They are."

"What about your parents? Are they in Alexandria?"

"Yeah." Technically, that wasn't a lie. His mother was buried in

Alexandria, and Mr. H. was a great father figure.

"Do you have any brothers or sisters?" Curtis asked, eager to put the focus back on her.

"One older brother. He's in the army."

Ben turned back to Curtis and Tania. He motioned to the particularly rowdy house on their right. "This is it."

Funky letters that resembled *E* and *X* were fastened to the façade of the white mansion with thick columns and black shutters. The Greek letters stood for Sigma Chi. The driveway was filled with sports cars, Jeeps, and pickup trucks.

The foursome meandered up the driveway, then across the brick walkway to the front door. Three fraternity brothers stood on the portico, acting as gatekeepers. All three of them were large and muscular. Curtis wondered if they were football players.

The largest of the three lifted his chin to Ben. "Invite or walk-in?"

The other two fraternity brothers leered at Tania, like she was a juicy steak.

"I'm a legacy," Ben said.

The large man said, "Girls get in free." He mean-mugged Ben and Curtis. "You two, ten bucks each."

Curtis frowned at Ben. "You said no cover."

"If you're a member of Sigma Chi, there's no cover," the large man said.

"I got you," Ben said to Curtis, reaching for his wallet.

Curtis refused the gesture and paid his own way, mainly because he had brought Tania and didn't want to appear poor and cheap, even though he was poor and cheap.

The large man stamped *Tweety Bird* on Ben's and Curtis's fists, in case they had to leave and wanted to come back.

Inside the fraternity house was pandemonium. Young men and women were packed into the house like sardines. Rap music blared from the speakers. The smell of sweat and beer permeated the air. Partygoers danced, made out, laughed, shouted, and drank from red plastic cups. To their left was a stage with a lonely microphone. A few female partygoers danced on stage in bikini tops and short shorts.

The crowd near the stage chanted, "Take it off. Take it off. Take it off."

Curtis and Tania followed Ben and Mallory through the crowd. Tania took Curtis's hand so they stayed together. Curtis held Tania's guitar tight to his chest with his other hand. Several guys ogled Tania, who wore a sundress that hugged her subtle curves. A few catcalled her.

"Lookin' good, girl."

"Damn. She's fine."

"Hey, what's your name?"

Tania kept her head down, ignoring the attention.

When they neared the kegs, the crowd was too dense to continue. Ben pivoted and shouted at them, "I'll get us drinks."

Ben forced his way through the crowd, taking Mallory with him.

Curtis leaned toward Tania's ear. "You okay?"

Tania nodded and leaned toward Curtis's ear. "It's crowded."

"I think this was a mistake."

"No. This is good. It's a crowd. Just like you said. I just need to figure out how to get on stage."

"I think we need to ask someone." Curtis spotted a handsome guy nearby, wearing a Sigma Chi T-shirt, and chatting up a tiny blonde. Curtis nudged Tania and pointed. "He might know."

"Good eye."

They waded through the crowd to the Sigma Chi guy, Curtis in front, Tania behind him.

"Excuse me," Curtis said.

The guy ignored Curtis, his attention on the blonde.

"Excuse me," Curtis shouted over the rap music.

The guy glared at Curtis. "What do you want?"

"How do we get someone on stage to play music?"

He glanced at the guitar case in Curtis's hand. "Not gonna happen." He turned back to the blonde.

Tania moved in front of Curtis and tapped the guy on the shoulder. He pivoted, red-faced, his fists clenched. At the sight of Tania, his eyes widened, and his scowl transformed into a leer.

"Are you in charge around here?" Tania asked, one hand on her hip.

"I might be," the Sigma Chi guy said, his eyes crawling over Tania's body. "Who's asking?"

The blonde crossed her arms over her chest, mean-mugging Tania.

"I'm Tania. I'm a singer," she said. "I was wondering if I could play a few songs on stage?"

The blonde left in a huff.

The Sigma Chi guy held out his hand. "I'm Declan."

Tania shook his hand. "Do you think I could play a few songs?"

Declan grinned. "For a kiss."

Tania shook her head. "Oh, I don't know."

Declan lifted his chin to Curtis. "You're not with him, are you?"

"Um, no."

Curtis gritted his teeth.

"You have a boyfriend?" Declan asked.

"No," Tania replied.

Declan tapped his lips. "Then you gotta pay the toll."

Tania rose to her tippytoes and pecked him on the lips. He tried to lean in for more, but Tania pulled back.

"Can I play now?" Tania asked.

"Are you any good?" Declan asked.

"She's great," Curtis said.

Declan ignored Curtis, his eyes locked on Tania. "Sing something for me."

"Right here?"

Declan nodded. "Why not?"

"It's loud," Tania said.

"It'll be loud on stage."

Tania swallowed hard and sang like an angel.

I can't imagine ever feeling this bliss.

I've got a feeling we'll never be closer than this.

I can't imagine ever being so fast.

But I've got a feeling this will never last.

The nearby partygoers stopped what they were doing and turned to the little singer with the big voice. Many of them clapped when Tania finished.

"Not bad. I'll see what I can do. Come with me." Declan took Tania's hand. Curtis tried to follow them, but Declan stopped and said, "He can stay here."

Curtis clenched his jaw. "I'm not leaving her."

"He has my guitar," Tania said.

Declan held out his hand to Curtis. "I'll take it."

Curtis glanced at Tania.

She nodded and said, "It's okay."

Curtis narrowed his eyes at Declan.

"Relax," Declan said. "I just gotta clear her with the Top G."

Curtis handed the guitar to the frat guy. Declan led Tania away from the large room. They disappeared down a hallway. Someone nudged Curtis in the back. Curtis pivoted to Ben and Mallory smiling, each holding two red plastic cups.

Ben handed a beer to Curtis. "Where's Tania?"

"I think she's gonna sing," Curtis replied.

"*Nice.*" Ben grabbed the extra beer from Mallory. "I'm double-fisting tonight." He took a gulp from each cup.

Curtis and Mallory sipped their beers too.

"Did you see Justin Love?" Ben asked Curtis.

"No," Curtis replied.

Ben gestured across the room to the bar area. "He's over there. Surrounded by chicks."

Curtis peered at the bar area. Justin had his arms around two beautiful coeds, smiling for a camera phone. CVU had beaten Wake Forest earlier that day. Justin had thrown four touchdown passes and rushed for another.

Mallory gave Ben a dirty look. "They're not chicks. They're women."

"Sorry."

Curtis, Ben, and Mallory drank their beers, chatting and waiting for Tania to return.

The rap music ceased. Partygoers booed.

Declan's voice came from the speakers. "We have a special musical guest for you this evening. Please welcome to the stage, making her debut, Tania Berry."

Curtis dropped his empty cup and rushed toward the stage, slicing through the crowd, moving as quickly as possible without pushing people.

"Curtis," Ben called out to his back.

Tania stood on stage, trembling, her face flushed. She opened her mouth but nothing came out. Curtis was about twenty-feet away, deadlocked by the crowd. Ben and Mallory were nowhere in sight.

Someone called out, "You suck."

Someone else yelled, "Take it off."

The guy next to Curtis yelled, "Show us your tits."

Curtis shoved the guy. "Shut the fuck up."

The guy stumbled but regained his balance. He wore a Sigma Chi T-shirt. "What the fuck?"

Curtis pointed at the guy. "Don't say that shit."

Many male partygoers chanted, "Take it off. Take it off. Take it off."

Four muscular Sigma Chi brothers surrounded Curtis. One of them said, "Get the fuck out, man."

"I'm not leaving without my friends," Curtis replied.

The Sigma Chi brothers converged, grabbing Curtis, pinning his arms behind his back. They dragged Curtis toward the front door, but

Curtis resisted.

"We don't wanna hurt you," one of the guys said.

"Fuck you," Curtis replied, still resisting.

"Don't be a dick," said one of the other guys.

The crowd still chanted, "Take it off. Take it off."

They managed to push Curtis outside onto the grass, then they blocked the front door.

"Get the fuck outta here, freak," one of the guys said.

Curtis straightened his T-shirt, glowering at the frat brothers.

Then the chanting crowd inside quieted, and Tania's angelic voice carried through the air.

> *I don't blame you. We got carried away.*
> *I try to laugh about it, like it's okay.*
> *I lie awake and think about it sometimes.*
> *What could've been. What would've been.*
> *But I don't blame you. We got carried away.*

CHAPTER 53

Hypergamy

Curtis waited for nearly two hours on the public sidewalk in front of the Sigma Chi fraternity house, watching partygoers enter mostly sober, and others exit mostly wasted. Tania sang for about forty minutes, ending with a thunderous applause, punctuated by wolf whistles. Curtis had expected to see her shortly after her set, but she was still inside.

Ben exited the frat house, red-faced, with Mallory hanging on to him. They staggered toward Curtis.

"Dude. What happened to you?" Ben asked.

"They threw me out," Curtis replied. "I pushed some asshole who was talking shit to Tania. Is she still in there?"

"I think so. I saw her about fifteen minutes ago."

"She's a star," Mallory slurred.

"She *is* a star," Ben said. "She fucking killed it. Did you know she was that good?"

"Yeah. I knew," Curtis replied.

"Everyone's trying to talk to her. She's the most popular girl in there. Every girl wants to be her, and every guy wants to be *with* her."

Curtis frowned.

Ben winced. "Sorry, dude."

"Don't worry about it."

Ben glanced down the sidewalk, the path they'd take back to the dorms. "We're gonna head back."

"I'm gonna wait for Tania."

Ben leaned close to Curtis. "Can you give us a few hours of alone time?"

Curtis exhaled. "Yeah."

Ben clapped Curtis on the shoulder. "Thanks, man."

"See ya, Curtis," Mallory slurred.

Ben and Mallory left, arm in arm.

Shortly thereafter, Tania exited the frat house with Justin Love. They strolled down the driveway toward the sidewalk, laughing and talking. Justin carried Tania's guitar. Curtis approached the pair.

"How did it go?" Curtis asked Tania, purposely not acknowledging Justin.

Tania beamed. "It was so great." She glanced at Justin. "They invited me back next weekend. "They're going to pay me like $500."

Justin lifted his chin to Curtis. "I've seen you before. Didn't you try out for football?"

Curtis ignored Justin, his focus on Tania. "That's good. I'm happy for you. Did you want me to walk you back?"

"I got her. Thanks, bro."

Curtis glared at Justin. "I didn't ask you, and I'm not your bro."

Justin glared back. "What's your problem?"

"Relax, Curtis," Tania said.

"Yeah, relax," Justin echoed.

"Did you want me to walk you back or not?" Curtis asked, his voice colder than he'd intended.

"Justin said he'd walk me."

Curtis nodded.

Tania reached out and squeezed Curtis's hand. "Thanks for inviting me out tonight." Then she and Justin walked away.

Curtis hiked in the opposite direction, taking the long way back to the dorm. But he didn't go to his room, as Ben was likely with Mallory. Instead, he climbed into the back seat of his SUV, replaying his exchange with Tania over and over again, trying to figure out where he went wrong.

CHAPTER 54

Nice Guy?

Billowy clouds blocked the sun, giving the student body of CVU a respite from the heat. Curtis trudged to class, his hands on his backpack straps, his hood over his head. He cut through the quad. Tania sang to a crowd of thirty, her guitar case overflowing with cash. He didn't stop. He certainly didn't leave a tip. He didn't even break stride.

As he continued to Psychology 101, he thought, *I was a fucking idiot to think she'd like someone as ugly as me.*

After psychology class, Curtis cut back across the quad, with the intention of studying at the library. Several young men and women chatted with Tania, as she packed up her guitar. Curtis covered his head with his hood and fast-walked past, not looking in Tania's direction. He had hoped to slip by unnoticed.

Quick steps approached from behind. "Curtis. Wait up," Tania said.

Curtis glanced over his shoulder. The petite singer jogged his way, lugging her guitar case.

"Curtis," she said again. "Wait."

Curtis stopped and pivoted to Tania.

She smiled, as she caught up to him. "Hey. How come you didn't stop by?"

Curtis shrugged. "You looked busy."

Tania cocked her head. "Are you mad at me?"

"Why would I be mad at you?" Curtis spoke in monotone.

"You know that Saturday wasn't a date, right?"

"I'm well aware that you're not interested in me."

She scowled. "I thought you were different."

Curtis laughed, but he didn't sound happy. "If I'm not different, I don't know who is."

"You're just like every other guy. It was all an act, wasn't it? Pretend to be a nice guy, so you could get with me."

Curtis glowered at Tania. "Is that what you think?"

"Am I wrong?"

"You wouldn't be saying this to me if I was Justin fucking Love."

Tania opened her mouth to speak, but nothing came out.

"That's what I thought." Curtis walked away.

CHAPTER 55

Six Months Later ...

The spring tryout was much the same as the fall tryout, except there were less prospective football players, as many of the guys who didn't make it the first time didn't return. Curtis waited in line with approximately one hundred other fit young men to be weighed and measured. Curtis and the other prospective football players wore CVU Football T-shirts and shorts, with number tags stuck to their chests.

At the front of the line, Curtis took off his cleats, and stood on the scale. Coach Marvin Williams checked his height and weight. Curtis had debated introducing himself, explaining his relationship with Mr. H., but the tryout ran like an assembly line. Not much time for conversation.

"Six feet even. Two hundred one pounds," Coach Williams said.

A student volunteer held a clipboard and wrote Curtis's stats on the page.

Curtis smiled, keeping his mouth closed. He had gained ten pounds of muscle since the fall tryout.

Unlike last time, Curtis wasn't nervous while waiting to run his forty-yard dash. He had practiced it so many times that it was second nature. A dozen scholarship football players watched the forties from the sideline. Justin Love was among them. Curtis didn't know if Justin and Tania ever got together. Curtis never saw them together around campus, not that he was looking. He avoided the quad like the plague, not wanting Tania to accuse him of stalking her.

When it was his turn to run, he shook out his arms and legs and bent down in his sprinter's stance. He inhaled. On the exhale, he exploded out of his stance. He sprinted smooth and fast, his feet barely touching the indoor turf. His momentum carried him an additional twenty yards as he crossed the finish line.

Curtis walked back to the finish line. Several coaches called out the times they had on their stopwatches, so the student volunteer could record the information.

"Four point four three," one coach said.

"Four point four six," said another coach.

"Four point four five," Coach Williams said, his eyes on Curtis. "What's your name, son?"

"Curtis Duffy."

Coach Williams creased his forehead, as if trying to remember where he'd heard that name before. Coach Williams was ripped, especially for a man with receding gray hair; even with his loose polo, his bulging biceps and chest couldn't be contained. He had perfect white teeth and even dark skin, two characteristics Curtis envied.

"You're Russel Henderson's boy," Coach Williams said.

"Yes, sir," Curtis replied.

"You've got the fastest forty so far." Coach Williams lifted his chin to the student assistant. "Put a check by his number."

CHAPTER 56

Tryout #2

Curtis sat at his desk, reading his Social Work Practice textbook. Ben played *Call of Duty* on the couch in their dorm room but was considerate enough to use his headphones. Curtis's laptop was open on his desk, his email account on the screen. Every minute or so, Curtis glanced at the screen, anticipating an email about the tryout.

It was 3:27 p.m. Coach Williams told them they would receive an email by 5:00 p.m. on Wednesday.

Curtis looked up from the page he'd been stuck on for twenty minutes. Still nothing. He returned to his textbook, determined to concentrate but couldn't. Instead, he thought about the tryout. He hoped he did enough. He had run the fastest forty-yard dash and the fastest three-cone drill. He'd lifted more than last time too. His bench was 335 and his squat was 465. And Coach Williams had told the student assistant to put a checkmark next to Curtis's name. That had to mean he had made it, but he wasn't certain. *I don't even have any varsity high school experience, and they know that.*

Curtis glanced at his email again. It was there. He held his breath as he clicked on the email.

From: CVUFootball@CentralVirginiaUniversity.edu
To: CurtisDuffy2323@gmail.com
Date: 3-30-2016
Subject: Football Tryout

Dear Prospective Football Player:

Thank you for trying out for the 2016 football season. We had over 100 prospective student athletes at the tryout. Our decisions were incredibly difficult, as we only have space for 6 new walk-ons this year.

Congratulations, you have been selected to the 2016 CVU Lions football roster. Spring practice begins Monday, April 4, at 3:00 p.m. If you need to get taped, please arrive to the training room at 2:00 p.m.

Curtis slapped his desktop and shouted, "*Yes.*"

CHAPTER 57

Spring Practice

It was the last spring practice before the intrasquad scrimmage. The team practiced on the outdoor turf fields, wearing shorts, shoulder pads, and helmets. It was overcast and cool. Curtis and the defensive backs practiced man-to-man techniques with the wide receivers.

Curtis lined up seven yards off Andre Willis, the best wide receiver on the team and possibly in the entire ACC. Curtis backpedaled, as Andre sprinted forward. When Andre neared, Curtis turned his hips and sprinted with the wide receiver. It appeared that Andre was running a post pattern. But after taking three steps to the post, Andre changed directions on a dime, breaking outside on a forty-five-degree angle. Instead of stopping and changing directions, which would've taken far too long, Curtis flipped his head around and turned, losing sight of the quarterback but ending on Andre's upfield hip. While Curtis made the turn, the quarterback launched the ball into the corner of the end zone, where only Andre could catch it. Andre's hands went up to make the catch. Curtis launched himself into the air. As the football touched the wide receiver's hands, Curtis ripped the ball from his grasp. Incomplete.

The defensive backs cheered the pass breakup.

Curtis popped up and jogged back toward the sideline.

Andre pushed his hands forward, signaling pass interference.

"Quit your crying. That was clean." Coach Williams smacked Curtis on the helmet, as he jogged by. "Nice job, Curtis."

After practicing fourteen times with one of the best college football teams in the nation, Curtis had learned two things. He still had a lot to learn, but he had the athletic ability to compete at this level.

At the end of practice, the players took a knee, huddling around Head Coach Frank Goodman. Coach Goodman was a large man—tall and heavyset, with a ruddy complexion and feathered hair.

"Men, that was an outstanding spring practice," Coach Goodman said. "National championships are won in the offseason. The time to get better is now. That's exactly what we've done. I'm proud of each and every one of you. Give yourself a round of applause."

Everyone clapped and cheered.

When the clapping ceased, Coach Goodman said, "We have the blue and white intrasquad scrimmage tomorrow. The teams are posted on the bulletin board in the locker room. Make sure you wear the appropriate jersey tomorrow. If you need treatment or taping, be in the training room by 10:30 a.m. I expect everyone else to be in the locker room by 11:00." Coach Goodman scanned his team. "Now don't go out doing anything stupid tonight. The scrimmage will help us determine the depth chart going into summer camp. Don't blow your big break by being an idiot." Coach Goodman stared at Justin Love.

"Why are you looking at me, Coach?" Justin asked.

Many of the players laughed, as Justin had a party-boy reputation.

Coach Goodman raised his eyebrows. "You know why."

"That's not me, Coach," Justin replied, with a smirk.

Coach Goodman gave him an I-don't-believe-that look, then said, "All right, Justin, break 'em down."

Justin moved to the middle of the team and held up his hand. The players crowded together, also with one hand raised. Justin said, "The natty on three. One, two, three."

The entire team shouted, "The natty."

The natty was slang for the national championship.

Curtis and the rest of the players lumbered toward the locker room, holding their helmets in hand. Shouts and laughter came from behind Curtis. He pivoted. A group of players surrounded someone, but Curtis had no idea who or why. A large offensive lineman wrapped Curtis up in a bear hug from behind. Curtis dropped his helmet, struggling in the man's grasp. Another player grabbed Curtis's feet. Curtis stopped resisting, as he knew this was likely his initiation. The other newbies had been discussing it, wondering when it would happen and what it would entail. The two men and a dozen more took Curtis to the goalpost.

Justin Love gave the orders. "Tape him to the goalpost."

They used eight rolls of athletic tape to secure him to the goalpost. The tape bit and squeezed Curtis's arms, legs, and stomach.

"Get the water," Justin said.

They dumped two coolers of ice water on Curtis's head. The cold water nearly took his breath away. He shivered in the cool breeze.

They shaved a big X into Curtis's head on Justin's orders.

"I don't know if we can make him any uglier," Andre Willis said.

They laughed.

Curtis laughed too, thinking that it didn't bother him one bit to have an ugly haircut.

After the haircut, they sprayed shaving cream over his face. Curtis couldn't wipe away the shaving cream because his hands were bound. He tried to open his eyes, but the shaving cream burned, so he shut them tight again.

"Welcome to CVU football," Justin Love said.

Someone punched Curtis in the stomach, taking his wind.

As Curtis wheezed for breath, Andre asked, "What are you doin'?"

"I didn't hit him that hard," Justin replied.

The voices and footsteps receded, until everyone was gone. Curtis struggled against the tape, trying to free his hands to clear the shaving cream from his eyes. After a few minutes, he relaxed, realizing it was futile. He figured someone would eventually cut him loose.

That person came about thirty minutes later.

"You, okay?" a woman asked.

Curtis nodded.

"I'm Jodie Hauser. I'm an assistant trainer. Let me get this shaving cream off your face." She used a towel to wipe away the shaving cream.

Curtis blinked several times, his eyes mildly burning. Jodie was a petite, athletic woman, who appeared to be in her forties.

"Are your eyes okay?" Jodie asked.

"I think so."

"I'm going to cut you free now."

Jodie cut the tape, and Curtis broke free from his bonds.

Curtis waved his arms back and forth, returning the blood to his veins. "Thank you."

"You're welcome." Jodie handed Curtis a plastic trash bag. "You also have to clean up the mess. Make sure you get all that tape off the goalpost."

As he peeled tape off the goalpost, he noticed the other newbies with their terrible haircuts doing the same thing to the other goalposts. It took Curtis nearly an hour to remove all the tape, but he didn't mind. He was officially a CVU football player.

CHAPTER 58

Scout Team

On a humid afternoon in late August, Curtis lined up twelve yards from the line of scrimmage, dead center of the formation. He played the deep safety on the scout team, mimicking the 3-3-5 defense used by their upcoming opponent.

As Justin Love and the first-team offense lined up in a trips formation, Curtis called out the strength to the rest of the defense. "Rip. Rip."

Rip meant the strength was to the right side of the formation, the same side as the three receivers. The defense shifted toward the strength, so the offense couldn't exploit the numbers advantage on the right side.

Justin called out the cadence. He used thirty-one to indicate the cover one coverage that the defense was likely running. "Blue thirty-one. Blue thirty-one. Hut. *Hut.*"

On the second *hut*, the center flicked the football between his legs, five yards through the air to Justin, who then handed it to the running back. The big guards pulled to the left and pancaked the defensive end and the outside linebacker. The running back toted the football around the left end, motoring for ten yards without being touched.

Curtis avoided the oncoming blockers and sprinted toward the running back. Curtis could've pushed him out of bounds, but he lowered his shoulder and launched himself into the running back. The *crack* reverberated through the outdoor practice fields, and the running back was upended and deposited on his back.

Oohs and aahs came from the players on the sideline.

The running back popped up and threw the ball at Curtis, who batted the ball to the ground.

"What the fuck, man?" the running back asked.

The two all-conference wide receivers joined the fray.

"Fucking scout team hero," Kavon Drake said.

Andre Willis shoved Curtis, and Curtis shoved him back.

Coach Goodman blew his whistle and shouted, "Cut the bull crap. Line up and run it again."

The offense ran the same running play. This time, two offensive guys blocked Curtis, and the running back ran for a touchdown.

On the next play, Justin dropped back to pass. Curtis backpedaled, reading Justin and his wide receivers at the same time. Kavon Drake ran a seam route. Justin threw a bullet, trying to fit the football over the linebackers but underneath Curtis, who was the deep free safety. But Curtis read the play, breaking on the ball as soon as Justin cocked to throw. The football sailed through the air. Kavon held up his hands for the easy catch, but Curtis jumped in front and snagged the ball from the air. He spotted an opening to his right, as he landed on the ground. Curtis sprinted toward the opening, running toward the opposite goal line.

It was rare that the scout team defense got an interception or picked up a fumble, but, when they did, they never ran it back for a touchdown. In fact, they never ran too far beyond the line of scrimmage, as the coaches and the second-team offense stood behind the first-team offense on the field. However, Curtis wanted to know what it felt like, so he kept running until he crossed the opposite goal line for the touchdown. Then he turned around and jogged back, the football still in the crook of his arm.

Coach Goodman yelled at Justin. "Why did you throw the seam? The out was wide open. Let's go. We can't have these mental mistakes."

Justin and much of the first-team offense mean-mugged Curtis, as he flipped the ball back to Justin.

★★★

After showering, Curtis dressed in front of his locker.

A linebacker from the scout team fist-bumped Curtis on his way out and said, "Nice job on that pick-six."

Curtis lifted his chin. "Thanks, man."

As Curtis tied his shoes, Coach Williams entered the locker room and made a beeline to Curtis.

"I need to talk to you in my office," said Coach Williams.

Curtis followed the defensive backs' coach into his tiny office. A dozen pictures of various NFL defensive backs hung on the wall, all former protégés of Coach Williams.

"Have a seat." Coach Williams motioned to the chair in front of his desk.

Curtis and Coach Williams sat across from each other.

Coach leaned forward, resting his elbows on his desk. "You looked real good this week."

"Thank you, sir," Curtis replied.

"I know you've been running with the scout team, but do you know our playbook yet?"

"I know it. I've been studying."

Coach Williams arched his eyebrows. "You sure?"

"Yes, sir."

"We're elevating you to the second team. That means you might see ten to fifteen snaps, as the dime back against West Virginia. You think you can handle that in addition to special teams?"

Curtis had already earned a spot on the kickoff and punt coverage units. He grinned. "I can handle it. Thanks, Coach."

"Don't thank me. You earned it."

CHAPTER 59

The Season Opener

The West Virginia Mountaineers proved to be a staunch opponent. The Central Virginia Lions were down |by three points, late in the fourth quarter. It was piping hot and humid. Several players from both teams had left the game because of exhaustion and dehydration. Curtis watched from the sideline at William T. Armstrong Stadium— or the more common nickname, the Lion's Den.

It was fourth and one at West Virginia's twenty-two-yard line. Despite eighty thousand fans in the packed stadium, it was dead quiet.

Justin Love and the Central Virginia offense lined up in a heavy formation with a single wide receiver, three tight ends, and one running back. Everyone expected a running play. Maybe a quarterback sneak or a dive to the running back. Justin lined up under center and called out the cadence. "Blue thirty. Blue thirty. *Hut.*"

The center snapped the ball. Justin took the football and went to hand off to the running back. The West Virginia defense swarmed, clogging the running lanes, but Justin faked the handoff and dropped back to pass. Andre Willis streaked to the corner of the end zone, the defender trailing by a few yards. Justin threw a perfect pass, hitting Andre in stride for the go-ahead touchdown.

The crowd erupted, cheering and high-fiving each other in the stands. It was Justin's fourth touchdown pass of the game.

Central Virginia kicked the extra point, extending their lead to 35–31.

With fifty-four seconds left in the game, Curtis trotted onto the field for the kickoff. Ten players lined up behind the kicker, evenly spaced across the field. Curtis lined up near the West Virginia sideline. His job was to contain the runner on that side, to not let him get outside of him.

The referee blew the whistle. The kicker trotted to the football and kicked it into the stratosphere. Curtis and his teammates sprinted downfield, trying to stay in their lanes. The West Virginia return team ran backward, coalesced, then blocked the incoming Lions.

The West Virginia runner caught the tumbling football at the one-yard line. He cut to his left, away from Curtis. There was an open seam and plenty of blockers. The shifty runner made a Central Virginia tackler miss, then ran up the Lion sideline with nothing but green in front of him. Curtis sprinted from the opposite side of the field, taking a good angle. The crowd held their collective breath. Curtis streaked across the field and slammed into the runner, knocking him out of bounds at the fifty-yard line, saving a touchdown and likely the game.

The crowd let out a collective gasp.

Curtis didn't get a break. He immediately ran out with the dime defense. A dime defense consisted of six defensive backs, two line-backers, and three defensive linemen. It was used when the defense expected the other team to pass. Given that time was short, and the West Virginia personnel on the field consisted of five wide receivers, it was likely they would pass.

Curtis watched Coach Williams from the sideline signal in the play. It was their base dime coverage—two deep, with man coverage underneath. Curtis played the weakside deep safety.

On the first play, the West Virginia quarterback threw a quick slant to the outside receiver for a ten-yard gain and a first down.

West Virginia only had one time-out left, so they hurried to the line, hoping to run another play quickly, before too much time drained from the clock. They did exactly that, running the same slant to the other side for another ten-yard gain and another first down.

On the next play, the quarterback dropped back to pass again, but he handed off the ball this time. The running back blasted up the middle for twelve yards, until Curtis and two others converged on the tackle. West Virginia used their final time-out.

During the time-out, a trainer brought water bottles to the defenders. Curtis sprayed water into his mouth through his face mask. The Central Virginia defenders huddled around Coach Williams.

"We're giving up too much," Coach Williams said. "If they line up in that spread formation again, cornerbacks, watch those slants. We were too loose before. I think they'll try to split the safeties right up the middle. Safeties, watch the backside post."

Curtis nodded, knowing he was talking about him and the other deep safety.

"Don't get caught staring in the backfield. Don't fall for any play-action. I doubt they'll try to run again without any time-outs. We're gonna stick with our base dime coverage." Coach Williams addressed the linemen. "Defensive ends, do *not* let the quarterback scramble outside of you." Coach Williams scanned the defenders, his eyes bulging with intensity. "This is it, men. We need a big play. Let's go now. It's time."

Coach Williams trotted off the field. West Virginia's offensive coordinator trotted off the field too.

It was now first down and ten on the Central Virginia eighteen-yard line with twenty-four seconds left. The crowd was at a fever pitch, doing their best to disrupt the West Virginia offense.

West Virginia lined up in a shotgun empty formation, with five wide receivers. On the snap, Curtis backpedaled, reading the two wide receivers on his side and the quarterback at the same time. The inside receiver ran a wheel route, headed for the back corner of the end zone, but he was well covered by the slot cornerback. The outside receiver ran a stop route that was covered by the linebacker. The quarterback didn't look to Curtis's side though. Instead, he checked the inside receiver on the other side, running the post that Coach Williams had warned them about. The other safety was beat by a step. If Curtis didn't close the passing window, the receiver would split the safeties for a touchdown.

Curtis planted and made a beeline for the receiver running the post pattern. The West Virginia quarterback threw a perfect pass. As soon as the ball touched the receiver's outstretched hands, Curtis collided with the receiver. The ball bounced off Curtis's helmet and hung in the air. Curtis fell to the turf, spraining his wrist while bracing his fall.

The other safety snagged the floating football for an interception and took a knee in the end zone, ending West Virginia's chance of an upset. The CVU sideline erupted in jubilation, along with eighty thousand fans.

★★★

After the game, Curtis met Mr. H. and his foster brothers outside the locker room, which was inside the CVU Athletic Center. Curtis still wore his football pants, a T-shirt, and a bag of ice wrapped around his wrist. The boys dapped Curtis and complimented his play. After he greeted and hugged his foster brothers, they wandered around the CVU Hall of Fame, looking at pictures of the greatest CVU football players, many of whom became NFL stars.

Mr. H. hugged Curtis. "You played great. I'm proud of you."

Curtis beamed. "Thanks."

Mr. H. gestured to the ice pack around Curtis's wrist. "You all right?"

"It's nothing. Trainer said it's just a sprain."

"Good."

"I still can't believe I was on that field today. It was crazy. All those fans. I've never seen anything like it."

"Believe it." Mr. H. poked Curtis in the chest. "This is what impressed me the most. Your heart. When you saved that touchdown on the kickoff team. And then that hit you made on the last play. That was all heart."

Coach Williams appeared with a big grin. "Russel."

Mr. H. hugged Coach Williams. When they separated, Mr. H. motioned to Curtis. "What did I tell you about my boy?"

Coach Williams nodded. "You were right."

"You could've had him last year."

Coach Williams showed his palms. "I know. I know. But we have him now, and he has a bright future ahead of him."

CHAPTER 60

Jodie Hauser

The following Tuesday, Curtis walked into the training room an hour before practice. It resembled a hybrid gym and hospital. Several cushy training tables spanned one wall, each with electrical stimulation and ultrasound machines, and all occupied by football players receiving treatment. Various rehabilitation equipment spanned another wall. In the back were multiple whirlpools and two ice machines.

The starting tight end waited before him. Curtis was there to have his wrist taped. Jodie Hauser finished treating one player's sore shoulder. The tight end sat on the open table, his bare feet dangling, while Curtis waited in a chair along the wall.

Jodie Hauser taped the tight end's ankles, working quickly and precisely. The tight end slid off the table, his ankles bound by tape. Curtis rose to his feet to take his place on the open training table. At the same time, Justin Love entered the training room.

Just before Curtis hopped on the table, Justin slipped in front of Curtis and said, "I got seniority."

Curtis went back to his seat without a word.

Justin lay on the training table, on his back, his hands behind his head. He turned his head to Kavon Drake, on the table next to him. "What's wrong with you?"

"Hammy," Kavon replied.

Jodie approached Justin. "Why don't you grab a heating pad."

Football players were expected to help the training staff by doing simple things that didn't require a trainer, like fetching their own heating pads.

"I just got comfortable. Will you get it for me?" Justin asked.

Jodie walked across the room.

To get his attention, Justin reached out and tapped Kavon. Justin lifted his chin to Jodie's backside, and whispered, "Check out that ass."

"Not bad for an old white lady," Kavon replied.

Justin frowned. "That ass is tight for any age."

Jodie fished a heating pad from the hot water receptacle with the metal tongs, and placed the pad inside a soft cover. The trainer returned to Justin and placed the heating pad on his left hip flexor area, part of the pad also on his crotch.

"That feels good." Justin winked at Jodie. "You got me all hot."

Jodie rolled her eyes and attended to another patient.

Kavon laughed.

Justin had been playing with a strained hip flexor since summer training camp.

Ten minutes later, Jodie removed the heating pad from Justin's hip, handed it to Justin, and said, "Put it back. Then I'll do your ultrasound treatment."

"*Really*?" Justin lifted his chin to Curtis, and the several other players waiting for treatment. "Make one of them put it back. They're not doing anything."

A freshman offensive lineman stood from the waiting area and said, "I'll take it." And he did.

Justin hiked the left leg of his shorts to his hip bone while Jodie fiddled with the ultrasound machine. Jodie squirted blue gel over his left hip flexor. She grabbed the wired ultrasound head and used the device in a circular motion on the injured area.

While Jodie worked, Justin leered at her. As she spread the gel with the circular motion of the ultrasound head, some of the gel got on Justin's shorts. Justin hiked his shorts some more, exposing himself in the process.

Jodie cleared her throat and placed a towel over Justin's exposed penis. Then Justin whispered something inaudible to Jodie.

She stepped back. "That's *enough*." She wiped off the ultrasound head and returned it to the machine. She walked away, her face beet red, and disappeared into the back office.

"I still have six minutes," Justin called out to her back.

"What's up with her?" Kavon asked.

Justin shrugged. "Fuck if I know. Must be on the rag."

Curtis wasn't sure if anyone else saw Justin expose himself. Jodie's location had screened Justin's penis from almost everyone in the training room, except for Curtis. Then she'd covered him up after only a few seconds.

A male trainer replaced Jodie, finishing Justin's treatment without incident.

★★★

The next day, Curtis jogged from the dorms to the athletic center after class. He hoped to arrive at the training room early to get his wrist taped before the rush.

When he entered the training room, he scanned the area for Jodie, as he liked the way she taped his wrist.

One male trainer approached Curtis. "What do you need?"

"My wrist taped. Is Jodie here?" Curtis asked.

"Haven't seen her."

CHAPTER 61

Clemson

Clemson Memorial Stadium in South Carolina was a sea of orange. The third-ranked Clemson Tigers were the toughest opponent that the Central Virginia Lions would face in 2016. The winner would likely move to number two in the college football rankings, behind top-ranked Alabama.

Eighty thousand fans screamed; their cacophony made it nearly impossible for the offense to hear Justin's cadence. Central Virginia had the ball, down by seven, with only three minutes to play.

On third and ten, the center snapped the ball to Justin Love. He rolled to his right and threw a perfect strike to Kavon on a corner route. But Kavon pulled up lame, grabbing his hamstring, and the football bounced off the lush Bermuda grass. Instead of going for it on fourth and ten, CVU elected to punt. With all three time-outs, they would have another crack at scoring, if their defense held.

Curtis lined up as the gunner on the punt team. He felt like Vince Papale, the former Eagles special teamer. They had watched *Invincible* on the plane ride to South Carolina, which had portrayed Papale's improbable rise to the NFL. Two blockers lined up in front of Curtis, determined to keep him away from the return man. Curtis turned his head inside, watching the football. As soon as the center snapped the ball to the punter, he jab-stepped outside, then cut inside, running around the blockers, then up the field.

The CVU punter held the ball for a moment, as Clemson wasn't rushing, instead electing to set up a return. Curtis heard the *thump* of the football off the punter's foot. The return man settled under the booming football. Curtis expected him to call for a fair catch, but he didn't, and Curtis made him pay for it. As soon as the ball touched his hands, Curtis slammed into the Clemson returner, sprinting at full speed. The hit jarred the football loose. The returner lay on his back, writhing, breathless. Curtis scrambled to his feet, his eyes on the loose football. He picked up the ball and sprinted for the goal line, all the while expecting someone to tackle him. But nobody did, and Curtis entered the end zone, the stadium dead quiet, except for the cheering CVU sideline.

Curtis didn't do a touchdown celebration. He handed the football to the referee and trotted back to his sideline, where his teammates engulfed him, slapping him on his helmet and shoulder pads. But it wasn't over yet. They could've kicked an extra point to tie the game, but Coach Goodman wanted the win. So, Justin Love and the offense jogged onto Frank Howard Field for the two-point conversion and the win—or the loss.

The Central Virginia offense lined up in a shotgun single back set, with two tight ends and two wide receivers. The Clemson faithful screamed, desperate to disrupt Justin and the CVU offense. On the snap, Justin Love checked right, then he threw a rocket to his left. Andre Willis made a diving catch on the slant route for the two-point conversion.

Curtis and the CVU sideline erupted in jubilation, while the rest of Clemson Memorial Stadium went silent.

CHAPTER 62

Fifteen Minutes of Fame

Curtis sat at his desk, reading his Psychology textbook, preparing for the quiz on Monday.

The lock turned, and Ben entered their dorm room. He shut the door behind him. His eyes were dilated and bloodshot. He smelled like marijuana. "Dude, what are doing?"

Curtis looked up from his book. "Studying. I have a quiz tomorrow."

Ben scrunched his face. "A quiz? Not even a test?"

"It still counts."

"Dude. There's a huge party at Sigma Chi right now."

Curtis shrugged. "I don't party on Sundays."

Ben frowned. "Or any other day."

"It's not my thing."

"You guys just won the biggest game of the year, and *you* were the fucking star. Don't you wanna celebrate with your teammates? A bunch of them are at Sigma Chi."

Curtis wasn't surprised by this. They didn't return from South Carolina until almost midnight, so most of the guys didn't party on Saturday night. In addition, Coach Goodman had given them a day off on Monday, so a bunch of football players had planned to party Sunday night.

"Come on, man," Ben said. "I hardly ever see you anymore."

Curtis thought about how high he felt when his teammates had mobbed him after his touchdown. "Yeah. All right."

Ben smacked Curtis across the back. "My man."

★★★

Curtis felt like a celebrity, when he entered Sigma Chi. He was mobbed by classmates and teammates, congratulating him on his late-game touchdown. Someone handed Curtis a beer in a red cup. They called him by name, even though Curtis had never met most of the partygoers. In fact, he'd never spoken to some of his teammates either.

Rap pumped through the speakers. A replay of the Clemson game played on all the flat screens.

A group of Sigma Chi fraternity brothers—most wearing khaki shorts, flip-flops, and rude T-shirts referencing drugs, alcohol, or promiscuous sex—accosted Curtis.

"Dude. You fucking destroyed that guy," one of them said. "I've never seen anyone get hit that hard."

"That was so badass," another one said.

"Dude, are you black or white? I'm not trying to be racial, I was—"

One of the guys nudged him. "Not cool, man."

"Thanks, guys." Curtis backed away from the fraternity brothers and pivoted. When he turned, he spotted Tania across the room, and she spotted him at the same time. Curtis nearly turned away, pretending he hadn't seen her, but he was in a good mood, so he held up his beer and smiled at her, keeping his mouth closed. They hadn't talked since their argument almost one year ago, but Curtis wasn't mad at her.

Tania smiled back and waded through the crowd toward Curtis. He did the same, meeting her in the middle of the room.

"Hey," Curtis said.

She was beautiful in her knee-length skirt and shiny silk blouse. "Hey, yourself. It's been a long time."

"Yeah, it's been a minute."

Tania pursed her full lips. "I saw you on TV yesterday, doing your thing."

"Yeah?"

"Yeah. I'm happy for you." She reached for his beer. "Can I have a sip?"

Curtis handed her the beer. "You can have the rest if you want."

Tania sipped the beer. "Thanks. I'm so thirsty. They never have bottled water here."

"Were you singing tonight?"

"You didn't hear me?"

"No, but I just got here. Are you planning to do another set?"

She shook her head. "My voice is starting to go. I really should go home and drink some tea."

The crowd parted for the conquering hero, and Justin Love appeared before them. He put his arm around Tania. "We're supposed to do some shots together."

Tania tilted her head up to Justin. "Only one."

"Only one? Shots are like potato chips. You can't have just one."

Tania giggled. She gave Curtis a discreet wave, as Justin led her to the bar area.

Curtis went to the basement, where it was quieter. A handful of fraternity brothers, football players, and coeds played pool, foosball, and sat on the couches, watching the replay of the Clemson game on the big screen.

Curtis sat on the end of the sectional couch.

One of his teammates handed him a beer. "The man of the hour, everybody."

A few people cheered and held up their beer to Curtis.

Curtis held up his beer, then took a swig.

Over the next hour, Curtis drank three beers and watched the replay of the Clemson game. His head buzzed from the alcohol. Three beers weren't a lot, but he rarely drank.

Ben descended the stairs. He scanned the basement, then hurried to Curtis.

"Hey, Ben. Where you been?" Curtis chuckled at his accidentally stupid pun.

Ben knelt next to Curtis and whispered, "I just saw Tania go upstairs with a bunch of football players. She was *messed* up. She could barely walk."

Curtis sprang from his seat. "Why didn't you stop them?"

Ben held out his hands. "What the fuck am I supposed to do? Those guys are huge."

Curtis ran upstairs to the first floor. He pushed through the crowd, causing a few drunk students to spill their beers.

"Hey. Watch out," one girl said.

Curtis sprinted up the circular staircase to the second floor. Most of the upstairs bedrooms were locked. Curtis knocked on each one, calling out, "Tania. Tania. Are you in there?"

Sometimes there was no answer. Sometimes they responded, "She's not in here." Or "Fuck off. She ain't in here."

Curtis banged on the last door at the end of the hall.

"Help me," Tania screamed.

Curtis lowered his shoulder, rammed the door, and busted the lock. The door flung open, and Curtis's momentum took him several feet into the room. Tania was face down on the bed, her skirt hiked to her waist, her underwear gone. Justin lay atop her, pumping her from behind, naked from the waist down. Four football players surrounded the bed. Kavon and Andre were two of them, along with the two starting offensive tackles, Preston Waylon, and Thomas Creese. Andre held his penis in hand, like he was on deck.

Tania screamed, "Help me." Her face was red and tear-streaked.

Kavon and the two offensive tackles tried to push Curtis out of the room.

"Get the fuck out of here," Kavon said.

But Curtis wouldn't budge. "Let her go."

Justin turned his head and glared at Curtis, still inside her. "Get him outta here."

The two offensive tackles managed to push Curtis into the hall-way, but Curtis threw a hard uppercut to the gut, causing Preston to double over. This gave Curtis a brief opening to run back into the room. He yanked Justin off Tania, dumping him on the floor. Curtis choked Justin, the quarterback's neck in the crook of Curtis's muscled arm. Curtis was a man possessed. Justin would've died in that bedroom if left to his own devices.

Tania rolled from the bed and fell to the hardwood. She scrambled to her bare feet and ran from the room. The four football players grabbed and punched at Curtis, until he let go of Justin. When he did, Justin wheezed for air. Then they kicked and beat Curtis until he blacked out.

Curtis woke when they tossed him on the front lawn of Sigma Chi.

CHAPTER 63

The Aftermath

"You sure you don't want me to take you to the hospital?" Ben asked, as he opened their dorm room.

Curtis shook his head and staggered inside, his ribs and back sore, along with a splitting headache and two swollen eyes. He glanced at his alarm clock—*11:37 p.m.* Curtis removed his prepaid phone from his pocket and sat on his bed. He only had a handful of minutes left.

"What are we gonna do?" Ben asked, pacing in front of Curtis's bed.

"*We're* not gonna do anything," Curtis replied. "*You* weren't there. *You* didn't see anything. *You* can't help me."

Ben blanched. "I'm sorry. I didn't know this would happen."

Curtis held up his hand like a stop sign. "I know." Curtis thought about calling Mr. H., but he was too far away to do anything tonight. He thought about calling the police, but he worried about being prosecuted for assault or even attempted murder. It would be their word against his. If he was gonna go to the police, he needed to go with Tania. They had to be a united front. "I need to talk to Tania. We can go to the police together. Tell our story before those motherfuckers lie. Do you have her number?"

"No. We barely see each other. I could go to her dorm. See if I can find her."

Curtis nodded. "That's a good idea."

"I'm on it. I'll be back." Ben left the dorm, locking the door with his key.

Curtis called the only other person who could help him, the only other person he trusted.

It took five rings, but Coach Williams finally answered with a groggy, "Hello."

"It's Curtis. I'm in big trouble."

Curtis explained exactly what had happened to Coach Williams, naming all who were involved.

At the conclusion of Curtis's account, Coach Williams let out a heavy breath and asked, "How are you physically? Do you need to go to the hospital?"

"I don't think so. I'm in bad shape, but I don't think I'm seriously injured."

"I'd like for Doc Harper to take a look at you tonight, if I can get him out of bed."

Doc Harper was the head athletic trainer.

"Okay." Curtis slipped off his running shoes.

"It's important that we're careful with this information," Coach Williams said. "This is a very delicate situation that will have far-reaching consequences. Do you understand that?"

"Yes, sir." Curtis lay on his bed, grunting in pain as he did so, his phone still to his ear.

"I need you to keep this information to yourself, until I talk to Coach Goodman and figure out exactly how to proceed. Can you do that?"

"What about the police?"

"Ultimately, that's up to the girl, isn't it?"

"What about what they did to me?"

"Didn't you throw the first punch?"

Curtis tensed. "Justin was *raping* her."

"That's what you thought. Justin may have another explanation. Maybe this girl's into that—"

"She's not." Curtis sat up again, pushing through the shooting pain coming from his midsection. "This isn't right. If you're gonna take his side, I'm going to the police. Let them sort it out."

"Hold on, Curtis. I'm on *your* side. I'm asking you the same questions the police will ask. Do you wanna go to prison for assault?"

"No."

"Look. I understand why you did what you did. I think you did the right thing, but the law and morality aren't the same thing. Based on your own words, the police could arrest you for assault or even attempted murder."

Curtis hung his head, his stomach turning.

"I'm not trying to scare you. I'm advising you to be smart. So, I'm asking you to keep this to yourself, until I can talk to Coach Goodman and figure out what to do next. Will you do that?"

"Yes, sir."

"Good. I'm gonna call Doc Harper. I'll call you right back."

"Okay."

Coach Williams disconnected the call.

Curtis lay on his bed again. When he closed his eyes, he saw Tania face down on that bed, begging for help, her face red and tear-streaked.

His phone chimed, jarring him from his nightmare.

It was Coach Williams. "Doc Harper's gonna meet us at the training room in twenty minutes. I'll pick you up at your dorm in fifteen."

"Okay."

After Coach Williams disconnected the call, Curtis struggled to his feet and slipped on his running shoes. He staggered to the communal bathroom. Thankfully, it was empty. He was shocked by his appearance in the mirror. *I didn't think it was possible to look any uglier.* Both his eyes were red and swollen, soon-to-be black eyes. He had an abrasion on his left cheek. From what? He didn't know. A boot? A fist?

He washed his face, hoping to improve his appearance. It didn't work. Before he left the bathroom, he peed and washed his hands. He staggered to the elevator. It was the first time he'd used the elevator, always electing to take the stairs.

Curtis waited for Coach Williams on a bench in front of the dorm, with a view of the parking lot. He couldn't stop thinking about Tania. Ben made it back to the dorm before Coach Williams.

Ben spotted Curtis on the bench and jogged to him. "What are you doing out here?"

"My coach is taking me to the training room to get checked out," Curtis replied.

"That's a good idea."

"Did you find her?"

"I found her room. Talked to her roommate. The roommate said she hasn't been back to her room, and her car's gone. Maybe she went home, or maybe she's with the police right now."

"Yeah. That makes sense. Thanks for looking."

"No problem. I can go by there tomorrow too."

Curtis nodded. "Yeah. That's a good idea."

Coach Williams's Toyota pickup entered the parking area.

"That's my coach." Curtis stood and lurched toward the curb.

Coach Williams parked along the curb, exited the truck, and helped Curtis into the passenger seat. Ben watched them drive away.

"Who's that?" Coach Williams asked.

"My roommate," Curtis replied.

"Does he know?"

"He saw Tania go up to the room with all of them."

As Coach Williams drove the short distance to the athletic center, he glanced at Curtis. "Have you talked to the girl since she ran off?"

"No. I haven't heard from her."

CHAPTER 64

From Bad to Worse

Curtis entered his dorm room, high on Aleve, his body cold and stiff from the ice the trainer had applied. Doc Harper had examined Curtis and had determined that he was unlikely to have any serious injuries. The head trainer had mentioned X-rays and a hospital visit, but Coach Williams was quick to dismiss the idea. After the examination, while Curtis iced his midsection and face, Doc Harper and Coach Williams had a contentious argument in the back office. Curtis couldn't hear the specifics, but he had wondered if it had to do with Doc Harper's hospital recommendation.

In the end, there was no hospital visit, which was just fine with Curtis. It was after 1:00 a.m., and Curtis wanted to sleep. The last thing he wanted was to spend hours sitting in the ER. Curtis shut the door behind him. His room smelled like skunk. Ben sat on the couch, sucking marijuana vapor from his bong.

Curtis kicked off his shoes and removed his jeans, grunting as he bent down.

Ben set his bong on the coffee table and stepped to Curtis. "What did they say?"

Curtis climbed into bed, under the comforter. "Not much. He doesn't think I have any broken bones. I just iced and took some Aleve."

Ben nodded. "I can't sleep. This shit is seriously fucked up."

"I can't think about it right now. I need to get some sleep." Curtis closed his eyes, his head on his pillow.

"Yeah. Me too." Ben hesitated for a moment. "Hey, Curtis?"

Curtis opened one swollen eye. "Yeah?"

"I'm sorry I got you into this. I never should've said anything."

Curtis opened his other swollen eye. "You were right to tell me. None of this is your fault. It's theirs."

"Thanks, man." Ben pivoted and went to his bed.

Curtis drifted off to sleep.

Hard banging on the door woke Curtis from his slumber. Sunlight slipped between the blinds in tiny slivers. Curtis glanced at the time on his alarm clock—*8:18 a.m.*

Ben poked his head up from his bed. "What the hell?"

The banging continued.

Curtis rolled out of bed, groaning from the soreness.

"Wait. Don't open it," Ben said, now sitting on the edge of his bed. "It could be Justin and his boys."

Curtis went to the door. "Who is it?"

"Police. Open up," the authoritative voice said.

Ben shot out of bed and said in a hushed whisper, "Don't."

Curtis figured Tania must've gone to the police, and they wanted a statement, which was a relief, as Curtis worried that the university might try to cover up the rape. Curtis opened the door. Two uniformed police officers and two campus police officers stood before Curtis. Ben rushed about the room behind him, his bare feet smacking the linoleum floor.

"Can we come inside?" asked the beefy Centre County police officer.

"Yeah," Curtis replied.

"No," Ben shouted, but they were already in the room. Ben hid his bong behind the couch.

Despite Ben's obvious concern, Curtis wasn't worried. He didn't think they would arrest a witness to a rape for marijuana. They weren't there for that.

Then the beefy officer said, "We've had reports of marijuana smell coming from this dorm room."

Curtis tensed.

The wiry Centre County police officer removed his flashlight from his utility belt, and walked to the couch, his boots reverberating off the linoleum. He flicked on his flashlight and peered behind the couch. "There's paraphernalia and what looks like marijuana in plain sight." He reached behind the couch, recovered the bong, and held it up to the other officers.

The beefy police officer faced Curtis. "Turn around. Put your hands behind your back."

Curtis swallowed hard and did what he was told.

"It's not his," Ben said, holding out his hands like a beggar.

The wiry police officer handed the bong to campus police and said the same thing to Ben. "Turn around. Put your hands behind your back."

As the officers handcuffed Curtis and Ben, the beefy officer said, "You're both under arrest for possession of marijuana and marijuana paraphernalia."

Curtis and Ben were removed from their dorm in handcuffs and taken to the back seat of a Centre County Police car. They were taken to the Centre County Police Department, where they were photographed, fingerprinted, and placed in a holding cell.

They were each given a single phone call. Ben had called his mother and explained the situation. She'd been hysterical but promised to meet Ben at the arraignment with an attorney. Curtis had thought about calling Mr. H., but he didn't have money for an attorney, and Curtis hated the idea of disappointing him. Furthermore, Curtis still held out hope that he could resolve the situation on his own. He was innocent, after all. Ben had promised to tell the judge exactly that and to share his attorney.

The holding cell was empty, except for Ben and Curtis. Apparently, it had just been emptied for transport to court for arraignment. Ben and Curtis would have to wait until tomorrow for arraignment.

Curtis sat on the metal bench, his head pounding. The Aleve was wearing off, and he had left his pills in his dorm room, although he doubted the police would've let him have them anyway. He thought about the odd timing of the police raid.

Ben paced in front of Curtis. "This is fucking bullshit. Lots of dorm rooms smell like weed, but I've never heard of anyone calling the cops for that." Ben stopped in his tracks. "Is this because of Tania?"

Curtis raised his gaze to Ben. "That's exactly what I was thinking."

Ben's eyes widened. "Holy shit. Who was in that room besides Justin?"

"The two best receivers in the ACC and our starting offensive tackles."

"*Fuck*. They're trying to shut you up."

"Maybe. I don't know. Either it's a big coincidence or …"

"Or CVU doesn't want the embarrassment."

Curtis leaned back against the cinderblock wall. "It might be more than embarrassment. Think about how much money CVU would lose if this gets out. What happens if they expel half the starting offense, including the Heisman candidate quarterback? We're not winning the national championship, that's for sure. The NCAA could impose sanctions too, which would impact recruiting and future scholarships. Then the booster money dries up. Who wants to give money to a football program of rapists?" Curtis blew out a ragged breath. "I think we're in over our heads, and I'm worried that my coach played me."

Ben slumped on the bench next to Curtis. "*Shit.* I'm sorry, dude.

There has to be something we can do."

"The only person who can help us is Tania. We need to get to her before they do."

CHAPTER 65

Arraignment

The next morning, Curtis, Ben, and a dozen other criminal offenders were transported to the courthouse. They were housed in another holding cell in the basement of the courthouse. While waiting for arraignment, Ben was taken from the holding cell to meet with his attorney. When Ben returned, he wore a crisp suit and was all smiles. Curtis still wore the orange jumpsuit issued by the jail.

Ben told Curtis, "Our attorney got us a deal. If we plead guilty to misdemeanor possession, all we have to do is pay a $250 fine. There's no jail time, no community service. Nothing. I'll pay your fine of course."

Curtis narrowed his eyes. "That's it? We plead guilty, and we walk?"

"That's it. He got the same deal for you as he did for me."

The deputy called out, "Curtis Duffy."

Curtis was escorted to a small room with a metal table and two chairs. Ben's attorney stood next to the desk. He was a portly middle-aged man, with a receding hairline and a ponytail. Curtis shook hands with the attorney, despite his bound hands. They sat across from each other at the metal table.

The defense attorney explained the deal he had negotiated with the prosecuting attorney. It was exactly as Ben had explained. No jail time. No community service. Only a $250 fine, which Ben's mother had promised to pay. If Curtis didn't plead guilty, he ran the risk of up to thirty days in jail and a $500 fine. Curtis figured if he went to jail, he'd be done. He wouldn't be able to find Tania in time to clear up this mess.

"What do you think?" the attorney asked. "Do you want to take the deal?"

"But I'm innocent," Curtis replied. "And Ben said he'd tell the judge that it was his marijuana."

"If you take the deal, this thing is over in a few hours." The attorney glanced at his gold watch to cement his point. "If you go to trial, an attorney will cost you at least five grand, and there's no guarantee of a *not guilty* verdict."

Curtis signed the plea agreement.

CHAPTER 66

The Easy Way or the Hard Way

After Curtis and Ben were released, they rode with Ben's mother back to the dorms. It was a beautiful day, with blue skies and cotton-candy clouds. Curtis sat in the back seat of her Volvo SUV, thinking about the arraignment. He wondered what it meant that one of the campus police officers was in the audience.

Ben's mother glanced in the rearview mirror at Curtis. "Are you sure you're okay? Your face …"

"I'm fine, really," Curtis replied. "It looks worse than it feels."

"Don't you wear a helmet?"

"My helmet came off." Curtis had told Ben's mother that his injuries had been from football.

Ben's mother glanced at her son, with a look that could kill. "I'm so disappointed in you, Benjamin. Now I know why your grades are so poor. I should get a hotel room nearby, so I can keep an eye on you for a few weeks. I need to make sure you're not a raging drug addict."

"*Mom.* I'm not a drug addict. Marijuana isn't addictive," Ben said, his head hanging and his shoulders hunched.

"Well, you could be doing other drugs, for all I know."

"I swear to God I'm not doing other drugs. I have a ton of work to do after missing two days of classes. I can't have you here."

Ben's mother turned into their dormitory parking lot. "Then I expect you to be on the straight and narrow from now on, mister."

"I will. I promise."

She parked the SUV, stopping unnecessarily hard. "*Fine.*"

Curtis and Ben exited the SUV.

As she left the parking lot, Curtis said, "I need to find Tania."

"I'll go with you," Ben replied.

Curtis checked the time on his phone—*1:15 p.m.* He was missing Social Work 370: Perspectives on Human Behavior and the Social Environment. He wondered if Tania was in class or in her dorm or maybe on the quad singing. On second thought, he doubted she was on the quad after what had happened to her. She had likely skipped class too. If Tania was still on campus, Curtis figured she was in her dorm room.

Curtis and Ben walked the short distance across campus to Tania's dormitory. A little whiteboard hung on the door. The names of the occupants, Tania and Rebecca, were scrawled across the board in pink cursive, along with bees and flowers for added pizazz. Ben knocked on the door. A short chubby young woman answered the door with a scowl. Curtis figured it was Rebecca.

She crossed her arms over her chest. "You again?"

"Is Tania here?" Ben asked.

"No." She glanced at Curtis. "Who's this?"

"I'm Curtis. I'm a friend." Curtis held out his hand, but she kept her arms crossed.

"Have you heard from her?" Ben asked.

"Maybe." She narrowed her eyes. "This is getting weird. Did you guys do something to her?"

"Did you hear from her or not?"

"That's none of your business."

Curtis sensed she had heard from Tania by text. "Could you give me her number?" He had her number for a brief time but had deleted it after their argument.

"I'm not giving you her number."

"Then would you please send her a message, letting her know that I need to talk to her?"

"I can't guarantee anything."

"Do you have her home address? I think she lives in Troy somewhere."

Rebecca glowered at Curtis. "I'm not telling you that either." She shut the door in their faces.

"I bet we can find her home address with a background check," Ben said.

Curtis nodded. "Good idea."

As they left the dorm, Curtis's phone chimed in his pocket. It was Coach Williams.

Curtis stopped in his tracks and said to Ben, "It's my coach." Then he answered. "Hello."

"Coach Goodman wants to talk to you in his office," Coach Williams said.

"When?"

"As soon as possible. He'd like to talk to you before practice. Where are you?"

"I'm on campus. I can be there in twenty minutes."

"All right."

Curtis's mouth was like cotton. "What does he wanna talk about?"

"I think it's best if he tells you." Coach Williams disconnected the call.

Curtis walked to the athletic center, while Ben vowed to find Tania's address via an online background-check service. During the walk, Curtis's head felt woozy from lack of sleep and food, not to mention his battered face. Stabs of pain came from his midsection with each step he took. He thought about what Coach Goodman would say. He was a religious man, who never swore. Curtis thought he might be horrified by what had happened. He might thank Curtis for helping Tania. Curtis wouldn't be able to practice for at least a few days. He doubted he could play effectively this Saturday with his injuries.

Curtis entered the athletic center and showed his ID to the student manning the front desk. He rode the elevator to the third-floor offices. From there, he walked down the blue-carpeted hallway, passing framed photos of former CVU football players who made good in the NFL.

He entered the waiting area for the coaches' offices. Curtis gave the receptionist his name.

She stared at his battered face for a beat and said, "They're expecting you."

She made a quick call on the desktop phone to announce Curtis's arrival, then she escorted him to a meeting room. She knocked once and opened the door. Coach Goodman and Coach Williams stood near the door, with two men in suits who Curtis had never met.

Curtis hesitated for a few seconds, then entered the meeting room. The receptionist shut the door behind him.

"Curtis. Thank you for coming," Coach Goodman said.

"You're welcome, Coach," Curtis replied.

Coach Goodman introduced the men in suits. "This is Dr. Callahan. He's the president of the university. And Mr. Forrest. He's an attorney for the university."

Curtis shook hands with the men, not making eye contact.

Coach Goodman gestured to the long table. "Why don't you have a seat."

Curtis sat in the nearest seat. All four men sat on the opposite side of the table, facing Curtis. The hair on the back of Curtis's neck stood on end.

"Coach Williams tells me that you've been through quite an ordeal," Coach Goodman said.

Curtis nodded, relaxing a little, feeling like Coach Goodman might be on his side.

"Why don't you tell us exactly what happened on Sunday night?"

Curtis told them everything, exactly how it had happened, and exactly who was involved. He didn't mention his misdemeanor arrest for marijuana possession. Throughout Curtis's testimony, the men on the other side of the table were dead silent and poker-faced.

Coach Goodman leaned forward when Curtis was finished, placing his elbows on the table. "Would you be surprised if I told you that those five young men said that it was *you* who had been hurting that girl and that *they* had intervened to make it stop?"

"That's not true," Curtis said, his voice amped with emotion. "Ask Tania. She'll tell you the truth."

"Unfortunately, she's not talking."

Curtis furrowed his brow. "What do you mean, *she's not talking*?"

"I don't know why except to assume that the poor girl is traumatized."

"This isn't right. Can't you just ask her? She doesn't have to go to court to tell you what happened."

"I'm afraid that's impossible. She doesn't wanna talk about it, and we can't make her."

Curtis gaped at Coach Goodman, at a loss for words. "What does this mean? Am I in trouble?"

"Do you know the difference between a problem and a predicament, Curtis?"

"No."

"Well, problems have solutions. Predicaments have outcomes. You, young man, are in a predicament."

"I don't understand."

"Well, given that it's your word against five of your teammates, I think this … *event* could go very badly for you, if you decide to move forward with your accusations."

Curtis looked at Coach Williams, hoping for a lifeline, but his face was like stone.

"Then there's the matter of your arrest," Coach Goodman said.

Curtis turned his attention back to Goodman, his eyes wide.

"Dr. Callahan."

"As you know, Curtis, this is a drug-free campus," Dr. Callahan said. "I'm sorry to inform you that there's an automatic expulsion for drug possession in the dorms."

"It wasn't mine. My roommate will tell you," Curtis said, his voice frantic.

"Then why did you plead guilty to drug possession this morning?"

Curtis opened his mouth to speak but nothing came out.

"You have one of two choices," Coach Goodman said, pushing a small stack of papers and a pen across the table. "This is a nondisclosure agreement. If you sign this agreement, you are agreeing not to talk about the events that transpired on Sunday night to anyone for the rest of your life."

Curtis shook his head; his face contorted as if in pain.

Coach Goodman showed his palms. "Before you say no, hear me out. If you sign the nondisclosure agreement, you can leave without a black mark on your academic record, and your tuition and room and board will be waived for the year. If you don't sign, you will have the drug offense on your academic record, and you will be responsible for the full year's cost of tuition and room and board."

Curtis slumped his shoulders in resignation.

"Take your time. Think about it," Coach Goodman said. "You might wanna read through the documents."

Curtis flipped through the pages, scanning the documents. He picked up the pen.

"You're making the right choice, son. Just sign and initial at the yellow tabs."

Curtis stared at the pen in his hand, then the papers. He balled his fist around the pen, stabbed the papers, the tip of the pen going through the paper to the wood grain of the table. Curtis jerked the pen back and forth, ripping the papers. He stood from the chair, sneered at Coach Goodman, and said, "Fuck you. I'm not your son."

CHAPTER 67

Sacrificed

Curtis grabbed his personal items from his locker and left the football equipment. Thankfully, the locker room was empty. Practice didn't start for an hour. Curtis wasn't sure he would be able to contain his rage if he saw Justin or any of the guys who had been in that room on Sunday night. With adrenaline still coursing through his veins, he shoved his personal items into his mesh bag, slung it over his shoulder, and left the athletic center. On the way out, he passed a few football players.

"Where are you going?" one of them asked.

Curtis didn't answer. He couldn't. Not without destroying the place or dissolving into tears.

Curtis returned to his dorm, like a cartoon hobo. All he needed was a stick attached to his bag. He entered his dorm room, expecting to see Ben, hoping he had found Tania's home address. But Ben wasn't there. Curtis dropped his mesh bag on the floor and sat on his bed.

He wondered how long they'd give him to leave. Curtis knew he could drag it out with the disciplinary hearing, but he knew how that would go. He'd be publicly disgraced and expelled in a few days, a week maybe. Why not save a week of his life and some shame? The only card he had left to play was Tania. *I need to get off my ass and find her. She's the only one who can fix this.*

Curtis stood from his bed and called Ben, but his call went to voice mail. After the prerecorded greeting, Curtis said, "Ben. It's me. Did you find Tania's address? Call me back as soon as you get this. It's an emergency."

Instead of sitting in his room, ruminating on his situation, and waiting for Ben to call, Curtis went to Tania's dormitory, hoping to find her.

Franklin Hall was a five-story apartment-style dormitory nearly identical to Curtis's dorm. A pickup truck was parked along the curb, the tailgate down, with a couch loaded in the back. Someone sat in the passenger seat. From the back, Curtis caught a glimpse of straight dark hair. *Is that her?* He circled the truck, nearly certain it wasn't her. Lots of people have straight dark hair. She must've sensed him, as he moved near the passenger window, because she turned her head. Tania's eyes were puffy and bloodshot. When she recognized him, she faced forward again, a nonverbal fuck-off. Curtis gaped at her, shocked she'd shun him. He regained his faculties and tapped on the window.

Tania shook her head. "I can't talk to you." Her words were muffled behind the glass.

Curtis pounded on the window and shouted, "They're kicking me out."

She faced him, her eyes glassy. "Go away. I can't deal with this right now."

"I need your help. Please talk to me."

She closed her eyes for a long moment. Then she powered down her window.

Curtis said, "Justin and them are saying that I hurt you."

"It doesn't matter. They can't prosecute anyone. I won't be talking about it. Not ever."

"But they *are* kicking me out."

She sniffled. "I heard, but your arrest doesn't have anything to do with me."

Curtis placed his hands on the window frame and leaned closer.

"Really? You think it's just a big fucking coincidence that they bust me for my roommate's weed the morning after?"

Tania stared through the windshield.

"Look. I'm really sorry about what happened. I know you're not in a good place to help anyone, but I really need your help. We can go to the papers. Tell them everything."

She shook her head again. "I can't talk about that. Not ever."

His eyes widened. He took a step back. "You signed the nondisclosure agreement."

"I had to. My dad thought …" She trailed off.

"They gave you money, didn't they?"

Tania hung her head.

"How much? How much did you get to ruin my life?"

Tania turned to Curtis, her expression hard. She blinked, and tears slipped down her face. "You think your life's ruined? What the fuck am I supposed to do? Take on the university? Justin and his buddies and all their lawyers? Do you know how fucking hard it is to prove rape? They'll say I wanted it. They'll say I was drunk. They'll say I'm a slut. I'll be humiliated in open court over and over again. It'll be five against two. Everyone will say I'm lying because nobody wants to believe that their fucking Heisman hero's a rapist."

Curtis slumped his shoulders. "It doesn't matter what they say. What matters is the truth."

"How's this for some truth? I could've pressed charges, but what would it have gotten me? How can I move forward if I'm rehashing this shit over and over again? Why shouldn't I take the money and run?"

"What about me?"

She exhaled. "I'm sorry. It's done."

Heavy boots approached Curtis from behind. "Can I help you?"

Curtis pivoted to a scowling man in his twenties with a buzz cut, carrying a cardboard box. Curtis figured this guy was Tania's brother. Curtis shook his head and walked away.

He returned to his dorm in a daze, his posture stooped. Curtis turned the dead bolt and entered his dorm room. He crawled into bed, still wearing his running shoes. He gripped his pillow, mashed his face into the cotton pillowcase, and sobbed. Less than forty-eight hours ago, he was on top of the world. Now it was all gone. He cried until he had nothing left, until his pillowcase was soaked. Then he rose from the bed, like a zombie.

For the next two hours, Curtis slowly packed his things into garbage bags, his old suitcase, and his laptop bag. Late in the afternoon, Curtis carried his belongings to the parking lot. With the sun orange and low on the horizon, he shoved his things into the rear hatch of his SUV. He slammed shut the hatch and turned to his dormitory.

Curtis called Ben, not wanting to leave without saying goodbye.

Ben answered, "Sorry, dude. I just got your message. I found Tania's home address."

"I don't need it," Curtis replied.

"Why not?"

"I already talked to her."

"What did she say?"

Curtis sat on his rear bumper. "She can't help me."

"*Shit*. I'm sorry."

"It is what it is." But that was bullshit. It was much more than that.

"What are you gonna do?"

"I'm leaving. They're gonna expel me."

"Right now?" Ben sounded panicked.

"I'm ready to leave. I'm in the parking lot. I was just waiting to say goodbye."

"Don't leave yet. We'll be back in like two minutes."

"All right." Curtis disconnected the call, wondering who Ben was with.

Shortly thereafter, Ben's mother's Volvo SUV entered the parking lot. Ben exited the SUV, said something to his mother, and scanned the parking lot. When he spotted Curtis, he jogged his way.

Ben approached, with a creased brow. "You're really leaving?"

Curtis stood from his back bumper, wiped the dirt off the seat of his jeans, and said, "Yeah."

"This is so fucked up."

Ben's mother drove away.

Curtis glanced at the Volvo SUV, disappearing in the distance. He turned his attention back to Ben. "Why did your mother come back?"

Ben averted his eyes. "A lawyer called her." He cleared his throat. "From the university."

Curtis crossed his arms over his chest. "You signed a nondisclosure agreement, didn't you?"

Ben held out his hands. "I had to. They threatened to expel me for the weed. It's not like I saw anything anyway. I never would've signed if I could've helped you."

Curtis frowned. "You had to have your weed."

Ben grimaced, as if he'd been slapped. "I'm sorry. I didn't think—"

"You're right. You didn't think." Curtis went to the driver's side door and entered his old Nissan.

Ben appeared at the driver's side window. "I'm sorry, Curtis."

Curtis reversed his SUV and drove away.

CHAPTER 68

Pay for It

The group home in Alexandria was a three-hour drive from Central Virginia University. Curtis drove on US 15 North, passing farms and forest, thinking about whether or not to call Mr. H. Curtis only had a few minutes left on his phone and felt the situation demanded an in-person conversation. In addition, there was Mr. H.'s inevitable disappointment, which Curtis dreaded and was eager to avoid for a little while longer.

★★★

It was almost ten when he parked behind the group home's van. He cut the engine and his headlights and sat in his vehicle, his stomach doing somersaults. He imagined Mr. H. admonishing his weakness for allowing Ben to smoke weed in their dorm room.

Mr. H. exited the side door, his face etched with concern. Curtis exited his SUV, his legs rubbery. He met Mr. H. on the driveway.

"What are you doing here?" Mr. H. asked, his head tilted.

Curtis bowed his head. "I messed everything up."

"What are you talking about?"

Curtis raised his gaze and took a deep breath. Then he told Mr. H. everything that had happened in the last forty-eight hours. Mr. H. listened, only interrupting briefly to clarify various facts. As Curtis talked, Mr. H. clenched his fists. His neck vein pulsed.

"Then I came here," Curtis said in conclusion.

"Why didn't you call me?" Mr. H. asked.

"At first, I didn't think I was in trouble. Coach Williams made me think that everything would be okay. Then, when I realized I was in trouble, I didn't wanna disappoint you. I'm nineteen years old. I'm not your responsibility anymore. I thought I could fix it myself." Curtis swallowed, his throat tight. "But I couldn't fix it. I ruined everything."

Mr. H. reached out and hugged Curtis.

"I'm sorry. I …" Curtis dissolved into tears.

Mr. H. squeezed Curtis tightly to his chest. "You have nothing to be sorry for."

"But I messed it all up."

They separated, but Mr. H. still held Curtis at arm's length. "Look at me."

Curtis swallowed hard and peered in Mr. H.'s dark eyes.

"Listen to me. You did the right thing, even though it cost you an awful lot. That says everything about who you are deep inside. I'm proud of you, son."

"What am I supposed do now?" Curtis asked, his voice shaky.

"The same thing you've always done. Your best. I know it's hard to see right now, but I believe you'll end up on top." Mr. H. poked Curtis in the chest. "You have more heart than anyone I know."

When Mr. H. let go, Curtis wiped his face with his T-shirt, embarrassed by his tears. "I don't have anywhere to go." Curtis knew the group-home rules. Once you were eighteen, you were on your own, legally an adult. He also knew Mr. H. had a full house, every bed occupied.

"I'll pull out the sofa bed for you tonight," Mr. H. said. "Then we'll figure out what to do tomorrow."

Mr. H. helped Curtis bring his belongings inside. The group-home boys were already upstairs, likely preparing for bed. Lights out was at 10:00 p.m.

They set Curtis's belongings in the living room, next to the sofa bed.

"Did you have dinner?" Mr. H. asked.

"I haven't eaten all day," Curtis replied.

"Let's start by fixing that."

They went to the kitchen. Mr. H. removed the leftover lasagna from the refrigerator and set it on the counter. "Help yourself. I need to make a phone call."

Curtis set a huge piece of lasagna on a plate, covered it with another plate, and heated it in the microwave. While he waited, he heard Mr. H. in his office, his words muffled by the wall. Curtis walked around the corner, near Mr. H.'s office door. His words were clearer there.

"You should be ashamed of yourself. I can't believe I ever considered you a friend." Mr. H. paused for an instant. "I don't give a shit if it's out of your hands. Find a way to fix it." Mr. H. listened for a few seconds. "Don't give me this bullshit about drugs. First of all, *none* of it was his. Second of all, you and I both know why the cops raided his room. God damn you, Marvin. You took my boy and threw him to the wolves, and you didn't even have the fucking courtesy to call me." Mr. H. listened again. "I don't give a shit that he's nineteen. You know you're wrong. You did what you did to keep your job. Coach Goodman did what he did to avoid the scandal. Can't have your Heisman hopeful arrested for rape. Curtis was the only one who did the right thing. I don't know how you can live with yourself. You're a disgrace." Mr. H. listened again. "Fuck your *sorry*. We're done, Marvin. You'll all pay for this. It may not be anytime soon, but, one of these days, you'll all pay for what you've done."

PART IV

The Real World

Everything starts with yourself, with you making up your mind about what you're going to do with your life. I tell kids that it's a cruel world and that the world will bend them either left or right and it's up to them to decide which way to bend.

—Tony Dorsett

CHAPTER 69

The New Normal

Curtis smacked his alarm clock, silencing the buzzing. The time read 4:30 a.m. He rose from the single mattress in the corner of his one-bedroom apartment. He trudged to the bathroom, peed, washed his hands, and brushed his teeth. He returned to his bedroom, grabbed his running gear from the crates along the wall, and dressed.

He drank a quarter glass of water before he left his apartment. It was too early to be hungry. He shouldered his backpack that held his cleats and descended the stairs of the apartment building. The stairwell smelled like urine. He exited the building into the night. The sidewalk and the parking lot were bathed in circular patterns of fluorescent light. The parking lot was filled with old economy cars and rusty pickup trucks.

Curtis glanced back at the three-story apartment building. He still wasn't sure if it was the exact same one. He often looked at his apartment building from different angles and times of day, trying to figure out if he was living in the same apartment building where he'd lived with his mother. He could ask Mr. H. He probably had the address in his files. But Curtis didn't want to go back. Nothing but pain was back there. He needed to move forward.

So he jogged out of the apartment complex. Slow at first. Then, once he was loose, he picked up the pace until he reached the park. Four Mile Run Park was a sprawling respite from the city that included baseball fields, athletic fields, basketball courts, biking and jogging trails, a playground, and a conservatory center.

Curtis stretched, then ran long sprints along the wetland trail, guided by the moonlight. Technically, the park was closed from dusk to dawn, but his early morning workouts had yet to be interrupted. He walked in between sprints, his legs heavy with lactic acid. In the dark loneliness of the early morning, he often thought about what had happened to him.

He was officially expelled. Central Virginia University didn't bill him for the spring semester like Coach Goodman had said they would. They also didn't refund his money for the fall semester, and he was responsible for paying back the loans. Mr. H. helped him get his apartment and a job to keep him afloat, until he got into another college, which would probably be in the spring semester of 2017. He had already applied for financial aid and for acceptance to Old Dominion University, a division 1-AA football program. Mr. H. had helped him get a preferred walk-on invitation in the spring.

After doing his sprint workout, he went to the grass fields and changed into his cleats. He worked on his defensive back drills, just as Mr. H. had taught him and then Coach Williams. Marvin Williams had thrown him to the wolves, as Mr. H. had said, but Coach Williams knew football, and Curtis was a much better football player because of his tutelage. Curtis backpedaled until his thighs burned. He worked on transitions—backpedaling, then turning and sprinting—concentrating on tracking the imaginary football without losing speed.

One of the things he'd learned at CVU was that defensive backs often slowed when tracking the football, which would lead to getting beat. Maintaining a full sprint while looking back over his shoulder was difficult, so Curtis practiced it often, until it was second nature.

As the sun rose in the east, Curtis jogged back to his apartment building, using the short jog as his cooldown.

★★★

After breakfast, Curtis drove to the Annandale campus of Northern Virginia Community College. He didn't park in the student section, instead parking at the maintenance building.

He entered the one-story brick building with an attached garage. Inside, he waved to his boss, who pecked on his computer. Curtis clocked in and checked the board for the day's tasks. With the recent rain, the grass was growing rapidly that October.

Curtis grabbed a pair of earmuffs and safety glasses and stepped into the garage. Mowers, line trimmers, edgers, blowers, wheelbarrows, snowplows, spreaders, and various hand tools were arranged in the garage. He gassed the zero-turn riding mower and checked the oil. He put on his glasses and ear protection, climbed aboard the machine, and turned the key.

The engine roared to life, and Curtis pressed the levers forward, exiting the garage. He spent the morning mowing the lower one-third of the campus, which sat on seventy-eight acres. Thankfully, only twenty acres were grass, so he was tasked with mowing about seven acres that morning. He started close to the buildings. They tried not to mow close to the buildings once classes started for the day, as the engine noise could be heard through the windows.

After lunch, he trimmed the edges and around the obstacles that he couldn't reach with the mower. After an hour or so, the bottom half of his khaki pants were stained green.

He trimmed near a walkway as the 2:00 p.m. classes were dismissed. He stepped back from the students, letting his trimmer idle, as he didn't want to accidentally kick rocks, grass, or debris in their direction. Nobody looked at Curtis. He couldn't help but think about his time at CVU. He couldn't help but think he was like them or used to be like them. Only a month ago he'd been expelled, but it felt like a lifetime ago.

CHAPTER 70

Don't Look at Anyone

After work, Curtis stopped by Gold's Gym. He forgot his workout gear, so he wore his maintenance uniform. It was an upper body day, so he could lift comfortably in his khaki pants, boots, and polo shirt. Curtis loaded another forty-five-pound plate. Then he secured the weights with collars. Mostly men occupied the nearby bench press stations. A rack of dumbbells spanned the mirrored wall in front of the benches. A mix of men and women stood before the mirror, doing dumbbell curls, lunges, shoulder presses, and front raises.

Curtis lay on the bench and lined up his hands on the bar, making sure they were even. In the background, pop music played on the speakers, punctuated by weights clanging together. Several men watched Curtis, interested to watch him bench press 225 pounds without a spotter. Curtis pressed the bar off the rack and pumped out ten repetitions without struggling. He reset the bar on the rack.

A few gymgoers gaped at him.

Curtis grabbed his notebook from the floor and added the weight and repetitions he had just completed. He kept detailed notes on his lifting workout, which helped him to know when to increase weights and by how much. Curtis set his notebook back on the floor, stood, and racked twenty-five-pound plates on each side, upping the weight to 275 pounds. He stretched out his upper body, checking himself in the mirror.

A young woman did lunges in place, while holding ten-pound

dumbbells. She wore spandex shorts and a black sports bra, her toned midriff exposed. Her dirty-blond hair was tied into a ponytail. Curtis stared for a long beat, distracted by her beauty. When she finished her set, she scowled at Curtis in the mirror. Curtis dropped his gaze to the rubber floor. He silently chided himself for staring.

It was dangerous for an ugly man to show any interest in an attractive woman. Curtis sat on the bench, wondering how the woman felt to be ogled by someone as ugly as him. *Scared probably.* He still had a face full of freckles, with beady eyes, a wide nose, and crooked teeth, but he wasn't a skinny little kid anymore. He was 205 pounds of thick ropy muscle. People didn't tease him much anymore, at least not to his face. They avoided him like the plague.

Curtis lay on his back and lined up his hands on the bar. More gymgoers gawked at the freak with grass-stained pants and snaggleteeth. Curtis pressed the bar off the rack. He sucked in a breath, as he lowered 275 pounds to his chest. He exhaled as he pressed the weight upward. After six repetitions, the last one requiring all his might, he racked the bar again.

The guy racking weights on the bench beside him lifted his chin and said, "Nice job, man."

"Thanks," Curtis replied.

"If you need a spot, let me know."

Curtis nodded. "I'll need a spot on the next one, if you don't mind."

"No problem. Just let me know when you're ready."

Curtis removed the twenty-five-pound plates, and replaced them with forty-five-pound plates. The bar now weighed 315 pounds. He glanced in the mirror, noticing that the beautiful blonde was gone.

After another short rest, he summoned his spotter and completed three difficult repetitions, the bar bending at the ends from the weight. His spotter was a good one, ready to help but never touching the bar, as long as the bar was moving in the right direction. He thanked his spotter, who then left the free-weight area. Curtis removed some plates and added some smaller ones, lowering the weight to 255 pounds.

A Gold's Gym employee, who resembled a young Sylvester Stallone, entered the free-weight area. Curtis loved the old Rocky movies. He identified with Rocky's perpetual underdog status. The young Sly scanned the room, while vigorously chewing gum. He made a beeline to Curtis. The guy wore a name tag that read Salvatore, Manager.

"We've had a complaint that you were harassin' a young lady," Salvatore said, his hands on his hips, still smacking his gum.

"I didn't harass anybody," Curtis replied.

The nearby gymgoers watched the drama.

"That's not what the young lady said to me," Salvatore said.

Curtis exhaled, more annoyed than angry. "What did she say I did?"

"She said you were starin' at her like a predator and makin' her extremely uncomfortable."

"This is bullshit."

"No. This is serious."

Curtis shook his head. "No, it's not."

"We take all complaints seriously, *sir*."

"You shouldn't. I suspect there's nothing you can do about staring, so I would appreciate it if you left me alone, so I can finish my workout."

Salvatore was dumbstruck.

Curtis stretched his arms, ignoring the manager.

Salvatore looked Curtis up and down. "You're not wearin' the proper gym attire. You're gettin' grass everywhere."

"I forgot my workout gear," Curtis replied, not making eye contact with Salvatore.

"You can't be here without the proper attire. You need to leave."

Without a word, Curtis snatched his notebook and water bottle from the floor and left the gym. On the way out, he saw the fit blond through Salvatore's office window.

Curtis drove to his apartment building, the short trip taking twice as long in rush-hour traffic. He parked in the lot. The afternoon sun was still high in the sky. Curtis went to his apartment, changed into his workout gear, grabbed a protein bar, and refilled his water bottle.

Curtis left his apartment and drove back to the gym, while munching on his protein bar. When he entered the gym, Curtis showed his membership card to the woman at the front desk. He went to the free-weight area, intent on finishing his workout.

Along the way, he passed Salvatore and the fit blonde, flirting near the treadmills. When the pair spotted him, Salvatore mean-mugged Curtis while the blonde scrunched her face, as if she'd eaten something bitter. As Curtis walked into the free-weight section, he wondered how their expressions of anger and disgust were any different from what he'd done. Of course, he knew why it was different. Attention from attractive people was mostly welcomed, but attention from ugly people was mostly unwanted.

By the time Curtis returned home from the gym the second time, he was exhausted. With the lot mostly full, he parked in the back corner, next to a Lexus with shiny chrome wheels. Post lamps dimly lit the parking lot, but the back corner was especially dark. It wasn't uncommon for drug dealers to break the bulbs so they could conduct their business under the cover of darkness.

Curtis exited his SUV. A muscular man, wearing a hoodie, exchanged something—likely drugs—with a gaunt woman. Curtis thought about his mother, as the woman staggered away, like a zombie.

"What the fuck you lookin' at?" said the drug dealer.

"Nothing. Sorry." Curtis walked toward his apartment.

"Bitch-ass nigga," the drug dealer said to Curtis's back.

Along the way to his apartment building, Curtis stopped by the cluster of mailboxes, using his key to open his tiny box. He retrieved a single letter from his mailbox. It was a letter from Old Dominion University. He nearly opened the letter right there, but the drug dealer from the parking lot walked toward the apartment building. Hoping to avoid another confrontation, Curtis went inside. The drug dealer used a bottom-floor apartment in the building as a stash house.

Curtis climbed the steps to his apartment, his feet aching from the long day, his upper body swollen from lifting. The next-door neighbor opened her apartment door as he fished his keys from his pocket. A middle-aged man exited the apartment with his shirttail untucked.

The neighbor smooched her hand and blew an imaginary kiss toward the man. "See you soon, baby."

The man saw Curtis, dipped his head in embarrassment, and hurried down the stairs.

The curvaceous neighbor stepped into the hall, wearing a silk robe, showing her deep cleavage. She cocked her head at Curtis, her hair extensions cascading over her shoulders. "You like what you see, sugar?"

Curtis gaped at her. "I, uh …"

She sauntered closer and held out her hand and her long red fingernails. "I'm Destiny."

"Curtis," he said, inhaling her flowery perfume, as he shook her hand.

She squeezed his biceps. "These are nice. You could wrap those big arms around me, if you want." She pursed her full lips. "It'll be worth every last dollar."

"Uh, … no, thank you." Curtis tried to insert his key into his dead bolt, but he dropped his keys on the floor.

Destiny stood, smirking, her hand on her curvy hip.

Curtis grabbed his key, unlocked the dead bolt, and pushed into his apartment.

"It was nice to meet you, sugar," Destiny called out, as Curtis shut the door behind him.

I really need to stop looking at people.

CHAPTER 71

A Face Only a Mother Could Love

Curtis dropped his keys and his wallet on the kitchen table. It had been an old card table from the group home. He inspected the thin letter from Old Dominion University, knowing thin letters were usually bad. His heart pounded in his chest as he opened the envelope.

Old Dominion University
Office of Financial Aid
5115 Hampton Blvd
Norfolk, VA 23529

Mr. Curtis Duffy
1200 Washington Avenue
Apartment 304
Alexandria, VA 22305

Dear Mr. Duffy,

Unfortunately, Federal Student Aid has denied your request for financial aid. Your FAFSA form contained the following question:

Have you been convicted for the possession or sale of illegal drugs for an offense that occurred while you were receiving federal student aid (such as grants, work-study, or loans)?

You answered yes to this question, which disqualifies you from federal financial aid.

Go to the following link to find out more: https:// studentaid.gov/understand-aid/eligibility/ requirements/criminal-convictions

Curtis slapped the letter on the tabletop. "*Shit.*"

He thought out what this meant. *It means I need more money to go to school. A lot more. No way I'll have enough for the spring semester without financial aid.* Curtis trudged to his bedroom, stripped, tossed his dirty clothes in the hamper, and padded to the bathroom.

Curtis was invited to dinner at the group home on Saturday. He would talk to Mr. H. about it then. They would figure out a plan, just like they always did. In the meantime, no point in getting depressed about it. He tried to think about something else, something more pleasant. His mind drifted to Destiny's curves. He still felt her touch on his arm. He still smelled her flowery perfume. He'd never had sex before. He'd never had much experience at all with women. He'd only kissed a woman once. Technically, Amanda wasn't a woman at the time. They were both teenagers.

Curtis turned on the shower. As he waited for the hot water, he thought of paying Destiny for sex. His mind and body buzzed with the real possibility. He had resigned himself to a life of celibacy. A face only a mother could love. Except his mother didn't even love him. His mind flashed back to his childhood. He remembered his mother taking him to McDonald's. Some teenagers sat near them.

One of them had said, *That boy's so ugly, when his mama breastfed him, she closed her eyes and thought about other babies.*

Curtis tried to think about something else. His mind served up another memory. The last thing his mother had said to him. *My life would've been so much better if I never had you.* Curtis climbed into the shower and thought, *I wish you never would've had me either.*

Dirt, grime, grass, sweat, and tears washed down the drain.

CHAPTER 72

Dinner at the Group Home

Curtis stepped into the kitchen of the group home, carrying a cake he'd picked up from the grocery store. The smell of garlic, oregano, and basil hung in the air. Mr. H. stood at the stovetop, stirring the meat sauce. Muffled shouts and high-pitched voices came from the boys playing in the backyard.

Mr. H. glanced at Curtis over his shoulder and smiled. "Just in time."

Curtis set the cake on the counter, not returning the smile.

Mr. H. turned the burner down to simmer and faced Curtis. He eyed the cake. "You didn't have to bring anything."

"I thought the boys might like some dessert."

"They'll like it all right. It's not good for them, but they'll like it." Mr. H. studied Curtis's face for a moment. "What's wrong?"

"I got some bad news. We can talk about it after dinner. I don't wanna ruin …" Curtis trailed off.

Mr. H. tilted his head. "No sense in waiting."

Curtis reached into his back pocket and handed Mr. H. the letter from Old Dominion University. Mr. H. read the letter for a minute, then handed it back to Curtis.

Mr. H. rubbed the back of his neck. He let out a heavy breath. "It's a setback, but it's not insurmountable. Have you checked that link yet?"

Curtis nodded. "If I complete an approved drug program, I can reapply for aid, but it's gonna take some time to save for the program and to go through it. I don't know if I can get it done before the spring semester."

"It's not the end of the world if you have to wait until next fall."

"I know, but ..."

Mr. H. raised his eyebrows. "But what?"

Curtis shrugged. "I don't know. I was thinking that maybe college isn't realistic for me. Maybe it's not meant for me."

Mr. H. frowned. The oven timer buzzed. Mr. H. stopped the timer, turned off the oven, and faced Curtis again. "College is jam-packed with lazy, entitled, and dumb kids." Mr. H. poked Curtis in the center of his chest. "But you're smart, hardworking, and you've had to scrape for everything you've gotten in this life. College is not only realistic but you're perfectly suited to be successful in higher education, provided that's what you really want. You have all the skills to do *anything* you want in this life. You just have to apply those skills consistently for a long period of time. People greatly *overestimate* what they can do in a year but greatly *underestimate* what they can do in a decade."

CHAPTER 73

Bread

On the drive home, Curtis listened to sports radio.

"Central Virginia destroyed Duke today, 56–7," the radio host said. "They maintained their perfect record and number two ranking, behind Alabama. Looking at their schedule, it's hard to see them losing in the regular season. I think they're ultimately the runner-up for the national championship, behind Alabama. But Justin Love is the front-runner for the Heisman. This young man is special. I haven't seen a quarterback talent as impressive as Justin Love, since John Elway at Stanford. Love's stat line today was unreal. He completed thirty of thirty-six attempts for an 83 percent completion percentage. Four hundred and seventy-nine passing yards with six touchdown passes and no interceptions. He added another thirty-eight yards on the ground. Like I said, this young man is special. He's a future number one overall NFL draft choice."

Curtis turned off his radio and gripped the steering wheel, his knuckles white. The traffic was light that night, as he navigated the Alexandria city streets. He thought about what Mr. H. had said about underestimating what he could accomplish in a decade. Curtis couldn't imagine ten years. It seemed like forever into the future.

A Lexus with tinted windows near his apartment complex cut him off. Curtis braked to stop from rearending the Lexus. Then the Lexus brake-checked him several times, as if angry that Curtis had been too close. Thumping bass came from the gold luxury sedan. The Lexus turned into Curtis's apartment complex. As it turned, Curtis caught a glimpse of the car's side and recognized the vehicle. Curtis wasn't certain, but he thought the car belonged to the drug dealer who operated a stash house in his apartment building.

The parking lot was mostly full, causing Curtis to park closer to the Lexus than he desired. Two men exited the Lexus, one of them being the drug dealer he'd seen two days ago. Curtis waited in his SUV, hoping the two men would leave, but they loitered by the car, smoking blunts, staring in Curtis's direction.

Curtis worried that he'd offended the guy by nearly rearending him. He'd seen simple misunderstandings result in severe beatdowns. Curtis exited his vehicle, knowing if they thought he was fearful, it might further embolden them. He walked toward his apartment building, trying to appear confident—his head up, his strides purposeful. Curtis didn't look directly at the men, and he gave them a polite berth that was close enough to show he wasn't fearful.

As Curtis passed the men, the drug dealer said, "Hey, you."

Curtis stopped and faced them.

The drug dealer motioned with his finger. "C'mere."

Curtis approached the men. The drug dealer wore a white tank top, jeans, and Timberland boots, the laces undone. He was built like a linebacker. His buddy was taller and thinner but also muscular. Curtis noticed a bulge at the man's hip, his handgun barely covered by his tank top.

"You almost hit my car." The drug dealer inhaled on the blunt.

"I'm sorry. I didn't see you," Curtis replied.

The drug dealer exhaled marijuana smoke into Curtis's face. He narrowed his eyes. "God *damn.* You're an ugly ass motherfucker."

Curtis looked through the drug dealer, trying not to show emotion.

The drug dealer lifted his chin to his buddy. "What you think, Dre?"

"I don't even know what this nigga is," Dre replied. "Looks like he's from space or some shit."

The men cackled.

"I'm sorry about your car," Curtis reiterated. Then he continued toward the apartment building.

The drug dealer mimicked Curtis, using a stuffy white man's voice. *"I'm sorry about your car."*

The men cackled again.

Curtis climbed the steps to his third-floor apartment. Soft R&B music came from Destiny's apartment. Curtis thought about knocking on her door and asking her about an appointment. *Is that what they call them?* He had been paid yesterday, so he had some cash on hand. Curtis stepped to her door, held his fist to knock, but stopped himself. *Whatever she's offering, it's not real.*

Destiny opened her door, wearing shorts and a deep V-neck T-shirt. "I thought I heard someone out here. What you need, sugar?"

"I, uh, … I was, uh, just wondering if you had any bread?"

She arched her eyebrows. "Bread? You need some bread?"

"If you don't have any, it's okay," Curtis replied.

"I got you, sugar." She tugged on Curtis's hand. "Come in."

Curtis stepped into her apartment and shut the door behind him. Her living room was framed by a leopard-print sectional couch, facing a wall-mounted plasma TV. Babyface played on the stereo that stood near the television. She disappeared into the kitchen.

Destiny returned with a half loaf of white bread. She handed him the bread. "This okay?"

Curtis forced a smile. "It's perfect. Thank you, Destiny. I'll buy you a loaf next time I'm at the store."

She smirked at him. "You sure you just want bread?" She leaned forward, giving Curtis a view down her shirt.

"Thanks for the bread." Curtis hurried from her apartment.

Destiny giggled in his wake.

CHAPTER 74

The National Championship

Three months later, Curtis walked behind a snow blower, clearing a sidewalk at the Annandale campus of the Northern Virginia Community College. The machine blew the snow away from the building. Curtis wore a one-piece snowsuit, gloves, and a ski mask that covered his face. The moon reflected off the snow, illuminating the campus.

After snow blowing all the walkways, he cleared the various steps around campus with a snow shovel. The snow was wet and heavy, giving his back a workout. It was quiet and lonely work, only the sound of his breath and the scraping of his snow shovel on the concrete. While he worked, he thought about his former teammates. On that night, January 9, 2017, his former teammates played the Alabama Crimson Tide at Mercedes-Benz Stadium in Atlanta, Georgia.

Curtis couldn't help but think about where he'd be if he'd never gone to that party. But he did go to that party. He did help Tania. Yet he was the only one who was punished. Tania got paid. Kavon, Andre, Thomas, and Preston were playing for the national championship, along with Justin Love. This past December, Justin Love had won the Heisman Trophy, after an undefeated regular season in which he threw sixty touchdown passes, which was a new NCAA record, two more than Colt Brennan threw at the University of Hawaii in 2006.

Everyone got what they wanted, but Curtis still wasn't back in school. He had missed the spring semester. He might've been able to make the spring semester, but he would've been strapped, especially if he didn't earn a scholarship during the spring football tryouts at Old Dominion, which was unlikely. He elected to play it safe, save his money, and wait until the fall. His drug program was scheduled in two weeks. The whole thing was infuriating and ironic because he had never done drugs in his life. But that's what was required to restore his financial aid privileges, along with regular drug tests to ensure he stayed on the straight and narrow. Of course, this was all on his dime.

Once the sidewalks and stairs were clear, he finished the job by treating the concrete with ice melt.

He clocked out at 11:56 p.m. He was the last maintenance employee to leave. There were only three of them, including his boss. Now that he was off the clock, he checked his phone, wondering about the game. He tapped his way to the game news, silently rooting for Alabama.

The headline read "Justin Love and Central Virginia Shock Alabama, 36–35."

CHAPTER 75

American Star

Curtis locked the maintenance garage and office, then drove home. The midnight drive was quiet, except for the dump trucks spreading salt, and scraping the asphalt with their plows.

He turned into his apartment complex. A pickup plowed snow, the blade tilted toward the curb. Given that the snow came fast and heavy in the late afternoon, and the parking lots were mostly full, there were limited places to pile the snow. The result was haphazard piles of snow, sometimes blocking vehicles. The morning would be a clusterfuck, with angry residents shoveling out their cars before going to work.

A small snow pile blocked one of the few remaining parking spaces near Curtis's apartment building. Curtis used his four-wheel drive to power through and over the pile, before pulling the parking brake and cutting his engine and headlights.

A light sleet fell from the sky, as Curtis trudged to his building. He hoped the ice melt he had applied at the college would be enough to prevent any ice from forming on the sidewalks. Otherwise, he'd receive an early morning call to return to work.

Curtis flashed his key card on the sensor, unlocking the front door of his apartment building. He climbed the stairs to the third floor, his shoulders hunched and his back sore from the snow shoveling and the deadlifts he'd done earlier that day. Pop music spilled into the hallway from Destiny's apartment. Her television and stereo were placed along the adjoining wall between her living room and Curtis's bedroom. He'd lost sleep the night before because of the noise. He was too tired to have his sleep interrupted again, so he knocked on her door.

The music ceased. Destiny answered the door, wearing a pink sweatsuit and a big grin. "Hey, Curtis."

"Your music's a little loud," Curtis said. "Would you mind turning it down?"

She placed one hand on her ample hip. "I ain't got music on."

"I just heard it."

"Oh, that? That's just *American Star*. Don't you just love the Star?"

"I've never seen it."

Destiny drew her manicured eyebrows together. "*Never*?"

Curtis shook his head.

She grabbed him by the wrist and pulled him into her apartment. "You gotta watch some with me."

"It's late," Curtis said, as she shut the door behind him.

"Just a few minutes."

"I should take off my boots. I have salt all over them." Curtis untied his boots and left them by the front door. Destiny's apartment felt cozier than Curtis's, with her purple shag carpet, cushy furniture, faux palm trees, and framed R&B concert posters on the walls.

As they walked into her living room, she glanced at his snowsuit and said, "You look like you're plannin' to go out in the snow."

"I just came back from work. I was shoveling the walks."

She plopped on the sectional couch. "Okay. I see you workin' hard." She gestured to the couch. "Take off your hat, stay awhile."

His hat was his ski mask that sat atop his head. Curtis removed it and set it on the glass coffee table. He fingered the zipper of his snowsuit. "Mind if I take this off?"

She cocked her head. "Depends on whatcha got under there?"

Curtis smirked. "Just sweatpants and a T-shirt."

"That's no fun."

He unzipped his snowsuit and stepped out of it. He sat near the corner of the sectional, six feet away from Destiny.

She eyed the young man paused on the plasma television. "You know it's a singin' show, right?"

"They pick the best singers, don't they?"

"That's right. Some of them are so terrible. I feel bad for them." She pointed the remote at the television and restarted the show.

The young man continued his rendition of Lionel Richie's "Hello."

At the end Destiny clapped and said, "He was *so* good. Don't you think?"

Curtis nodded. "I wish I could sing like that."

The *American Star* judges agreed, passing the young man to the next round of the contest.

Curtis and Destiny watched several more singers. A housewife from Oklahoma sang "Firework" by Katy Perry, who was surprisingly good. A rapping college student was astonishingly awful. And then came a teacher from Florida, who sang "Wrecking Ball" by Miley Cyrus. She was decent but not quite good enough to make the cut. Curtis gaped at the fourth singer—Taylor Wilde—a beautiful waitress from North Carolina. She appeared nervous, as she told the judges she'd never sung in public. When she told them she was singing "Lovin' You" by Minnie Riperton, the judges gawked at her.

One of them said, "That's a very difficult song for your first live performance."

Taylor nodded.

The judge held out his hands, as if to say, *It's your funeral.* "Okay. Take it away."

The acoustic guitar played. Taylor approached the microphone, placing her hands around the base. She closed her eyes, swaying to the music. She sang like the most beautiful bird, her voice rising and falling effortlessly, hitting the high notes, fluttering about, going even higher. All without ever cracking or singing off-key. When she finished, half the judges were in tears, and so was Curtis.

"Oh, my God. That was so beautiful." Destiny glanced at Curtis.

"You okay over there?"

Curtis stood from his seat and discreetly wiped his glassy eyes. "I should go."

"Don't go." Destiny paused the program and stood from the couch too. She stepped closer to Curtis, her hips swishing back and forth. She touched the base of his neck with two fingers. She slowly ran her hand down his body, stopping at his waist and venturing a little farther, just before his penis. Her touch sent a jolt of electricity through his body. She placed her hands on his hips, gazed up at him, and said, "Why don't you stay? Please?"

Curtis swallowed hard. "I should go to bed."

"You can sleep here."

His heart pounded in his chest. "I don't have a lot of money."

"Can you afford a hundred dollars?"

Curtis nodded. He stepped around the coffee table and opened the zipper pocket of his snowsuit.

"What are you doin', sugar?"

Curtis grabbed his wallet and faced Destiny. "Getting your money."

Destiny padded to him. "Don't worry about that right now. I trust you."

Curtis returned his wallet to his snowsuit pocket.

"Focus on me," Destiny said, placing her hands on his hips again.

Curtis peered down at her.

"Pretend I'm your girlfriend, and I'll pretend you're my boyfriend. Okay?"

Curtis nodded again.

She took his hand. "You must be so tired after working all night."

"A little."

"Come on, baby." She led him to the bathroom and turned on the shower. "Let's get you cleaned up." She helped him out of his T-shirt and sweatpants.

Curtis removed his socks and stood before Destiny in his boxer briefs.

She smiled and ran her hands over his upper body, as if mapping the peaks and valleys of his muscular physique. "I love your body, baby." She bit the bottom corner of her lip. "So sexy."

Curtis blushed. "Thanks."

Steam came from the shower. Destiny removed her sweatshirt and T-shirt at the same time, exposing her full breasts. His eyes bulged. She giggled, grabbed his hands, and placed them on her chest. "How does that feel?"

Curtis squeezed her breasts, not hard. "Soft."

She stepped back, and Curtis let go. Destiny slid her sweatpants past her curvy hips and down her legs, revealing pink cotton underwear. "Why don't you take these off for me?"

Curtis stepped closer. With trembling hands, he slid her underwear down her thighs, bending as he went, revealing a landing strip of dark pubic hair now at his eye level. Curtis stood upright. She stepped out of the little pile at her feet, holding on to Curtis's forearm so she didn't trip. Destiny grabbed a fresh washcloth from under the sink, bending over and giving Curtis a view of her round butt and thick labia.

Destiny faced Curtis again, glancing at his boxer briefs. "I think you're forgetting something."

Curtis fingered the waistband of his boxer briefs, feeling self-conscious.

She touched the outline of his erection. "No need to be shy, baby. I can tell you have a nice one."

Curtis was beet red, as he removed his boxer briefs.

She simpered at his erection, pointing at the ceiling. She pulled back the shower curtain. "You first."

The warm water peppered Curtis's back. Destiny faced him, lathering the washcloth and rubbing soap over his body, paying particular attention to his penis. After washing him, Destiny dried them both, and led Curtis to her bedroom. A king-size bed dominated the room, topped with a leopard-print comforter. She turned on the infuser, which sat on the bedside table. Lavender filled the air.

She pulled back the comforter and faced Curtis. "What do you like?"

"I, uh, ... I don't really know," Curtis replied.

She narrowed her eyes. "Have you ever done this before?"

Curtis looked away.

She stepped closer and grabbed his hand. "Don't you worry, baby. Just relax." She led him to the bed. "Lay down. On your back."

Curtis climbed into bed. He lay on his back, his head on a pillow.

Destiny climbed into bed with him. She cuddled next to him, her naked body against his. She stroked his penis, slow and gentle. "Does that feel okay?"

Curtis nodded.

"Do you want me?" she whispered into his ear.

He nodded again.

Destiny opened the bedside table drawer and retrieved a condom. She opened the square package and rolled the rubber disk onto his erection. She mounted him, grabbed his penis, and rubbed her labia and clitoris against the head of his erection. Then she sat back and moaned, taking his length inside her. Curtis groaned in ecstasy, desperately trying to avoid his orgasm. Destiny placed her hands on his chest and rode up and down and back and forth at the same time, squeezing and releasing her vagina while she did so. Curtis gripped her hips, leering at her breasts swinging before him, his entire body buzzing with pleasure.

Less than a minute later, he exploded in ecstasy. Destiny rode harder, enhancing his orgasm until it was over, and she dismounted. She snuggled next to him. His chest rose and fell with his elevated breathing.

She pecked him on the cheek. "How was that, sugar?"

"Thank you," Curtis replied.

CHAPTER 76

Just a Trick

The next morning, Curtis worked for a few hours at the community college, clearing sidewalks that had been covered by snowdrifts. Then he treated himself to lunch at McDonald's. He ordered his favorite—a quarter-pounder with cheese and fries.

After lunch, he went to the gym. He was there for several hours, lifting weights and doing his cardio. Given that the park was still buried in snow, he couldn't do his cardio there, so he settled for the gym treadmill.

Curtis floated through his day, thinking about Destiny and what they'd done together. He remembered their shower. Her naked body. He remembered her on top of him, grinding. She had shown him the girlfriend experience. It had felt so real that he almost believed the fantasy. As he drove home from the gym, he still thought about her. But the fantasy was fading, usurped by reality. *She's good at what she does. You were just a trick. You'll never do that again without paying. Nobody will ever love you like that for real.*

He drove by the corner store near his apartment complex, and he remembered he was out of milk, so he parked along the street and walked the short distance to the store. Curtis entered the corner store, and the bell jingled. The Asian man at the counter glanced at him. Curtis lifted his chin in recognition. He went to the fridge, grabbed a gallon of whole milk, then browsed the aisles. He grabbed a box of Fruit Rings—a cheaper generic version of Fruit Loops—and two cans of chicken soup. The bell jingled. The drug dealer entered the store, wearing a puffy black coat. Curtis avoided eye contact and took his groceries to the counter. The clerk scanned his items, while watching the drug dealer over Curtis's shoulder.

"Nine twenty-one," the clerk said.

Curtis handed the man a ten-dollar bill. The clerk opened the cash register, stuffed the ten inside, and handed Curtis his change.

"Thanks," Curtis replied, as he took his grocery bag.

The drug dealer strutted past the register—holding an energy drink and a bag of pork rinds—and left the store.

"I think he just stole that stuff," Curtis said.

The clerk frowned. "He does it all the time."

"Did you call the police?"

"They do nothing. Said it's too small. I told him to stop, but he said he kill my whole family."

Curtis winced. "I'm sorry."

"Not your fault."

Curtis left the store, carrying his groceries.

The drug dealer stood on the sidewalk, near his Lexus, eyeballing Curtis. "Hey, you."

Curtis stopped and faced the man.

The drug dealer swaggered toward Curtis, a smirk on his face. "I been tryin' to figure out what the fuck you are. I finally figured it out."

Curtis gripped his groceries, staring through the drug dealer.

"You wanna know what you are?"

Curtis still stared, expressionless.

"You're white as fuck, with red-ass hair, but you got that wide nose and them big-ass lips, and kinky hair." He paused for effect. "You're a ginger nigger." The drug dealer cackled.

Curtis walked away.

The drug dealer called out to Curtis's back. "I ain't done talkin' to you."

But Curtis didn't turn back.

CHAPTER 77

What Have I Done?

A few days later, Curtis spotted Destiny walking home from the corner store, carrying two bags of groceries. He parked along the curb and tapped his horn. Destiny turned, recognized Curtis, and smiled.

Curtis powered down his front passenger window, leaned toward the open window, and asked, "You need a ride?"

Destiny climbed into the front passenger seat. "Thank, God. I'm freezin' my ass off."

"That wind is brutal."

"I know. I should've driven, but I was tryin' to get some exercise."

Curtis drove the short distance from the corner store to their apartment building.

"I haven't seen you in a few days," Destiny said. "I thought you might come back for more."

Curtis parked in the lot. "I can't afford you."

"It's a shame. We're so good together. Don't you think?"

Curtis turned in his seat to face her. "It was the best night of my life, but I think it's better if we're just friends."

Destiny leaned over and kissed Curtis on the cheek. "I bet you'll never forget me."

"I bet you're right."

They exited Curtis's SUV.

He eyed her grocery bags. "You want me to carry those?"

She handed him the bags. "Thank you."

"What are friends for?" Curtis smiled, keeping his mouth shut.

She smiled too. "I like this arrangement."

Destiny scanned her key card and opened the door to their apartment building. The drug dealer was in the hall, pacing and talking on his cell phone. Curtis stepped inside and headed for the stairs, hoping not to be noticed.

The drug dealer spotted Curtis and pocketed his phone. "Ginger nigger."

"What did you call him?" Destiny asked.

"You heard me."

Destiny wagged her finger in his face. "We ain't doin' that, *Leon*. His name's Curtis."

"You better get that fuckin' finger outta my face."

"It doesn't matter," Curtis said, standing six feet away from the argument, but neither of them acknowledged Curtis's statement.

Destiny retracted her hand. "Why you always gotta be like that?"

"Like what?"

Another resident entered the building—an older gentleman.

"Like all ghetto and shit. Always *tryna* be hard," Destiny said.

Leon crowded her, his chest puffed out. "You think I'm *tryin'* to be hard?"

The older man walked past Curtis.

"All you do is talk shit, like a little *bitch*," Destiny said.

Leon threw an overhand right, connecting with Destiny's jaw, and sending her down for the count.

Curtis dropped her grocery bags and attacked Leon, throwing a deadly combination. Left jab, right cross, and left hook, just like Mr. Vasquez had taught him. They all landed in quick succession. Leon dropped to one knee, woozy, blood spilling from his nose. With Leon unprotected, Curtis wound up and threw a haymaker, sending him to the floor. But Curtis wasn't finished. He mounted Leon and continued hammering him until his face was a mangled mass of blood and tissue.

By now Destiny stirred and regained her faculties. She shouted, "Curtis. Stop it!" Her voice broke the spell.

Curtis stood from Leon's motionless body. He stared at his bloody hands, like they weren't his own.

The old man watched them from the second floor. He was on the phone. "Hurry. I think he killed him."

Curtis looked at Leon, then his bloody hands again. "What have I done?"

CHAPTER 78

Closing Arguments

Six months later, Curtis sat behind the defense table, next to his attorney.

District Attorney Teresa Palmer paced in front of the jury. "This case is about the evidence. Pure and simple. And the evidence is quite clear. You heard eyewitness testimony from Arnold Hopkins, who watched the entire incident. Mr. Hopkins said that the defendant continued to punch Leon Tolliver *after* Leon had been knocked unconscious. This testimony was corroborated by the defendant's friend, Destiny Mays."

Curtis glanced over his shoulder at the mostly empty courtroom. Nobody gave a shit about Leon, except for the scowling middle-aged woman who was likely Leon's mother. Nobody gave a shit about Curtis either, except for Mr. H., who sat right behind the defense table. Mr. H. nodded to Curtis, offering encouragement with his intense stare. Curtis nodded back and faced forward. Mr. H. had been the one to pay for Curtis's attorney. Curtis had protested, not wanting Mr. H. to waste his money. But Mr. H. had insisted on helping, explaining to Curtis that he knew an excellent defense attorney who would represent Curtis for very little.

DA Palmer rested her hands on the jury box. "You heard from the medical examiner, Dr. Fielding, who testified that the brain damage suffered by Leon Tolliver resulted from the severe beating perpetrated by the defendant, who just so happens to be a trained fighter." Palmer gestured to Curtis at the defense table. "And as a trained fighter, he should know when to stop. He should know when a man is beaten, which, according to Mr. Hopkins, was quite obvious when Leon fell to one knee after a furious combination of punches by the defendant. But the defendant didn't stop there. He continued to punch Leon, even though Leon was unresponsive and offered *no* resistance."

Curtis dropped his gaze, thinking the DA wasn't wrong.

Palmer gestured to the defense table again. "The defense seeks to prey on your emotions and empathy. The defense wants you to ignore the facts and to focus on intentions, possibilities, and conjecture. The defendant grew up in a broken home and was likely subjected to violence as a child. Sadly, many people have had this experience." DA Palmer surveyed the jury. "Given the prevalence of child abuse, I suspect several of you on the jury know exactly what it feels like to be an abused child. It's absolutely heartbreaking, yet the vast majority of abused children do *not* grow up to beat someone to the point of severe and permanent brain damage."

Curtis wondered what was wrong with him. It had been like an out-of-body experience. It was like he had watched himself beat that man, but he couldn't stop it.

"Leon Tolliver never should've punched Destiny Mays. Nobody is arguing that was okay. If there was an alternative universe where Leon caused Destiny to have permanent brain damage, he would be the one on trial for first-degree aggravated assault. But the defendant and Destiny Mays are 100 percent healthy. Leon Tolliver may be technically alive, but he's an empty shell of his former self. That's a fact. The defendant caused the damage. Also a fact. Therefore, the defendant must pay for his crime. It's the law. Plain and simple. When you're deliberating, I ask you, the jury, to follow the *truth*, to do the *right* thing, to do the *lawful* thing, and to *convict* based on the evidence presented." DA Palmer paused for a long moment, making eye contact with each juror, letting her closing argument marinate. "Thank you." The DA returned to her seat at the prosecution table.

Attorney Gerald Watts stood from the defense table, buttoned his suit jacket, and swaggered to the jury box. "Good morning."

A few jurors nodded. A few mouthed, *Good morning.*

Gerald Watts had been an orphan in Mr. H.'s group home seventeen years ago. He had been adopted though and had lived happily ever after, with enough love and support to become a successful defense attorney, known for swaying a jury with his charisma. It didn't hurt that he resembled a young Denzel Washington.

Watts said, "This is a tragedy. No doubt about it. But we wouldn't be here if Leon Tolliver hadn't sucker punched Destiny Mays. Leon Tolliver is a big man, far taller, heavier, and stronger than Ms. Mays. But that didn't stop him from punching her so hard that he knocked her out with one punch."

Gerald Watts motioned to Curtis. "My client testified that he didn't know what Leon would do next. Leon might've stomped Ms. Mays to death if Curtis hadn't intervened. And that's a reasonable assumption, based on the fact that Leon punched her with such ferocity and venom. What if Destiny Mays was your wife or daughter? Would you have wanted Curtis to walk away? To leave Leon Tolliver to do as he pleases?"

Gerald motioned to Curtis again. "My client testified that he intended to protect Ms. Mays, not to injure Leon Tolliver permanently." Gerald scanned the jurors. "The prosecution wants you to disregard important details of this case, but it matters that Curtis Duffy is only nineteen years old. It matters that he's an orphan who has experienced unspeakable violence. It matters that Curtis has never been convicted of a felony. It matters that Curtis was saving up for college. It matters that Curtis wants to be a social worker to help orphans just like him. It matters that Leon Tolliver was harassing Curtis with racial slurs. It matters that Leon is the type of man to sucker punch a woman. It matters that Curtis reacted, not out of malice, but out of a desire to help a woman in peril, his friend, Destiny Mays."

Gerald Watts took a deep breath and scanned the jury again. "I hope each of you will look inside your heart and make the choice not to compound this tragedy by sending a nineteen-year-old to prison for protecting a young woman from attack." Gerald nodded to the jury. "I trust that you'll do the right thing and vote not guilty. Thank you."

CHAPTER 79

The Verdict

The jury filed into the courtroom. Mr. H. sat in his customary spot in the audience, right behind Curtis and Gerald Watts at the defense table. Curtis watched the jurors, searching their faces for signs of their verdict. None of them made eye contact with Curtis, which he figured was an ominous sign.

The jury foreman—a white-haired woman with a pannus stomach—handed a folder to the bailiff, who handed the folder to the white-haired judge with droopy jowls. Judge Akers opened the folder, read the form for a minute, and then handed it back to the bailiff. The bailiff returned the form to the foreman, giving her a few muted instructions.

"Curtis Duffy, please stand for the reading of the verdict," Judge Akers said.

Gerald Watts stood. Curtis stood, his knees weak, and his stomach twisting.

"You may read the verdict," Akers said to the jury foreman.

The old woman stood in front of her seat on the jury, holding the folder open. She read from the form without emotion. "For the charge of aggravated assault in the first degree, we find the defendant ... guilty."

Curtis's knees buckled. He grabbed the table to steady himself.

CHAPTER 80

Sentencing

The next day, Curtis was back at the defense table with his attorney, Gerald Watts. The judge sat behind his desk on high, the state flag of Virginia and the American flag hanging limp behind him. Like the trial, only a few people came to watch the sentencing.

Judge Akers said, "Yesterday, the defendant was convicted of aggravated assault, a first-degree felony, which carries a maximum sentence of up to twenty years in prison." The judge addressed the prosecution. "Mrs. Palmer, in the matter of the sentencing, is there anyone who would like to speak on behalf of the victim in this case?"

DA Teresa Palmer spoke from behind her prosecution table. "Yes, Your Honor. Beatrice Tolliver, the victim's mother, would like to make a statement." Palmer gestured to the middle-aged woman sitting in the first row of the audience behind the prosecution table.

"Mrs. Tolliver, you're welcome to stand where you are and address the court, or you may use the podium," Judge Akers said.

Beatrice Tolliver stood from her seat, made her way to the podium between the defense and prosecution tables, and faced the judge. She was a tall heavyset woman, wearing a black dress fit for a funeral. She unfolded a piece of paper and spread it out on the podium. She read from the paper without looking up. "My name is Beatrice Tolliver. My son is Leon Tolliver." She cleared her throat. "My son made his mistakes, but he never hurt someone so bad, like the defendant did. Deep down, my Leon's a good boy. Took care of me when I got sick.

Gave me money when I couldn't work. I had complications when I had Leon. Couldn't have no other babies. Leon is my only child"—Beatrice pointed at Curtis—"and that man *took* my baby and messed up his brain so bad that my Leon is gone." Beatrice grabbed a tissue from the box on the podium and dabbed the corners of her eyes. "Truth be told, it might've been better if the defendant killed my Leon. The way he's livin' now ain't no kinda life." Beatrice looked up from her paper to the judge. "If you ask me, this should be a murder trial. Twenty years ain't enough, but, if that's the maximum, at least give him that." She returned to her seat.

Curtis stared forward, blank-faced.

"Thank you, Mrs. Tolliver." The judge addressed the defense. "Mr. Watts? Do you have anyone who would like to speak on behalf of the defendant in this case?"

Gerald spoke from his seat. "Russel Henderson would like to speak on behalf of my client, Your Honor."

Mr. H. stood from the front row pew.

"Mr. Henderson, you're welcome to stand where you are and address the court, or you may use the podium," Judge Akers said.

Mr. H. went to the podium. He glanced at Curtis, then spoke directly to the judge. "Curtis came to my group home as a ten-year-old, when his mother couldn't care for him anymore. His mother was skinny, with track marks on her arms. All of his belongings fit into a trash bag. Everyone in his life abandoned him at ten years old. He was bullied mercilessly and ostracized."

Curtis stared at the tabletop, remembering the day his mother had dropped him off at the group home.

"Through it all, he never became bitter and cruel. All he's ever done is the best he can, which is more than I can say for most of us, me included." Mr. H. dropped his gaze for a few seconds, as if collecting his thoughts. He addressed the judge again. "I've cared for hundreds of children at my group home. Most of them had suffered abuse prior to my care. Some went on to do great things." Mr. H.

gestured to Gerald. "I had the pleasure of caring for Mr. Watts at one time. He's become a fantastic attorney and, more important, a wonderful husband and father."

Gerald Watts nodded to Mr. H.

"But I deal with high-risk children," Mr. H. said. "They don't always walk the straight and narrow. Sometimes their demons are too much. Curtis has demons that would overwhelm the best of us, but Curtis was on the right path. He was doing all the right things. If given a chance, Curtis will be a force for good in this world. I know this because I know he has a big heart. I humbly ask you for leniency. Thank you."

"Thank you, Mr. Henderson," Judge Akers replied.

Mr. H. returned to his seat.

The judge turned his attention to Curtis. "Mr. Duffy, is there anything you would like to say, before I impose your sentence?"

Curtis stood from his seat and turned to Beatrice Tolliver. "I'm sorry for what I did to your son and for the pain I caused you and your family."

Mrs. Tolliver stared at Curtis through glassy eyes.

Curtis sat and faced forward.

"This case has been particularly tragic. The senseless violence and wasted youth," Judge Akers said, addressing the courtroom. The judge turned his attention to Curtis. "Mr. Duffy. I sympathize with your past. I sympathize with your current situation. I believe Mr. Henderson's assessment of your character. Your crime wasn't premeditated. You weren't the first one to throw a punch. However, you went too far. *Much* too far. The crime began when Leon Tolliver was immobile, yet you continued to punch him with such ferocity that he will never be the same. For that, you must pay a penance." Judge Akers took a deep breath. "I sentence you to five to ten years in a state correctional facility. You will serve a minimum of five years and a maximum of ten years in prison. You will be eligible for parole consideration, after you've served your minimum sentence." Judge Akers banged his gavel.

CHAPTER 81

Fresh Fish

The Greensburg Correctional Center was located in southeastern Virginia, far enough that visits from Mr. H. would be few and far between. Inmates were housed in pod-style buildings. Each pod was unofficially segregated by race and gang affiliation. Curtis had overheard this bit of gossip on the bus. He had wondered where they would put him. He wasn't white. He wasn't black. And he wasn't in a gang.

After the intake process, Curtis and approximately fifty other inmates were divided into eight groups, based on which cell block they would be assigned to. The prison administration decided this at intake. It certainly appeared that they were divided by race. Curtis was the outlier—by far the whitest man among a group of black men.

Curtis marched in single file with five other freshly incarcerated men, following the black line on the hallway floor to Cell Block C. Several corrections officers escorted them. Curtis and the men were silent, their eyes darting about. An ID badge with Curtis's picture was clipped to the breast pocket of his orange smock. He carried his bedroll, a laundry bag, and his intake paperwork. The bedroll contained fresh sheets, a pillow case, and a blanket. His laundry bag contained extra prison uniforms, underwear, socks, and toiletries.

They were buzzed into Cell Block C, a two-story rectangular building capable of housing 160 inmates. The door shut behind them, along with their escorts. The center of the building resembled an indoor courtyard, with stainless-steel tables and chairs bolted to the floor. A handful of guards patrolled the perimeter.

A cacophony of voices came from the inmates, loitering at and around the tables. The inmates self-segregated. The majority of the men were black. Many had visible tattoos, containing the letters *BGF*, with a crossed sword and rifle. BGF stood for Black Guerilla Family, a well-known black power and prison gang. Curtis was the only white person in Cell Block C, although he thought this was a better option than being dumped in the Aryan Nation cell block.

Some of the BGF members joked and laughed. Others leered and pointed at the incoming inmates. A few catcalled and threatened them.

"Fresh fish comin'," someone announced.

A few BGF inmates blew kisses at the newbies.

"Look at these motherfuckers," said another BGF inmate.

"Look at that albino nigger."

Curtis ignored the comment meant for him. He followed the other newbies, his underarms sweating, trying not to make eye contact with anyone.

Prison guards watched the scene through the thick windows of the control room, which was a half-moon shaped observation area, situated along the west wall, with a wide view of Cell Block C. Along the perimeter of the cell block were two stories of open cells, and two metal staircases to access the cells on the upper floor.

Several of the new inmates went directly to the BGF and greeted their brothers. Curtis and the other fresh fish searched for their cell assignments. Curtis gripped his bedroll to stop his hands from shaking. A few men deliberately stepped in front of Curtis, forcing him to walk around or to cause a collision.

A mountain of a man who resembled an NFL offensive tackle sneered at Curtis and said, "Punk-ass bitch."

Curtis saw a tear drop tattoo under his right eye and a neck tatt. BGF was tattooed atop his bald head. Curtis pretended not to hear him and slipped by in the chaos.

He climbed the stairs on rubbery legs to the second-floor landing. He found cell number 208. The sliding cell door was wide open. Curtis stood in the doorway and stuck his head inside, bracing himself for the worst. An older black man lay in the bottom bunk, reading a paperback.

"I'm supposed to be in here," Curtis said, his voice wavering. "Is it okay if I come in?"

The older man set his bookmark, closed his book, and stood from the bed. The man was wiry and average height, with deep grooves around his forehead and mouth. He narrowed his eyes at Curtis. "What's your name, youngblood?"

"Curtis."

"I'm Virgil."

Curtis still stood in the doorway.

"You scared?" Virgil asked.

"No."

Virgil chuckled. "You, me, and the man upstairs knows that ain't true."

Curtis opened his mouth to speak, but he didn't know what to say.

"It's okay, youngblood. You should be scared, but you'll be all right—if you follow the rules. Now come in. Let's get you squared away."

Curtis stepped into the nine-by-twelve space, relieved that his roommate wasn't intimidating. It was only three steps from the door to the stainless-steel toilet and sink in the far corner. Bunk beds were built into the concrete wall. There were two lockers, each with built-in combination locks.

Curtis tossed his stuff on the top bunk, held out his hand to the older man, and said, "It's nice to meet you."

They shook hands.

"Likewise." Virgil gestured to the empty locker. "I suggest you put your stuff in there and lock it up. Stuff goes missin' all the time 'round here."

Curtis slipped past Virgil to the empty locker. Curtis consulted his orientation paperwork for the combination, committing it to memory. He mastered the combination, tried it twice, then locked his valuables inside.

Virgil sat on the edge of their little desk, watching Curtis, as if sizing him up.

Curtis pivoted from his locker. "What are the rules?"

Virgil cocked his head, confused.

"You said, if I followed the rules, I'd be okay …"

"Right. The rules." Virgil stood from the desk. "Listen up, youngblood. This'll save your butt." Virgil held up one finger. "Don't ever accept favors or get into debt or gamble. That's the quickest way to end up as a prison wife. Got me?"

Curtis cringed and nodded.

Virgil held up two fingers. "Don't disrespect anyone." Virgil held up three fingers. "If someone steps to you, you have to fight. You don't have to win, but you have to put up a good fight."

Curtis nodded again. "How long have you been here?"

"Ten years next week."

"What did you do?"

"Careful with that question. You never know how an inmate will respond. Like everyone else here, I can't go back and fix what I did. I spent years wishin' I could, but what's done is done."

CHAPTER 82

The Resource Center

Curtis had been assigned to the resource center as Virgil's assistant, a job that paid thirty cents per hour.

Virgil gave Curtis a tour of the resource center, gesturing to the six round tables and plastic chairs. "Sometimes guys come in here and play cards at the tables. As long as they stay quiet, it's fine. Don't let anyone write on the tables. It's a real pain to clean off the ink."

The tabletops were scratched and dinged, with initials carved in various places. Curtis wondered if they'd used a knife.

Virgil showed Curtis the computer stations, which were all occupied by neo-Nazis of the Aryan Nation. Like the pod segregation, the resource center was also segregated, with each racial group or gang having a designated day and time to visit. The cream-colored desktop computers were dingy and yellow-tinted from constant use, sometimes by men with questionable hygiene.

"Guys mostly come here for the computers," Virgil said. "We only have ten stations, and sometimes we have more than ten guys who wanna be online. I usually have 'em draw numbers out of a bowl. If it's twelve guys, I'll put numbers one through twelve in the bowl. Whoever draws the eleven and twelve has to wait to use the computer. If you don't do that, you'll have a fight."

Curtis nodded. "Do we have to monitor anything, or can they look at whatever they want?"

"We don't have to worry about that. The prison staff censors the internet. No pornography or violence. Basically, anything with an age restriction is prohibited. All incomin' and outgoin' emails are read and approved or censored by the prison staff."

"That's messed up."

"Shoot, they even charge twenty cents for every incomin' email. If the sender doesn't pay, it doesn't get through."

"That's not right."

"No. No, it ain't."

They meandered through the jam-packed bookcases.

"How do you know where to put the books?" Curtis asked.

"I used to use the Dewey decimal system with a card catalogue, but most guys had no idea how to use it, so now I group books by subject. Notice I have stickers with numbers on each bindin'." Virgil touched a book in the nonfiction section about World War II, with a number twelve sticker. "Anything that starts with the number one is nonfiction, then the second number breaks it down more. In this case, the number two refers to military nonfiction." At the end of the row, Virgil tapped the laminated poster taped to the end of the metal bookcase. "This shows everyone what's on this row."

The poster was a map of the bookshelf, showing which numbers were on the shelf, where, and what the numbers meant.

"That's smart," Curtis said.

"I appreciate that, youngblood," Virgil replied. "Took me many years to get it done. But when all you got is time …"

They moved from the bookshelves to the sitting area, brightened by a long bank of windows with a view of the gravel track and the forest beyond. Magazine racks surrounded the ratty couches. Well-worn magazines were shoved into the racks: *Sports Illustrated, Time, National Geographic, Popular Mechanics, Road & Track, Motor Trend,* and others.

One neo-Nazi sat on a couch, reading a paperback—*By Any Means Necessary* by Malcolm X. The neo-Nazi appeared to be in his forties, with a little gray in his long beard. He was a large barrel-chested man, with tattoos covering his forearms. A swastika was inked to the side of his neck.

The neo-Nazi looked up from his book, nodded, and said, "Virgil."

Virgil nodded back. "Sam. Interestin' book you got there."

Sam smirked. "Gotta know how you people think." Sam squinted at Curtis, as if trying to understand what he was looking at.

Virgil led Curtis back to the front desk and demonstrated the checkout procedure. Three large boxes of books sat under the front desk.

Curtis pointed to the boxes. "What about these books?"

"That's busy work. When the guards come in, we shelve the new books. Otherwise, they'll yell at us and tell us to get to work. But there isn't much to do but read. This job is the best-kept secret 'round here. I've read hundreds of books in this library. Kept me sane for ten years. Maybe it'll do the same for you."

CHAPTER 83

The Big Dog

After work, Curtis and Virgil entered the pod, intent on relaxing in their cell until dinner. The stench of body odor and raucous voices greeted their senses. The courtyard was chaotic with inmates joking, clowning, posturing, and plotting. Several groups of the Black Guerilla Family monopolized the tables, many sitting on the tabletops, their feet on the chairs.

As they neared, the largest BGF member—the one with the BGF tatt on his bald head—stood from the table. He lifted his chin to Curtis and said, "Hey, Red. Lemme holla at you."

Curtis stopped and faced the three-hundred-pound behemoth.

Virgil stopped too. "He doesn't want what you're sellin'."

One of the BGF members said, "Shut the fuck up, old man."

Another BGF member said, "Big Dog wants to eat."

"Let the man speak for himself," the behemoth said.

"Leave him alone." Virgil grabbed Curtis's elbow and pulled him toward the stairs that led to the second-floor cells.

"You don't own him."

"Neither do you," Virgil said over his shoulder.

The behemoth replied, "Yet."

Curtis and Virgil continued to their cell. The door was wide open, and it would be until the nightly lockdown, but it provided some privacy, as most inmates understood not to enter another man's cell, unless invited.

Once inside their cell, Virgil said, "That man who wanted to talk to you is Deontae Simmons. Everyone calls him Big Dog. He runs the Black Guerilla Family in here."

"Why do you think he wanted to talk to me?" Curtis asked.

"Same reason he wants to talk to any new inmate. Recruiting. He recruits new members to do all the dirty work. Dealin' drugs. Assaults. Collections. Murder."

Curtis furrowed his brow. "Murder?"

Virgil nodded. "Last year, a young brother came here on a one-year drug charge. Got caught up with Big Dog. Shanked an Aryan. He would've been back home by now. Instead, he's doin' life." Virgil stared at Curtis, emphasizing his point. "Don't fall into that trap."

CHAPTER 84

BGF for Life

During rec time, Curtis walked to the outdoor weights. Heat reverberated off the asphalt. Many inmates lifted without shirts, their sweaty muscles glistening in the sun.

Curtis found an empty bench, already racked with 135 pounds. He stretched his arms and shoulders, then did an easy warmup of ten repetitions. He racked another forty-five-pound plate on each side, upping the weight to 225 pounds. He waved his arms back and forth and rolled his shoulders, loosening up.

A group of BGF members surrounded Curtis. They were all built, most of them not wearing shirts, their bodies covered in prison tattoos.

The one with tight cornrows said, "What the fuck do you think you're doin'?"

Curtis showed his palms. "I can do something else if you want the bench."

"Shut the fuck up," one of the other BGF members said.

Cornrows stepped closer to Curtis. "I should fuck you up right now. Ugly ass bitch."

"Yeah," another BGF member said.

The crowd moved closer, the metaphorical noose tightening around Curtis.

Cornrows gestured to the outdoor gym. "All this shit is ours. You gotta *pay* if you wanna use it."

Big Dog approached the huddle. "He's with me."

Everyone backed off.

Big Dog lifted his chin. "What's your name?"

"Curtis."

"I'm Big Dog Simmons. You can call me Big Dog or Big Simmons."

Curtis glanced at his bench. "Is it okay if I work out?"

Big Dog nodded. "I'll spot you."

The bald behemoth stood behind the bench, as Curtis pumped ten repetitions. Curtis racked the weight with a little guidance from Big Dog.

"You're strong," Big Dog said.

"Thanks," Curtis replied. "I used to play football at Central Virginia."

Big Dog raised his eyebrows. "CVU. That's big-time football. I played defensive tackle at Virginia Tech. Didn't work out though."

"Virginia Tech's big-time too."

Big Dog stared at Curtis for a long moment. "I'm a long way from there, and you're a long way from CVU."

Curtis nodded.

"I like you, Red. I'd like for you to join my esteemed organization." Big Dog tilted his bald head down, showing Curtis his BGF tattoo.

"I appreciate that, Mr. Simmons—"

"Big Simmons or Big Dog."

"Big Simmons. I appreciate the offer, but I just wanna do my time. I don't wanna get involved in any gang ... activity."

Big Dog crossed his beefy arms over his chest. "All right."

"Thanks."

Big Dog motioned to the bench press. "You gonna do another one?"

"Yeah."

"You should add some weight. Last set was too easy."

Curtis added twenty-five-pound plates to each end, upping the weight to 275 pounds. He lay on the bench. Big Dog stood behind him again, as the spotter. Curtis spaced his hands and lifted the bar off the rack, the bar bending from the heavy weight. Curtis inhaled as he lowered the weight to his chest, then exhaled as he pressed the weight up. He struggled on the fifth repetition, but the bar still moved upward.

Big Dog leaned forward and added resistance to the bar, halting Curtis's progress. Curtis reddened, his back arching, as he desperately tried to complete the rep and return the bar to the rack. But Big Dog didn't relent. He pushed the weight back to Curtis's chest, pinning him on the bench.

Curtis groaned, the heavy weight crushing his chest.

Big Dog leaned over Curtis, pressing on the bar, adding to the weight. "If you join the BGF, you're family. For *life*. If you don't, ... you better watch your fuckin' back." Big Dog pushed off on the bar, as he stood upright.

Pain radiated from Curtis's chest. Curtis turned to his side, letting the twenty-five-pound plate fall off one side to the asphalt. With the weight disparity, the bar pulled him in the opposite direction, dumping all the weights from that side. Then it whipsawed him back to the other side, dumping the remaining two forty-five-pound plates.

CHAPTER 85

The Demand

The resource center was empty, except for Curtis and Virgil. Curtis stood behind the front desk, organizing books by subject, then organizing them on the metal cart for eventual reshelving. A bar-size bruise had formed on his chest since yesterday's lifting session, and it hurt to take a deep breath, but he didn't think anything was broken.

Virgil sat in his swivel chair, reading *Man's Search for Meaning* by Viktor Frankl.

Curtis sorted the last book, then set the piles on the cart. He addressed Virgil. "Is that any good?"

Virgil set his bookmark and shut the book. Several Post-it notes protruded from the pages. "Might be the best book I've ever read. Not quite finished but I'm almost done."

"Really? What's so great about it?"

Virgil tapped the paperback in his lap. "It's the meanin' of life."

Curtis cocked his head. "What's the meaning of life?"

Virgil flipped through the book, stopping at one of his Post-it notes. He scanned the page, then said, "I think this sums it up best." Virgil read from the book. "*As each situation in life represents a challenge to man and presents a problem for him to solve, the question of the meanin' of life may actually be reversed. Ultimately, man should not ask what the meanin' of his life is, but rather he must recognize that it is he who is asked. In a word, each man is questioned by life; and he can only answer to life by answerin' for his own life; to life he can only respond by being responsible."*

"That's it. Be responsible?"

Virgil shut the book again. "Bein' responsible is no small thing. We start with bein' responsible for ourselves, for a job. Then maybe we're responsible for a family. Then maybe a community. Without responsibility, life's meaningless. The more responsibility we carry, the more meanin' our lives will have."

Curtis nodded, thinking about Virgil's point. "What about prison? Are we being responsible for the crimes we committed by being here?"

"I don't think so. Unfortunately, prison's more punitive than redemptive."

Curtis stared at the carpet. "I beat a man so bad he doesn't even know his own name. How do I take responsibility for that?"

Virgil stood from his chair. "I don't think you can."

Curtis leaned on the counter. "I took it too far. It was like I was possessed."

Virgil leaned on the counter next to Curtis. "I know what you're goin' through. Those regrets are tough to swallow. I get it. But you only have two choices. Let that guilt and regret eat you from the inside out, or move forward and be the best person you can be. You still have a helluva lotta life to live. How you do that matters."

"Is that what you're doing? Moving forward? Being the best person you can be?"

Virgil let out a heavy breath. "Sometimes. Sometimes it's too much. Did I ever tell what I used to do?"

"No."

"I was a truck driver. Long haul. I used to drink too. A bad combination. One night … I had some whiskey. Too much to be drivin'. Went over the double yellow line." Virgil swallowed hard. "Hit a minivan head-on. A mother and her two girls …"

Curtis winced. "I'm sorry, Virgil."

"Don't be. Ain't your sin to carry." Virgil took a deep breath. "A big part of me wanted to die for what I did, but I got a wife and four kids. They're grown now, but I still gotta be the best husband and father I can be, knowin' it'll never make up for what I did. I owe it to my family and myself to be responsible, just like *you* owe it to your people and yourself to be responsible. You understand?"

"I think so."

Virgil placed his hand on Curtis's shoulder and squeezed.

Curtis pushed the cart through the bookshelves, thinking about Virgil's revelation, while shelving the books by subject. Heavy footsteps and a cacophony of voices entered the resource center—the next group of inmates. Curtis continued to shelve books. Most of the voices and footsteps went to the computers.

One unmistakable voice loitered at the front desk. "Where he at?" Big Dog asked.

"You made your point," Virgil replied. "Leave him alone."

"What you gonna do about it, old man?"

Big Dog appeared between the bookcases, the narrow aisle barely wide enough to contain his massive frame. He recognized Curtis and marched his way, with Virgil hot on his heels.

Curtis stood like a deer in headlights, his eyes wide.

"I was lookin' for you," Big Dog said.

"Don't talk to him," Virgil said.

Big Dog glanced over his shoulder at Virgil. "Shut the fuck up." He faced Curtis again. "I need you to do somethin' for me."

Curtis showed his palms. "I don't want any trouble. I just wanna do my time."

Big Dog spoke through gritted teeth. "You gotta choice. You can be my prison wife—wash my clothes, clean my cell, suck my dick."

Curtis cringed.

"That's enough," Virgil said.

Big Dog pivoted to Virgil and shoved him with a flick of his wrist. Virgil fell to the ground, like a flea on Big Dog's ass. Big Dog faced Curtis again. "Or you can stick that cracker, Sam Shaw. I heard he comes here to read every week."

Virgil stood from the floor.

"The Aryan?" Curtis asked.

Big Dog nodded, reached into his waistband, and removed a crumpled paper towel. He handed the crumpled mess to Curtis. "You do this, we're square."

Something hard was inside. Curtis opened the crumpled paper towel to reveal a plastic toothbrush that had been sharpened to a fine point.

"He's not doin' this," Virgil said.

"I can't," Curtis reiterated.

Big Dog poked Curtis on his sore chest. "You don't have a choice." Big Dog pivoted and purposely brushed past Virgil, nearly knocking him to the ground again.

CHAPTER 86

The Commissary

Once per week, the inmates of Cell Block C were allowed to visit the commissary. Ten inmates were escorted at a time throughout the day at scheduled intervals. Eligible inmates were expected to sign up in advance, so the prison could allocate the appropriate number of guards. Curtis and Virgil had signed up for the latest time slot after dinner.

The commissary was divided by a concrete wall with an open window for transactions. A daily printed list of prices and items in stock hung on the wall. A long counter beneath the price list held order forms with pens chained to the counter. Curtis, Virgil, and the other inmates grabbed order forms and scanned the price list. The price list was alphabetized and divided into categories: foodstuffs, pharmacy, toiletries, entertainment, electronics, and stationary. Curtis was shocked by the prices. Everything was two to three times more expensive than normal. Sodas were $3. So were candy bars. Ramen noodles were $4. A single roll of toilet paper was $1.50.

"These prices are crazy," Curtis said, holding his empty laundry bag.

"You're right," Virgil replied.

Curtis and Virgil filled out their cards and turned them in to one of the inmates working behind the counter. The inmate collected their order and set it in front of the corrections officer, who ran the computer and register. The CO deducted the items and funds from their prison accounts. Curtis packed his purchases in his empty laundry bag. He had purchased a roll of toilet paper, soap, floss, a candy bar, and a bag of potato chips. His total came to $19.50, which was $9.90 more than he'd made working at the Resource Center over the past four days, but he had some additional money that Mr. H. had added to his account.

Virgil purchased similar items.

Curtis, Virgil, and the eight other inmates were escorted back to Cell Block C. As soon as they entered the cell block, everyone was accosted, and Cell Block C turned into a market. Inmates haggled, begged, and cajoled for their desired goods.

"What did you get?"

"Lemme have some."

"I'll trade you for that candy."

"I'll pay you back next week."

Curtis and Virgil walked toward the stairs, intent on locking up their goods in their cell. Virgil had already explained the importance of immediately locking up their commissary items. Curtis held his laundry bag tight to his body, not making eye contact with the beggars and potential thieves. Big Dog and six other members of BGF blocked the stairs. The hair on the back of Curtis's neck stood on end, and his heart thumped in his chest. Curtis sensed they were about to get jumped, but he was fully prepared to go down swinging.

Big Dog lifted his chin to Curtis and Virgil. "What'd you get?"

"Some necessities." Virgil pointed up the stairs. "Mind if we get through?"

More BGF members approached from behind, surrounding Curtis and Virgil.

"Gimme those bags," Big Dog said.

Curtis clenched his fists, thinking about knocking out Big Dog. He glanced at Virgil, trying to figure out if he had a plan. Virgil shook his head, almost imperceptibly, as if he knew what Curtis was thinking. Big Dog reached out and snatched Virgil's bag. Another BGF member snatched Curtis's bag. Big Dog grabbed a Snickers candy bar from Virgil's bag. He opened the wrapper and took a big bite.

"I love me some Snickers," he said, with his mouth full.

Curtis watched Big Dog chewing, his entire body rigid with rage.

The BGF stole all the food, then tossed their laundry bags at their feet. Thankfully, they left the toiletries.

Big Dog chuckled and said, "Bitch-ass niggas."

Curtis and Virgil grabbed their bags from the floor and trudged to their cell.

As soon as they entered their cell, Curtis slapped his bag on his bunk. "They're gonna keep doing this shit."

"Ain't nothin' we can do about that," Virgil replied.

Curtis held out his hands. "I thought we were supposed to fight. You said that's the prison rule. If someone steps to you, you have to fight. You don't have to win, but you have to fight. Remember that?"

"One on one, yes. Fifteen on two? No. That's suicide."

"We should've kept that shank," Curtis said.

CHAPTER 87

Visiting

Curtis hugged Mr. H., holding on to him for a few beats longer than a typical hug. When they separated, they sat across from each other at a stainless-steel table. Mr. H. had dark circles around his bloodshot eyes. Curtis figured the visit was a hardship for Mr. H., given the long drive and his busy schedule at the group home.

The visiting room was filled with inmates sitting and talking with their friends and families. A few vending machines lined the walls with overpriced snacks and soda. Corrections officers patrolled the room, making sure nobody acted inappropriate or aggressive.

Curtis forced a smile. "Thank you for coming."

Mr. H. narrowed his eyes, his hands folded on the table. "You okay?"

"I'm fine."

Mr. H. leaned forward. "You forget who you're talking to. What's wrong?"

Curtis looked away.

"Curtis?"

He faced Mr. H. and whispered, "Have you ever heard of the Black Guerilla Family?"

Mr. H. grimaced. "I have. They giving you trouble?"

"I think they want me to join—"

"Don't do it. They'll get you involved in criminal activity. Then you'll never see the outside of this prison."

"I already told them no, but …"

"They're threatening you, aren't they?"

Curtis nodded. "I don't know what to do. I'm not sure I can avoid them for a month, much less ten years."

Mr. H. ran his hand over his face. "If you do all the right things, there's a chance you get parole in five."

"That's still a long time."

"This isn't the first time I've visited one of my kids in prison. This isn't the first time they had issues with gangs either. Usually, they're already in one. I can say one thing with absolute certainty. If you join a gang, you'll be a criminal in word and deed, and you're in for life. It's not a social club."

"What am I supposed to do?"

"A man has to stand on his own, especially when it's hard."

Curtis exhaled, his shoulders slumped. "And if they come after me?"

Mr. H. cracked his knuckles. "You still got the hands of a trained fighter."

"I can't fight the whole gang."

"You don't have to. You just have to win one against a worthy opponent."

CHAPTER 88

Rec Time

Curtis walked around the gravel track with Virgil. Most of the inmates played basketball, watched basketball, or lifted weights.

After two laps, Curtis said to Virgil, "I'm gonna run."

Virgil grinned. "Go ahead, youngblood. I'm gonna sit."

Curtis jogged, and Virgil headed for the aluminum bleachers, which were only five high, and could accommodate no more than fifty people. Curtis's slip-on shoes weren't exactly running shoes, but they weren't terrible. As he jogged, he remembered recovering that fumble against Clemson and scoring the game-winning touchdown, or at least the touchdown that led to the game-winning two-point conversion. Curtis replayed the moment over and over in his mind. He remembered the jubilation from his teammates, while the rest of Clemson Memorial Stadium was shocked silent. They would've lost that game without Curtis, and Central Virginia University never would've won the national championship.

Curtis picked up the pace, stretching his legs with each stride. Virgil leaned back on the bleachers by himself, enjoying the sun on his face. Two Latino inmates strolled on the track, talking in Spanish. Curtis pushed himself harder, running faster, feeling the breeze on his face. His breathing was labored, but his feet were light, barely touching the gravel. Sweat beaded at his hairline and under his arms. He continued around the circle, pushing harder, imagining he was in a race. His legs and lungs burned, but he didn't stop. Curtis pushed through the pain. Part of him hoped his heart would burst, and he'd die on that track. As he rounded the corner, he spotted Virgil, still leaning back on the bleachers, his face to the sky, and his eyes closed.

A group of BGF members approached the bleachers from behind. Their posture was all wrong. They weren't boisterous and strutting. They were stiff, walking with purpose, while looking around. They surrounded Virgil.

Curtis used the last of his breath to call out, "Virgil!"

Virgil sat up, noticed the BGF members, and said something.

Curtis sprinted toward the bleachers, but he was nearly one hundred yards away.

One of the BGF members appeared to punch Virgil in the stomach repeatedly. Then they all scattered like roaches. Virgil slumped to his side.

Curtis reached Virgil and stood over the older man, still breathing heavy from his sprint. "Virgil, are you okay?"

Virgil groaned, his face contorted in pain. Curtis noticed that Virgil's smock was covered in tiny holes. He lifted Virgil's smock, revealing his blood-soaked T-shirt.

Curtis screamed, "Help. Somebody help me!"

CHAPTER 89

Lockdown

Curtis paced in his locked cell, replaying Virgil's stabbing. The guards did come shortly after Curtis screamed for help. The medical staff had acted quickly. Curtis hoped it was enough to save Virgil's life. Curtis wasn't religious, but he said a silent prayer for his friend.

Please, God. Please help my friend Virgil. He's fighting for his life, and he needs your help. He has four children and a wife who need him. I need him. I know he made a big mistake, but he's a good man. Please help him. Please, God. The world is a better place with Virgil in it.

A guard banged on his door three times, opened it, and entered. "You need to wait outside, while we conduct the search."

Curtis stepped out of his cell. One guard frisked him, while the other turned his cell upside down, searching for the shank. Curtis thought of the shank Big Dog had given him. Virgil had taken it from Curtis and said he'd get rid of it, but Curtis didn't know for sure if he did. For all he knew, the shank was hidden in his cell. Curtis's stomach did somersaults. Sweat beads formed on his hairline.

After Curtis was frisked, he asked the guard, "Have you heard anything about Virgil?"

"They took him to the ER, but that's all I know," the guard replied.

"Thanks." Curtis glanced into his cell. The other guard stripped the sheets off Curtis's mattress. A bead of sweat slid down Curtis's cheek, then another. He faced the guard again. "What happens if you find the shank?"

"Depends."

"Depends on what?" Curtis asked.

"Court. I've seen cons get ten years added to their sentence."

Curtis trembled as he imagined the guard finding the sharpened toothbrush handle.

The other guard exited Curtis's ransacked cell and said, "It's clean."

CHAPTER 90

Tellin' It Like It Is

On Monday morning, Curtis still hadn't heard any news about Virgil. All he knew was Virgil had been taken to the ER and he hadn't returned. Curtis stood at the front desk of the resource center, affixing numbered stickers to the appropriate books.

Two guards led a group of Aryans into the resource center. Most of the Aryans went to the computers. A few browsed the magazines. One of the guards approached the front desk.

Curtis looked up from his work.

"Virgil's stable," the guard said. "I thought you'd wanna know."

Curtis smiled wide, showing his crooked overbite. "Thank you. That's great news."

The guard smiled back, tapped the countertop with his knuckle, then exited the resource center, taking his post just outside.

Sam Shaw approached the front desk. He rolled his neck, like he was preparing for a fight. Instead, he said, "I'm glad Virgil's okay."

"Me too," Curtis replied. "Is there something I can help you with?"

Sam stared at Curtis for several seconds. "What are you anyway? Some kinda mixed breed?"

"My mother was white—"

"Lemme guess. Your daddy was black."

Curtis nodded.

Sam shook his head. "This is the problem with America. Too much race mixin'. We're better off keepin' with our own. You're a perfect example of why blacks and whites shouldn't mix."

Curtis stiffened.

"I bet you were never accepted by blacks *or* whites. I wonder what that does to a child. It's no surprise you ended up here. Your mother should've fucked her own kind."

Curtis glowered at Sam.

Sam showed his palms and chuckled. "Don't shoot the messenger. I'm just tellin' it like it is." He walked away.

CHAPTER 91

Shank

Curtis sat at the little desk in his cell, writing a letter to Mr. H. He didn't write about Virgil's stabbing or his trouble with the BGF. Curtis didn't want Mr. H. to worry. *What's the point in making him worry? It's not like he can do anything to help me.*

As if on cue, Big Dog appeared in his open doorway, casting a hulking shadow. His freshly shaved head glistened in the fluorescent light.

Curtis stood from his desk.

Big Dog crowded Curtis, who was wedged between the desk and the bunk bed. Curtis clenched his fists, watching Big Dog's massive mitts. Big Dog reached into his waistband and produced a shank, this one with a metal blade and electrical tape covering the handle. The blade was larger and sharper than the sharpened toothbrush Curtis had been given in the resource center.

Big Dog held the blade to Curtis's face. "I could stick your ugly ass right now."

Curtis leaned back, his eyes bulging.

Big Dog chuckled and stepped back. He held out the shank. "You still gotta job to do. I bet that old-ass nigga took the other one."

Curtis stared at the shank.

"Take it, nigga."

Curtis took the blade.

"You gotta week. If Shaw ain't dead by then, it'll be you and that old-ass nigga."

CHAPTER 92

The Fork in the Road

Curtis followed the black line on the floor to the resource center. A guard followed close behind. The shank was wedged in his waistband, just above his rear end. His heart pounded, sure the guard could see the shank imprinted on his lower back.

At the locked door to the resource center, the guard said, "Hold out your hands."

With his back to the guard, Curtis held his arms perpendicular to his body. Sweat beaded on his lower back and armpits. The guard ran gloved hands down Curtis's body and between his legs, then patted his empty pockets. It was a cursory frisk the guards gave when they didn't want to touch the inmate or trusted the inmate or were lazy. Curtis hadn't been in prison long, but he'd been respectful to the guards, and they'd respected him. Thankfully, the guard didn't touch the shank.

The guard opened the resource center and took his post in the hallway.

Curtis went to the front desk and double-checked the schedule. Just as he thought. Cell Block D was scheduled for resource center time that afternoon. Cell Block D housed the Aryans and most of the incarcerated white men. Sam Shaw never missed resource center time. Curtis stared at the couches near the magazine racks. Sam liked to read there. Curtis imagined sneaking up behind Sam, while he's reading, and slicing his carotid artery in one quick motion.

Curtis wondered if he could do it, if he had it in him. He thought about what Sam had said yesterday. *Your mother should've fucked her own kind.*

The Aryans did what they always did. Most of them went to the computers, while Sam Shaw sat on the couch and read his paperback. He was nearly finished with Malcolm X's book, *By Any Means Necessary.* Curtis glanced toward the computers. The Aryans were occupied with their emails and entertainment.

Curtis crept toward the couch. Sam sat there, his back to Curtis, his nose buried in his book. Sam's head was down, exposing the back of his neck. Curtis removed the shank from his waistband. His entire body buzzed in anticipation. As he neared Sam, Curtis heard snoring. He was asleep. Perfectly vulnerable. One quick swipe, then it would be over. Curtis leaned over Sam, gripping the shank in his right hand. Curtis heard Mr. H. in his head, like he was there, watching over him.

A man has to stand on his own, especially when it's hard.

Curtis retracted the blade and slipped it into his pocket. He pivoted and stepped back to the front desk. He grabbed an old envelope from the trash can and placed the shank inside. Then he turned the shank in to the guard, telling him that he found it hidden on a bookshelf.

CHAPTER 93

Bully

Curtis walked toward the weights and the muscled members of BGF. Heat reverberated off the asphalt in a haze. Six BGF members surrounded Big Dog on the bench press. They encouraged him, barking and shouting, as Big Dog pressed 405 pounds off his chest. Big Dog racked the weight and sat upright. The barking and shouting continued, as if Big Dog's strength was shared among the gang.

As the commotion dissipated, Curtis said to Big Dog, "I need to talk to you."

Everyone pivoted to Curtis.

"Get the fuck outta here," said one BGF member.

"Ugly motherfucker," said another BGF member.

Big Dog stood from the bench. The crowd parted as he stepped to Curtis. "Your time's runnin' out."

"I know," Curtis replied. "I'm gonna do it, but there's something you need to know."

Big Dog frowned. "Say what you gotta say."

"In private."

Big Dog surveyed his crew. "Look at this pushy nigga."

"You'll wanna hear this in private," Curtis said, his head level, and his voice strong, showing as much confidence as he could muster.

Big Dog narrowed his eyes at Curtis for a long time, then nodded. Big Dog led Curtis a short distance away from his crew.

"This better be important," Big Dog said.

"You're a bitch," Curtis said, watching Big Dog's right shoulder for the telltale sign of his overhand right.

Big Dog twisted his face in confusion. "What the fuck did you say?"

"You heard me. I could fuck you up right here in front of your boys."

Big Dog clenched his fists and jaw. His neck vein pulsed.

Still watching Big Dog's shoulder, Curtis said, "Punk ass—"

Before Curtis finished his statement, Big Dog's shoulder flexed. He reared back and threw a haymaker, but Curtis anticipated the punch and ducked underneath. The haymaker exposed Big Dog's jaw, and Curtis threw his best left hook, connecting with Big Dog's chin. Curtis's hook caused Big Dog to stumble backward, in a daze, his hands down. Curtis threw a nasty combination—a right cross, another left hook, and another right cross. The final right cross tagged Big Dog, as he fell to the ground, the back of his head bouncing off the asphalt.

It had all happened so fast.

Just a few seconds after Big Dog threw that haymaker, he was on the ground, out like a light. Curtis turned his attention to Big Dog's crew. They gaped at Curtis, standing over Big Dog. Curtis expected BGF to jump him, but they didn't move. The siren came from the PA system. The inmates lay on their bellies, arms and legs spread out like an X.

When the corrections officers came for Curtis, he went willingly. They took Curtis to seg, short for segregation. They took Big Dog to the infirmary.

CHAPTER 94

Seg

The six-by-nine cell had a single metal bunk and a toilet with an attached sink. Light came from the fluorescent tube overhead, and a small sliver of a frosted window offered no view.

Curtis paced in his solitary cell, which amounted to walking three steps, turning around, walking three steps, and turning around again. He wasn't sure if his plan had worked. He had knocked out the most intimidating man in his cell block, hoping it would earn him respect and peace. But he wasn't sure if that was the case. Maybe Big Dog would come after him much harder. Maybe BGF had a hit on Curtis. Either he was safe and feared or he was in more danger than before, with an entire gang seeking revenge. He also worried about the possibility of doing extra time. Big Dog was alive. He had seen him stirring, right before the guards had hauled away Curtis. But, for all Curtis knew, Big Dog could have brain damage, like Leon Tolliver. Big Dog had hit his head pretty hard on the asphalt.

The bigger they are, the harder they fall.

The yard, like the rest of the prison, had surveillance cameras. Curtis hoped the prison had video of the altercation, as it would show Big Dog swinging first. Despite the uncertainty, Curtis smiled, thinking Mr. H. would've been proud of him. Mr. Vasquez too.

The food pass opened, and a covered plastic container appeared. Curtis went to the door. A guard's stoic face was in the door window. Curtis grabbed his lunch and turned around.

The guard rapped on the window with his billy club.

Curtis pivoted to the guard.

"You did a good thing." The guard nodded to Curtis and disappeared from the window.

Curtis sat on his bunk and opened his tray. In addition to his spaghetti, he had three pieces of pound cake.

CHAPTER 95

Back on the Block

Curtis was escorted from seg to Cell Block C by CO Holliday. He and the kitchen had given Curtis extra desserts with his meals. CO Holliday had made sure Curtis had whatever he wanted to read, whenever he wanted it.

They entered the vestibule, the door locking behind them. Holliday said, "Anybody gives you a hard time, let me know."

Curtis thanked the CO, but he had no intention of being a snitch. Big Dog had been transferred out of Cell Block C, as soon as he'd recovered from his beatdown. Thankfully, he'd made a full recovery. The prison hadn't pursued charges against Curtis, apart from the mandatory month in seg for fighting. Despite Big Dog being neutered, Cell Block C was still BGF territory, so Curtis had no idea what he would be walking into.

The door to Cell Block C buzzed open, and Curtis stepped inside, his laundry bag with his personal items over his shoulder. A cacophony of voices and the smell of body odor greeted Curtis. It was just before dinner, so the courtyard was packed with inmates. The voices quieted, and everyone gawked at Curtis. He avoided eye contact and walked toward the stairs.

A dozen BGF members loitered by the stairs. Curtis clenched his fists, anticipating an altercation. As he neared the stairs, the group of BGF members parted like the Red Sea. Curtis felt like Moses, as he passed them without a word.

Curtis climbed the stairs to access the second-story cells. Then he ambled across the landing and entered his cell. Virgil lay in his bunk, reading a book.

"I'm supposed to be in here. Is it okay if I come in?" Curtis asked, purposely saying the exact same thing he'd said to Virgil when they had first met.

Virgil chuckled and stood from his bed, struggling and holding his midsection.

Curtis stepped into his cell. "How are you feeling?"

Virgil smiled from ear to ear. "I'm gettin' better. Doc says I should make a full recovery."

Curtis gave Virgil a hug, careful not to squeeze him too hard.

The Parole Hearing

It had been five years and six weeks since Curtis had been arrested and detained. Curtis had spent six months in jail before being sentenced to a maximum of ten years and a minimum of five years in prison, pending parole. Thankfully, those six months in jail counted against his sentence, giving Curtis his first opportunity at a parole hearing.

Curtis sat in an interview room at the Greensburg Correctional Center, peering into a laptop screen, with a view of the Virginia Parole Board. He wore a loose smock and hunched forward, not wanting to show his chiseled physique. A technology person for the prison stood behind the laptop, in case the remote meeting failed. A corrections officer stood near the door.

Through the laptop, Curtis observed five middle-aged white people, all sitting at a high desk, reminiscent of a judge's desk. He couldn't see Mr. H. or his attorney, Gerald Watts, but Curtis knew they were there. Mr. H. had said he would be in the audience, and, if Mr. H. said he would be there, it was a lock he was there. And Curtis had heard his attorney's voice, as he made a statement in favor of his parole.

Curtis's stomach turned as Beatrice Tolliver addressed the parole board.

Mrs. Tolliver said, "Five years ago, I told the judge that it might've been better if Curtis Duffy had killed my Leon. Now I'm *certain* that it would've been better. After the beatin', Leon was never the same. With his brain damage, he could barely go to the bathroom by *hisself.* The way he was livin' was no kinda life." Mrs. Tolliver cleared her throat. "My Leon died three years ago. They said it was a heart attack, but I know the truth. Curtis Duffy killed my son. Five years ain't near enough for what he did. Curtis Duffy needs to serve his full sentence."

Curtis swallowed hard.

"Thank you, Mrs. Tolliver," said the Chairman of the Virginia Parole Board, Judge Harrison Danforth. "Are there any other statements from family and friends of the victim?"

The prosecuting attorney replied, "No, Your Honor."

Judge Danforth was a bloated man with snow-white hair and red cheeks. He peered into the camera at Curtis. "Mr. Duffy. How does it feel to know that Leon Tolliver's brain was permanently harmed because of your violent actions?"

Curtis took a deep breath and peered into the camera. "I did a terrible thing that I wish I could take back. It's something I'll carry with me for the rest of my life. I wish I could go back in time and ..." Curtis sniffed. "I'm sorry, Mrs. Tolliver. I'm so sorry."

The five board members stared at Curtis on the screen, poker-faced.

"Do you feel that you've been rehabilitated?" Judge Danforth asked.

"Yes, Your Honor," Curtis replied.

"What are your plans? How will you live your life, if you're granted parole today?"

"I know I'll have to abide by the rules of my parole. I'd like to get a job as a groundskeeper. That's what I was doing before. If I can save enough money, I'd like to go back to school and finish my degree in social work."

Two of the board members nodded as Curtis spoke.

Judge Danforth held up a few papers. "We received and read your parole application letters. Russel Henderson vouched for your character and wrote about your childhood and the struggles you endured. CO Brent Holliday wrote about your exemplary behavior as an inmate at Greensburg Correctional Center. Warden Tomlinson wrote about your participation in the prisoner tutoring program." Danforth frowned. "It's hard for me to imagine the man described in your parole application letters doing what you did to Leon Tolliver."

Curtis dipped his head, sure that his parole would be denied.

Judge Danforth turned to his fellow board members. "Do you have any questions for Mr. Duffy, before we vote?"

The board members shook their heads or said no. This was also a bad sign.

They started at the far end of the desk, working their way toward Judge Danforth.

"Mrs. Helms. How do you vote?" Judge Danforth asked.

"Release," she said.

"Mr. Childress?" Danforth asked.

"Serve out," Childress replied.

Curtis winced.

Serve out meant a denial of parole. He needed three votes to be granted parole. The next two board members were also split, leaving the decision to Judge Danforth.

The judge narrowed his eyes at Curtis on the screen for a long moment. Then he said, "Congratulations, Mr. Duffy."

CHAPTER 97

The Big Day

Curtis waited another month for freedom, while the slow prison bureaucracy churned out paperwork and procedures. On the big day, Curtis paced in his cell, waiting for the CO. Virgil sat at their tiny desk.

"Do you need me to send you anything?" Curtis asked.

"That's not necessary," Virgil replied.

"As soon I get some money, I can send it to your commissary."

Virgil stood from the desk and met Curtis near the bunk beds, now blocking Curtis from pacing. "I don't want you sendin' me money."

"What are you talking about?" Curtis asked. "I know what it's like to make thirty-cents an hour."

"I don't want you sendin' me money."

"Then I can bring you whatever you need when I come to visit."

Virgil shook his head, his face resembling a sad basset hound. "You won't be on my list."

Curtis drew back. "I don't understand."

"I've been thinkin' about this a lot. You're like a son to me, and I wouldn't want my son comin' back here under any circumstances—"

"But—"

"No buts. Your life is out there in the world. Your life ain't in here. Not anymore. The best thing you can do for me is to live your life and don't look back. You don't need to be reminded."

"What about you?"

Tears welled in Virgil's eyes. "When my time's up, I'll come to see you under the bright blue sky." Virgil hugged Curtis.

"Thank you for everything."

Heavy boots stopped at their open doorway. "It's time," CO Holliday said.

They disengaged. Curtis pivoted to the guard and nodded. He turned back to Virgil again.

Virgil forced a smile that didn't reach his eyes. "Get outta here."

Curtis smiled back, then left with CO Holliday. He carried nothing, leaving his things with Virgil to do with as he liked.

Along the way out of Cell Block C, many inmates patted Curtis on the back and wished him well. CO Holliday led Curtis to an interview room.

"What this?" Curtis asked.

CO Holliday opened the door. "You can't leave here dressed like that."

On the metal table, folded neatly, were new clothes and a pair of shoes.

"How did …" Curtis trailed off.

"Russel sent 'em to us."

CO Holliday shut Curtis inside the interview room, giving him privacy while he changed. Curtis thought of Virgil while he dressed, happy, yet already missing his friend.

Curtis emerged from the interview room wearing a button-down shirt, black slacks, black shoes, and a coat.

"Much better," CO Holliday said.

Curtis held out his hand. "Thank you, Officer Holliday."

Holliday shook his hand. "It's Brent. And I hope I never see you again."

After some paperwork, and a few more doors, Brent opened the last door that led to the prison parking lot. The cool air nipped at Curtis's ears, but the sky was bright blue and cloudless. It was technically spring, but only by eight days.

Mr. H. exited his van, grinning from ear to ear.

Curtis waved to Brent and a few other guards, then walked to Mr. H. with a spring in his step. Mr. H. gave Curtis a rib-crushing hug and a back slap that would've taken down a lesser man. Despite the power of his hug, Mr. H. felt a little skinnier and slightly shorter than Curtis remembered. He was nearly seventy after all.

When they separated, Mr. H. said, "I'm proud of you."

Curtis averted his eyes, embarrassed. "It was my fault. I didn't do anything ..."

"Look at me, son."

Curtis raised his gaze.

"You made a serious mistake, but you didn't start that fight. It was a bad situation for everyone, but you did the best you could with the hand you were dealt. That's all anyone can ask."

On the three-hour trip to Alexandria, they jabbered back and forth about Curtis's future plans, the group home, and the current crop of kids. The kids Curtis had known prior to his arrest were long gone, adopted, or in a foster home.

Mr. H. had invited Curtis to crash on the group-home couch, until he secured employment, at which point, he would move into an apartment.

As they neared the group home in Alexandria, Mr. H. asked, "You hungry?"

"Starving," Curtis replied.

"That's good. It's lasagna night."

"Thank you for letting me crash. I won't stay long."

Mr. H. glanced at Curtis, then back to the road. "You're welcome."

With the afternoon sun high in the sky, Mr. H. parked in the driveway of the group home, next to Curtis's old Nissan SUV.

Although, it didn't appear old. It was freshly detailed, with four new tires.

"My car," Curtis said, his eyes bulging. "I thought it was falling apart."

Several years ago, Mr. H. had mentioned that his car was falling apart, with nobody to drive or maintain it.

"I know a good mechanic. He owed me a favor." Mr. H. winked at Curtis. "Besides, without a car, you'll be living on my couch forever."

"It looks great. Thank you." Curtis exited the van and circled his SUV.

Mr. H. exited his van and watched Curtis, with a small grin on his lips.

"Does it run okay?" Curtis asked.

"Runs great. I drove it around the block yesterday. It has a new battery. Spark plugs. Tune up. Some other things I can't remember."

Curtis had planned on walking and riding a bus to work, thereby limiting his job prospects to bus lines and walking distances. A working car was a huge advantage in the job market. "I don't know what to say."

PART V

Chasing the Dream

I know from experience that you should never give up on yourself or others, no matter what.

—George Foreman

CHAPTER 98

Parole

On the last day of March, Curtis drove through Alexandria. Landscape trucks parked across the city, their workers spreading mulch on the beautiful day. Yesterday, Curtis procured a job with Virginia Roadside Mowing, which did exactly as their name implied. They mowed roadsides for the state of Virginia. The grass was still too short to mow, but Curtis was due to start on Monday, picking up the roadside trash that had accumulated over the winter.

Curtis neared his old apartment complex. On impulse, he turned into the neighborhood and drove to his old apartment building. He parked along the curb, his SUV idling, inspecting the three-story apartment building. He thought about Destiny, wondering if she still lived in the same apartment. Curtis glanced at the time on his dashboard—*9:12 a.m.* His appointment with his parole officer was at 10:00 a.m.

So he drove to the nearby lot and parked in a visitor spot. He exited his SUV and went to the front door of the apartment building. He loitered out front for about ten minutes, until a mother and her baby struggled to exit the building, with her stroller wedged against the door. Curtis held open the door, allowing the mom to exit.

"Thank you," she said.

"You're welcome." Curtis entered the apartment building, as the mom pushed her stroller along the sidewalk.

He climbed the stairs to the third floor and knocked on Destiny's apartment—or at least where she had lived five years ago. Footsteps approached the door. The dead bolt unlatched. A woman opened the door a sliver, the chain taut.

"Who are you?" she asked, her brow furrowed, curlers in her dark hair.

"I'm Curtis Duffy. I used to live next door. I was looking for my friend Destiny. She used to live in your apartment."

"Ain't no Destiny here." She slammed the door in Curtis's face. The dead bolt latched.

Curtis let out a heavy breath. As he descended the stairs, he thought about the old man who had witnessed his fight with Leon Tolliver and had testified against him at his trial. Curtis thought he lived on the second floor. *Mr. Hopkins.* Curtis knocked on several second-floor apartments. Two didn't answer. One was a middle-aged man who worked nights and was annoyed that Curtis had woken him from his slumber.

At the fourth one, Mr. Hopkins opened the door. He stared at Curtis for a split second, then slammed shut his door, and latched the dead bolt. "I'm calling the police," he yelled through the door.

"Please don't," Curtis replied. "I'm not mad at you. It wasn't your fault I got into that fight. I was just looking for Destiny. She was the woman I was defending. Do you know where she is?"

"The one who lived upstairs?"

"Yes."

There was a long pause. Then he said, "She died in her apartment about two years ago."

"She died? Of what?"

"I think it was an overdose."

Curtis hung his head. "Sorry to bother you."

Curtis left the apartment building and returned to his SUV. In the driver's seat, he closed his eyes and tried to picture Destiny's face. It was blurry. He opened his eyes again and checked the time. *Almost 9:30.* Curtis started his Nissan, and drove to his meeting.

He found a parking lot for five bucks per hour. He walked the short distance to the probation and parole office—a nondescript five-story building. Curtis entered the building, signed in with the security guard, then rode the elevator.

On the ride to the top floor, he heard Taylor Wilde's angelic voice through the speakers.

He took what he wanted, but I'm still fighting.

He took what he wanted, but I'm still surviving.

He took what he wanted, but now I'm thriving.

Curtis clenched his fists.

The elevator door opened. Curtis stepped into the hall, oriented himself, and walked to the probation and parole office. He gave his name to the receptionist, then sat in the waiting room, along with seven other men and one woman. Nearly everyone tapped on their phones. Nobody made eye contact. Nobody appeared happy to be there.

Fifteen minutes later, the receptionist said, "Curtis Duffy."

Curtis stood from his seat and approached her desk.

"Officer Edmunds is ready for you." The receptionist pointed down the hall beyond her desk. "Last door on the right. His name's on the door."

"Thank you."

Curtis walked down the hall to the last door on the right. The placard on the open door read, Lorenzo Edmunds, Parole Officer. Curtis peeked into the office. "Officer Edmunds?"

Edmunds was on the desktop phone. He was middle-aged and stocky, with his polo shirt buttoned to his throat. He waved Curtis into his office. Then said into the receiver, "If you don't fill out the proper paperwork, you're in violation." He paused for a beat. "I don't wanna hear any excuses. You know the rules. I'm not your babysitter. Figure it out." Edmunds hung up the phone.

The parole officer glanced at the file on his desk and stood. "You must be Curtis Duffy."

"Yes, sir," Curtis replied, as he approached the wooden desk.

They shook hands.

"I'm Officer Edmunds, and I'll likely be your parole officer for the duration." Edmunds gestured to the chairs in front of his desk. "Have a seat."

Curtis sat before the parole officer, noticing his cleft palate repair scar on his upper lip.

"I know this is your first time on parole, so I suggest you pay attention to what I'm about to tell you, because, if you screw up, I have no problem sending you back to prison. Got it?"

"Yes, sir."

"Now listen up." Officer Edmunds rested his elbows on his desktop. "First, you must maintain a residence and a full-time job at all times." Edmunds opened the file on his desk. "I see you have a residence but no job yet."

"I got a job yesterday. Landscaping. I start next week."

"You'll need to fill out the paperwork in regard to your employer. If you change jobs, I need to know about it. Got me?"

"Yes, sir."

"You're required to report to me every other week in person, in my office. I suggest you make your appointments before you leave here today. The best times fill up fast."

Curtis nodded.

"I can and will show up to your residence or your place of employment at any time. I will *not*, under any circumstances, be denied entry. I can search your belongings anytime I want. Understand?"

"Yes, sir."

"You are not allowed to leave the state without written permission. You are not allowed to use drugs. You will submit to urinalysis or blood testing when instructed. Don't think you can get away with a little weed. It'll show up on your piss test, and I'll send you back to prison so fast it'll make your head spin." Edmunds raised his eyebrows. "Got me?"

"Yes, sir." Curtis deflated in his chair with each edict.

"You are not allowed to buy or possess a firearm or any other dangerous weapons. No knives. No guns. No Tasers. No stun guns. No blackjacks. No clubs. No brass knuckles. I don't even wanna see nunchucks. If it can be used to hurt someone, you can't have it. Got me?"

"Yes, sir," Curtis replied in monotone.

"You are not allowed to associate with anyone who has a criminal record. You are expected to obey all state and local laws." Edmunds handed Curtis a pamphlet. "Everything I just told you is in here."

Curtis took the pamphlet, entitled Rules and Regulations of Parole.

"I'm not your friend. I'm not your brother. And I'm not your daddy. You follow all the rules, we'll get along fine. You screw up, and I'll send you back to prison without hesitation. You got me?"

Curtis swallowed hard. "Yes, sir."

CHAPTER 99

Together Again

Chiming woke Curtis from his slumber. He stood from the couch, rubbing the sleep from his eyes. He grabbed his phone from the end table and silenced the alarm. The time read 4:30 a.m. He folded his sheet and blanket and tidied the couch. Curtis went to the downstairs bathroom, peed, and brushed his teeth. He changed into his running gear, downed a glass of water, and left the group home.

It was cool and dark, the temperature in the fifties. By streetlight and moonlight, he ran to West Potomac High School. He hopped the fence and entered the stadium and track area. He wondered if trespassing could get him sent back to prison. He jogged to the back corner of the track, as far away from potential school security guards as possible. He leaned against the chain link fence and stretched. He did a few active warm-up drills, like high knees, butt-kicks, bounding, shuffling, and lunges.

Once he was loose, he completed ten one-hundred-meter sprints, with thirty seconds rest in between. His goal was to complete the sprints with little to no degradation in speed from the first sprint to the last. He could do five without much fatigue. After the sprints, Curtis worked on football specific footwork—transitioning from a backpedal to a full sprint, simulating turning and running. He planted and changed directions, simulating driving on a running play or covering a short passing route. He finished with a grueling 800-meter backpedal, keeping his butt low, his thighs and hip flexors burning.

Curtis hopped the fence to exit the stadium and jogged back to the group home. His legs were heavy and on the verge of cramping as he returned. He entered through the kitchen door. He grabbed the ripest banana and ate it, hoping to prevent cramping. He washed it down with several glasses of water. He opened the trash can lid and tossed his banana peel.

Something caught his eye. Or rather *someone* caught his eye. He opened the trash can lid, brushed aside a napkin and his banana peel, to reveal a *Sports Illustrated* magazine. Curtis grabbed the magazine. It was in perfect condition, as if it had never been opened. The headline read "Together Again." The cover featured three smiling men wearing Philadelphia Eagles gear. The heavyset man in the green sweater was Curtis's former college head coach, Frank Goodman, now the new head coach of the Philadelphia Eagles. The wide receiver wearing number 80 was Kavon Drake. The quarterback wearing number 7 was perennial pro-bowler and Eagles legend, Justin Love.

Curtis tossed the magazine back into the garbage.

CHAPTER 100

Super Bowl Bound?

Cars and trucks zipped past at seventy-five miles per hour and faster. Diesel and gasoline permeated the air. Curtis hiked on the roadside, wearing an orange vest, holding a black plastic bag. He bent over and picked up cans and bottles and anything else that might cause a hazard when they mowed next week. He picked up fast-food bags too, even though they would eventually biodegrade.

His mind wandered while he worked. He thought about Justin Love and Coach Goodman. Coach Frank Goodman had won two national championships with Justin Love in three seasons. After Justin Love had declared early for the draft, Coach Goodman and the Central Virginia University Lions were ranked in the top ten each season, but they didn't win another national championship.

Justin Love was drafted number one overall by the Philadelphia Eagles. Despite playing on a bad team, with a terrible defense, Justin Love collected enough passing stats to win the NFL Offensive Rookie of the Year. His second season was much improved, with Justin making his first pro bowl, and the Eagles winning as many as they lost. His third season was another improvement, with the Eagles fielding the best offense in the NFL, and Justin leading the league in every passing statistic. Unfortunately, the Eagles barely missed the playoffs because of another historically bad defense. After the disappointing season, Justin had been secretly recorded criticizing the head coach and the defensive coordinator, saying, "They don't know what they're doing. Give me an average defense, and I'll deliver a Super Bowl."

The clip went viral. The owner of the Eagles, Jeffrey Lurie, appeared to be listening because he fired the head coach and the entire defensive staff. At Justin's likely urging, he hired two-time national championship coach, Frank Goodman, a renowned defensive mind. It was a match made in Super Bowl heaven. Coach and quarterback back together again.

Curtis wondered if Coach Williams would serve as the new Defensive Coordinator with the Eagles. It was likely, as new head coaches often brought their staffs with them, as they moved up the football ranks.

Curtis cinched his full trash bag. A honk jolted him from his thoughts. An SUV sped past. Someone threw trash from the passenger door. *Fuck them.*

At the end of the day, the foreman drove the quad-cab truck on the shoulder, picking up the full trash bags and retrieving the employees who had collected trash from twenty-five miles of roadside along I-95.

Curtis was the first to be picked up. The foreman was a scrawny white guy, his arms and neck filled with tatts, and a dip in his lower lip. Curtis sat on the tailgate, as the foreman drove at about thirty miles per hour. Each time he stopped at a trash bag, Curtis hopped off the tailgate, grabbed the bag, and tossed it in the truck bed. They continued like this until they found the next employee, at which point, that man took Curtis's place on the tailgate, and Curtis sat in front with the foreman.

The foreman spit in a disposable cup. "This is the best part of your day. Now you get to sit on your ass and get paid, until we get back to the shop."

A *Washington Post* newspaper sat on the bench seat between them.

Curtis touched the paper. "You mind if I read this?"

"Be my guest. You're prob'ly the only motherfucker out here besides me that can read English."

Curtis read the paper, while the foreman picked up the rest of the employees. The rest of the guys were Latino. They were mostly quiet on the ride home, but they spoke in Spanish to each other. As Curtis neared the sports section's end, he fixated on an advertisement.

Do you dream of playing in the NFL?

Are you more than a fan?

Would you like the real NFL experience?

Would you like a tryout with the Washington Commanders?

Three winners will be invited to training camp this summer.

CHAPTER 101

Fan Fiction

Curtis entered the Washington Commanders practice facility in Ashburn, Virginia, along with a small crowd of fans and men dressed in athletic gear. They were ushered to a line of tables to sign in with staff from the Washington Commanders. Curtis filled out the paperwork, signed the release form in case of injury, and paid his two hundred bucks. In return, he was given a Washington Commanders T-shirt, and a number to attach to his shirt, like he was in a track meet.

Curtis had borrowed the money from Mr. H., promising to pay him back as soon as he received his first paycheck. Mr. H. had expressed reservations about the tryout, telling Curtis that open tryouts were not typical for the NFL. Curtis had cited Vince Papale, the former Eagles special teamer who had been discovered at a tryout—just like this one.

Once he had finished his paperwork, Curtis and the other athletes were ushered to a waiting area that overlooked the practice field. Through the massive panorama windows, the men laughed and joked and gawked at the turf fields. Curtis scanned his competition, surprised by their lack of fitness. Most of them looked like they'd spent the last decade on the couch.

After signups were completed, they were ushered to the locker room. The carpet was burgundy and gold. The wooden lockers were like small closets. Flat screens hung from the walls, broadcasting highlights from the great Washington teams of the eighties. John Riggins was currently on the screen—affectionately known as the Diesel—who ran over a Dolphins defender en route to a critical Super Bowl touchdown.

The other men gaped at the locker room, carrying on like awestruck fans. Curtis wasn't there as a fan. He was there to earn a trip to training camp. If he could do that, he might be able to earn a spot on the roster.

Curtis and the men claimed their lockers. They dressed in their cleats, shorts, and Washington Commanders T-shirts. They affixed their numbers to their shirts. Curtis's number ended with the letters DB, which stood for defensive back, his position. Curtis used the restroom, drank some of his water, then walked out to the practice field.

The morning sun shone in their faces. They were greeted by the same support staff who had helped sign them in, along with a few assistant coaches who Curtis had never heard of. A local NBC affiliate set up their camera on the sideline.

One of the coaches, a bear of a man, said, "Welcome to the Washington Commanders Training Facility. Thank you all for coming. We're gonna do a series of drills to determine your speed, strength, agility, and your overall football skills. Many of these drills are the same drills used at the NFL Combine. The top three football players will be invited to training camp this summer. Do your best and don't forget to have fun. It's football. It's supposed to be fun."

They were divided into eight groups: quarterbacks, running backs, offensive linemen, wide receivers or tight ends, defensive lineman, linebackers, defensive backs, and kickers or punters.

Eight stations were set up around the practice fields. The defensive backs went to the forty-yard dash first. Curtis was horrified that they didn't have time to warm up and stretch. *Shit. I should've warmed up and stretched before I checked in.* Curtis took his spot at the end of the line, doing some active stretches on the turf, while the thirty or so men in front of him ran their forties. As Curtis stretched, he noticed some of the results on the automatic timer forty-yards away. The times were dreadful, with very few defensive backs even breaking five seconds. By the time Curtis's turn came, he was still a little stiff. Curtis felt the stiffness when he tried to explode from his sprinter's stance. It felt like his legs were in concrete. His time reflected his stiffness, as he ran a 4.62, which was slower than the 4.4 he had run in college and even in recent workouts.

Despite his slow time, one of the coaches said, "Nice job, 112." He referred to Curtis's number. "That's the fastest so far."

After his one sprint, they moved to the next drill, which was the three-cone drill. Curtis was disappointed that he didn't get another crack at the forty, knowing he would do better with his legs a little warmer.

The three-cone drill was used to test agility. Three cones were placed five yards apart from each other, forming a right angle. One of the coaches demonstrated the drill, moving at a slow speed. He started in a sprinter's stance. He jogged to the first cone, touched the line, pivoted, jogged back to the start, touched the line, pivoted again, jogged around the outside of the second cone, and continued to the third cone. He jogged around the third cone and jogged back to the start.

Curtis was familiar with the drill. He had done it at CVU and had practiced it independently. Again, Curtis waited at the back of the line, doing some static stretches and shaking out his legs to keep warm. This drill was a shit show, with many of the athletes forgetting how to perform the drill. Several men fell to the turf, laughing, like it was all a joke.

When Curtis's turn came, he was warm and ready. He sprinted through the drill, staying low to change directions rapidly.

When he finished, the coach said, "Whoa. Six point seven-eight. That's impressive."

Curtis nailed the rest of the drills. He was clearly superior to the others in his position group. By the end of the day, he was confident he had earned a trip to training camp. They were given water and herded onto the bleachers, while the coaches chose the winners.

With the cameras rolling on the bear-like coach, he said, "First, I'd like to thank everyone for all their hard work this morning. I saw some real fire out there. You're all winners in my book, but three men stood out above the rest." He reached into an envelope and read from the paper. "Congratulations, Floyd Reeves, Izell Joseph, and Curtis Duffy."

Curtis and his fellow winners stood from the bleachers, grinning from ear to ear. Everyone clapped. They descended the bleachers and shook hands with the coaches. They were given special passes to training camp and tickets to the first preseason game against Minnesota.

"What's this?" Curtis asked one of the coaches, while holding up his tickets.

"The tickets are a bonus," he said. "They figured you guys would like to see a game too. There's an extra one to bring a friend. Pretty cool, *huh*?"

Curtis furrowed his brow. "I thought this was to go to camp, like to actually be in camp."

The coach cocked his head. "You mean, as a player?"

"Yeah."

The coach laughed.

Curtis clenched his jaw and handed the coach his tickets and training camp pass. "Give this to someone else."

The coach stopped laughing and took the tickets and pass. "Are you serious?"

Curtis walked away.

CHAPTER 102

Dream or Delusion

Curtis ate dinner with Mr. H. and the group-home boys. The dining room had seen better days. The carpet was stained, and the table was chipped, courtesy of thousands of meals with unruly boys.

"How did you do in the forty?" Mr. H. asked, sitting across from Curtis at the dinner table.

Curtis swallowed a bite of his cheeseburger. "Four six two."

Mr. H. frowned. "You're faster than that."

"I'm the fastest in the whole school," ten-year-old Marcus said with a gap-toothed grin.

"Are not," one of the other boys said.

"Am too."

Marcus was chubby and short for his age, likely not the fastest kid in school.

"You're slower than doodoo," one of the other boys said.

"You're slower than poop," Marcus countered.

"You're slower than dookie."

"You're slower than *s-h-i-t*."

"That's *enough*," Mr. H. said. "We're trying to eat."

The group-home boys giggled.

"I wasn't warmed up," Curtis said. "We did the forty right away, without even stretching."

Mr. H. nodded, while chewing.

"I did better in the three-cone. I got a six point seven-eight."

Mr. H. wiped his mouth with his napkin. "That's more than good enough to play defensive back in the NFL. What else did they have you do?"

"We benched. I did nineteen reps with 225."

"That's above average for a defensive back."

"We did some ball drills too."

"How did that go? Did you feel nervous?"

"No. I felt great. Didn't drop a single ball." Curtis let out a heavy breath. "Too bad none of it mattered. I feel really stupid."

"You're not stupid," Marcus said.

"Thanks, Marcus," Curtis replied.

"You're thinking about this all wrong," Mr. H. said. "The fact that you believed this tryout was for real is a good thing. You were able to simulate the pressure involved with trying out for the NFL, and you passed with flying colors."

"What good is being good at trying out if I never get a shot to really try out?"

"NFL teams are constantly looking at free agents, even undrafted ones. In fact, tons of guys on NFL teams were never drafted. You just need to find a way to get on somebody's radar."

"How do I do that?"

"You need to stay in shape and stay ready. You need to play football. Competitive football. Hone your skills. Working out alone isn't enough. I know some guys who play in a flag league—"

"*Flag?*"

"It's competitive. It'll sharpen your skills."

Curtis slumped his shoulders. "I don't see how playing flag gets me anywhere."

"It's a start," Mr. H. said. "It might be fun. Remember that? Remember when you played football in the backyard for fun?"

"That was a long time ago." Curtis swirled a fry around his pool of ketchup.

"I'm gonna be a running back for the Cowboys," Marcus said.

"The Cowboys suck," said one of the other boys.

Mr. H. pointed at the boy. "What did I tell you about using that word?"

The boy shrank. "Sorry."

Curtis wondered if he was as delusional as Marcus.

CHAPTER 103

The Mount Vernon Marauders

On Tuesday after work, Curtis met the flag football team at Mount Vernon District Park. There was no football field, no lines, just a massive expanse of grass.

Before practice, Curtis talked with Byron Church, Mr. H.'s friend and the captain of the Mount Vernon Marauders. Byron was average height, well-built, with a wide nose and a toothy grin. According to Byron, they were the defending champs of the Northern Virginia Flag Football League, or NVFFL for short. It was a five-on-five passing league.

Byron gestured to the six other guys on the team, all fit young men in their twenties and early thirties. "The tall guy, Beau, he played at Old Dominion. He was a helluva tight end. Maurice—the short guy—he was a Division III All-American running back at Emory & Henry. Quick as hell."

Everyone on the team had college experience. Byron had played wide receiver at the University of Richmond and in the CFL for three seasons for the Saskatchewan Roughriders. He was an athletic trainer now.

"Russel said you played safety at CVU," Byron said.

"For about a minute," Curtis replied. "In 2016."

Byron's eyes bulged. "You won a national championship."

Curtis shook his head. "I didn't finish the season."

Byron nodded. He didn't speak for a moment, no doubt wondering why Curtis hadn't finished the season. "Well, let's see what you got."

CHAPTER 104

It's a Start

On the game's final play, the Arlington Eagles lined up with three receivers on one side, a single receiver against Curtis. The single receiver was their best player. Curtis thought the other receivers would run short routes to keep the Marauder defenders near the line of scrimmage, negating the possibility of double coverage against their best receiver.

On the snap, Curtis was proven right. The receiver sprinted deep, running a post pattern. Curtis ran with the speedy wide receiver, stride for stride. The quarterback launched a bomb in their direction. It was a perfect pass. One that should've landed in the receiver's outstretched hands for the touchdown. One that should've won the game for the Eagles. But Curtis leaped into the air and snagged the football. As he landed in the opponent's end zone, he noticed that the receiver's momentum had carried him out of the end zone. Curtis should've taken a knee. They had already won. But Curtis planted hard and sprinted the other way. His teammates blocked the Eagles, clearing a path for Curtis to run the length of the field for a meaningless Marauders touchdown.

But it didn't feel meaningless to Curtis.

The man in the striped shirt raised his hands over his head. Curtis handed the football to the referee. His teammates mobbed him in the end zone. He couldn't help but smile, showing his crooked overbite. It was the same high he felt when he'd scored against Clemson almost six years ago.

The stands were mostly empty, but he heard the group-home boys cheering his name. Mr. H. stood in the stands, clapping.

CHAPTER 105

Opportunity Knocks

In the back seat of his SUV, Curtis changed from his work pants into a pair of sweatpants. He slipped on his sneakers, grabbed his cleats, and exited his vehicle. A cool breeze chilled his ears. Dark clouds moved in from the north, threatening rain. It had been that way all day. Curtis had thought they might cancel work, but they had managed a full day of mowing along I-95, without a single drop of rain falling from the sky.

The Mount Vernon Marauders huddled near Byron's BMW, shooting the shit. Curtis approached his teammates and was greeted warmly.

Curtis glanced at the clouds. "We're still practicing, right?"

Byron checked the clouds too. "Might as well. We're here. A little rain never hurt anybody."

"I'm gonna warmup," Curtis said.

"I'll go with you," Beau said. "I need to stretch out my legs. Been at a desk all day."

Beau wore a headband, like Patrick Mahomes, to corral his long brown locks. Curtis and Beau jogged around the expansive grass field at Mount Vernon District Park. Beau had an effortless gait, his long legs taking gigantic strides.

As they jogged, Curtis said, "Byron told me you played tight end at Old Dominion."

"That was a long time ago," Beau replied. "I graduated in 2012."

"He said you were really good. Did you try to go pro?"

"I was in camp with the Giants, but I was out with the first cuts. I was in over my head. The jump in talent from ODU to the pros was like trying to jump over the Grand Canyon. You went to Central Virginia, right?"

"Yeah."

"I would've been better prepared had I gone to a Power 5 school. You know what it's like. At CVU, you practiced with a dozen guys every day who play in the NFL now. A few were probably high draft choices. And you played teams with the same caliber of players. At ODU, we had one or two guys who might make a practice squad."

"I only played one season and didn't even finish the season, so I'm not sure I know much of anything."

Beau glanced at Curtis. "Don't sell yourself short. You were good enough to get there, and you looked pretty damn good on Saturday. That pick you made at the end of the game was some Deion shit."

"Thanks." Curtis smiled, keeping his mouth shut. As they neared their starting point, Curtis asked, "You wanna run another one, or are you good?"

"I'm good."

They sat in the grass and stretched.

The rest of the Marauders approached them. Maurice carried a mesh bag filled with footballs. Another guy carried orange cones. Most of the Marauders started active stretching, doing high knees, bounding, high kicks, and side squats.

Byron kneeled next to Curtis and Beau, tightening and retying his cleats. "How did your brother's tryout go?"

Curtis stopped stretching, his interest piqued.

"It's at the end of this month," Beau replied, as he bent forward, stretching his hamstrings.

"Who's the tryout with?" Curtis asked.

"The Carolina Panthers. My brother's a long snapper. They invited a bunch of UDFAs. I doubt they'll sign him, but you never know."

"You think I could try out?" Curtis asked.

Beau stood from the grass and brushed off his rear end. "It's invitation only."

Curtis stood too. "Is it at their practice facility?"

"I think so."

"When is it exactly?"

Byron stood too.

"You can't just show up, if that's what you're thinking," Beau said.

"Why not?" Curtis asked.

Byron laughed.

Curtis frowned.

"I'm laughing, but it's not a terrible idea," Byron said.

"I'll give you the details but don't drop my name or my brother's," Beau said, pointing at Curtis.

After practice, Curtis walked with Byron to the parking lot. A misty rain fell from the sky, so light that the tiny drops appeared to levitate.

"Hey, man. I'm sorry for laughing at you earlier," Byron said.

"It's okay. It *is* a crazy idea," Curtis replied.

"Maybe. Maybe not. I went to a tryout with Atlanta that was probably a lot like the one in Carolina. Now this was nine years ago, but I doubt things have changed that much. When I got there, I signed in with someone who worked for the Falcons. I don't know what he did, but he wasn't a coach or an executive. I didn't see the coaches until I got onto the practice field." They stopped in front of Byron's BMW. "I think you could finesse your way into this workout."

"I don't understand," Curtis replied.

"The people that sign you in will have a list—"

"Which I won't be on."

Byron nodded. "True. But all you have to do is name-drop the GM. Tell them that so and so told me to come down and try out. Tell them that you traveled a long way. Tell them that you have an email from the GM or something."

"What if they call the GM?"

"They might. Then again, they might not. What's your forty?"

"I can run a 4.4 if I get a decent start."

"If you can do that before they figure out who you are, I bet they'll at least let you finish the workout."

Curtis nodded, pondering his crazy idea.

Byron continued. "I know it's less than two weeks away, but if you need some training, I can help. We can work on your start, make sure you run that 4.4."

"That would be great, but I can't afford you."

"This isn't about money. I'm offering my help as a friend."

CHAPTER 106

The Permission Slip

Curtis sat across from his Parole Officer. A framed poster hung on the wall behind the PO's blockhead that read No Excuses. No Drama. No Complaints.

"How's the job going?" Officer Edmunds asked, his elbows on his desktop.

"It's fine," Curtis replied.

"Any problems with your boss or coworkers?"

"No."

Edmunds squinted at Curtis. "I don't know anyone who does landscaping or construction that doesn't have some complaints."

"It's not what I wanna do for the rest of my life, but I understand that I don't have many options, so I'm trying to be grateful for what I do have."

Edmunds drew back, his eyebrows arched. "I don't get too many responses like that." He paused for an instant. "How's your living situation?"

"It's cramped at the group home, but I'm saving some money. I should have an apartment in a month or so. Of course, I'll fill out the paperwork and get approval before I move."

Officer Edmunds closed Curtis's file. "Well, that's about it. I'll see you in two weeks."

Curtis cleared his throat. "I have a football tryout coming up on April 30. It's in North Carolina."

Officer Edmunds scowled. "Football tryout? For what? A pro team?"

"For the Carolina Panthers."

"You're telling me that you gotta tryout with the Carolina Panthers after spending five years in prison?"

Curtis wrung his hands in his lap. "It's not specifically for me. It's for a bunch of undrafted free agents. I don't think I have much of a chance of being invited to training camp, but I wanted to try."

Edmunds leaned back in his chair and crossed his arms over his barrel chest. "You really trying to see some girl in North Carolina?"

"No, sir. It's a tryout."

"It's short notice."

"I know. I'm sorry, but I was really hoping to go. It would only be overnight. I would leave on Friday, and I'd be back on Saturday night."

Edmunds sighed and rested his hands on his desktop. "If you can get the paperwork to me by the end of the day tomorrow, I'll consider it."

"Thank you," Curtis replied. "I'll email it tomorrow."

"I don't know who's running this tryout, but don't give me some generic phone number. I need to talk to whoever invited you to make sure it's legit. I'll be double-checking their credentials, so don't try anything stupid."

CHAPTER 107

Crossing State Lines

Curtis drove past the sign that read Welcome to North Carolina. A sinking feeling came from deep in the pit of his stomach. Curtis hadn't filled out the parole paperwork for the tryout. That was a nonstarter, as Officer Edmunds had made it clear he would check the veracity of the tryout. Curtis had two choices—don't go or go in secret. He chose the latter.

Technically, there was no way for Edmunds to know that Curtis was violating his parole. Curtis didn't have an ankle monitor. He figured the only way he would get caught would be if he got a ticket. He checked his speedometer reflexively.

His phone nested in a suction-cup mount, displaying the directions to Charlotte, North Carolina. It was about six hours away, with a little traffic. He had taken off Friday from work, not wanting tired legs for the tryout on Saturday, provided he got the opportunity. His rational side thought it was a waste of time, money, and gas, not to mention a serious parole violation. The dreamer in him thought, *You never know.*

Late in the afternoon, Curtis parked at the Motel 6, fifteen minutes from the practice field in downtown Charlotte. He would've preferred to stay closer to the tryout, but he would save one hundred bucks with the discount lodging in the suburbs.

Curtis checked in and paid with cash. He hadn't booked a room in advance because he didn't want a record on his credit card. He took his old suitcase to his room. It was a standard room, with two double beds and a television.

He walked to the Cracker Barrel a few blocks away and ordered dinner—roasted chicken, mashed potatoes, and salad. He sat at a table for two along the wall. The walls were cluttered with signs, paraphernalia, and knickknacks from a bygone era. A sign above Curtis's head read Standard Oil. Several framed black-and-white photos of forties' and fifties' era cars surrounded the sign.

The restaurant was mostly full that Friday night, with weary travelers eating with slumped shoulders. Curtis tapped on his phone, while he waited for his food. He was on the Carolina Panthers official website. He read the webpage that detailed the staff, further cementing the names and titles to memory. Over the past week, he had memorized the sixteen staff members in football operations and their titles. If someone asked him a question about a particular staff member, Curtis could then respond, *Oh, so and so. Yes, I talked to the director of football operations last week. He told me to come down. He said that it would be fine.*

He had also done a deep internet dive on all of them, searching for a possible in. He had found one thing that might come in handy. The Vice President of Player Personnel, Morris Dickenson, had a nephew who played running back for Central Virginia University. He didn't know the nephew personally, as Curtis had left CVU prior to the nephew's arrival.

CHAPTER 108

The Tryout

Curtis arrived at the practice facility in downtown Charlotte thirty minutes early. The facility consisted of two grass football fields and an indoor turf field. He exited his car and stretched in the parking lot. Curtis watched the other athletes arrive and enter the indoor practice field, which resembled a giant tent. Curtis waited, then entered the indoor practice facility right before the arrival time. This way, he thought, they would have less time to figure out if he was supposed to be there.

At least ten athletes loitered in the waiting area near the entrance, talking among themselves. Many of the large men wore athletic gear from their former colleges. Several guys were from the University of North Carolina. Several more were from Coastal Carolina. One wore an orange shirt from Clemson. They all wore name tags on their chests. One guy resembled Beau and wore an Old Dominion University T-shirt. Curtis guessed it was Beau's brother, but Curtis didn't dare introduce himself, as he didn't want to get anyone into trouble.

Two young women stood behind a desk, with a sign that read, Welcome Sign in Here. Curtis approached the women, his heart thumping in his chest.

"Welcome," the young blonde said, with a smile. "Are you here for the tryout?"

"Yes, ma'am," Curtis replied.

The brunette glanced at her clipboard.

"Your name?" the blonde asked.

"Curtis Duffy."

"Everyone's already signed in," the brunette said.

The blonde glanced at her clipboard, her brow furrowed. "I'm sorry. We don't have your name on the list. Did you receive an invitation?"

"Mr. Dickenson invited me. It was last-minute," Curtis said.

The blonde turned to the brunette. "Is he here this morning?"

"I think so. I'll call his office." The brunette stepped away from the table and tapped on her cell phone.

"I'm sorry about this," the blonde said.

"It's okay," Curtis replied, watching the brunette out of the corner of his eye.

The brunette returned to the table and addressed the blonde. "He's not at his desk. Just write him a name tag. Let them sort it out on the field."

"What was your name again?" the blonde asked.

"Curtis Duffy."

"Your position?"

"Defensive back."

The blonde wrote his name on a blank name tag along with DB, then handed Curtis the sticker. "Put that on whatever shirt you're planning to wear."

"Thank you." Curtis slapped the name tag on his gray CVU T-shirt.

Then she handed him a clipboard with a pen attached. "You'll need to fill these out too."

On the clipboard was a liability waiver and a contact information form.

They were given thirty minutes to warm up and stretch. Curtis jogged around the indoor football field three times, stretched, then did some active stretching. Once he was loose, he worked on his start, knowing his forty time would likely be the most important test.

Several coaches rounded up the athletes. They all wore black polo shirts with the Carolina Panthers logo on their chest.

A heavyset coach said, "I'm Coach Gogan. I'm the assistant offensive line coach. We're gonna start by getting your height and weight and wingspan. Then we'll run the forty and the three-cone. Then we'll break you up by position group for some position-specific agilities."

Curtis was last in line to be measured and weighed. When it was his turn, Curtis stepped on the scale.

An assistant coach checked his height too. "Six feet even. Two hundred ten pounds."

One of the staff members scanned the paper on his clipboard. "There's nobody named Curtis Duffy here."

"Mr. Dickenson called me. It was late-notice," Curtis said, sweat accumulating under his armpits.

"Write his name at the bottom," said the assistant coach.

As they queued for the forty-yard dash, several men in suits entered the football field and coalesced near the finish line, along with the assistant coaches. Curtis recognized Morris Dickenson from his photo, with his grayish-white hair and manicured beard to match. Curtis hid in the back of the line, trying not to think about the fact that he'd likely only get one shot at the forty. The executives would wonder who he was, and the coaches would say Dickenson had invited him, and then the ruse would be over. His only hope was to run fast, very fast.

When Curtis's turn came, he jumped several times, getting his legs ready. He took the sprinter's stance that he'd worked on with Byron. He took a deep breath and exploded out of his stance like a missile. Curtis knew right away he would run a good time. His legs felt light and fast. His feet barely touched the turf. In an instant, he blasted through the finish line, not stopping for twenty more yards. Curtis pivoted and jogged back toward the finish line. The coaches and executives gaped at him. The automatic timer read 4.38. Curtis grinned at the timer, shocked and thrilled that he'd broken 4.4.

He slowed to a walk, as he heard someone ask, "Who is that?"

"Curtis Duffy. He said you invited him," one of the coaches said.

"I've never heard of him." Morris Dickenson marched to Curtis, his face like stone. "We need to talk. Over here." Morris led Curtis to the sideline, out of earshot of the coaches and executives. "What is this?" He glanced at Curtis's CVU T-shirt. "Do you know my nephew?"

"No, sir," Curtis replied.

"Why did you tell Coach Gogan that I invited you here?"

"I found your name on the Panthers website. I'm sorry. I was hoping for a chance to try out."

Morris shook his head, incredulous. "Let me get this straight. You found my name on the internet, then used it to lie your way into this tryout?"

Curtis nodded. "I'm sorry, sir. I just want a chance."

Morris chuckled to himself. "I've seen a lot in this league, but this is a first. Did you play at CVU?"

"Yes, sir."

"Safety or corner?"

"Safety."

Morris stared at Curtis for a long beat. "I'm pretty familiar with CVU. I've scouted them for years. How come I've never heard of you?"

"I only played one season. I was expelled for marijuana." Curtis didn't bother telling him that it wasn't his marijuana, which he knew made him sound like a liar.

Morris let out a heavy breath.

"If you give me a chance, you won't regret it."

"You can finish the tryout."

CHAPTER 109

Ex-Con

Curtis sat on the sideline bench, changing his shoes. He smiled to himself, recreating the tryout in his mind. He remembered the forty, which was a full tenth of a second faster than anyone else. He killed the three-cone drill too. His agility and ball drills had been nearly flawless.

Morris Dickenson approached, his face stoic.

Curtis stood from the bench in his socks.

Morris held out his hand. "Nice job."

Curtis shook his hand. "Thank you, sir."

"You only played one year at CVU?"

"Yes, sir."

"Did you play anywhere else? JUCO?"

"No, sir. I tried to go to a JUCO school but ..." Curtis trailed off, not wanting to reveal any more.

"You obviously have the raw ability. I'm surprised you couldn't get into a JUCO program, especially after playing at CVU." Morris narrowed his dark eyes. "You get into trouble?"

Curtis dipped his head, embarrassed.

"We do background checks on our players."

"I was arrested."

Morris exhaled. "For what?"

Curtis cleared his throat. "Aggravated assault."

"How many years were you in prison?"

"Five." Curtis raised his gaze. "But that's all behind me. I was paroled early for good behavior."

"How old are you?"

"Twenty-four."

Morris paused for a moment, doing the math in his head. "You must've just gotten out."

"It's been a month."

"You obviously kept yourself in good shape."

"I did my best to train while I was inside."

Morris nodded. "Well, good luck to you." The executive walked away.

"Thank you for the opportunity," Curtis said to the man's back.

Morris raised a single hand in acknowledgment, but he didn't look back.

Curtis thought, *I'll never hear from him again.*

★★★

Curtis left the indoor practice facility and stepped to his SUV. He climbed into the driver's seat and tossed his duffel bag on the passenger's seat. His phone buzzed again from the side pocket of his bag. He retrieved his cell phone and checked his notifications.

> **Byron:** Good luck this a.m. U can do it. Remember. Loose is fast. Fast is loose
> **Byron:** How did it go? The guys are pulling for u
> **Mr. H.:** Are you on your way home? How was it? Call me when you get a chance.

Curtis texted Byron.

> **Curtis:** It went great. I ran a 4.38. Auto time. Thank you for your help. I don't think I could've done it w/o u

Curtis set his phone in the cradle, started his vehicle, and drove toward the interstate. Once he was out of downtown Charlotte and on I-85 North, he settled in the right lane and watched his speed. Curtis scanned his rearview mirror, making sure no police car was in sight.

He grabbed his cell phone and called Mr. H. on Speakerphone. Then he set his phone back in the suction-cup cradle on his dashboard.

"Hey, Curtis," Mr. H. said through the phone. "Where are you?"

"I just left Charlotte. I should be home in five or six hours," Curtis replied, his voice monotone.

"How was everything? Did they let you work out?"

"I went through the workout."

"That's great. How did you do?"

"I ran a 4.38 forty with auto time."

"That's *outstanding*. What about the rest of the workout?"

Curtis spotted a police car in his sideview mirror, approaching at a high rate of speed, its lights flashing. He let off the accelerator, despite not speeding. Curtis gripped the steering wheel, his knuckles white, as the police car sped past.

"Curtis? You still there?" Mr. H. asked.

"I'm here. Sorry. A police car just passed me," Curtis replied, his voice still subdued.

"We can talk when you get home. I don't want you getting a ticket because you're on your cell phone."

"It's fine. You're on Speaker. The rest of the workout was better than I expected."

"You all right?"

"Yeah. I'm fine. Why?"

"Sounds like it went great, but you don't seem happy."

"After the workout, I spoke with the VP of Player Personnel. He wanted to know why I only had one year of college ball." Curtis took a deep cleansing breath. "I told him everything. Now I'm regretting it because, after that, he walked away from me, like he wasn't interested."

"You did the right thing," Mr. H. replied. "They'll find out anyway. It's better to be upfront and honest."

Curtis rubbed the back of his neck. "I know. But I thought I nailed the tryout, and now I don't think they'll give me a chance. Is this what it's like to be an ex-con? People hold it over my head for the rest of my life?"

"Some people. But you can't worry about those people. You can only control what *you* do. Your effort. Your heart. Your perseverance. It took guts to go down there without an invitation. It took effort, preparation, and heart to do what you did this morning."

CHAPTER 110

Back to Work

Curtis hiked along I-95, the line trimmer rumbling in his hands. He trimmed the grass around signs and posts, anything the tractors couldn't reach. His pant legs below his knees were stained green from the lush spring grass. Cars and trucks zipped by at seventy miles per hour, leaving gasoline and diesel fumes in their wake.

With the grass growing like gangbusters, Curtis worked late in the afternoon, until the foreman finally appeared in his truck. Curtis hung the trimmer on the rack and climbed into the front passenger seat of the pickup. His head hurt from hours of noxious fumes and noise pollution from the traffic and the line trimmer.

The Latino guys were already in the back seat, chatting in Spanish. Curtis glanced back at them and nodded.

The foreman must've noticed because he said, "They don't like to sit up here with me."

Curtis stared out the windshield, wondering if this would be his life.

The foreman continued. "What happened to you on Friday?"

"I had an appointment."

"I figured you were done." He lifted his chin to the rearview mirror and the guys in the back seat. "They're the only ones who can take this shit."

Curtis gestured to the *Washington Post* on the seat. "Mind if I read your paper?"

"Go ahead."

Curtis scanned the paper, reading some of the front page, most of the sports section, and hardly any of the business section. He gaped at the picture on the front page of the entertainment section, portraying a glamourous singer onstage. The headline read "Taylor Wilde gives five million dollars to help survivors of sexual violence."

★★★

By the time Curtis clocked out and climbed into his car, it was nearly 7:30 p.m. He still had a two-hour weightlifting workout to complete. Thankfully, his gym was open until midnight. He planned to drive home, eat some leftovers for dinner, then go straight to the gym. If the traffic cooperated, he might make it to bed by eleven, which would give him six hours of sleep.

He opened his center console and retrieved his cell phone. Virginia Roadside Mowing didn't permit personal cell phones while working. Curtis glanced at his notifications. He had a few texts, calls, and messages. Nothing from his contacts, so they were likely spam calls. He checked his texts first. He deleted the texts and blocked the person trying to sell him health insurance and another offering a credit card.

Curtis checked his phone messages. One message was from Nissan—or someone posing as a Nissan representative—offering an extended warranty. Another message was from someone offering him a business loan. The final message was from the Panthers.

"Hello, Curtis. This is Morris Dickenson. Please call me when you have a chance. My direct number is 704-555-9122."

Curtis sat upright, his face taut. He checked the time of Morris's call. It was less than two hours ago. Curtis tapped Morris's phone number.

"This is Morris Dickenson," he answered.

"Mr. Dickenson, this is Curtis Duffy. I was returning your call."

"Yes. I was calling to invite you to training camp."

Curtis was stunned, his mouth ajar.

"Curtis?"

"Yes, sir. What does this mean exactly?"

"Well, it means you'll need to be here for rookie minicamp, which begins on May 16th and ends on the 18th. After rookie minicamp, we'll have OTAs, which runs from the end of May until mid-June. Then we're off until summer training camp, which starts in late July."

OTA stood for organized team activities, which was the NFL version of spring practice.

"Does this mean I have a chance to make the team?" Curtis asked.

"This is an opportunity to compete for a spot on the roster," Morris Dickenson replied.

Curtis beamed. "Thank you, sir. You won't regret this."

"You're welcome."

"Will I get paid during camp? I'm not asking for anything. I just need to know how much money to save."

Morris chuckled. "It's $850 per week."

"That's a lot. That's good for me. Where am I supposed to stay?"

"Most free agents get a short-term apartment near the facility."

Morris answered a few more questions about housing and how many days in advance Curtis should arrive in Charlotte. After the call ended, Curtis's smile receded, replaced by nausea.

CHAPTER 111

What's Fair

Officer Edmunds scowled. "What do you want? Spit it out."

Curtis sat across from his parole officer at the wooden desk. "I was offered a spot in training camp for the NFL."

"Which team?"

Curtis wrung his hands in his lap. "The Carolina Panthers."

Edmunds leaned back in his chair, nodding to himself. "That's interesting. Didn't you just ask me to go to North Carolina for a tryout with the Panthers?"

"Yes, sir."

"And did you fill out the proper paperwork?"

"No, sir."

"Yet you must've gone to North Carolina anyway."

Curtis squirmed in his seat.

Edmunds shook his head. "I don't know why you people have to be so *stupid*. I gave you the paperwork. I even said you could file the paperwork on short notice. Why the hell did you do that?"

"I didn't think you'd let me go."

Edmunds slammed the side of his fist on his desktop. "You're a damn fool. Now I gotta send you back to prison. All because you can't follow simple directions."

Curtis winced. "I'm sorry. I couldn't fill out the paperwork—"

"Why the hell not?"

"Because I wasn't actually invited to the tryout. I heard about it from a friend, and I went down there and told them that the Vice President of Player Personnel invited me."

Edmunds leaned forward, placed his meaty forearms on his desktop, and stared at Curtis. "Let me get this straight. You weren't even invited to this tryout, and you still risked your freedom?"

"Yes, sir."

"What chance did you think you had of even getting into the tryout?"

"Not a very good one."

"Yet you did it anyway."

"Yes, sir."

"And, even if you were able to tryout, you had to know that they'd figure out you weren't invited. You had to know that your chances were slim to none."

"Yes, sir."

Edmunds rubbed his temples. "But you did it anyway. Why?"

Curtis shrugged. "I figured the chances were better than zero."

"If you didn't get this invitation, I never would've known." Edmunds dropped his hands to his desktop. "You've put me in a terrible position. I have to be the bad guy. The dream killer."

Curtis swallowed the lump forming in his throat. "It's not your fault. It's mine. I knew the rules. I doubt I'd make the team anyway."

Officer Edmunds frowned. "You must've had a helluva workout to get invited."

"I did my best."

Edmunds exhaled. "If I'm gonna let this slide, I expect a little more confidence in yourself. If I forget about this, do you think you'll make the team?"

Curtis furrowed his brow. "I think so."

"No. That's not good enough. You need more confidence. I'll ask you one more time. If I forget about your parole violation, do you think you'll make the team?"

"I guarantee it, sir."

Edmunds smiled wide, showing the gap between his teeth.

On the way home, Curtis sang along with cheesy pop tunes and drummed on the steering wheel. At the commercial, Curtis changed the station to sports talk radio.

As he cruised down Route 1, the broadcaster said, "Philadelphia Eagles superstar, Justin Love, will not attend OTAs or camp without a new contract. He is in the final year of his rookie contract, but he has been vocal about wanting a new contract prior to the 2022 season."

The broadcast cut to Justin's voice. "I've outperformed my rookie contract. I was the offensive rookie of the year. I've been to two pro bowls. I want what's fair. I won't practice or play without a new contract."

CHAPTER 112

Last Practice

"Last one," Byron said.

Curtis lined up seven yards away from Beau's inside shoulder. They were practicing man-to-man coverage in the park. As soon as Beau moved, Curtis backpedaled, weaving to mirror the inside release. Beau head-faked inside and cut outside at a ninety-degree angle. Not biting on the fake, Curtis planted and sprinted to Beau's upfield shoulder. Beau flashed his hands, as if the football was coming, but Curtis didn't bite on the second fake. Beau turned upfield. The out and up route was supposed to bait the defensive back into going for the interception on the out route, causing him to be wildly out of position, and likely beat for a touchdown on the up route. However, Curtis was in good position. He simply turned with Beau and sprinted upfield, matching the former ODU tight end, stride for stride. The quarterback launched a high arcing pass to the back corner of the end zone, where only Beau could reach it. Beau used his height and long arms to jump and snag the football, just out of reach of Curtis. But, on his way down to earth, Curtis reached between Beau's arms and knocked the football to the grass. Curtis signaled *no catch*, waving his arms back and forth like a referee.

Curtis and Beau jogged back to the guys, Beau with the football in the crook of his arm.

The guys razzed Beau.

"Why are you so slow?" Maurice asked.

"Why are you so short?" Beau replied.

They had been working Curtis hard, doing their best to challenge him, but Curtis had locked them all down, never giving up a pass beyond five yards.

The quarterback lamented, "I thought we had him that time."

"Huddle up," Byron said. "I have an announcement to make."

The Mount Vernon Marauders coalesced around Byron.

Byron said to Curtis, "Since this is your last practice with us, we wanted to send you to Carolina with some parting gifts." Byron opened his duffel bag. He handed Curtis two pairs of receiver's gloves and a Visa gift card. "These are from all of us. There's five hundred bucks on that card. We wanted to make sure you had enough money to eat while you're in Carolina."

Curtis took the gloves and the gift card. "I don't know what to say." Curtis surveyed his teammates. "Thanks, guys. I really appreciate it."

Beau put his arm around Curtis. "Now you gotta make the team. I still can't believe you went down there and got a camp invitation. I thought you were crazy."

"That *was* crazy," Maurice said.

"But it worked," Byron said.

Curtis's teammates shook his hand and wished him well. Maurice gave him a hug.

Byron gave Curtis a hug too. When they separated, Byron poked Curtis in the chest and said, "You're gonna be a Carolina Panther. You have what it takes."

CHAPTER 113

Parting Words

Curtis sat at the patio table with Mr. H., watching the boys play football in the backyard. The umbrella overhead was frayed and tinged green from mold. Like the old umbrella, Mr. H. was fraying at the edges too. A few errant hairs grew from his ears. His old T-shirt was faded from too many wash cycles.

Mr. H. lifted his chin to the boys. "That was you not that long ago."

Curtis chuckled. "I remember."

"You ready for tomorrow?"

Curtis was leaving for minicamp tomorrow. "I think so."

"You have enough money?"

"I'm good. They're paying me $850 a week."

"Good. Are you all set with a new PO?"

"Yeah. I've already talked to him twice. He's willing to work around my practice schedule."

"Good. Don't mess around with that," Mr. H. said.

"I won't," Curtis replied.

The ten-year-old quarterback threw a beautiful spiral to a wide-open receiver for a touchdown. The quarterback turned to the patio. "Did you see that pass?"

"Nice spiral," Curtis called out.

Mr. H. clapped, and the boy beamed. The quarterback ran to the end zone, celebrating with his teammates.

"Did you hear about Justin Love holding out?" Curtis asked.

Mr. H. nodded. "I did, and I don't care. He's rotten to the core."

"I read that he wants to be the highest-paid player in NFL history."

"I'm sure he'll get his money, but that doesn't change who he is."

Curtis let out a heavy breath. "It would be nice not to worry about money."

"All that money won't change the fact that he's a liar and a rapist." Mr. H. turned in his chair, to better face Curtis. "You have something he'll never have, something that's worth more than all the money in this world." Mr. H. paused for a beat. "You're a good, decent person."

Curtis dipped his head. "My record says otherwise—"

"I don't care what your record says. *I* know who you are. Look at me."

Curtis raised his gaze to Mr. H.

"I'm proud of you, son. You haven't had it easy in this world. You could've blamed society or your parents or racism or poverty or any number of things. But you never did. Life has thrown you more than a few knockout punches, but you keep getting up, and you keep fighting. That's who you are. Don't forget that."

CHAPTER 114

Rookie Minicamp

"Tight mike strong inverted two," said the rookie linebacker.

Curtis and the defense broke the huddle on the last day of rookie minicamp. They practiced on an outdoor field, wearing half pads—shoulder pads and helmets, with shorts. The offense—also consisting of rookie draft picks and undrafted free agents—lined up. Based on the formation, Curtis lined up as the box safety, five yards from the line of scrimmage. With an inverted cover two, Curtis's responsibility would be the outside force player if it's a run and to cover the flats if it's a pass. He lined up on the receiver, who was bunched close to the tight end.

At the snap, Curtis noticed the offensive line pass blocking. The receiver and the tight end exploded from their stances. Recognizing the pass, Curtis tried to shove the receiver, to reroute him, but the receiver was too quick. Curtis sprinted to his zone, noticing the running back on a swing route into the flats. Figuring the running back was his man, Curtis covered him. The quarterback threw it over Curtis's head, completing a fourteen-yard out route to the receiver.

Coach Clay shouted at Curtis, "*Duffy*, you can't do that."

Coach Clay was a recently retired Carolina cornerback who looked like he could still play.

Curtis jogged to the defensive backs coach. "I don't understand."

"If you're the flat player in cover two, you can't just jump anything in the flat. You gotta make the quarterback work for that turkey hole.

Don't give him that easy throw. You gotta play man in the middle. Make him make the perfect throw, and, if he checks it down, you gotta be in position to make a tackle on the running back. Got it?"

Curtis nodded. "Yes, coach."

But he didn't have it. He was out of his league. The speed of the NFL was unlike anything he'd seen before. He couldn't even keep up during rookie minicamp. What would happen during OTAs, with the veterans? He wondered how he could possibly cover superstars like DJ Moore and Christian McCaffrey.

Curtis jogged back to the huddle and listened to the play.

"Tight will weak two," the linebacker said. "Tight will weak two."

The defense broke the huddle.

Curtis lined up on the right hash, ten yards from the line of scrimmage. In regular cover two, he was one of two deep safeties, responsible for the deep halves of the field. The Panthers offense lined up in a pro set, with two wide receivers, one tight end, and two running backs. One receiver was split wide on Curtis's side, along with a tight end. The offensive linemen appeared to be leaning forward, indicating a possible running play.

On the snap, the quarterback faked a handoff to the running back. Curtis bit on the fake, planting and exploding forward. He quickly realized his error, and sprinted back, reading the quarterback's eyes. The QB threw a perfect pass to the receiver, streaking down the field on a go route. Curtis sprinted to the receiver, pushing him out of bounds, just as he caught the ball for a thirty-yard gain.

Coach Clay slammed his clipboard on the ground and shouted, "God damn it, *Duffy*. What are you *doing*?"

After the team period, they were given a water break. Curtis squeezed the water bottle, spraying water into his mouth. He thought about his dreadful performance in team. *I'll be gone with the first cuts, if I keep this up.*

An older coach, tall and lanky with a ruddy complexion, approached Curtis. His legs appeared unnaturally long because his shorts were pulled up too high. "You're not in college anymore." His voice was raspy.

"No, sir," Curtis replied.

"I'm Coach Woody. Special teams. I'm your best chance of making this team. I've seen you run. You're as fast as anyone here. You could be a helluva special teamer." The coach walked away.

During the special teams period, Curtis remembered what Coach Woody had said. On kickoff and punt coverage, Curtis sprinted full speed, over and over again, his training and conditioning paying dividends. He made several tackles, although with half-pads, they didn't tackle anyone to the ground.

After his third tackle in a row, where Curtis pushed the return man out of bounds, he overheard Coach Woody say, "That young man wants to be here."

CHAPTER 115

Nothing to Celebrate

Curtis hung his head, letting the warm shower wash over him. He replayed the blown coverages over and over in his mind. Coach Woody was right. *If I'm gonna make this team, it'll have to be on special teams.* Curtis turned off the water, dried himself, wrapped the towel around his waist and exited the shower. He returned to the locker room, shower shoes on his feet.

The locker room was empty. The rest of the rookies had rushed to leave the practice facility, intent on hitting the Charlotte nightlife to celebrate the end of rookie minicamp. Curtis could've tagged along, but he didn't feel much like celebrating, and his potential teammates had largely ignored him during minicamp. There had been a hierarchy among the rookies, with the draft picks above the undrafted free agents, and those UDFAs with decorated college careers over those without. Curtis hadn't even played a single season at CVU. He hadn't played football outside of flag football in almost six years. He was a nobody, destined to be cut, never to be heard from again. Why would his potential teammates waste their time with someone who would be gone soon?

The carpet was silver, black, and blue, with the Panther emblem in the center of the locker room. Leather couches faced various flat-screen televisions. Curtis went to his locker. His name was scrawled across the cardboard insert over the locker in black Sharpie. The veterans and highly drafted rookies had metal placards with their names printed. It was just a name tag, but one signaled permanence, the other transience.

Curtis dressed in sweats and a CVU Football T-shirt. A fit man wearing workout gear entered the locker room. He walked to a veteran's locker. Curtis did a doubletake, recognizing the man. It was all-pro cornerback, Felix Gamble, who had played at Central Virginia. Curtis slung his duffel bag over his shoulder and trudged toward the exit. He thought about saying something to Felix, but he didn't want to relive his time at CVU.

"Hey, man," Felix said.

Curtis stopped and turned to Felix.

The star cornerback gestured to Curtis's shirt. "You went to CVU?"

"For one year," Curtis replied.

"Do I know you? I feel like I've seen you before."

Curtis thought, *My ugly face is hard to forget.* "I was a freshman when you were a senior, but I didn't make the team until the spring, so we never played together." Curtis held out his hand. "Curtis Duffy."

Felix shook his hand. "Felix Gamble." When Felix let go, he snapped his fingers. "Now I remember. I saw you at the walk-on tryout."

"I think so."

"I also saw you on TV. The Clemson game, right? You destroyed that punt returner at the end of the game. Made him fumble. Ran it back for a touchdown."

Curtis nodded. "Good memory."

"They never would've won the natty without you. Man, you brought the wood. I don't remember seeing you in any more games though."

Curtis broke eye contact. "I didn't play after that."

Felix furrowed his brow. "Why not?"

"I got into some trouble with marijuana. Got kicked out."

Felix frowned. "Sorry to hear that. I don't understand the marijuana rules. Alcohol and cigarettes are far more dangerous."

"I didn't have much choice."

Felix tilted his head, confused. "You're here now. That's good. What's your position?"

"Safety."

"You'll like Coach Clay. He's a good dude."

"He's a good coach. I didn't have the best minicamp though."

"It's a big jump from college to the NFL, even coming from CVU. It takes time. You need any help, let me know."

CHAPTER 116

Candy Asses

The day after rookie minicamp, Curtis woke at 5:00 a.m. and went to the Panthers practice facility. With his ID badge, he had 24/7 access. With the first rays of sunlight, and morning dew still on the grass, Curtis did his running workout, incorporating many of the drills he'd learned from Coach Clay during minicamp. He didn't see anyone that morning, not even the coaches. Curtis and the rookies had been given twelve days off between minicamp and OTAs. Most of the rookies had gone home to their families or had slept in after their night on the town.

After his morning workout, Curtis returned to his temporary one-bedroom apartment. Along the way, he passed an office building with an orthodontist on the first floor—Solomon Orthodontics. Testimonial posters hung in the window. He peered at the before-and-after pictures of crooked teeth transformed into sparkling smiles with straight teeth. None of the before pictures were worse than Curtis's teeth.

Free Consultation was printed at the top of each poster. Curtis thought about scheduling a consultation. He imagined the orthodontist telling him that they couldn't help him, his teeth were too crooked. Curtis continued to his apartment building—a ten-story high-rise. He took the elevator to his one-bedroom apartment. It had come fully furnished, the perfect arrangement for rookie Panthers, especially ones likely to be cut. No need for a complicated move out with bulky furniture.

Curtis showered, ate breakfast at the kitchen table for two, and watched ESPN. They showed a clip of Justin Love backing his Mercedes G-Wagon out of his driveway. He stopped the SUV next to the attractive female reporter and powered down his window.

The ESPN reporter asked, "Has there been any progress with your contract?"

Justin frowned. "Unfortunately, no. My agent is negotiating in good faith. I'd like to stay in Philly. I love my teammates. I love the fans here. Hopefully, we can work it out."

"We've had reports of multiple teams inquiring about a trade."

"I don't know anything about that."

"Are you open to being traded?"

"It's a last resort. I have to go. Thanks." Justin drove away, leaving the reporter in the street.

Curtis turned off the television, grabbed his workout gear, and left his apartment. On the way back to the practice facility, he stopped at the orthodontist office. He went to the reception desk, his mouth sealed shut. Several teenage patients, with mouths full of metal, sat in the waiting area with a parent.

The young receptionist smiled her perfect smile and said, "Welcome to Solomon Orthodontics. How can I help you?"

Curtis spoke, careful to keep his teeth covered. "I'd like to schedule a consultation."

Curtis scheduled his consultation for the next available appointment, which was tomorrow morning. According to the receptionist, they often had openings in the morning, while school was still in session.

He left the office, with a little card reminding him of the date and time of his appointment. Curtis returned to the practice facility, intent on lifting weights, his second workout of the day.

★★★

Curtis was the only person in the weight room. He ducked under the bar, placing his traps and shoulders against the bar. He wiggled a little, finding a comfortable spot for 405 pounds to rest. Then he lifted the bar off the squat rack and took two mini-steps backward. The bar bent at the ends. Curtis looked up as he squatted, his thighs horizontal before he pushed upward, standing again. He did ten repetitions without too much trouble, then racked the weight. He noticed Coach Woody in the mirror.

Curtis pivoted.

The old coach stood with his arms crossed over his chest.

Curtis smiled with his mouth closed. "Hey, Coach."

"Curtis. You stickin' around for the break?"

"Yes, sir."

The old coach nodded. "Your competition's sittin' on their candy asses."

Curtis stared at the coach, unsure of what to say.

Coach Woody walked away.

CHAPTER 117

The Orthodontist

Curtis lounged in the dental chair, waiting for the orthodontist.

A woman appeared at his side. "Mr. Duffy?"

"Yes." Curtis sat up. As he raised his gaze to the woman, he noticed her toned calves, pencil skirt, and white dental coat. Her name was stenciled on her coat pocket—Gabriella Solomon, DMD. She smiled, showing perfect white teeth, like everyone else who worked at the office. Like Curtis, she appeared to be biracial, but she was beautiful, with wavy black hair just past her shoulders, tan skin, almond eyes, and high cheekbones.

Curtis was speechless.

"Mr. Duffy, I'm Dr. Solomon. Mr. Duffy?"

Her singsong voice brought him back to reality. "Sorry. Um, … hi. It's nice to meet you."

She smiled again. "What brings you here today?"

"I'd like to straighten my teeth. Not sure if it's even possible …" He trailed off.

"Let's take a look. Can you lean back for me?"

Curtis leaned back in the dental chair.

Dr. Solomon shone the light into Curtis's mouth and sat in the nearby roller chair. "Open wide."

Curtis opened his mouth, blushing from embarrassment, expecting her to gasp. She leaned over him, examining his teeth with a little mirror. A faint smell of lavender wafted into his nostrils. An electric charge coursed through his body.

She leaned back, moved the light from Curtis's face, and raised the dentist's chair so it was upright. "I would love to straighten your teeth."

Curtis faced her. "You think you can? My teeth are"—Curtis looked down—"really bad."

"You should've seen my teeth before I got braces. I didn't smile for like ten years."

Curtis smiled with his mouth closed. "You can fix my teeth?"

"Absolutely. It'll take about two years, but I'm very confident. The first step is to take X-rays and to set up an appointment to install the braces. Luckily, you have plenty of space, so we don't need to use spacers. The total price should be around $3,500. I can get you an exact quote before you leave. What do you think?"

"I'm a rookie with the Carolina Panthers—"

"I'm a big Panthers fan. That's so cool."

"The only problem is, I don't know if I'll make the team. I might not be here very long."

"You can always have another orthodontist finish the work. I'll only charge you for what we've done."

Curtis nodded. "Do you have a payment plan?"

"We sure do."

CHAPTER 118

The New PO

The parole office was only two miles from Curtis's apartment, so he jogged to his appointment on Monday morning. It was a beautiful morning, and he'd barely broken a sweat when he arrived at the three-story office building. Curtis found the parole offices on the second floor and signed in with the receptionist. He sat in a waiting room with other parolees, waiting for his name to be called.

Fourteen minutes later, his name was called. He was led to a back office by an administrative assistant who struggled to make the short trek, partly from age and partly from obesity.

A smiley middle-aged man with leathery-tan skin met Curtis at the office door. He held out his hand. "I'm Trevor Alcott. You must be Curtis Duffy."

"Yes, sir," Curtis replied, as he shook the man's hand.

"You don't need to call me sir or Officer Alcott. You can call me Trevor."

"Thank you, sir."

Trevor mock-frowned. "Come on, Curtis."

"Sorry, sir—I mean, Trevor. Between prison and parole, it's a habit."

"No apology needed." He gestured to a sitting area, with a round table and four chairs. "Have a seat."

Curtis sat at the table. Trevor joined Curtis at the table with a single manila folder.

The office walls were decorated with framed inspirational pictures. One picture showed a pier, ending in bright blue waters. Under the picture was the word *Dreams*, followed by one sentence: *If one advances confidently in the direction of his dreams and endeavors to live the life which he has imagined, he will meet with a success unexpected in common hours.* Another picture showed a rock climber, dangling from a rock face. Under the picture was *Make it happen,* followed by *There is no challenge too great for those who have the will and the heart to make it happen.*

Trevor opened the manila folder and scanned the paperwork. "I'm excited to talk to you, Curtis. How was rookie minicamp with the Panthers?"

"It was hard. I have a lot to learn."

Trevor looked up from the folder. "Well, I think what you're doing is great. I'm a bit of a football fan, and I don't know if there's ever been anyone who's made an NFL roster after being in prison for five years. I think Michael Vick was only in for two years, and he *struggled* after he got out. He had a couple of nice seasons with Philly, but prison still really hurt his career. Brian Banks was in for five years, but he never made an NFL roster. You could make NFL history. What do you think of that?"

"I hadn't thought about it like that," Curtis replied. "I'm just fighting for a roster spot, like everyone else. I'm trying to put prison behind me."

Trevor nodded. "That's good. It's my job to help you transition. Think of me as a resource, as someone you can come to for help. My goal is for you to be a successful free citizen. Of course, you have to follow the rules, but I don't think that'll be hard for someone like you."

Curtis knitted his brow. "What do you mean, *someone like me?*"

"You're a football player. Obviously, a very good one. To be a good football player, you must understand the rules. You must be disciplined and hardworking. With those traits, I'm very confident that you'll make a successful transition."

CHAPTER 119

Organized Team Activities

On the second day of OTAs, Curtis dressed for practice, his mouth sore from his braces. A cacophony of voices surrounded him, almost one hundred guys joking and jeering each other. The veterans were the most boisterous, with rookies like Curtis mostly quiet. They were like children of yesteryear. Seen and not heard.

Curtis tried not to think of the numbers. They had ninety guys, but only fifty-three would make the roster. He highly doubted he was better than thirty-seven of the guys. Curtis had been starstruck on the first day, practicing with pro-bowlers, such as Christian McCaffrey, Brian Burns, and Felix Gamble, but now he was indifferent to the veterans. He had a job to do, just like they did.

Felix Gamble approached Curtis and lifted his chin. "You ready, rook?"

Curtis reached under his jersey and fastened his shoulder pads. "I hope so." Curtis let his mouth hang open, the braces making it harder to shut his mouth comfortably.

Felix noticed his new hardware. "Look at you with the grill."

Curtis flushed. "Yeah. My teeth …"

"Nothing to be ashamed of. I'll see you out there."

They started practice with active stretching, followed by individual drills. Curtis practiced with the defensive backs, working on their footwork and ball skills. Coach Clay held a football, pointing this way and that way. They turned and sprinted, planted and changed directions, all at Clay's command. Curtis had practiced the drills, and it showed.

Even Coach Clay noticed, saying, "That's nice, Duffy."

After individual drills, they met the receivers for one-on-one drills. Two quarterbacks stood in the middle of the field, at the twenty-yard line, facing the end zone. They threw to one receiver on each side. Curtis waited in line to cover a receiver.

He ended up covering DJ Moore. The star receiver gave Curtis a hard jab step outside, then cut inside, making an easy catch on the slant.

When Curtis returned to the line, Felix Gamble said, "Don't over-commit. You gotta slow-play that shit at the line. Let them make all the moves."

The next time, Curtis covered an undrafted rookie. Curtis didn't bite on the first jab step, instead running stride for stride with the receiver, until the receiver slowed and cut outside, creating a step of separation between them. The pass was on the money, but Curtis had been quick enough to recover and to deflect the pass. Incomplete.

His fellow defensive backs cheered his victory.

Felix smacked him on the helmet, when Curtis returned to the line. "That was better. Still you gotta notice when his hips drop like that. Had you reacted to that out cut sooner, you could've picked it off."

CHAPTER 120

Proud

Three weeks later, Curtis sat in the dental chair, while Dr. Solomon tightened his braces. He gladly endured the tooth pain to be close to Gabriella, to smell her lavender perfume. Of course, they weren't on a first-name basis. They were still Mr. Duffy and Dr. Solomon. She was Gabriella only in his dreams.

Dr. Solomon moved the light aside, leaned back, and set the dental chair upright. "All done."

Curtis moved his jaw back and forth, feeling the tension on his teeth. "This is gonna hurt tomorrow, isn't it?"

"Probably. I tightened pretty aggressively. You'll be okay." She winked. "You must be tough to be a football player."

Curtis smiled, showing his braces.

"Your smile's already starting to look better."

"Really? It still looks like a snaggletooth mess."

"I wouldn't describe it like that."

"How would you describe it?"

"A work in progress. A beautiful work in progress."

Curtis frowned. "You're too nice, Doc."

"You might not think I'm so nice when you wake up tomorrow."

Curtis chuckled. "Do you mind if I ask how old you are?"

Dr. Solomon tilted her head.

"I was just thinking you look really young to be a doctor, with your own practice."

"Well, I am young. I'm twenty-six, but this was my dad's practice. He retired last year and left me to do all the work."

"Your parents must be really proud of you."

She smiled. "Thanks. I hope so. Although, I'm pretty sure my dad would be more impressed if I played for the Panthers. *Your* parents must be ecstatic. You're in the NFL. I bet it's a lot easier to become an orthodontist."

"I haven't made it yet."

He hadn't even made it past the first cuts. He had finished rookie minicamp and OTAs, but cuts didn't start until summer camp, which didn't begin until August 1st.

"Either way, I bet your parents are very proud," Dr. Solomon said.

Curtis nodded, noncommittal.

On the short walk home from the orthodontist, Curtis thought about his mother. He wondered if she would've been proud of him. *She never was when she was alive. She didn't even want me.* He wondered if his father still lived in DC. He thought about the time his mother had taken him to see his father. He remembered his mother had begged for help. His father hadn't said one word to Curtis. His father had called his mother a crack whore and had sent them away with nothing.

No, Dr. Solomon, they're not proud.

CHAPTER 121

Gabriella

Curtis left the Panthers practice facility just behind Coach Woody. Curtis and his Panther teammates had been off since OTAs had finished five weeks ago. He had been working out twice daily on his own at the Panthers practice facility. The old coach held the door for him.

Curtis hurried to the door, so Coach Woody didn't have to wait. "Thanks, Coach."

"Need to get you a lunch pail and a hard hat." Coach Woody walked away, headed for the parking lot.

"Have a good night, Coach," Curtis called out to the old coach.

Coach Woody didn't respond.

With the afternoon sun high in the sky, Curtis went the opposite way, toward his apartment. As he walked, he checked the time on his phone. His orthodontic appointment was in thirty minutes, Dr. Solomon's last appointment of the day. He felt like a creep for scheduling the late appointment, when he could've easily scheduled it for the morning. But he wanted to ask Dr. Solomon out and hoped to do it when her office was least busy. He also had a fantasy that she'd be so flattered they might go out for a drink or coffee right then and there. If not, there would be fewer people to watch him crash and burn.

Curtis hurried to his apartment, showered, and dressed in his nicest pants and a button-down shirt. Then he left his apartment and walked to Dr. Solomon's office. The middle-aged assistant led him to the dental chair. Soft music played from the speakers in the ceiling. He sat in the dental chair, his wallet making his rear end uncomfortable.

Curtis leaned to his left and grabbed his wallet from his back pocket. He showed his wallet to the assistant. "Would you mind putting my wallet on the counter? I hate sitting on it."

"Of course." She placed his wallet on the counter, out of the way. "Don't forget it."

"Thanks."

"Dr. Solomon will be right with you." The assistant walked away.

Less than a minute later, Dr. Gabriella Solomon sat in the rolling stool next to Curtis, and said, "You're late."

"Am I?" Curtis replied. "I thought my appointment was at six."

"You're on time. I meant, you usually come in the morning."

"Uh, … I was working out at the practice facility."

"Aren't you supposed to go to camp soon?"

"Next week. We're going to Wofford College, but I'll be back for my next appointment."

"That's good. Are you excited?"

"Excited. Worried. I'm trying not to worry too much. I'll do my best. That's all I can do."

"That's very true." She stared at him for a long beat. "I bet you'll do great." Then she moved the light into position, causing Curtis to shut his eyes. "Let's get to work."

As Dr. Solomon tightened his braces, she said, "Your teeth really are looking better. We still have a long way to go, but I'm pleased with how you're progressing."

"*Uh-huh,*" Curtis said, doing his best to reply, with her hands in his mouth.

An angelic voice came from above.

> *My life's filled with pain and regret.*
> *And I don't know what to do about it.*
> *I just want you to love me.*

I just want you to own me.

Curtis winced.

Dr. Solomon removed her hands from his mouth. "Did I hurt you?"

"No. Sorry. It's the music."

She furrowed her brow. "You don't like Taylor Wilde?"

"Not really, but it's okay."

She stood from her chair. "I love Taylor Wilde." Dr. Solomon went to the panel on the wall, cut the music, and returned to her seat.

"I'm sorry," Curtis said. "You didn't have to turn it off."

"The customer's always right."

They didn't talk for the rest of the tightening. Curtis chided himself in his mind for acting like a crazy person. *Of course she loves Taylor Wilde. Everyone does.*

Dr. Solomon moved the light aside, leaned back, and raised the dental chair upright. "That's it."

"Thank you," Curtis said.

"You're very welcome."

Dr. Solomon escorted Curtis to the exit. The rest of the staff had gone home. Curtis sensed she was nervous to be alone with him, so he aborted his plan to ask her out. He didn't want to make her more uncomfortable. *No way she'd be interested in someone as ugly as me anyway.*

"You said you were from Virginia, right?" Dr. Solomon asked, as they neared the front door.

"Yes."

"Do you get to see your family much?"

They loitered by the glass front door. The occasional car drove by. The far side of the street was shaded, a consequence of the setting sun.

"Not since I came down here," Curtis replied, thinking of Mr. H. "Even when we're off, I've been focused on working out at the facility."

"Hopefully, you'll get to visit soon," Dr. Solomon said.

"I think we're both hoping not. At least not until the season's over."

She smiled. "Right. Hopefully, you can visit after making the team."

"What about you? Do your parents live nearby?"

Dr. Solomon peered out the glass door, distracted. "About fifteen minutes from here."

"You must see them all the time."

Dr. Solomon gazed outside, her eyes wide. "Too much sometimes." She sounded distracted.

Curtis gazed outside too, checking what had distracted Dr. Solomon. A man stood across the street, obscured by the shade, but clearly staring in their direction. Curtis faced Dr. Solomon. "Are you okay?"

"I'm fine."

"You sure?"

Dr. Solomon opened the glass door. "Have a good evening, Mr. Duffy."

Curtis stepped through the door, held it open, and pivoted to Dr. Solomon. "You can call me Curtis."

She forced a smile.

It was on the tip of his tongue. Despite his reservations, he almost said, *Would you like to go out with me sometime*? But instead, he said, "See you next time." As Curtis walked away, he thought, *See you next time? That was real smooth. Dumb-ass.*

Curtis had walked two blocks to his apartment building when he realized he'd left his wallet at the orthodontist's office. He jogged back, worried that Dr. Solomon might've already left for the day. When he rounded the corner, he heard sharp voices talking back and forth. Dr. Solomon stood with her back against her glass office door, her face taut. The man who had been staring at them, crowded her, his fists clenched.

Curtis crept closer, his eyes on the guy's hands, ready to intervene.

"You threw me away like *fucking* trash," the man said. "Now look at you. Everything's great for you, but my life's a mess. You don't get to walk away without repercussions."

Curtis startled them both when he asked, "Is everything okay?"

The man glared at Curtis. "It's none of your fucking business."

"Dylan, stop," Dr. Solomon said.

Curtis stared back, unintimidated. Dylan appeared to be in decent shape but was several inches shorter than Curtis and probably forty pounds lighter. However, Dylan was a handsome guy, with wavy brown hair and a stubbly beard.

Dylan turned his glare back to Dr. Solomon. "Is this mutant your new boyfriend?"

"*Stop it.* He's a client, not that it's any of your business," Dr. Solomon said. "I need you to leave. Don't make me call the police again."

Dylan put his finger in her face. "*You* did this to me." He stalked away.

Dr. Solomon faced Curtis. "Thank you."

"I didn't do anything, but you're welcome." Curtis tilted his head, noticing her glassy eyes. "You okay?"

She wiped the corners of her eyes. "I'm fine. I'm sorry that you got caught up in that. You must think I'm so unprofessional."

"I'm not thinking anything, other than you have an angry ex-boyfriend."

Dr. Solomon let out a heavy breath. "It's not all his fault. We were supposed to get married after dental school, and I broke it off four months before the wedding. He didn't take it well. He quit school. He ..." She trailed off.

Curtis grimaced. "Sorry. That must've been a tough decision."

She frowned. "No, I'm sorry. I shouldn't be telling you all this."

"It's okay."

She cocked her head, confused. "Why are you here?"

"Oh, I forgot my wallet. It's on the counter by the dental chair."

"Wait here. I have to do the alarm."

Curtis waited outside, while Dr. Solomon went into her office, disarmed the alarm, grabbed his wallet, armed the alarm again, and locked the front door.

She handed Curtis his worn leather wallet. "This is it, right?"

"Yes, thank you." Curtis thought about asking her out again, but he sensed she was wary of him, making him wait outside while she grabbed his wallet. "You want me to walk you to your car?"

She gestured to the white Honda Accord parked on the street, directly in front of the building. "This is me."

"Have a good night, Dr. Solomon." Curtis turned to leave.

"Curtis?"

He pivoted back to her.

"You can call me Gabriella."

CHAPTER 122

Training Camp

Curtis exited the shower, his towel around his waist and shower shoes on his feet. A purple *W* was etched into the carpet, the Wofford College logo, and the Carolina Panthers training camp site. Massive muscular men talked and dressed at their lockers. A few of the veterans eyed Curtis as he walked to his locker. His close-cropped red hair was still damp. Curtis removed his towel and put on his boxer briefs. He slipped on a pair of shorts and a T-shirt.

Bryce 'Wilks' Wilkinson occupied the locker next to Curtis. He was an undersized rookie cornerback from TCU, who had been invited to camp after one of the other UDFA cornerbacks tore an ACL during rookie minicamp.

Wilks lifted his chin to Curtis. "They're coming for us."

Beefy arms wrapped Curtis in a bear hug from behind. The deep voice said, "Time for your haircut."

Another veteran grabbed Wilks too.

Curtis, Wilks, and the other rookies were forced to the open bathroom. They queued behind three chairs, while the rest of the team crowded around them. Curtis was first in line.

The big lineman who had bear-hugged him said, "Have a seat, Ginger Braces."

Curtis sat in one of the chairs.

"You too, little man," the big lineman referred to Wilks.

Wilks and another rookie took the other seats.

The team cheered when the big lineman turned on the electric clippers. Two other veterans, Brian Burns and DJ Moore also grabbed electric clippers from the counter.

"What kinda haircut should we give Ginger Braces?" the big lineman asked the crowd.

"Doesn't matter," one veteran said. "Whatever you do won't make him any uglier."

The crowd cackled.

Curtis didn't react, knowing his reaction would only make it worse.

"Inverted mohawk," Felix Gamble called out.

Curtis figured Felix was doing him a favor, as there were far worse haircuts.

The big lineman shaved a path right down the middle of Curtis's head. "Next."

Curtis watched his fellow rookies receive various haircuts. They shaved squiggly lines in Wilks's head. A rookie lineman with long hair received the Friar Tuck. They shaved the top of his head bald but left the rest long. A rookie linebacker who had fought one of the veterans earlier that day received the Dick Cut. They shaved everything except for three penis shaped patches of hair, one on top of his head, and another on each side of his head. A rookie fullback got the Hitler. They shaved his beard, leaving only the Hitler mustache. Others got zigzag patterns or even derogatory words shaved into their head.

At the end, Curtis and the rookies were left to clean up their hair.

Later that night, Curtis lay in bed, reading his playbook. The Wofford dorm room wasn't much different than his dorm at CVU. His roommate, Wilks, also lay in bed, reading his playbook.

"How do you think you did today?" Wilks asked.

Curtis turned his head to his roommate. "I think I did okay. How about you?"

"Guys were big at TCU, but some of these guys are huge. And everybody's fast. I feel like I'm behind."

"I thought you did good during one-on-ones."

"I don't think I can make the roster as a corner. They want taller corners. If I'm gonna make it, it's gonna be on special teams."

Curtis thought special teams was his ticket to a roster spot too. But they only carried a few designated special teamers on the roster.

CHAPTER 123

Two-a-Days

Curtis trotted out to the Wofford College practice field, wearing full pads, his helmet in hand. His exposed arms and calves and face were covered in sunblock. Coach Woody stood on the sideline, alone. His T-shirt was tucked into his shorts, which were pulled up too high.

"Hey, coach," Curtis said.

Coach Woody nodded.

Coach Woody held a voluntary special teams practice thirty minutes before practice began. Very few players attended, but Curtis hadn't missed yet. Curtis put on his helmet and jogged around the field. He was twenty minutes early for the pre-practice. He used the time to warm up and stretch, as Coach Woody didn't allow any time for that. Curtis's legs were sore, and his body was bruised from nearly three weeks of two-a-day practices in the South Carolina heat. After two laps, he stretched on the sideline. By the time Curtis finished stretching, Wilks and a few other rookies joined him.

The kickers, punters, long snappers, and holders strolled to the field with bags of footballs. Without any instruction, they set up at the far end of the field. The kickers booted footballs through the uprights. Punters booted footballs into the stratosphere. Several ball boys shagged the balls.

Coach Woody took Curtis, Wilks, and the other rookies to the opposite end of the field. They practiced their techniques as punt team gunners.

Coach Woody spread the rookies across the goal line. "Let's see your stance."

Curtis and the rookies all took a balanced athletic stance, slightly wider than shoulder width, just as they'd been taught.

Coach Woody shoved Wilks, causing him to stumble backward. "About eighty percent of your weight needs to be on the balls of your feet." Coach Woody shoved Curtis in the chest, but Curtis didn't move. The old coach stepped back and addressed the group. "On the whistle, everyone take an inside release for five yards, before sprintin' up field." Coach Woody blew the whistle.

Curtis pushed off with his left foot, running along the line of scrimmage for five yards before turning and sprinting upfield. This drill simulated avoiding the blockers en route to the punt returner. They did this several times, going inside and outside. Coach Woody watched each repetition intently, offering correction where needed.

"That's good, Curtis," Coach Woody said, "but don't give it away. When you were in your stance, I could tell that you were puttin' more pressure on your right foot. That'll tell the blocker you're goin' left. The other team will see that shit on film."

"Yes, Coach," Curtis replied.

After practice, Curtis went to the training room, his entire body sore. In the back, near the whirlpools, ten ice baths were setup. As a rookie, Curtis had to wait for the veterans to finish their ice baths, before Curtis had his turn in the now-dirty water.

As he finally sat in the ice-cold water, Curtis's entire body constricted, and he sucked in a sharp breath.

Wilks jogged into the training room. He sat in the ice bath next to Curtis. "Woo. Damn. I hate this shit."

Through chattering teeth, Curtis replied, "Me too."

"You know what today is?"

"Thursday, the eighteenth."

"*Nah*, man. It's the first day of cuts. They have to cut down to eighty-five by the end of the day."

They had ninety guys in camp, so five had to go.

Curtis's stomach lurched. He wondered if this was his last day with the Panthers.

"I saw the Turk coming down the hall," Wilks said. "I ran in here. I don't wanna see that dude. Not today."

The Turk was the assistant to Head Coach Grant Mellon. He was tasked with tracking down guys who had been cut.

After eight minutes in the ice bath, Curtis stood from the frigid water, his entire body numb. Curtis and Wilks returned to the locker room, wrapped in towels, still freezing from the ice bath.

The Turk approached them at their lockers.

Curtis felt like his heart had stopped.

The Turk glanced at Curtis, then said to Wilks, "Coach Mellon wants to see you. Bring your playbook."

CHAPTER 124

King Ugly

On the last day of camp, the Carolina Panthers held a goofy award ceremony. It was meant to be a team-bonding experience and a few laughs. While this was the end of training camp at Wofford College, they still had two preseason games to determine the final roster. They still had to cut twenty-seven guys, which would happen after the final preseason game.

Curtis, his seventy-nine teammates, coaches, and staff crowded into the large meeting room. Felix Gamble stood at the front of the room, MCing the event. Curtis sat in the back corner of the room, hoping to be ignored. He thought about the game they had played four days ago. They had defeated the Washington Commanders 23–20 in their first preseason game, but Curtis had played very little, which was a bad sign.

If a player didn't play much in the preseason, it usually meant the coaches knew what they had and didn't need to see more. For superstar veterans, they didn't play much because the coaches didn't want to risk injury. For unknown rookies, they didn't play much because the coaches didn't think they had a shot to make the roster.

Despite the sinking feeling in the pit of his stomach, Curtis laughed with his teammates as Christian McCaffrey received the Instagram Award for dating the hottest women on the Gram. A nose tackle received the Stank-Ass Award for the guy who smelled the most like shit.

Coach Woody received the Jacked Shorts Award, for his shorts being pulled up over his stomach. They showed pictures on the big screen for emphasis. With a chuckle, Coach Woody accepted his award—a certificate and a pair of pink short shorts. Like a geriatric line dancer, he presented one bare leg to the audience and said into the mike, "This is pure jealousy. Y'all wish you had legs like mine."

The room erupted with laughter.

The highlight of the evening, as it had been for years, was the King Ugly Contest. The winners were the ugliest three guys, as voted by their peers. It was the one award that came with a cash prize. The veterans had collected one thousand dollars from the rookies for the prize. The twenty rookies split the bill, each contributing fifty bucks. Eight hundred dollars went to the third-place winner. Two hundred dollars went to the second-place winner. Nothing went to the ugliest guy in camp. He was so ugly, he didn't deserve a prize.

Felix Gamble was given three envelopes by DJ Moore. The envelopes contained the prize money and the names of the winners. Curtis felt nauseated, knowing he would likely win the cashless award. He steeled himself, thinking about managing his reaction and what to say.

Felix opened an envelope and peeked at the paper inside. He spoke into the mike. "The third-place winner of the King Ugly Contest is Alvin Beathard."

The crowd hooted and hollered.

A beefy mountain of a man lumbered to the front of the meeting room. He snatched the cash prize from Felix, and flashed the money to the audience. "I'll take this money, but most of you are way uglier than me."

The crowd laughed.

Felix checked the second-place envelope. "The second-ugliest man in camp is Coach Woody."

With a smirk, Coach Woody took his money. "We'll see what y'all look like in thirty years."

Felix checked the final envelope.

Curtis swallowed the hot bile creeping up his throat.

Felix said, "And the winner of the 2022 King Ugly Contest is … Curtis Duffy."

The crowd laughed and cheered.

Curtis trudged down the center aisle, everyone gawking at him.

Felix put a Burger King paper crown on his head. When he did so, he whispered, "I'm sorry, man."

Curtis shook his head, almost imperceptibly, just enough to let Felix know it was okay. Felix wrapped a sheet around him and handed him a plunger, the items meant to represent his robe and scepter.

The crowd chanted, "Speech. Speech. Speech."

Curtis took the mike from Felix. He stared at the crowd for a few seconds. Then he said in a very somber tone, "My whole life I was told I'd never amount to anything because I was too ugly."

The room went dead quiet.

"But look at me now." Curtis held up his scepter and smiled wide, showing his braces and crooked teeth. "I'm the king."

They gave him a standing ovation.

CHAPTER 125

The Invitation

The Carolina Panthers were back in Charlotte, after camp at Wofford University. Yesterday, they'd lost to the Patriots 20–10 in their second preseason game. Like the first preseason game, Curtis had played very little—kickoff and punt team, but zero snaps on defense. He did make a tackle on the punt team.

That Monday, after the Patriots game, was the first day off for the Panthers' players since the start of training camp. Curtis again scheduled his orthodontist appointment for the latest possible time, although he had a plausible excuse this time. They had arrived by plane from New England late the night before. Curtis had been exhausted and had slept late on Monday. He had lounged around the house all day, watching television, surfing the internet, and eating.

Now Curtis sat on the dental chair, waiting for Gabriella.

She appeared at his side with a smile. "Hi, Curtis." Her smile evaporated as she noticed his appearance. "What happened to your hair?"

Curtis ran his hand over his stubbly red hair. "They gave me an inverted mohawk in camp, so I had to shave it off."

She inspected him, her brow furrowed. "And your arms are all bruised. It looks like you've been in a car accident. Are you okay?"

"I've been in fifty car accidents every day for like a month." Curtis smiled. "But I'm okay."

Gabriella sat on the swivel chair, close enough to smell her lavender perfume. "How was camp? Apart from all those car accidents."

"Hard but good. I don't know if I'll make the team, but I did my best."

"That's exactly what you said you would do. They'd be stupid to cut you."

"You've never seen me play. Maybe cutting me is a smart idea."

She frowned. "I doubt that."

Curtis reached into his back pocket and removed an envelope. "Our last preseason game is on Saturday. Would you like to go?"

Gabriella cocked her head. "Oh, I, um …"

He held up the envelope. "I got you two tickets. You could take a friend. It's my last shot to impress the coaches before final cuts."

"This game is a pretty big deal for you, *huh*?"

Curtis nodded.

"Don't you want to give those tickets to your parents?"

Mr. H. had attended the preseason games against the Commanders and the Patriots, but he couldn't make the final preseason game.

"I wanna give them to you, but, if you don't wanna go, it's not a problem." Curtis dipped his head, no longer making eye contact with Gabriella. "The Panthers gave us all free tickets. I didn't have to buy the tickets or anything."

"I would love to see you play," Gabriella said.

Curtis raised his gaze, smiled wide, and handed the envelope to Gabriella. "I'm not sure how much I'll play."

CHAPTER 126

Last Chance

With two minutes left in the game, the third-string quarterback for the Panthers threw a short touchdown pass. After the extra point sailed through the uprights, the Panthers led the Bills, 20–15.

On the ensuing kickoff, Curtis trotted onto the field with the rest of the kickoff team. They'd had four kickoffs that afternoon, but all of them had been touchbacks, negating Curtis's opportunity to make a tackle. Curtis glanced to the stands, checking the first four rows near the forty-yard line. If Gabriella had come, she would be in that section, but he hadn't seen her. He had seen someone who might be her, but it was hard to tell because they were wearing a Panthers hat.

The kicker again booted the football into the end zone, but the return man didn't down it. He was a rookie, like Curtis, wanting to be noticed, so he ran it out. Curtis streaked down the turf field of Bank of America Stadium. The stadium was half filled with die-hard Panthers fans, cheering on a bunch of undrafted rookies who were unlikely to have jobs in a few days.

Curtis split two blockers, using his speed to avoid contact. He took a good angle toward the return man, before launching his shoulder into the man's chest. An audible *pop* echoed through the stadium. The return man fell backward, head over feet, as if he'd run into a brick wall. The fans oohed and aahed after the big hit. Curtis's teammates on the sideline cheered and jumped up and down, excited by the collision. Curtis stayed on the field, as he was in at free safety on defense.

The third-string Buffalo Bills started the drive at their fifteen-yard line, with 1:54 left in the game. The Bills moved thirty yards in three plays with a slant pattern, an out route, and a draw play. They burned their final time-out on the draw play.

It was first and ten, the Bills on their forty-five-yard line, with 1:15 left in the game. Curtis and the Panthers played a prevent defense with three safeties, but the prevent allowed shorter passes and effective run plays. The Panthers were betting the Bills didn't have enough time to score on running plays and short passes.

The Bills ran a screen pass to the wide receiver, which resulted in a twelve-yard gain. Curtis ran across the field to tackle the wide receiver, to keep him in bounds, and to keep the clock running. The Bills hurried to the line, not wanting to waste precious time. They ran another draw play. The offensive line of the Bills created a gaping hole for the runner, as the running back blasted into the secondary. Curtis sprinted to the runner, breaking down, and making another sure tackle after an eight-yard gain.

With the clock still moving—fifty-two seconds left and counting down—the Bills offense hurried to the line. The quarterback dropped back to pass. He threw a bullet to the wide receiver on the slant pattern, in between the linebacker and cornerback for a ten-yard gain and another first down. They hurried to the line again, running another draw play. This one was stopped by the defensive line after only a two-yard gain.

The clock ticked down from thirty-five seconds. Thirty-four, thirty-three, thirty-two. Curtis watched Coach Clay signal the defensive play from the sideline. *Offset stack two robber.* The Bills hurried to the line of scrimmage, now on the Panthers twenty-three-yard line. Curtis lined up on the hash, as one of the deep safeties. He keyed on the tight end and wide receiver.

The Bills quarterback dropped back to pass. The wide receiver ran a five-yard speed out, and the Panthers cornerback covered him tight. The tight end sprinted directly at Curtis. The tight end faked inside, then cut outside for the back corner of the end zone. On the fake, Curtis lost a step. The tight end was open. Curtis sprinted to catch up, adrenaline coursing through his veins. The football spun with a tight spiral, a perfect pass. But Curtis leaped and tipped the ball out of bounds at the last split second.

The home crowd cheered. The Panthers sideline cheered too, especially Felix Gamble, who was in street clothes. The pro-bowl cornerback was too valuable to play in the final preseason game.

On the incompletion, the clock stopped at twenty-six seconds. It was third and eight, the ball still on the Panthers' twenty-three-yard line. With the clock stopped, the Bills huddled and took their time to call the play.

On the next play, the quarterback dropped back to pass again. This time the tight ends ran double hook routes at ten yards, intent on finding the soft spot in the zone between the linebackers and safeties. And they did, catching a ten-yard pass in the middle of the field.

With the first down, the clock stopped, until the referee spotted the football at the thirteen-yard line. With the clock ticking, the Bills hurried to the line of scrimmage. They ran another wide receiver screen, this time for seven yards, before the receiver ran out of bounds, stopping the clock.

It was second and three from the six-yard line, with fourteen seconds left. The crowd shouted at the top of their lungs. The Bills ran a read option, with the quarterback handing the ball to the running back, the bowling-ball-like runner plowing ahead for four yards, another first down.

The clock stopped momentarily, until the referee spotted the football.

The Bills hurried to the line of scrimmage. The quarterback shouted over the crowd noise, "Kill, kill, kill."

The Bills center snapped the football, and the quarterback threw the ball into the turf, stopping the clock with six seconds left.

The Panthers called a time-out, and Coach Clay jogged to the defensive huddle. Two defensive linemen followed him onto the field. The lineman replaced two safeties, leaving Curtis as the lone safety.

Coach Clay stood before the huddle and said, "Expect a pass play. If they run it and don't get it, game's over. They're out of time. But if they throw an incompletion, they'll have another shot. If they do throw an incompletion, they might come back with a running play. Maybe another read option. Watch out for the pick plays. Let's go with goal line, gap, stack, zero. If they have time to run another play, same call." Coach Clay scanned the motley crew of undrafted free agents and undertalented veterans. "Let's make a stand here. Get the win." Coach Clay jogged back to the sideline.

After the time-out, the Bills lined up at the two-yard line. The crowd was at a fever pitch. Curtis stood five yards from the line of scrimmage, covering the tight end, but also responsible for the run. The Bills quarterback lined up in the shotgun. The center snapped the football. The tight end pass-blocked. The quarterback caught the ball and immediately tossed a perfect spiral to the back corner of the end zone. The cornerback was beat on the fade route. The wide receiver jumped and grabbed the football, but it squirted through his hands, incomplete.

The crowd let out an audible gasp of relief.

With two seconds left on the clock, the Bills had one final play to score and to win the game. When the Bills lined up for the final play, the crowd noise was so loud that Curtis couldn't hear the linebacker next to him. The Bills quarterback shouted the cadence at the top of his lungs. The center snapped the football. The quarterback faked the handoff to the running back and ran the ball himself on the read option, just as Coach Clay had predicted. The quarterback ran the ball to the left. Then he planted his foot, lowered his head, and turned up the field. The quarterback saw the running lane between the tight end and the left tackle. So had Curtis.

As the quarterback tried to sprint through the hole to pay dirt, Curtis exploded through the hole at the same time. They met at the one-yard line with a colossal collision. Curtis was a little lower and stronger. He stopped the quarterback cold, then Curtis picked up the man and slammed him to the turf.

The crowd cheered. The Panthers sideline erupted in jubilation, as if they'd won the super bowl. Veterans, like Felix Gamble, led the cheers, like proud papas who had helped develop young guys, like Curtis.

The Bills slunk back to their sideline, while the Panthers celebrated on the field. Once the celebration died, Curtis and the Panthers shook hands with their opponent. Then the players meandered to the locker room or to the sideline, to the friends and family section. Curtis followed his teammates to the friends and family section, wondering if Gabriella had come.

Friends and family stood in the front row, waiting for their favorite player to appear. They were stuck in the stands, about six feet above the field, a security guard nearby to prevent people from climbing down to the field. They leaned over the wall, talking to the players below them.

Curtis scanned the people. He found Gabriella at the far left, next to a young woman.

Gabriella waved and smiled, as he approached. She was clad in a throwback Steve Smith jersey and a Panthers hat.

Curtis looked up at her and smiled. "Hey."

"You did so great," Gabriella said. "That was awesome at the end. You totally saved the game."

Curtis blushed. "Thank you for coming."

"Thank you for the tickets." Gabriella gestured to the curvy white woman, wearing a Panthers T-shirt. "This is my friend Kayla."

Curtis waved. "It's nice to meet you."

"Congratulations," Kayla said.

"Thanks."

"We're going out to World tonight," Gabriella said. "Would you like to come?"

"What's World?" Curtis asked.

"It's a club."

CHAPTER 127

World Nightclub

Curtis knew it was a mistake the second he entered World Nightclub in uptown Charlotte. Men leered at Gabriella and Kayla. Gabriella wore a white shirt that practically glowed in the dim light, along with a knee-length skirt that showed off her toned legs and flats. Curtis thought Gabriella was the most beautiful girl in the club. Every other guy seemed to agree. Kayla also drew her share of male attention, with her skintight jeans and low-cut top, her curves on full display.

Electronic dance music pumped from the speakers. Smoke spilled into the audience during intense drumbeats. Directional lights changed color and zipped through the crowd, creating a trippy feel. Young people danced, grinding on each other, many wearing multicolored glow sticks around their necks.

They climbed the metal stairs to the loft area and found a standing table, overlooking the dance floor and DJ area. They watched the people dancing to the techno beat.

Curtis leaned over the table toward Gabriella. "You want a drink?"

Kayla interrupted. "I'd love a vodka cranberry."

"You don't have to get us drinks," Gabriella said.

"It's okay," Curtis replied.

"I guess I'll have a rum and Diet Coke. Let me give you some money." Gabriella dug into her purse.

"I got it."

"I'll get the next round."

Curtis was happy to get the drinks. He didn't know how to dance and dreaded trying to dance in front of Gabriella. So he was happy to do anything that wasn't dancing.

It took him ten minutes to wade through the bar crowd and another ten minutes to get the bartender's attention. Curtis didn't bother buying a drink for himself, since he couldn't carry three drinks. He waded through the crowd again, back to the loft. He returned to the standing table, but Gabriella and Kayla were gone, replaced by three young men pounding beers.

Curtis scanned the loft area, thinking he had the wrong table, but he didn't see Gabriella or Kayla anywhere. He found another empty standing table and set down the drinks. Curtis peered over the railing at the expansive dance floor below. The techno beat thumped through the speakers. The crowd danced, pumping like a single heartbeat.

After scanning the crowd for several minutes, he spotted Gabriella's white shirt. She danced with a guy who reminded Curtis of Jimmy G, the pretty-boy Italian quarterback who played for the San Francisco 49ers. Kayla was nearby, grinding with another handsome white guy. Her guy resembled a surfer with a mop of blond hair. Gabriella looked up periodically, her gaze on their old table, possibly searching for Curtis. She eventually spotted him and waved.

Gabriella said something to her dance partner, the guy leaning in close to hear her. Then she said something to Kayla and left the dance floor.

A few minutes later, Gabriella appeared alone at the table across from Curtis. She smiled. "Sorry about that. Kayla was begging me to dance."

"That's okay." Curtis slid her rum and Diet Coke across the table. "Here's your drink."

"Thank you." Gabriella sipped her mixed drink.

"You're welcome."

"Do you like to dance?"

Curtis shook his head. "Not really."

Gabriella frowned. "I love to dance."

Kayla appeared with the two handsome white boys in tow. "I can't believe you left us."

The Jimmy G look-alike sidled up to Gabriella, his body brushing against hers. Kayla and the surfer dude huddled around the table. His arm was wrapped around her waist, his hand resting on her hip. Kayla grabbed her drink, chugged half of it in two big gulps, then winked at her new man.

"Damn, girl," Surfer Dude said.

Kayla mouthed a kiss.

Gabriella presented the Jimmy G look-alike, like a game show host presenting the grand prize. "Curtis, this is Joey." She motioned to the blond. "And that's Tyler."

Curtis shook hands with the guys.

"Curtis plays for the Panthers," Gabriella said.

"Right on," Tyler said.

Joey narrowed his eyes at Curtis, sizing him up. "What's your name again? Like your full name?"

"Curtis Duffy," Curtis replied.

"I'm a pretty big Panthers fan, but I've never heard of you," Joey said.

"I haven't made the team yet."

Joey nodded, nonplussed.

Tyler leaned toward Curtis. "Dude, do you have braces?"

Curtis nodded, not showing his teeth.

"How old are you?"

"Twenty-five."

"Dude. I had braces when I was like thirteen."

"Lots of adults get braces. It's not a big deal," Gabriella said to Tyler. "I'm actually Curtis's orthodontist."

"That makes sense." Joey lifted his chin to Curtis. "I was wondering how you knew this guy. I thought he was your stepbrother or something."

Kayla and Tyler laughed.

Curtis clenched his jaw.

"I don't see what's so funny," Gabriella said. "I would love to have a brother like Curtis."

Gabriella's *brother* reference stung like a quick jab to the nose.

Kayla chugged the rest of her drink and said, "This is boring. Let's go back to the dance floor."

"We're talking," Gabriella said.

Kayla grabbed Gabriella's hand. "Come on. We can talk anytime."

Gabriella asked Curtis, "Are you coming?"

"In a minute," Curtis said.

Curtis watched the foursome leave the table. Joey guided Gabriella through the crowd, his hand on her lower back. Once they were out of sight, Curtis left the club, thankful he had met them there and had his vehicle to make a quick getaway.

CHAPTER 128

The Truth

Curtis's phone buzzed with a text, as he drove home from the club. He glanced at the text.

Gabriella: Where are you?

While he parked his car, he received another text.

Gabriella: Did you leave?

As he entered his apartment, his phone chimed. It was Gabriella. He rejected the call. Curtis slouched on his couch, reflecting on the disaster at the club. *I'm so stupid. I should've known she didn't like me. Was probably using me for free tickets. Why would she even bother inviting me out if she didn't like me?*

Curtis turned on the television, the channel already on ESPN. He watched highlights from the NFL preseason games, distracting himself from thinking about Gabriella.

★★★

Thirty minutes later, a knock came at his door. The knock startled Curtis upright. He went to his door and checked the peephole. Gabriella stood there, wringing her hands.

Curtis opened the door, his face a hard mask. "What are you doing here?"

"I was worried about you. I tried texting and calling you."

Curtis blocked the doorway. "How did you get my address?"

Gabriella frowned. "I send you a bill every month. Why did you leave?"

Curtis shrugged.

Gabriella glanced over his shoulder. "May I come in?"

Curtis stepped aside. "If you want."

Gabriella stepped into his living room. Curtis shut the door and joined her, standing in the middle of the room.

"Why did you leave?" she asked again.

"I don't know," Curtis replied, without making eye contact.

"I think you left because of those guys."

Curtis shrugged again. "What difference does it make?"

"I'm not interested in either of those guys. Kayla was the one who brought them to the table."

"You seemed interested. You didn't have to dance with the guy."

Gabriella put her hands on her hips. "I was dancing with Kayla. Those guys just started dancing with us. It's a dance club. That's what happens. I wanted to dance with you."

"I don't know about that." Curtis went to his couch and sat.

Gabriella followed him, standing in front of him, talking with her hands. "What do you mean, you don't know about that?"

"It's hard for me to believe that you'd rather dance with me than that guy."

"Why? Why is that so hard to believe?"

Curtis eyed the carpet.

Gabriella stepped closer. "Don't shut me out. Answer the question. Why?"

Curtis raised his gaze. "What do you want me to say?"

"The *truth*."

Curtis stood from the couch abruptly. "Oh, you want the truth? Look at me, Gabriella. You think I don't know what I look like? I've been *ugly* my whole life."

Gabriella stepped back.

Curtis continued. "You think I don't know how women view me?

They're either disgusted or afraid of me. Did I tell you about the award I won in camp? Out of over one hundred guys, guess who they voted as the ugliest?"

Gabriella blanched. "I didn't know that. I'm sorry. It's not true to me. I think you're very cute."

"It doesn't matter."

She grabbed his hand. "It *does* matter."

Curtis retracted his hand from hers. "I was stupid to think someone like you would be interested in someone like me."

"What's that supposed to mean?"

"Every guy in that club wanted you because you're beautiful. And you're a nice person too. You're smart. Successful. You have a nice family. I'll be unemployed in less than forty-eight hours. Then I can go back to my previous job, picking up trash and mowing roadsides."

She grabbed his hand again. "I think you'll make the team, and, if you don't, that doesn't change how I feel about you."

Curtis stared at her, speechless.

"I like you, Curtis. You're a good person. You make me feel safe. My whole life I've picked guys who weren't good for me. My ex, Dylan, …" Tears welled in her eyes. "I broke up with Dylan because he hit me. If you hadn't been there that day, I don't know what he would've done."

"I'm really sorry that happened to you."

"Don't be." She inched closer, staring at him with unblinking eyes.

He leaned down and pressed his lips to hers, tentative, worried about his braces. She wrapped her arms around him, forcefully pressing her lips against his. A wave of euphoria washed over him. His entire body buzzed as he kissed her.

CHAPTER 129

Definitely

Morning sunlight streamed into Curtis's living room. His eyes fluttered and opened. He sat up on the couch, his back a little sore from the game and the uncomfortable sleeping place. He padded down the hall to the bathroom, checking his bedroom along the way. His bedroom door was shut. He peed, washed his hands, and brushed his teeth. On the way back down the hall, he thought about knocking on his bedroom door, checking on Gabriella, but he didn't want to disturb her. They had stayed up past two, talking, and she was too tired to drive home, so Curtis had offered his bed. Curtis went to the kitchen and cut some apples and bananas, scrambled some eggs, and made some toast.

As he pushed the eggs around the pan with a spatula, Gabriella appeared from the bedroom. Despite no makeup and Curtis's sweats swallowing her figure, she was still beautiful.

Curtis smiled, with his mouth closed. "Good morning."

She smiled that perfect smile. "Good morning. Smells good."

"You hungry?"

"I'm starving."

"Have a seat." He motioned to the kitchen table for two. "It's almost ready."

Gabriella sat at the table.

Curtis finished the eggs, set the table, and filled glasses with water and orange juice. Luckily, the apartment came with a small set of

398

dishes and pans.

Curtis sat across the table from Gabriella.

"Thank you. This looks so good," Gabriella said.

"You're welcome."

They chatted while eating, making plans to hike at the park later that day. Gabriella wanted to go home and shower and change first though.

"Who taught you to cook?"

"Mr. H. taught me the basics …" Curtis trailed off, realizing he had inadvertently revealed something he wasn't ready to reveal.

"Who's Mr. H.?" Gabriella asked, then took the last bite of her eggs.

"He's pretty much my father."

Gabriella set down her fork. "I don't understand. Is he your stepfather?"

Curtis shook his head. "He …" Curtis stared at his plate.

"Curtis?"

"He runs a group home for boys in Alexandria." Curtis raised his gaze to meet Gabriella. "I was an orphan. I *am* an orphan."

Her mouth turned down. "Oh, I didn't know that."

"I'm an orphan, but I'm not all alone. I have Mr. H. I used to have Mr. Vasquez too, but he died."

"What happened to your parents?"

Curtis hesitated.

"I'm sorry," Gabriella said. "You don't have to answer that."

"It's okay. My dad's probably still alive. I haven't seen him in fifteen years. He didn't want anything to do with me. My mother had a drug problem." Curtis stabbed his half-eaten eggs with his fork, no longer hungry. "She dropped me off with Mr. H. when I was ten."

"Oh, Curtis."

"She did what she had to do." Curtis took a deep breath. "She died of a drug overdose six months later."

"I'm so sorry for your loss." Gabriella stood and went to Curtis.

Curtis held up his hand, blocking her. "It was a long time ago. It's fine."

"It's not fine. That must've been unbelievably traumatic." She bent over and wrapped her arms around him.

He fought his emotions, holding back the tears.

Gabriella rubbed his back, still holding him. "You were just a little boy, and you were all alone."

That was when the tears came.

★★★

After breakfast, Curtis escorted Gabriella to her car. She had parked in a visitor's space. As they entered the parking garage, hand in hand, Curtis saw movement out of the corner of his eye. He stopped and scanned the parking garage.

Gabriella stopped too. "What is it?"

"I thought I saw something," Curtis said, staring between two SUVs in the distance.

"What did you see?"

"I don't know. It must be nothing." Curtis thought he saw a man watching them, but now he was second-guessing himself.

They continued to Gabriella's Honda Accord.

At her car door, Curtis said, "I'm sorry for getting overly emotional at breakfast. I don't talk about my parents much."

"Don't apologize to me. You didn't do anything wrong." She kissed his cheek. "I'm glad you told me."

Curtis forced a smile, still feeling raw from the emotions. "Thank you for listening."

She took his hand. "Of course."

"I'll see you soon then."

She kissed him on the lips and said, "Definitely."

CHAPTER 130

The Final Cut

Early on Monday morning, Curtis received a text.

> **The Turk:** Coach Mellon wants to see you at 1:00 p.m. today. Bring your playbook and iPad.

Curtis felt sick to his stomach.

Curtis handed his playbook and iPad to Coach Mellon.

The beefy head coach took the items and gestured to the leather chairs before his desk. "Have a seat, Curtis."

Curtis sat across from the head coach. Various trophies and signed footballs decorated a glass case behind the coach's cherrywood desk.

The coach rested his meaty forearms on the desktop. "I have to say that you surprised me. I didn't expect much from you, but you proved me wrong. I've never had a more hardworking player. Coach Woody has nothing but good things to say about you. I think you have the raw ability to play in this league, but you need more seasoning. You don't have the experience, and it shows, especially on defense."

Curtis nodded along with his coach.

"Unfortunately, we're gonna release you today."

Curtis winced. He envisioned going back to mowing roadsides. He swallowed hard and said, "I appreciate the opportunity." Curtis stood from his seat and started for the door.

"Hold on, Curtis," Coach Mellon said, standing and meeting Curtis by his office door. "You didn't let me finish. We're releasing you, *but*, if you clear waivers, we'd like to add you to the practice squad. Do you understand how the practice squad works?"

"I won't be on the game-day roster, but I'll practice with the team to help them get ready each week."

"Exactly. It pays $12,000 a week, and there's also the possibility that you could get called up to the active roster. It's a long season with a lot of injuries."

Curtis gaped at his coach. "Twelve thousand per week?"

"Yep."

Curtis hugged his coach, then separated immediately after, feeling foolish. "Sorry, Coach."

Coach Mellon chuckled. "It's okay." They shook hands. "If you keep working like you do, I believe you have a future in this league."

CHAPTER 131

What You Deserve

On his way out of the building, he stopped at Coach Woody's office. The old coach watched film, while wearing his reading glasses. Curtis knocked on the open door.

Coach Woody turned from his laptop. "Curtis. How did it go with Coach Mellon?"

"Good. I'll be on the practice squad, if I clear waivers," Curtis replied.

Coach Woody stood from his desk and held out his hand. "Congratulations, young man. You earned it."

Curtis shook his hand. "I know you put in a good word for me. Thank you."

"I didn't do anything except tell the truth."

"Do you think there's a chance another team will claim me?"

"Anything's possible, but I doubt it. We're the only ones who know who you are, and we ain't tellin' anybody."

Curtis savored the sun on his face, as he strolled home from the Panther's stadium. Along the way, he stopped by Gabriella's office.

"Hi. It's Mr. Duffy, right?" the receptionist asked.

"Good memory," Curtis replied. "I was wondering if I could talk to Dr. Solomon for a minute."

"I'll see if she's available." The receptionist dialed Gabriella's extension. "Mr. Duffy's in the waiting room. He wanted to speak with you. ... Okay. I'll tell him." She hung up the phone. "She's in her office. She said you can go back."

"Thank you." Curtis walked beyond the reception desk to Gabriella's corner office.

Gabriella pecked on her keyboard, a bag of baby carrots open before her.

Curtis knocked on the open door.

Gabriella looked up from her computer and smiled. "What are you doing here?"

"I have some news."

She stood from her desk, her eyes like saucers. "You heard, didn't you?"

Curtis nodded. "I didn't make the team, but they want me on the practice squad."

"What does that mean?"

Curtis explained what it meant to be on the practice squad.

"This is good, right?"

"Not as good as making the fifty-three-man roster, but"—Curtis grinned, showing his braces—"it's still very good."

She stepped around her desk, hugged him, and said, "I'm so happy for you."

When they separated, he said, "The best part is, it means I should be here for at least a year."

They sat again and talked for a few minutes, Curtis recounting his interactions with Coach Mellon and Coach Woody. Gabriella giggled when Curtis described his impromptu hug of the burly head coach.

"I should get out of your hair," Curtis said. "I'm sure you have a ton to do."

Gabriella glanced at the clock on her laptop. "I have an appointment in about two minutes.

Curtis stood. "Would you like to go out to dinner tonight to celebrate?"

She beamed. "I'd love to."

"I'll pick you up at 7:30, if that's okay."

"Perfect."

Curtis wanted to kiss her but refrained, not wanting to embarrass her at work.

He returned to his apartment and called Mr. H., sharing his news.

Mr. H. said, "That's *outstanding*, Curtis. I'm so proud of you, son. I hope you take some time to celebrate. You deserve it."

"I'm going out to dinner with my orthodontist." Curtis then told Mr. H. about Gabriella.

"She sounds like a wonderful woman." Mr. H.'s voice caught.

"Mr. H.? You okay?"

Mr. H. cleared his throat. "I'm really happy for you."

CHAPTER 132

The Past Won't Let Go

The Fig Tree Restaurant was a craftsman-style home that had been converted into a fine dining restaurant. He had never been to a nice restaurant before. He had never had the money, the occasion, or the date. For the first time in his life, he had all three. Gabriella followed the hostess through the quaint country-style dining area with wooden accents and white linen tablecloths. Curtis followed Gabriella, who wore an off-white peasant dress with a black cardigan. Curtis wore his nicest slacks and a white button-down shirt. The hostess sat them outside, on the patio, as they had requested. Lights twinkled overhead, strung from one Turkey fig tree to another. The temperature was in the low-seventies. The hostess pulled out Gabriella's chair, and she sat. Curtis sat across from her.

"Your server will be right with you." The hostess handed them menus and a wine list before leaving.

"Thank you," Curtis replied.

Gabriella scanned the outdoor dining area. "It's so beautiful here."

A gazebo covered half of the patio area. Potted plants and flowers added to the ambiance. Arborvitae trees surrounded the patio, adding to the privacy.

"It is," Curtis agreed. "Have you ever been here?"

"Once or twice with my parents, but it was a long time ago. This was a great choice."

Curtis smiled. "It was on Yelp."

Their server appeared. He took their drink orders and disappeared.

Curtis and Gabriella studied their menus.

The server returned with a white wine for Gabriella and a beer for Curtis. "Are you ready to order?"

Curtis peered across the table at Gabriella. "Are you ready?"

"I think so," Gabriella replied.

Gabriella ordered a mixed-greens salad and the pan-roasted Scottish salmon served over zucchini, yellow squash, roasted cherry tomatoes, and farro with broccoli rabe and dill beurre blanc. Curtis ordered the brown-butter-crusted grilled elk chop with parmesan polenta cake, bacon-braised brussels sprouts, and dijon demiglace. He had thought about ordering a steak, but he'd had steak before. He'd never had elk.

After the waiter left, they chitchatted about their day. Gabriella talked about her business. Curtis talked about his conversation with Mr. H.

"He's done so much for me," Curtis said. "I think he was happier than me."

Gabriella smiled. "He sounds like a wonderful man. I'm glad you have him. Does he still run the group home?"

"Yeah. He's been at the one in Alexandria for like thirty years." Curtis sipped his beer.

"What was it like growing up there?"

Curtis set down his beer. "At the group home?"

"Yes."

"It was hard at first. The other boys picked on me. I remember my first day there like it was yesterday. I had a garbage bag with my clothes, and I was putting my clothes in the dresser Mr. H. had assigned for me. I was still upset that my mom left me, and I was crying. Some other boys came in and saw me crying, and they started teasing me, you know?"

Gabriella nodded.

"Then they saw my teeth, and the teasing got worse, and I wasn't equipped to handle myself. I didn't know how to fight. I didn't know how to reason."

"You were just a little boy."

Curtis nodded. "Mr. H. came in and saw what they were doing, and he was pissed. Everyone got into trouble except me, which wasn't good. That night, they pulled me out of bed from the top bunk. I woke up on the floor, and all these kids surrounded me. Every single one of them punched me that night. Some didn't wanna do it, so they hit me in the arm, but some did. They only hit me in places that adults wouldn't see, so nobody punched me in the face. But my body was covered in bruises."

Gabriella's eyes were glassy. "That's awful. Your mother had just abandoned you."

"It was awful at the time, but being bullied taught me a lot. I learned that I can take anything. The biggest bully became my best friend, if you can believe that." Curtis sipped his beer. "It took some time, but the group home became my home. It was better than the environment I had been in with my mother. I used to be angry with her, but I think she did the right thing leaving me with Mr. H."

"I don't know if I could've coped with something like that as a ten-year-old."

"You're a lot tougher than you think. I think you would've figured it out."

"I don't know. Maybe."

They sipped their drinks, silent with their thoughts for a time.

Gabriella set down her wineglass and asked, "Is it normal for kids to stay in the group home for a long time, or do some kids get adopted?"

"I don't know about other group homes, but, at mine, pretty much every kid was adopted or at least put in foster care. I would say the average stay was like a year."

"But you were never adopted?"

Curtis shook his head. "Nobody wants the ugly kid."

Gabriella stood from the table. "Excuse me." She hurried inside the restaurant.

Curtis sat by himself for ten minutes, replaying their conversation, wondering what he had said wrong and if she was coming back. He reasoned she was, since he'd driven, but then he wondered if she had called an Uber. Curtis was about to go inside to search for her, when she appeared on the patio.

She sat across from Curtis. Her eyes were puffy.

"Are you okay?" Curtis asked. "Did I say something wrong?"

Gabriella shook her head. "It's my fault. I'm sorry. I asked and you answered. I guess I wasn't expecting it to hit me so hard. I'm embarrassed to admit that I cried in the bathroom."

Curtis reached across the table and took her hand. "There's nothing to be upset about. I'm good. How could I not be good? I'm here with you. We're supposed to be celebrating. All that happened a long time ago."

Gabriella forced a smile. "I guess it's my privilege showing through. I grew up going to private schools, with plenty of money. Two parents at home. It's really hard for me to understand your experience."

"I think you understand my experience perfectly well. I don't think you have to live the same life as someone to understand. You just have to care."

Gabriella squeezed his hand. "May I ask you for a favor?"

Curtis sat up straight. "Sure, anything."

"I don't want you to refer to yourself as ugly." She touched her chest with her free hand. "It hurts my heart, and it's not true. You're adorable."

On the way home, Curtis drove with one hand on the wheel, the other holding Gabriella's hand. A vehicle approached from behind rapidly. The vehicle tailgated them, despite Curtis driving five miles per hour over the speed limit. It appeared to be an SUV.

Gabriella turned around, peering out the rear window. "What does this guy want?"

"I'm not driving any faster, if that's what he wants." Curtis almost mentioned his parole but remembered that Gabriella didn't know he'd been to prison. He had planned to tell her, but they hadn't known each other that long. He didn't want to ruin their burgeoning relationship with talk of his criminal record. He had vowed not to lie to her if she asked, but he wasn't ready to tell her. The relationship was too new. He felt he had already revealed too much, too soon about his past.

The driver turned on their high beams, the lights reflecting in Curtis's rearview mirror, causing him to squint.

"This is ridiculous," Gabriella said.

"Hopefully, he'll turn off soon," Curtis replied.

Gabriella scowled. "What an asshole."

"I just had the best meal of my life with the best date. He's not getting under my skin." Curtis glanced at Gabriella and grinned.

Gabriella lifted his hand to her mouth and kissed it. "You're right."

The black SUV raced past them, gunning the engine, passing them on the wrong side of the road. Curtis caught the make and model before it disappeared into the distance. It was a GMC Yukon Denali.

Curtis glanced at Gabriella.

She stared through the windshield, dumbstruck.

"Are you okay?" Curtis asked.

"I think that might've been Dylan's car," she said. "Did you get the license plate?"

"No, sorry. Did you?"

"No."

Curtis glanced back and forth from Gabriella and the road.

"Should we call the police?"

She shook her head. "I've already been down that road. They can't do anything until he hurts me."

CHAPTER 133

The Contract

During the first game week of practice, Curtis helped his teammates prepare by playing safety on the scout team defense. After practice on Thursday, Curtis lay on the bench, pressing 245 pounds with ease. After ten repetitions, he racked the weight and sat upright.

Rap music played from the speakers. ESPN with subtitles played on the weight room flat screens. A handful of Panthers also lifted weights. *Breaking News* appeared on the screen. A smiling Justin Love appeared at a podium.

Curtis stood from the bench and approached the nearest flat screen.

The following information appeared at the bottom of the screen: *Justin Love ends holdout. Signs most lucrative contract in NFL history. Five Years, 260 Million Dollars. 100 Percent Guaranteed.*

Curtis gritted his teeth, as he watched Justin Love talking at his press conference.

According to the subtitles, Justin said, *I'm happy it's over. I'm excited to get to work. I'm excited to be with my teammates. I'm excited to be in Philly. I plan to live up to every penny of this contract. For me, anything less than a Super Bowl will be a disappointment.*

ESPN cut to a commercial. Curtis returned to the bench press. As he sat on the bench, his phone chimed in his duffel bag. He fished his phone from his bag, checked the number, and answered, "Hey."

"Hey yourself," Gabriella replied. "I'm sorry to bother you. I just had a quick question."

"It's no bother. Practice is over. What's up?"

"I was just wondering if you were going to the game on Sunday. I didn't know how the practice squad works for game day."

"We're not allowed to attend. I can sit in the stands like anyone else, but I can't be on the sideline. I was planning to watch it at home. You're welcome to join me."

"My parents invited me over for a cookout on Sunday. My dad will have the game on for sure."

"That's fine, if you wanna watch it with your parents. Maybe we can meet up later for dinner."

Gabriella hesitated for a moment. "Actually, I was hoping you would go to the cookout with me. I'd like for you to meet my parents."

CHAPTER 134

Meet the Parents

Gabriella's parents lived in a gated community. Their house was a Cape Cod, with gray shingles, black shutters, and dormer windows.

Shortly before kickoff, Gabriella helped her mother in the kitchen. Curtis stood next to her father, Dr. Wayne Solomon, while the retired dentist worked the grill. The rectangular pool rippled in the warm breeze.

"I read that the average career length for an NFL player is 3.3 years," Wayne said. "Assuming you're average, what do you plan to do three years from now?"

A crescent of salt-and-pepper hair surrounded Wayne's bald head. Sweat beaded on his sun-kissed dome. His polo shirt was tucked into khaki shorts, and he wore sandals with socks.

"I'm not sure, sir," Curtis replied, holding a bottled water.

"Well, you should think about it. For all you know, this might be your first and last season in the NFL. Where did you go to college?"

"Central Virginia University." Curtis took a sip of his water.

Wayne pressed his spatula on a burger, causing the meat to sizzle. "That's a pretty good school. What was your major?"

"Social work."

Wayne turned from the grill, his brow furrowed. "Social work? Social workers barely make a living wage. How do you plan to support a family?" Wayne flipped the burgers.

"I don't know."

Wayne turned from the grill again and pointed his spatula at Curtis. "This is the problem with young men today. No direction. Let me give you a piece of advice. Gabby is a smart and successful woman. She deserves a smart and successful man. I'm sure she's enthralled with the idea of dating a Panther, but football is a short-term endeavor. In the end, Gabby, like most women, will want a man at least as successful as her. I don't think you're on a good path to success, therefore, I don't see you sticking around long-term."

Curtis gaped at Wayne, speechless, his face hot with shame.

Wayne added cheese to the burgers.

Gabriella and Regina exited the house, each carrying covered dishes.

"I should give them a hand," Curtis mumbled.

Wayne grunted.

Curtis approached the ladies, as they arranged the dishes on the patio table. "You need any help?"

Regina smiled at Curtis. "Could you bring the plates, glasses, and silverware out here? Everything's in the kitchen on the center island."

Gabriella's mother, Dr. Regina Solomon, was a practicing psychologist. She resembled a model—tall and thin, with high cheekbones, and smooth dark skin. Gabriella's beauty came from her mother.

"Sure." Curtis went inside. He grabbed the plates, intent on returning for the glasses and silverware.

Gabriella approached Curtis. "Hey. Are you okay?"

Curtis forced a smile. "I'm fine. Why?"

"Your face is red. You seem distracted or upset all of the sudden."

"Your dad was grilling me about what I plan to do after football. I don't think he likes it that we're dating."

"You're not dating my father. It's *my* opinion that matters, and I'm *very* happy that we're dating." Gabriella kissed Curtis on the lips.

★★★

Curtis was quiet on the drive toward Gabriella's townhome.

Gabriella placed her hand on his thigh. "Are you okay?"

Curtis didn't take his eyes of the road, as he replied, "I'm fine."

"You don't seem fine. Are you upset about the game?"

The Panthers had lost by two to the Browns. An interception thrown by Sam Darnold had ended their late-game attempt to drive into field goal range.

Curtis shook his head.

"Are you still bothered by what my dad said to you?"

Curtis glanced at Gabriella. "He makes some valid points."

Gabriella frowned. "No. He doesn't. It's not your fault that the NFL is a short-lived career. This is your dream. You have to put everything into it for whatever time you have. After it's over, you can be a social worker, if that's what you want."

Curtis stopped at a stoplight and turned in his seat to Gabriella. "Social workers don't make much money."

"I don't need money. I need a good honest man."

Curtis swallowed hard. "I need to tell you something."

She knitted her brow. "What?"

The light turned green.

Curtis drove through the light. "I should probably wait until we park."

"You're scaring me. I feel like this is something bad. Is it?"

Curtis nodded.

They were near Gabriella's neighborhood, so they drove in silence for a few minutes.

Curtis parked his old SUV in a visitor's space. He cut the engine and turned in his seat to face Gabriella. "After I tell you this, I'll understand if you want me out of your life. I wanted to tell you right away, but everything's so new, and I didn't know what to say so early in a relationship. I don't have a lot of experience with dating."

Gabriella stared at Curtis, her eyes like saucers. "Just tell me."

"I never graduated from CVU."

"Why not?"

"My roommate had weed in our room. We got caught with it, and I was expelled." Curtis thought about telling her the whole story, but he worried that it sounded like a lie, especially given the celebrity status of the participants.

"Oh." She let out a heavy breath. "It's not good, but it's not your fault."

"I'd like to go back to college and finish my degree someday."

"You should."

Curtis nodded.

She reached out and grabbed his hand. "You had me really worried."

Curtis dipped his head. "There's more."

Gabriella retracted her hand.

"Haven't you ever wondered why I'm a twenty-five-year-old rookie?"

"You said you were working as a landscaper."

"I was, but that's not why." Curtis took a deep breath. "I was in prison for five years."

Gabriella stiffened, her eyes glassy. She shook her head. "I can't believe this. I can't believe I keep doing this. Please tell me you didn't hurt anyone."

Curtis understood the pattern she feared and knew that the truth would likely end their relationship. "I stole a car."

She nodded. Her shoulders slumped. "Okay. Okay. Is that everything?"

"That's everything."

CHAPTER 135

Bullies Understand Violence

After practice on a Tuesday, Curtis walked to Gabriella's office from the Panthers practice facility. He stopped there briefly, letting her know he was headed home to shower and change and would return in approximately thirty minutes. They had plans to make dinner together at Gabriella's townhome.

Curtis left Gabriella's office, headed for his apartment. Along the way, Curtis spotted a black SUV parked around the corner from Gabriella's office. It was a GMC Yukon Denali, the same make and model of the SUV that had tailgated them on the way back from their dinner at the Fig Tree Restaurant five weeks ago.

Curtis ran back to Gabriella's office. He scanned the area in front, checking for her ex-boyfriend but didn't find him. Gabriella's Honda Accord wasn't parked on the street. She parked in the adjacent parking garage if she couldn't find a good space on the street in the morning. He stepped inside the office. The waiting room was empty, except for the receptionist. It was almost closing time, so no patients were waiting to be seen.

Curtis greeted the receptionist.

She smiled. "Back already?"

"I just needed to tell Gabriella something. Do you mind if I go back?" Curtis asked.

"Go ahead."

Curtis found Gabriella working on a patient. "I'm sorry to interrupt. It's important."

Gabriella stood from the rolling stool. "Is everything okay?"

"Can I talk to you in private for a minute?"

"Excuse me for a moment," Gabriella said to her client.

They went to her office and closed the door.

"What is it?" Gabriella asked.

"I saw a black GMC Yukon Denali parked around the corner," Curtis said. "It's probably nothing, but I think you should lock the door now. I'll wait outside and keep watch."

"Okay."

Gabriella escorted Curtis to the front door, locking the door as soon as he stepped onto the sidewalk. Curtis waved to Gabriella. She waved back and returned to her patient. Curtis scanned the area again, seeing nothing out of the ordinary. There were plenty of black GMC Yukons on the road. *Maybe it's just a coincidence. Maybe I'm being paranoid.* Curtis tried to think like a predator. *If I wanted to get Gabriella alone, what would I do?* He remembered what Dylan had done last time, accosting Gabriella in front of her office. It hadn't gone well for him, as Curtis had been there. It was too public. Dylan would likely choose someplace else to accost her. Then it hit him like a bolt of lightning. *The parking garage.*

Curtis searched the three-story parking garage for Gabriella's white Honda Accord. He found it in the back, wedged between two SUVs. He peered into the narrow lanes on either side of the Honda, between the SUVs. Nobody was there. He bent down and peered underneath the Honda. No feet behind the car. He did the same for the SUVs. A rush of adrenaline hit him when he saw black sneakers behind the Ford Edge.

That's gotta be him. Curtis crept alongside the Honda and the Ford Edge. When he neared the back corner of the Ford, he jumped behind the vehicle. A man crouched behind the vehicle, wearing a dark hoodie, the hood concealing his identity.

"What are you doing?" Curtis asked, his voice authoritative.

The man tried to run, but Curtis lunged after him, grabbed his hoodie, and yanked him backward. The man pivoted and swung, but Curtis ducked, causing the punch to glance off Curtis's head. Curtis countered with a right cross that dropped the man like a sack of potatoes. The man writhed on the ground in a daze.

Curtis stared down at the man, realizing it was Dylan. Gabriella's ex tried to stand, but Curtis kneeled on his chest and said, "What the fuck are you doing here?"

Dylan struggled under Curtis's knee. "Get off me, you fucking mutant."

Curtis spoke through gritted teeth. "Not until you tell me why you're here."

"Why do think?"

"You're here for Gabriella."

Dylan's lips curled into a sneer. "No shit."

Curtis shook his head. "You're not gonna do this anymore."

"Fuck you." Dylan tried to punch Curtis, but it had no power or effect from the prone position.

Curtis punched Dylan in the face, causing blood to spew from his nose.

Dylan held his nose, blood seeping through his fingers. "*Ow.* Get the fuck off me."

"You're not gonna do this anymore," Curtis repeated.

"Get off me."

"You're not gonna do this anymore."

"What are you gonna do about it?"

Curtis put his hands around Dylan's throat and squeezed. Dylan turned beet red.

"I could kill you right now," Curtis said.

Dylan flailed and pried at Curtis's hands, but Curtis was too strong. Curtis let go, and Dylan sucked in a large gulp of air, wheezing.

Curtis stood from Gabriella's ex. He pointed down at Dylan. "If I see your fucking face again, I'll kill you. Believe that." Curtis walked away.

As soon as Curtis emerged from behind the Ford Edge, he worried about the police. He checked for cameras but didn't see any, until he reached the parking garage entrance. Curtis doubted Dylan would go to the police. Hiding and stalking in a parking garage didn't look good. Not to mention Dylan threw the first punch, although that wasn't provable. Curtis doubted he had a mark on himself.

As he approached Gabriella's office, he worried she'd be upset with him, given her disdain for violence. He had choked Dylan and threatened to kill him. Under the circumstances, it felt justified to Curtis, but he doubted Gabriella would see it the same way. He'd already lied about his aggravated assault conviction.

Curtis knocked on the glass door. The receptionist was gone. Gabriella appeared from the back and unlocked the door.

It must've been written on his face because Gabriella asked, "What happened?"

"Nothing."

PART VI
Settling the Score

Everybody has a plan, until they get punched in the mouth.

—Mike Tyson

CHAPTER 136

Six Months Later ...

"That's amazing," Mr. H. said, while inspecting Curtis's teeth.

Curtis still wore braces, but his teeth were much straighter, and his overbite was nearly gone.

On a lazy Saturday in April, Curtis, Gabriella, and Mr. H. sat around the patio table at the group home.

"I regret that I didn't get him braces when he was younger," Mr. H. said to Gabriella, as if Curtis wasn't sitting next to her.

"With what money?" Curtis asked.

Mr. H. frowned. "I should've found a way."

"Good thing you didn't," Gabriella said, flashing her engagement ring. "We never would've met."

The group-home boys played Five Hundred in the backyard. The quarterback called out a number. "Fifty." Then he tossed the football into the crowd of boys. One tall boy jumped and snagged the football from the sky, gaining fifty points. The first boy to five hundred won the right to be quarterback.

"Do you two have a wedding date yet?" Mr. H. asked.

Curtis and Gabriella glanced at each other, then Curtis said, "We're planning to get married right after the football season in February ... in the Bahamas."

Mr. H. raised his eyebrows. "The Bahamas?"

"We're planning to pay for everyone's plane ticket and hotel," Gabriella said.

"Including yours," Curtis added.

"Absolutely not," Mr. H. said. "I'll pay my own way, thank you very much. I hope you two have a small guest list. It'll be expensive. I hate to see young people starting out with a big bill."

"It's a very small guest list," Gabriella said. "My parents refused to let us pay too, so it won't be that much."

"Plus, Coach Woody thinks I have a good shot at making the fifty-three-man roster this year," Curtis said. "If that happens, we'll have plenty of money. The minimum salary for a second-year player is $870,000."

Mr. H. pointed at Curtis. "Be careful with that. It doesn't go as far as you think, and professional football is a very short-term proposition."

"Don't worry"—Curtis glanced at Gabriella—"I'm marrying a successful business woman. A frugal one too. How many doctors do you know drive a Honda Accord?"

"You're a smart woman," Mr. H. said. "Cars are a depreciating asset."

One of the group-home boys sauntered to the patio table. He grinned at Gabriella and said, "Bobo likes you. He wants you to hold his hand at the zoo."

Curtis and Gabriella had planned to take the boys to the zoo tomorrow.

"He wants your Snapchat too." The boy pumped his eyebrows.

Mr. H. glared at the boy. "None of you even have a phone. Get outta here. Go play, Darnell."

Darnell giggled and ran back to the other boys.

Gabriella laughed. "Which one's Bobo?"

"The little one in the purple shirt," Mr. H. said.

"He's adorable."

"He's a pain in my ass. Always up to something."

"Is that his real name?"

Mr. H. shook his head. "His mom named him Robert Bob Hamlin. She didn't know Bob was short for Robert, so people started calling him Bobo."

They left the group home late, after a great dinner with great company. Curtis drove toward their hotel. Gabriella dozed against the passenger window of the rental car, exhausted from the early morning flight.

Curtis felt a stirring deep in the pit of his stomach. Despite his good fortune, Curtis often felt uneasy, when his mind and body were still. He had told Gabriella two big lies and hadn't been caught. There hadn't been a Dylan sighting since Curtis had beat him up in that parking garage, but it only made Curtis paranoid that Dylan would come back and ruin his life by pressing charges—or worse, hurt Gabriella.

Curtis found a sports talk station on the radio to distract his thoughts, keeping the volume low.

The broadcaster said, "Philly has a real problem. I think there's something to these Justin Love rumors. If you watch the divisional playoff game, where they got shellacked by the 49ers, you can see it in his body language, you can see it on the sideline, when he was yelling at his line. His offensive line couldn't protect him. His defense was improved, but it was still middle of road. Then they cut his buddy, Kavon Drake, after his Achilles tear. I'm telling you there's bad blood between Justin Love and the Eagles organization. I think the rumors are true. I think he wants out."

CHAPTER 137

He's Back

Curtis lounged on the couch with Gabriella, their feet sharing the same ottoman. They watched ESPN on Gabriella's big screen. Curtis had spent most of the summer at Gabriella's townhome. They had planned for Curtis to move in with her full-time, as soon as his apartment lease was up in October. ESPN cut to a commercial break.

Curtis grabbed the remote and muted the television. He kissed Gabriella on the cheek and said, "I'm gonna miss you." He was referencing the start of training camp, which began in three days.

Gabriella turned her head to face him. "At least you don't have to go away this time."

Last season, training camp had been held at Wofford College in South Carolina, but this year's training camp would be held at the practice facility in Charlotte.

"We can still see each other at night," Gabriella said.

"I don't know if I'll have time," Curtis replied. "I should probably stay at my apartment. It's closer."

"I could come by after work and cook you dinner," Gabriella said. "You have to eat, right?"

Curtis arched his eyebrows. "You would do that for me?"

"Why wouldn't I? I love you."

Curtis smiled, showing his braces. "I love you too."

She pecked him on the lips.

An Applebee's commercial played on the screen, reminding Curtis of his dinner reservations. "By the way, I made those dinner reservations for our birthdays. The Fig Tree at 7:30 on Friday."

Curtis would be twenty-six on Friday, August 4th, and Gabriella would be twenty-eight three days later.

"You sure you'll have time?" Gabriella asked. "We can always celebrate our birthdays after camp."

"It's just dinner," Curtis said. "I can make a little time. Like you said, I have to eat."

ESPN returned from the commercial break. Breaking News appeared at the bottom of the screen. A picture of Justin Love appeared in the upper right corner. Curtis pressed the Mute button, the sound returning.

The ESPN news anchor said, "We have breaking news from the NFL. Justin Love has been traded from the Philadelphia Eagles to the Carolina Panthers for a first- and second-round pick in 2024, 2025, and 2026. The Eagles have agreed to pay half of Love's fifty-two-million-dollar salary in 2023."

Curtis gaped at the screen. His hands trembled.

"What's wrong?" Gabriella asked.

Curtis sprang from the couch. He paced in front of the television, no longer hearing the broadcaster. "No, no, no, no, no. This can't be happening."

Gabriella muted the television and went to Curtis. "What's wrong? I don't understand."

Curtis shook his head. "I can't fucking play with him. I can't do it. I can't."

Gabriella grabbed his hands. "Why not? Talk to me."

Curtis nearly told her everything, but he worried she wouldn't believe him. The story was objectively unbelievable. Five people were in that fraternity bedroom who would swear on a stack of Bibles that it had been Curtis who had raped Tania. He didn't want Gabriella to doubt him, to think for a second that he might be a rapist. So, he said, "Justin Love was at CVU when I was there. He bullied me because of my looks."

CHAPTER 138

First Day of Training Camp

Curtis sat at his locker before practice, his knee bouncing rapidly. He glared across the locker room at Justin Love. The gregarious quarterback shook hands and dapped up his new teammates. He was already a celebrity in Charlotte. The missing piece to the Super Bowl. Carolina had a great defense, a good offensive line, and excellent skill position players. What they lacked was a franchise quarterback. Until now.

Curtis thought about Justin raping Tania in that fraternity bedroom, with four of his teammates watching. Andre held his penis in his hand, like he was on deck. Andre Willis was the number-one receiver for the Jacksonville Jaguars. Kavon Drake had been in the room too. He tore his Achilles last season and was cut by the Eagles, but he'd recently signed with the Dallas Cowboys. Preston Waylon was a swing tackle with the NY Giants. Thomas Creese was a starting right tackle for the Cleveland Browns. Curtis imagined punching Justin in the face.

When the crowd finally dispersed, Curtis stood and walked across the locker room to Justin. The superstar quarterback took off his shirt, displaying his athletic build. Justin faced Curtis. The quarterback's eyes widened.

"You remember me?" Curtis asked, his face a hard mask.

"No. Should I?" Justin replied.

"We played together at CVU for a short time."

Justin cocked his head. "What's your name?"

"Curtis Duffy."

Justin blinked. "Sorry, man. Don't remember you. College was a long time ago." He held out his hand. "It's nice to meet you though."

Curtis ignored Justin's outstretched hand. "It wasn't that long ago." Curtis walked away.

CHAPTER 139

Happy Birthday

On Curtis's birthday, he exited the locker room. Fans stood behind temporary fences, cheering their favorite players as they emerged from the locker room. The crowd cheered but not for Curtis. The crowd clamored for Justin Love's attention, as he signed autographs before practice.

Curtis glowered at Justin, as he trotted to the practice field, wearing shoulder pads and shorts, his helmet in hand. Curtis jogged two laps around the practice field, then stretched alone. While he stretched, he mean-mugged Justin Love as he warmed up his billion-dollar arm. Justin's contract was 260 million, fully guaranteed, but he would likely earn much more off the field with endorsements.

Justin stared at Curtis for a beat, then marched his way. Justin's face was like stone. "What the fuck is your problem? You've been looking at me like you got beef this whole week."

Curtis narrowed his eyes. "Yeah."

"Who the fuck do you think you are? You're damn lucky to even be here."

Curtis clenched his fists. "Those questions are better suited to you."

Justin lifted his chin to Curtis. "Keep it up, motherfucker. It'll end just like it did at CVU."

"You know exactly who I am, don't you?"

Justin walked away.

Curtis watched the quarterback, now joking with his fellow quarterbacks, as if nothing had happened.

During the team period, the first-team offense practiced against the third-team defense. Curtis played free safety on the third-team defense. Justin Love showed off for the fans, completing nearly every pass, without worry of a pass rush. Justin wore a red jersey, signifying he was off-limits for contact. As they were in half-pads, they weren't tackling anyway, but instead hitting and stopping the momentum of the runners and receivers. Since the defenders couldn't take players to the ground, the runners and receivers stopped as soon as they were hit. There was an unwritten rule. Defenders wouldn't take them to the ground, and the ball carriers wouldn't try to run over the defenders.

On the next play, Justin Love lined up in the shotgun and called out the cadence. On the second *hut*, the center snapped the ball to Justin. Curtis lined up on the right hash, playing a two deep zone. The tight end took an outside release and sprinted up the hash on a seam route. Justin threw a rocket to the tight end, in front of Curtis, and just over the linebacker's head. Curtis sprinted downfield. He could've destroyed the tight end, as Curtis arrived just as the tight end caught the football. Instead, Curtis avoided the hit, letting the big man catch the ball unmolested. His role on the scout team wasn't to hurt his teammates. Those hits were reserved for games and full-contact practice periods.

As Curtis jogged back to the defensive huddle, Justin Love said, "Hey, 41." Justin was referencing Curtis's jersey number.

Curtis glared at the quarterback.

Justin said, "This is the NFL, which stands for Not For Long, when you're getting roasted like that."

Three plays later, the call was offset, stack, inverted two, strong fire. The inverted two meant the corners would play the deep halves, and the safeties would play the flats, but the strong fire meant Curtis would blitz, and the outside linebacker would play the flats in his place. This all had to be choreographed and timed with expert precision, so the quarterback and the offensive line didn't see the safety blitz coming.

Justin and the Panthers offense lined up in a shotgun pro set, with one tight end and two running backs. On the cadence, the outside linebacker inched toward the flats. Curtis waited for Justin to check his side. As soon as Justin looked to the other side, Curtis sprinted down the line of scrimmage. Curtis was at full speed when the center snapped the football. He had timed it perfectly. The running back missed Curtis entirely, and Curtis slammed his shoulder pad into Justin's chest at full speed, causing a loud *crack*. The football squirted from Justin's grasp and rolled on the turf.

The practice went silent. The 260-million-dollar quarterback writhed on the ground, the wind knocked out of him. Curtis stood over him and spit through his facemask. An offensive tackle shoved Curtis. Several more crowded Curtis, protecting their quarterback.

"What the fuck, Curtis?" asked one of them.

"What the hell are you doing?" asked another one.

Trainers sprinted onto the field to tend to Justin.

Head Coach Mellon ran onto the field, his keg-size stomach jiggling under his gray T-shirt. "You're done, Duffy. Go home. *Now*."

Curtis scanned his teammates. They gaped at him, shocked by what he had done. Curtis jogged to the locker room, the fans booing him along the way.

CHAPTER 140

7HEAVEN

Curtis showered and dressed in shorts and a T-shirt. The locker room was nearly empty, his teammates still at practice, except for the watchful security guard. Curtis grabbed his personal items from his locker and shoved them into his duffel bag. He hurried, figuring practice would be over soon. He didn't want to face his teammates.

Curtis left the locker room, just before his teammates entered. The security guard followed Curtis, until he left the practice facility. Curtis walked through the parking lot to his SUV. He normally walked to practice, but he was trying to save his feet the extra mileage during training camp. Curtis climbed into his old Nissan and slammed the creaky door.

Was I cut? Is that why the security guard was following me? Coach Mellon had said, You're done, Duffy. Go home. *Shit.* Curtis smacked his steering wheel. *I'm so stupid.*

He started his vehicle and peered through the windshield. Directly in front of his SUV, in the next row, was a shiny Mercedes G-Wagon with a license plate that read 7HEAVEN. Curtis gripped his steering wheel with white knuckles. He cut his engine and said aloud, "*No.* I'm not doing this again. That motherfucker is gonna fix this."

Twenty-five minutes later, a handful of Curtis's teammates trickled into the parking lot. They climbed into their luxury vehicles and drove away, while Curtis waited for Justin Love. Justin appeared ready for a night on the town, with his slacks and silk shirt. Curtis exited his SUV, leaving the door open, and stalked to Justin. Curtis met him in the middle of the parking lot, in front of Justin's G-Wagon. A couple of Curtis's teammates watched the scene from a safe distance.

"You're gonna fix this," Curtis said, through gritted teeth.

"Get the fuck outta my face." He tried to walk around Curtis, but Curtis blocked him.

"Tell the coaches that we're good, or I'll tell every motherfucker with a microphone that you raped Tania."

Justin froze, his entire body taut. He spoke in a low tone, aware of a few teammates watching from afar. "Nobody will believe an ex-con."

Curtis clenched his fists, now wary that Justin had investigated his arrest record. "Someone might. Either way, I got nothing to lose. But you? You'll always have the stench of a rapist."

Justin raised one side of his mouth in disgust. "That's not how this works. You of all people should know that. Five witnesses will tell the world that *you* raped Tania. You're the one with a criminal record. You're the one who was expelled for drugs. You'll be the one with the stench of a rapist."

Curtis's shoulders slumped.

Justin smiled, but it didn't reach his eyes. "You're done here. I already told Coach Mellon that I want you gone. You'll be cut tomorrow. Why don't you go back to whatever shithole you came from—"

Curtis threw a powerful right cross, catching Justin squarely on the jaw, sending the quarterback down for the count. Felix Gamble ran toward the scene. Justin lay on his back, his mouth open and red with blood.

Felix called across the parking lot to another player, "Get the trainer!"

The probable repercussions of his actions filtered into Curtis's consciousness. He ran back to his car, climbed inside, and drove away.

CHAPTER 141

Repercussions

On the short drive to his apartment, Curtis was shaky, his heart pounding, wondering if the police would be waiting for him. *No, that's too quick, but they're coming soon.* Curtis drove past his apartment building, preferring someplace safe to figure out his next move. So he drove to a nearby park.

Frazier Park was a 16.5-acre urban park with soccer and football fields, basketball and tennis courts, a playground, a dog park, and creek-side trails. Curtis parked in the lot and exited his SUV, purposely leaving his phone behind. He needed to think without any distractions.

The afternoon sun was high in the sky, as he walked to the creek. The smell of freshly cut grass hung in the air. He meandered on the concrete sidewalk, moving at a snail's pace. In the distance, young men played basketball on the asphalt courts. He crossed the footbridge, the lazy creek underneath.

Curtis ambled along the creek until he found a lonely bench. He sat on the wooden bench, watching and listening to the creek. Being alone with his thoughts didn't make the situation any better. If anything, after reflecting on his actions, he realized how badly he had fucked up everything. He was about to make an NFL roster. He was about to realize his dream. With two split second acts of violence, he had thrown away his dream job and his freedom. He would have to return to prison to complete the remaining five years of his aggravated assault conviction, not to mention the new charge for punching Justin.

Why do I keep making the same fucking mistakes? I can't ever have anything good. I always find a way to ruin it. It's like I'm broken. Something in me doesn't want anything good. Why do I keep sabotaging myself? Fuck. I am so fucked.

Curtis thought about Mr. H. *He believed in me. He stood by me when I was expelled from CVU, when I went to prison. He's so proud of me, but I ruined everything.* Tears welled in his eyes. *What am I gonna tell Gabriella? She'll call off the wedding. The wedding is the least of it. She'll never talk to me again.*

Curtis hung his head. Tears dripped from his eyes to the grass, disappearing into the soil like raindrops. He stayed there on that bench for a long time, imagining the worst of it. Losing Mr. H's respect. Losing Gabriella. Losing his freedom. He imagined spending the next ten years in prison. There would be no NFL comeback this time. He'd be much too old.

With the sun low on the horizon, Curtis stood from the bench, ready to face the music. He trudged back to his SUV and checked his phone. He had a flurry of texts from his ex-teammates checking on him, asking him if he was okay. There were multiple texts from the President of Player Personnel.

> **Morris Dickenson:** I need you to come to the stadium offices tomorrow and sign some paperwork and meet with legal at 11:00 a.m. This is for your benefit. We would like to keep this out of the press.
>
> **Morris Dickenson:** Do not tell anyone what happened until you talk to legal. There is an offer that might keep you out of prison and from being sued, but it is contingent on your silence.
>
> **Morris Dickenson:** Please confirm that you will be at the stadium at 11:00 a.m. tomorrow.

The possibility of avoiding prison buoyed Curtis. If he could stay out of prison, maybe he could explain everything to Mr. H. and Gabriella. Curtis replied to Mr. Dickenson's text, letting him know that he'd be there.

He went back to his texts. Two were from Gabriella, wondering where he was. *Shit.* Curtis had forgotten about their birthday dinner reservations at 7:30. He checked the time on his phone. It was 7:14 p.m. They'd never make it, not that it mattered. They had a lot to talk about.

Curtis sent Gabriella a quick text.

> **Curtis:** I'm sorry. We won't make dinner. Something bad happened today. I'll be at your house in 20 min to talk.

Curtis drove to the suburbs, to Gabriella's townhome. Her parking lot was inundated with police cars. Two police officers stood sentry by her front door. His stomach turned, and his palms were sweaty. *Are they here for me? Did Gabriella tell them I was coming?* Curtis parked his SUV in a visitor spot. He took a deep breath. *I can't run from this.*

He exited his SUV and walked to Gabriella's house, feeling nauseated. Along the way, he noticed her father's white BMW in a nearby space. The police officers held up their hands, like stop signs. One of them put his hand on the butt of his handgun.

Curtis showed his hands in surrender. "I'm Curtis Duffy. I think you're looking for me."

The officers looked at each other quizzically.

"What's your relation to Gabriella Solomon?" one of the police officers asked.

"I'm her fiancé," Curtis replied.

"Hold on," the officer said. "Wait here."

One police officer went inside, while Curtis waited outside with the other officer. Curtis expected the officer to handcuff him, but instead the officer said, "You can put your hands down."

Curtis lowered his arms to his sides, confused.

Less than a minute later, the officer returned to the front stoop, and said, "Can I see some ID?"

Curtis showed the police officer his driver's license. Then he let Curtis inside Gabriella's townhome. Two plainclothes officers talked in the kitchen. Dr. Wayne Solomon paced in the living room. Dr. Regina Solomon sat perched on the edge of the couch.

Curtis went to the living room. "What's going on?"

Regina stood from the couch.

Wayne glared at Curtis. "Dylan broke in and held Gabby at knife-point."

Curtis was stunned for an instant. "Oh, my God. Is she okay?"

"She wasn't *physically* harmed."

"Where is she?"

"She's in her office, giving her statement to the detective."

Curtis breathed a sigh of relief. "Did they arrest him?"

Wayne nodded.

Regina touched Curtis's forearm. "She's a little shaken up. A neighbor heard her scream and called the police. If he hadn't ... I don't want to think about what might've happened."

"How did he get in?" Curtis asked.

Wayne crossed his arms over his chest. "She thought it was you. Thought you forgot your key."

Curtis ran his hand over his face. "I'm so sorry."

Wayne shook his head. "Don't apologize to me. Apologize to her."

The home office door opened, as if on cue, and a female detective exited, followed by Gabriella. Curtis went to Gabriella, meeting her just outside her home office. Her hair was disheveled, and her eyes were red-rimmed.

Curtis took her hands. "Are you okay?"

"Where were you?" she asked, anger in her voice.

"I'm sorry. Something happened at practice." Curtis gestured to the office. "Can we talk in private?"

They went into Gabriella's office. Curtis shut the door behind them.

"You were supposed to be here." Tears welled in her eyes. "I never would've opened the door, but I thought it was you."

Curtis hugged her. "I'm so sorry." Curtis rubbed her back, as she cried softly.

When her tears subsided, she sniffed and stepped back from Curtis. "What happened at practice?"

Curtis told Gabriella about tackling Justin Love in practice and being ejected.

"What does that mean? Are you cut?" Gabriella asked.

"There's more to it." Curtis cleared his throat. "This next part is confidential, so you can't tell anybody. If they find out I talked, I could go to prison. Truthfully, I still might."

Gabriella sucked in a sharp breath. "*Prison*? What did you do?"

"I waited for Justin in the parking lot. I was worried that he'd tell Coach Mellon to cut me. I wanted to reason with him, but he didn't care. Told me that he had already told Coach Mellon to cut me. Said I was done." Curtis looked down. "So I punched him."

Gabriella took two steps back. "Oh my God. He was telling the truth."

Curtis stepped closer to Gabriella. "Who was telling the truth?" He reached for her.

Gabriella took another step back, her hands held up like a stop sign. "*Don't* touch me."

"I don't understand."

"Did you beat up Dylan in the parking garage by my office?"

Curtis froze, like a deer in headlights. "I …"

Gabriella shook her head. "I can't believe I keep doing this."

Curtis held out his hands. "Doing what?"

"Falling for violent men."

"I'm not violent. I love you. I would never hurt you."

Her eyes were glassy. "That's exactly what Dylan said."

"I'm not Dylan. I'm not violent."

"You're not?" She put her hands on her hips. "You just waited in the parking lot to beat up your quarterback after you hit him in practice when you weren't supposed to."

Curtis opened his mouth to speak, but nothing came out.

"You beat up Dylan and didn't even tell me. Did you ever stop to think he might come after me because of that?"

"I was trying to protect you."

"By *lying* to me?"

Curtis winced, her words like a slap to the face.

She pointed toward the office door. "Get out. I don't want you here."

Curtis was stunned.

"Get out!"

Curtis pivoted and left her home office. He fast-walked from her townhome without a word, not making eye contact with Gabriella's parents or the police officers.

CHAPTER 142

Legal

Two security guards escorted Curtis upstairs to a conference room. Morris Dickenson and three attorneys stood in front of a shiny mahogany table. The guards waited outside. Morris made the introductions, his face a hard mask, his tone harsh. Curtis shook hands with the attorneys but didn't remember their names. They sat across from each other at the table—Morris and the attorneys on one side, Curtis on the other. His stomach fluttered with nerves, feeling like he was being setup in some way, just like before. It was everyone on their side, and nobody on his side.

"Are you cutting me?" Curtis asked Mr. Dickenson.

"You will be released today," Mr. Dickenson said, his jaw set tight.

Curtis slumped his shoulders and looked away.

The female attorney slid a small stack of papers across the table with a pen. "This is a nondisclosure agreement or an NDA. Do you know what an NDA is?"

Curtis nodded. "I'm assuming it says, I can't talk about what happened yesterday with Justin Love and me, or I'll be arrested and sued."

"Partly. It also says that you can't talk about the event that transpired on September 11, 2016, in the fraternity house of Sigma Chi."

Curtis furrowed his brow. He addressed Mr. Dickenson. "How did you know about that?"

Mr. Dickenson said, "I can't divulge that information."

"What did Justin tell you?"

Mr. Dickenson glowered at Curtis. "I will say that I'm against this agreement. You should've gone to prison then, and you should go back now. You're a thug and a rapist. Prison is where you belong. I never should've given you a chance."

Curtis gaped at the President of Player Personnel. "I didn't rape *anyone.*"

Mr. Dickenson stood from the table. "I'm done with you. I suggest you sign that NDA and reevaluate your life choices. You're extremely lucky Justin agreed not to press charges in return for your discretion." Mr. Dickenson left the room.

Curtis read through the documents, confirming that the deal was as advertised. He signed the NDA.

As Curtis left the Carolina Panthers facility, he thought about Justin Love. *Why wouldn't he press charges?* Just outside the building, Curtis stopped in his tracks. *He doesn't want everything coming out in court.*

CHAPTER 143

Leaked

Curtis drove back to his apartment. He called Gabriella, but his call went straight to voice mail. He sent her another text.

Curtis: Please talk to me. I'm so sorry.

Curtis went to his bedroom, undressed, and climbed into bed. He hadn't slept much the night before. He put his phone on silent and drifted off to a fitful sleep.

★★★

Curtis sat on the couch, watching Scooby-Doo. His mother was in the kitchen, talking to Derek.

Sara said, "He wouldn't pay. He wanted it raw."

Derek grabbed her by the throat. Her face turned scarlet. She pawed at his muscular arms to no avail.

Curtis ran to the kitchen. "Let go of my mom."

Derek scowled at Curtis. "What you gonna do about it, nigga?"

Curtis ran to Derek and pounded on his lower back with his little fists, but it had no effect.

Derek sneered at Sara. "How many times do I have to tell you to get the money up front?" Then he let go, and Sara fell to the linoleum in a heap, wheezing for breath.

Curtis rushed to his mother's side, wrapping his arms around her.

Derek disappeared, and his mother's face turned dark and skeletal.

She said, "Get off me. I don't love you. I don't want you. Ugly motherfucker."

Curtis woke in a cold sweat, thrashing under his covers. His eyes adjusted to the darkness, the only light coming from the streetlights outside. He calmed as he realized it was just a dream. Then he felt sick to his stomach, remembering how he'd fucked up his life.

He rose from his bed, not wanting to revisit his nightmares. He dressed in shorts and a T-shirt and grabbed his cell phone from his bedside table. Curtis padded to the living room, flipped on the overhead light, and sat on the couch. He checked his notifications. He had a few more texts from his teammates. One from Coach Woody. But nothing from Gabriella. He tossed his phone on the coffee table, the ringer still on Silent.

Curtis turned on the television with the remote. It was already on his favorite channel, ESPN, but there was a commercial. He surfed through the channels, searching for something to take his mind off what had happened. He couldn't find anything good, so he surfed back to ESPN.

Curtis gaped at his own image on the screen.

An ESPN broadcaster spoke, with Curtis's ugly mug in the corner of the screen. "Second-year practice squad player for the Carolina Panthers, Curtis Duffy, assaulted quarterback Justin Love yesterday in the parking lot of the Panthers practice facility. According to our sources, Curtis Duffy tackled Justin Love during a noncontact drill and was kicked out of practice. Mr. Duffy then waited in the practice facility parking lot for Justin Love, where Mr. Duffy sucker punched the newly acquired star quarterback. During the attack, Justin Love sustained a broken jaw and will likely miss the next ten weeks. Previously, Curtis Duffy had served five years in prison for aggravated assault."

Curtis turned off the television, wondering if his teammates had leaked the story to the press, or maybe the Panthers organization had leaked it on purpose, knowing Curtis couldn't tell his side of the story.

It's not like they could hide Justin's broken jaw. His cell phone didn't chime, but its screen went from black to *Mr. H Calling*. Curtis didn't answer. Instead, he waited for Mr. H.'s call to go to voice mail. Then Curtis tapped his own name into the Google search bar. He clicked on an article from the *Charlotte Gazette* titled "Justin Love Out for Ten Weeks after Criminal Assault by Teammate."

Curtis scanned the article containing the same information as the ESPN report. He scrolled down to the comments.

> **PanthersFan334:** This is why you don't let criminals near your 52 million dollar per yr QB
>
> **DougieG12:** This franchise is cursed!!!!!! We finally get a good QB and some f-ing criminal punches him in the face.
>
> **LukeKFan59:** We had a good one. He was too soft to jump on a fumble. But I hear you. This franchise is cursed. Who the hell hires someone who was in prison for five years? Has that EVER happened in the NFL?
>
> **The_Real_Deal:** Curtis Duffy is ugliest dude I've ever seen. No wonder he's so angry.
>
> **Your_Uncle_Bob:** I don't even know what he is. He's like a black ginger but somehow he's whiter than me. Weirdo

CHAPTER 144

Curtis Can't Stop the Bleeding

Curtis tried calling Gabriella again, but his call went directly to voice mail. He sent her another text.

> **Curtis:** I have to explain. I just need you to hear me out. If you want me to go away after that, I will. I'm coming over. Please talk to me.

Curtis drove to Gabriella's townhome. He parked in a visitor's space. Her Honda Accord was there, which was a good sign, but the house was dark, except for the porch lights. He glanced at the time on his phone. It was only 9:12 p.m. *She can't be asleep yet.*

He exited his car and jogged to her front door. Curtis rang the doorbell several times, but nobody stirred inside. *She's probably staying with her parents.*

Curtis drove to the Solomons' gated community. He couldn't remember the gate code, so he parked along the road shoulder, hopped the fence, and hiked to their house. The neighborhood streets were quiet that Saturday night. Lights were on inside the homes though, filled with people who belonged.

He reached their Cape Cod after a half-mile walk. As he neared the front door, his throat felt dry, and his underarms felt wet. Curtis took a deep breath and pressed the doorbell. He peered through the sidelight window but didn't see anyone. Muffled voices came from the living room.

Dr. Wayne Solomon appeared in the sidelight window. He glowered at Curtis and opened the front door. "You have a lot of nerve showing up here, after what you've done."

Curtis dipped his head. "I know. Can I please talk to her? There's a lot more to the story."

Wayne frowned. "I bet."

"Please, sir. Five minutes, and I'll leave her alone."

"Hold on." He slammed the door in Curtis's face.

Curtis waited on the front stoop for several minutes, before Gabriella stepped onto the stoop and shut the door behind her.

"What are you doing here?" Gabriella asked, her hands on her hips.

Despite the anger in her eyes, he wanted to hug her, but he didn't dare.

"I'm assuming you saw the news," Curtis said.

Her face was a hard mask. "You lied about your conviction too. It wasn't auto theft. It was aggravated assault."

"I'm sorry that I lied to you. I know how you feel about violence. I was worried you'd break up with me if you knew."

"You'll never know now because there's one thing I hate more than violent men, and that's a liar."

Curtis held out his hands like a beggar. "Please. There's a lot more to this. My aggravated assault, I was trying to protect my friend, Destiny. I went too far, but I was afraid. She was afraid. I didn't start anything."

"And Dylan?"

"He was waiting in the parking garage for you. I was worried that he would attack you."

"And Justin Love hurt your feelings, so you were justified in breaking his jaw?"

"I'm not supposed to talk about this because I signed an NDA, but Justin raped someone, and I tried to help. Then Justin and the other guys in the room said it was me. The girl wouldn't talk, so they expelled me. It was easier to get rid of me than to face the truth."

She shook her head. "You're unbelievable. First, you tell me that Justin was bullying you because of your looks, and now you're telling me that he raped someone, but somehow you were the hero. It was a conspiracy to get rid of you, and now you can't talk about it because of some nondisclosure agreement. I thought you were expelled because of your roommate's drugs."

"I was. They never would've sent the cops if all the other stuff hadn't happened. Please. You have to believe me."

She narrowed her eyes, studying Curtis for a long beat. "There's a common thread through all of this. Notice how none of this is ever *your* fault. You're a liar and a con man. For all I know, *you* raped this poor girl."

Curtis stepped back at the accusation. His face scrunched. His entire body drooped.

"I want you out of my life. I never want to see you again. You understand me?"

Curtis nodded.

She removed her engagement ring and held it out, her nose up, like it was an offensive object. "Take your ring back."

Curtis took the ring and shoved it into the front pocket of his jeans.

"I want my house key."

Curtis reached into his other front pocket and grabbed his keys. He fumbled with the key ring, his hands trembling as he removed the house key, and handed it to Gabriella.

She snatched the key and said, "If I ever see you again, I'll assume you're stalking me, and I *will* call the police. Do you understand me?"

Curtis nodded again. Then he walked away.

CHAPTER 145

The First Attempt

Curtis woke late on Sunday morning. He stayed in bed, trying to fall back to sleep, preferring his nightmares to reality. But he couldn't sleep anymore, so he rolled out of bed and went to the bathroom. He went through the motions of brushing his teeth in a haze.

He tried to eat breakfast too, but he wasn't hungry, despite having eaten very little the day before. Curtis returned to his bedroom and changed into his running gear. His phone sat on his bedside table, but he had no desire to touch it. He left his apartment without his keys, leaving the door unlocked in his wake.

Curtis took the stairs to the lobby of his building, not wanting to see anyone in the elevator. He left his apartment building, stepping into the heat and humidity of Charlotte in August. Waves of heat emanated from the asphalt streets.

"Mr. Duffy," a female called out. "Mr. Duffy."

Curtis pivoted to the voice. A well-dressed woman holding a microphone fast-walked toward him, with a cameraman right behind her. They appeared to come from a white van emblazoned with *WBTV On Your Side*. Curtis ran away from the woman on the concrete sidewalk.

People gawked at Curtis as he sprinted down the sidewalk. He wasn't sure if they gawked because he was sprinting or because his ugly face was now infamous. Curtis ran until he hit the railroad tracks, a few miles from his apartment. Then he turned left, running on the gravel alongside the train tracks. He ran for another mile or so, until he reached the train overpass.

Curtis stopped in the middle of the overpass, leaning on the chain-link fence, catching his breath, and watching the I-77 traffic below. Engine and tire noise drowned out his heavy breathing. Diesel and gasoline fumes wafted from the highway. He closed his eyes and imagined climbing to the top of the fence and jumping in front of an eighteen-wheeler. He imagined timing it perfectly, falling from the bridge, the truck hitting him at seventy miles per hour before he hit the ground.

He scaled the fence, sat at the top, and perched, ready to jump. From the top of the fence, the drop appeared severe. Maybe forty-feet. He waited for the right truck, his entire body tense. He imagined the aftermath, the pileup of cars his body would likely cause. *How many other people will die because of me?*

Curtis climbed down from the fence, telling himself how he need-ed to find a better way that would only kill him. Curtis wasn't sure if that was really the reason or if he was just scared. Maybe it was both.

CHAPTER 146

The Inspection

Knocking noises woke Curtis from his slumber. He rolled out of bed, grabbed his shorts and T-shirt from the floor, and dressed. He stepped to his front door, the knocking still insistent.

Curtis peered through the peephole to see his parole officer, with his orangey-tan face and bug eyes. Curtis opened the door and said, "Good morning, Trevor."

Trevor frowned. "That's all you got for me? I've been calling and texting you."

"I'm sorry. I haven't been checking my phone."

Trevor entered Curtis's apartment. "I guess I can understand why."

Curtis shut the door and faced his parole officer. "Are you gonna send me back to prison?"

"Depends on what Justin Love does. If he presses charges, I have no choice. If he doesn't, then I'll let it lie."

Curtis nodded. "Thank you."

"Don't thank me." Trevor scanned the apartment. "I'm here to do an inspection."

"Go ahead, not that you need my permission."

Curtis sat on his couch, while Trevor searched his apartment for contraband. Curtis thought about the things he wasn't allowed to have. *Drugs, weapons of any kind. A gun.* He imagined putting a gun to his temple and pulling the trigger. It would be so simple, like pushing a button or flipping a switch. Then it would all be over. *Would I even be able to buy a gun? Felons aren't allowed to have guns.* Curtis thought about the ex-cons he knew who carried guns.

A few minutes later, Trevor emerged from the bedroom. He stood before Curtis and said, "You look like shit."

"It's been a rough few days."

Trevor sighed. "Why did you do it?"

After Gabriella's reaction to the truth, Curtis went with a lie. "Because I'm stupid and immature."

"That's a start." Trevor sighed. "I'm assuming you're leaving town soon?"

"At some point. I'll let you know of course."

"Make sure you do." Trevor paused for an instant. "I'm sorry it ended like this."

"So am I."

"Make sure you answer my calls in the meantime."

"Yes, sir."

Trevor left the apartment.

CHAPTER 147

Help

Curtis entered the gun shop, wearing a baseball hat. The bell attached to the door jingled, attracting the attention of the bearded man at the glass counter. Curtis brushed past the T-shirt rack. One prominently displayed shirt featured a revolver with the message, *Due to the high price of ammo, do not expect a warning shot.* He approached the glass counter, filled with handguns. Rifles and shotguns were mounted on the wall behind the counter.

"Can I help you?" the bearded man asked.

Curtis cleared his throat. "I'd like to buy a handgun."

"You have a particular manufacturer in mind? A particular caliber?"

"No."

"What do you plan to use it for?"

Curtis furrowed his brow. "Uh, I need it for home defense."

The man nodded. "I'd recommend a Glock 17 nine-millimeter. It's reliable. You don't have to worry about external safeties."

"That sounds good."

The man tilted his head. "You have any experience with guns?"

"No, sir."

"Well, we have a class for beginners once a month." He grabbed a flyer from the counter and handed it to Curtis.

Curtis glanced at the flyer. "Do I need to take the class before I can buy a gun?"

"No, sir. You can buy it today. We just need to do a background check."

"What's involved with a background check?"

"Basically, I take your information, name, address, social security number, and we run it through the FBI database to make sure you're not a felon."

Curtis nodded.

The man grabbed a triplicate form from under the counter. "Would you like to start on the paperwork?"

"I need to think about it."

"Okay."

Curtis left the gun shop. On the drive home, he didn't wear his seat belt. He drove fast and erratic, eliciting several honks. He thought about yanking the wheel into oncoming traffic or speeding into a brick wall. Despite his suicidal thoughts, and driving like he was playing *Grand Theft Auto*, he returned to his apartment building in one piece. He parked and rested his forehead on the steering wheel. He cried for a long time. When he was out of tears, he wiped his face with his T-shirt and exited his SUV.

On the way into his apartment building the same reporter from yesterday called out, "Mr. Duffy. Mr. Duffy."

Curtis ignored her, entered the lobby of his apartment building, and hurried to the stairs. A few residents gawked at Curtis. He ran up the stairs and rushed to his apartment, not wanting to see anyone.

He shut and locked his apartment door behind him. Curtis went to his bedroom and retrieved his silenced phone from the bedside table drawer. He didn't check the notifications. Instead, he searched for Dr. Regina Solomon. Curtis found her office phone number and dialed.

A pleasant voice answered, "Dr. Solomon's office. How may I help you?"

"I was wondering if I could talk to Dr. Solomon?"

"Are you a current patient?"

Curtis sat on the edge of his bed. "No, but I think this is an emergency."

"What is your name?"

"Curtis Duffy."

The woman hesitated. "Hold please."

Less than a minute later, Regina came on the line. "Curtis?"

"Hi, Regina. I'm sorry to bother you. I, uh, I think I need some help with …"

Her tone was harsh. "I won't be a conduit to my daughter. That ship has sailed."

"I know. I'm not calling about her. I'm calling about myself." Curtis gripped his phone like a lifeline. "I think I need help. I'm struggling with …"

"I can't help you, considering we have a personal relationship. You need someone unbiased."

"I understand. I was hoping you could tell me who to call."

CHAPTER 148

The Lynx

Just after dark, Curtis walked along the city streets to the nearest light rail station, his hood covering his head. The Lynx Blue Line was an aboveground train for people transit and part of CATS, the Charlotte Area Transit System. Curtis climbed the steps to the elevated train platform. The rail station was outdoors, but a tinted glass cover overhead shielded the waiting passengers from the sun and the rain. The station was mostly empty, only a dozen or so people waiting for the train. Curtis stood close to the edge, peering down at the train tracks. He peered left and right, wondering when the train would arrive and what direction it would come from.

Curtis went to the nearest digital screen and checked the schedule. A train would be coming from the south in about five minutes. Curtis moved to the southernmost end of the platform, far beyond the awaiting passengers. He reasoned that the train would slow down, as it neared the station, but he wanted to catch it at full speed, so the farther south he was, the faster the train would likely be traveling.

He inched closer to the edge of the platform, imagining jumping in front of the oncoming train. Quick and deadly, with no other casualties. He closed his eyes, thinking about the last thing his mother had said to him. *My life would've been so much better if I never had you.*

The train appeared in the distance, barreling toward the station. His toes were over the platform edge. His muscles were taut, ready to jump at the last possible split second, giving the conductor no time to stop or even slow the train.

"Sir. Excuse me, sir?" a man called out. The voice grew louder and closer.

Curtis ignored the man, the train mere seconds away. Curtis clenched his fists, his heart thumping in his chest.

The voice was very close. "Hey!"

Just before the reckoning, a large hand grabbed his shoulder and yanked him backward two steps. The train blasted past, bringing a flurry of wind.

"Careful," the man said. "You were a little close."

Curtis pivoted to the heavyset man wearing a Carolina Panthers jersey—Christian McCaffrey's number 22.

"Hey. Aren't you that guy who punched Justin Love?" the man asked.

Curtis ran from the train station.

CHAPTER 149

Therapy

Two days later, Curtis sat at the end of a tweed couch. Vanessa sat across from Curtis in a matching tweed chair, a pen and a notebook in hand. A clock ticked in the background.

"What brings you in today?" Vanessa asked.

Vanessa Padgett was older than Curtis but young for a therapist. Curtis guessed she was in her mid-thirties. She wore a nose ring and had muscular calves below the hem of her pencil skirt.

"I've been …" Curtis cleared his throat. "I've had some bad luck recently."

"Tell me about it," Vanessa said, leaning in a little.

"It's not really bad luck. It's … I don't know." Curtis hesitated for a long moment. "This is confidential, right?"

"Whatever you say in here, stays here. I am bound to uphold patient confidentiality, unless you are a danger to yourself or others. For example, if you told me that you were planning to hurt someone, I would have to report that."

Curtis nodded, making a mental note not to tell her about his suicide plans. He took a deep breath. "I punched Justin Love in the face, and I lost my job because of it. I'm assuming you know who he is."

"You've both been in the news lately."

Curtis wrung his hands in his lap. "Then you already know what I did."

460

"I know what the news said, but I would prefer to hear it from you."

Curtis told her about tackling Justin in the noncontact team period, then punching him in the face after Justin said he had told Coach Mellon to cut Curtis.

Vanessa scribbled a few notes in her notebook. "Why did you tackle Justin in practice? Were you angry with him?"

Curtis stared through Vanessa, thinking about Tania's rape. "If I told you, I doubt you'd believe me."

"Why not?"

"Because it sounds crazy."

"Try me. I promise to keep an open mind."

Curtis wiped his sweaty palms on his jeans. "I went to Central Virginia University. I walked on to the football team. Took me two tries to make the team, but I made it. Justin Love was a scholarship athlete, the starting quarterback. It was the night after we beat Clemson, on September 11th, 2016. If that didn't happen ..." Curtis stared beyond Vanessa, as if being transported back to the Sigma Chi fraternity house. "My life would be different."

"If *what* didn't happen?" Vanessa prompted.

"I did something that I thought was right, but I'm still paying for it, like I did something wrong."

Vanessa tilted her head. "Can you be more specific?"

"Like I said, it happened that night after the Clemson game. I rarely went to parties, but my roommate talked me into going to this fraternity party. A lot of football players were there. Justin was there." Curtis fidgeted in his seat. "There was this girl, Tania. She was there too. She used to sing at the parties for money. She had the most beautiful voice I've ever heard. She was really special. My freshman year, I ... I really liked her, but ..." Curtis looked down.

"But what?" Vanessa asked.

Curtis raised his gaze. "She didn't feel the same. What the hell did I expect?"

"What should you have expected?"

Curtis shrugged. "I don't know."

Vanessa raised her eyebrows. "I would like to circle back to that, but please continue with your story."

"I was in the basement, watching a replay of the Clemson game, and my roommate came downstairs in a panic. He said that a bunch of football players took Tania upstairs, and she was wasted, so I went upstairs and knocked on every door until I found—" His voice caught. Tears welled in his eyes.

"What happened when you found her?" Vanessa asked, her eyes wide open.

Curtis wiped his eyes with the sleeve of his T-shirt. He shook his head. "She was begging for help. Justin was on top of her. Four of my other teammates were there, like they were waiting their turn." He swallowed the lump in his throat. "I ... I helped her get out of there. She ran off, but Justin had already ..."

Vanessa made a note in her notepad. "How did you help her?"

Curtis clenched his fists, imagining the beating he took. "I fought 'em."

"All five of them?"

Curtis nodded.

"Were you hurt?"

"I was banged up, but I healed okay."

Vanessa edged forward in her chair. "Did you tell the police or a coach?"

"I told my coach, but he ..." Curtis rubbed the back of his neck. "My coach acted like he was on my side, but, the next day, the police raided my dorm, said someone complained about smelling marijuana from my room. They found my roommate's bong, and we were arrested. My roommate's attorney advised me to take a plea to make it go away, and that's what I did, but then they used the conviction to expel me. Justin and the other guys lied, said *I* was the one hurting Tania. I tried to get Tania to set the record straight, but they gave her a bunch of money to shut up and go away." Curtis crossed his arms over his chest. "That's why I tackled Justin in practice, and that's why I punched him in the face in the parking lot."

Vanessa let out a heavy breath. "I'm assuming you worked very hard to make it to Central Virginia University and to make it on the football team. Then the coaches sacrificed you for doing the right thing because it was inconvenient for the football program and the university's reputation. I'm trying to be professional here, but just hearing this makes me so angry on your behalf. Your anger is understandable."

"You believe me?"

"Yes, I do."

Curtis looked away, his eyes glassy. "I don't know what—" His voice caught. "I don't know what to do."

"About your job?"

"About my job. My fiancé. My father."

"Please forgive my ignorance, but can you get another job with a different football team?"

"If I was a former pro-bowler or a first-round pick, someone would take a chance on me, but I'm a nobody. I was lucky the Panthers gave me a chance."

Vanessa nodded along, her brown eyes focused on Curtis. "And your fiancé?"

"Technically, she's not my fiancé anymore. She ended it."

"Because of the incident with Justin Love?"

"Partly." Curtis explained how he had fought with Dylan in the parking garage and how he'd kept it from Gabriella. He told Vanessa about Dylan holding Gabriella at knifepoint and telling Gabriella about Curtis's previous fight with Dylan. He talked about lying about his prison time. "I know lying was wrong, but she has an abusive ex-boyfriend. I thought, if she knew I went to prison for aggravated assault, she'd end it, so I lied. I didn't wanna lose her." Curtis hung his head. Several tears snaked alongside Curtis's nose. "But I lost her anyway."

"Have you had any contact with her since she broke it off?" Vanessa asked.

Curtis stared at the plush white carpet. "She said, if she sees my face, she'll assume I'm stalking her, and she'll call the police." He wiped his face with his T-shirt and raised his gaze. "That's the last thing I need with my parole."

Vanessa knitted her brow. "Did this incident with Justin violate your parole?"

"He didn't press charges. In return, I had to sign an NDA agreeing never to talk about this or what happened with Tania in 2016."

Her eyes were like saucers. "It must feel like it's happening all over again, just like at college."

Curtis looked away, Vanessa's observation hitting the mark.

"You mentioned your father. What does he say about all this?"

"He's not really my father. I mean, I consider him to be my father, but he's not my father by blood. Mr. H. was my guardian."

"What does Mr. H. say about all this?"

Curtis shrugged. "I've been avoiding his calls. I've been avoiding everyone."

"That's understandable. Is Mr. H. supportive?"

"He is. That's why I don't wanna talk to him. He did so much for me, and I ruined—" His voice caught. "I ruined everything."

"I don't think that's a fair statement," Vanessa said. "You reacted out of anger, but your actions had justification. I wish you weren't in this situation, but it's unfair to heap all the blame on yourself. Does Mr. H. know about what happened in college?"

"Yes."

"Then I imagine he'll be a great support for you. He's probably very worried about you."

"I know. I need to call him back."

Vanessa shut her notebook. "I'm worried about you, Curtis. You've endured tremendous trauma. I imagine not just this incident with Justin Love. I would like to see you next week."

"Okay."

"I would also like you to do two things before we meet again."

"Okay."

"Make a family tree for me, so I can understand your history and the people who are important to you.

"It won't be a big tree."

"It doesn't have to be just blood relatives. You can include friends too. Anyone who's important to you."

"What's the other thing?"

"Please call Mr. H."

CHAPTER 150

Don't Give Up

Curtis checked Mr. H.'s texts. He also checked for anything from Gabriella, but there was nothing. He purposely avoided checking any others. Mr. H.'s last text had been from one hour ago.

> **Mr. H.:** I'm very concerned that I haven't heard from you. I'm planning to drive down there tomorrow. I'm debating calling the Charlotte police to do a welfare check. Call me back. We'll figure this out. I love you, son.

Curtis tapped his Contacts and sat on the couch.

Mr. H. answered on the first ring. "Curtis?"

"It's me," Curtis replied.

"Are you okay?"

"Under the circumstances, I guess."

"What happened?"

Curtis frowned. "You didn't see it on ESPN?"

"I don't believe what they're saying. I'd like to hear it from you."

"Justin was acting like he didn't know me, but it was all bullshit. He thought he could pretend that I didn't exist and that I would go along with that." Curtis stood from the couch and paced in his living room. "He threatened to have me cut, told me that I was lucky to be where I was. Lucky? I wanted to punch him in the face right then. But I tackled him in practice instead. Drilled him on a safety blitz. I have to admit, it felt good, but I knew I messed up. Coach Mellon was pissed. Kicked me out of practice. I wasn't sure if I was cut or not at that point. When I was in the parking lot, I noticed I was parked near

466

Justin's car. I decided right then that I wasn't gonna let him ruin my life again, so I confronted him in the parking lot, told him that he needed to tell Coach Mellon that we were cool. Otherwise, I'd tell anyone with a microphone what he did to Tania."

"How did he react to that?" Mr. H. asked.

Curtis clenched his fist reflexively. "He wasn't worried about me going to the press. He reminded me that there are four guys who will back up his story. He reminded me of my record. He told me that he already told Coach Mellon to cut me. That's when I knocked him out."

Mr. H. blew out a heavy breath. "God damn it. I'm sorry, Curtis. I should've known this was gonna be a problem. We could've worked on some strategies to handle your anger around that piece of shit. Listen to me. I can barely contain my own anger."

"Do you think I have an anger problem?"

"I think you've experienced a lot of violence and neglect in your life. I don't want you to take this the wrong way, but I should've gotten you into therapy a long time ago. That's on me. But I'm gonna come down tomorrow, and I'll bring you back here. I'll get you into therapy. You can stay at the group home for as long as you need."

"I'm already in therapy. My first session was today."

"That's good. I can still come down and stay with you for a while, whatever you need."

"How are you gonna do that? You have eight boys to take care of."

"I've already talked to my boss about getting a temporary re-placement."

Curtis slumped on the couch. "I appreciate it. I really do, but I don't want you doing that. I have enough guilt. I remember how much I needed you when I was their age. A substitute won't be the same, and you know it. I have it under control."

"Are you sure?"

"I'm sure."

"I know you wanna shut out the world, but I need you to get back to me," Mr. H. said.

"I know. I will," Curtis replied.

"I need to know you're safe and coping."

"I'm sorry about all this. I never wanted to disappoint you. You've done so much for me, and I keep ..." Curtis trailed off. His chest tightened.

"You didn't disappoint me," Mr. H. said. "You've never disappointed me. I know your heart. I know who you are."

Curtis sniffed. "If you wanted to walk away from all this ..."

"I'm not going anywhere. You're my son, and nothing will ever change that. You're gonna find your way in this world, and it's all gonna be worth it. It might not be on the football field, but it'll be important."

CHAPTER 151

Digging Deeper

Curtis sat on the tweed couch across from Vanessa in her tweed chair.

"I was quite fascinated by your background," Vanessa said. "You have my undivided attention."

Curtis fidgeted in his seat. "Not sure if that's a good thing."

"It's neither good nor bad. It does say a lot about who you are and how you've gotten to this place."

"How have I gotten to this place?"

"I'm not entirely sure yet. That's why you're here. We have quite a bit of work to do."

Curtis nodded.

Vanessa opened the notebook in her lap and unfolded a piece of paper that had been inside. She held up a copy of the email Curtis had sent, detailing his family tree, or lack thereof. "Thank you for sending your family tree."

"You're welcome."

"I was wondering when was the last time you talked to your biological father?"

"It was right before I went to the group home. I guess I was ten, although he didn't talk to me at all, and I didn't talk to him. My mother was in bad shape. She was hooked on crack. She couldn't take care of me, so we went to see my dad in DC. She wanted him to help, but he didn't want anything to do with us. He was living with another woman, or maybe he was married to her. I don't know. I just remember the woman coming out and telling us to leave."

"How did that make you feel?" Vanessa held her pen at the ready, but her eyes were on Curtis.

He shrugged. "I don't think I cared. I didn't even know him."

Vanessa jotted a note. "What happened next? Did your mom get help from someone else?"

"No. She dropped me off at the group home."

Vanessa scrunched her face, as if in pain. "That must've been incredibly hard."

Curtis wrung his hands in his lap. He shrugged again.

"Can you talk about the day she dropped you off? I would like to hear about whatever you can remember."

Curtis hesitated, then asked, "Can we come back to that another time?"

"Of course. You wrote on your family tree that your mother was deceased. How did she die?"

He bit the inside of his cheek. "Overdose."

"How old were you when she died?"

"Ten. She died six months after she dropped me off at the group home."

Vanessa scrunched her face for a split second, as if in pain. "I'm so sorry, Curtis. You must've been very sad and lonely. You must've felt like you lost her twice."

Curtis leaned back on the couch. "Can we talk about something else?"

"Of course. Last week, you talked about being incarcerated for aggravated assault. I would like to hear about what happened, if you're willing to share."

"I beat a man bad enough that he was brain damaged."

Vanessa raised her eyebrows. "I'm sure there's more to the story."

"After I was expelled from CVU, I got a job working on a grounds maintenance crew at a community college, and I moved into an apartment. There was this guy, Leon. He was always hanging around the apartment building, dealing drugs, hassling people."

Vanessa leaned toward Curtis ever-so-slightly. "Did he hassle you?"

Curtis nodded again. "He did, but I ignored him for the most part. Except for the day I didn't."

"What happened on that day?"

Curtis closed his eyes for a few seconds, remembering that frigid day. "I was driving home, and I saw my friend and neighbor Destiny walking home from the corner store. It was really cold and windy, so I stopped and offered her a ride. I helped her carry her groceries into our apartment building. Leon was just inside, and he started running his mouth, taunting me, calling me a ginger nigger. This wasn't new. I was planning to ignore him, but Destiny got in his face. I told her it didn't matter, but she didn't hear me. She called Leon a bitch or something, and that's when he punched her, knocked her out cold." He stared at the carpet. "I dropped her groceries, and I attacked him. I threw a combination of punches and kept hitting him, even when he was knocked out. It all happened so fast." He raised his gaze. "I was arrested, tried, and sent to prison."

"How many years did you spend in prison?"

"Five."

Vanessa jotted a note. "What was prison like for you?"

"It was like high school for psychopaths. Everyone's in a gang based on race, but I don't fit in an easily defined racial category. I'm this ugly guy who got the worst traits from white people and the worst traits from black people."

"Do you believe you're ugly?"

"Look at me. Don't you?"

"No. I don't. I see a very fit young man with a handsome face."

"Most people would disagree with you."

"What about you? What do *you* think?"

Curtis focused on a far-off memory, as he said, "I remember going to McDonald's with my mother. I think I was like eight. I was so excited. We got our food, and we were eating at this table, away from everyone else. This group of boys came and sat near us. They were probably fifteen or sixteen. One them said, 'That boy's so ugly, when his mama breastfed him, she closed her eyes and thought about other babies.'" Curtis shook his head. "You know what's weird? I didn't think of myself as ugly, until I was told I was ugly."

CHAPTER 152

Everyone's Beautiful from Afar

On Sunday afternoon, Curtis hiked along the creek-side trail at Frazier Park, his baseball cap pulled low over his eyes. The park was mostly free from prying eyes. He listened to the honks of the geese and watched the ducks dunk their heads, letting the creek water roll down their backs.

Curtis wished he could replay that one day. Punching Justin Love set in motion a chain reaction, upending Curtis's life, ending his engagement with Gabriella, destroying his football career before it began, and unearthing unwanted feelings that had long been buried.

Curtis sat on a lonely bench, overlooking the creek. He thought about Gabriella. He closed his eyes and imagined her sitting next to him on that bench. He imagined her hugging him, telling him that she loved him, and telling him that it would all be okay. He could almost smell her lavender perfume. She whispered in his ear, *I want you out of my life. I never want to see you again.* Then she disappeared from his imagination, as if he had no right to conjure her.

He watched the ducks and geese, until the sun was low on the horizon. Then he returned home. It was several miles to walk, but he didn't mind. He had nowhere to be and no one to see. He had been avoiding television and the internet, and, without a job, he had little to do but think.

When Curtis returned to his apartment building, he gazed up at the high-rise, imagining a ten-story free fall, his ugly head splattering on the concrete sidewalk. He entered the lobby and walked to the elevators.

Two young women waited for an elevator. Curtis stood back, not wanting to be recognized or to intimidate them. The door opened, and the women entered the elevator. They stared at him expectantly, but Curtis didn't move, letting the door shut. He figured they were probably relieved they didn't have to share that confined space with him.

Curtis pressed the up arrow and waited for the next elevator. This one was empty. He rode the elevator to the tenth floor. The elevator dinged, and the shiny doors slid open. Curtis stepped into the hall. He walked around the top floor of his apartment building, checking for access to the rooftop, but found nothing.

He entered the stairwell, and found a steel ladder attached to the wall, leading to a hatch in the ceiling. Curtis climbed the ladder and pushed open the hatch, surprised it wasn't locked. He climbed through the hatch to the rubber rooftop. Curtis scanned the roof area. Large metal air conditioners sat in a cluster, the fans spinning in the humid night air. Curtis stepped to the edge and surveyed the bright lights of Charlotte. Little cars and trucks motored about. A spattering of tiny people strolled on the sidewalks. He wondered if everyone was beautiful from afar.

But the city was mostly quiet. People had settled in with their families on a Sunday evening. Curtis imagined people having dinner with their spouses and children. He imagined families sitting around the television. Maybe they were watching preseason football.

Curtis climbed onto the edge of the building and gazed down. It was high. The death would be instantaneous. Nobody would give a shit. Not Gabriella. Not his biological father. His mother was long gone. Not his ex-teammates. Certainly not the public. After all, Curtis had ruined their season by breaking Justin Love's jaw.

He closed his eyes. All he had to do was fall forward. To let go. And it would all be over. He thought of the one person who would care. Curtis heard Mr. H. in his head. *I'm not going anywhere. You're my son, and nothing will ever change that. You're gonna find your way in this world, and it's all gonna be worth it. It might not be on the football field, but it'll be important.*

CHAPTER 153

Should've Been Aborted

"What was life like with your mother, before you went to the group home?" Vanessa asked.

Curtis fidgeted in his regular spot on the couch. "I watched a lot of cartoons. My mother was … She was mostly good to me. At least she was until she became an addict."

"Did you see your father much?"

He shook his head. "I didn't know him at all."

Vanessa jotted a note in her notebook. "So it was just you and your mother?"

"Yeah."

"Did she have any boyfriends?"

Curtis wrung his hands in his lap. "She didn't have boyfriends. She had clients. The closest thing she had to a boyfriend was her pimp, Derek."

Vanessa's eyes widened. "What was Derek like?"

"He was like you'd expect a pimp to be. I have this recurring dream. The memory has stuck with me all these years. I think I was eight years old. It was the last day of summer break, and I was immersed in this Scooby-Doo marathon because I was afraid to go to school. The kids had been pretty cruel to me the year before. I just wanted to stay home with my mom, but my mom told me it would be better, that I just needed to be nice. That doesn't work, by the way." Curtis forced a smile. "Anyway, she was making me a peanut butter and jelly sandwich. I remember that she asked me if I wanted grape or strawberry. I chose strawberry."

Vanessa smiled small, sitting across from Curtis in her chair.

"Then Derek came over. He had a key, so he just came and went, whenever he wanted. My mom didn't get the money from some guy, and Derek was pissed." Curtis stared at the carpet. "Derek grabbed my mother by the throat and choked her. Her face turned red. She hit his arms, but it didn't do anything. Derek was a big guy. I ran into the kitchen and said something like, 'Let go of my mom.' But Derek kept choking her. My mom was very fair-skinned, like me, and her face was bright red. I ran to Derek and punched him on his lower back over and over again, but it did nothing. I thought—" His voice caught. "I thought he was gonna kill her. He finally let her go, and my mother collapsed. She was wheezing for breath. I remember running to her and hugging her." Curtis raised his gaze to Vanessa. "That's what Derek was like."

"Did you feel it was your job to protect your mother?"

"I tried, but I didn't do a good job."

"Sounds like you were incredibly brave."

"I didn't know anything. I think I was doing what the heroes in my cartoons would do. Real life isn't like that though."

"How did you feel when your mother dropped you off at the group home? Were you relieved to be away from Derek?"

Curtis shook his head. "My mom had gotten so skinny from the drugs that Derek didn't want her anymore. I didn't know that I was going to the group home to live. Not until she was about to leave."

Vanessa winced. "That must've been a shock."

Tears welled in his eyes. "I begged her not to leave me. It didn't matter. She had already made up her mind. She was a drug addict, and people might say she was a bad mother, but I loved her, and she was all I had." Curtis wiped the corners of his eyes, stopping the tears at the source.

"Was that the last time you saw your mother?"

"No." Curtis swallowed hard. "I ran away from the group home after I'd been there for like a week. I went back home to our apartment in Alexandria, but she wasn't home, so I waited in the hall for hours. She finally came home with some guy on her arm." Curtis wiped the corners of his eyes again. "She wasn't happy to see me. Told the guy to give her a minute. She wanted to know what I was doing there. I begged her to let me stay with her. Told her I wouldn't ask for anything. Told her she wouldn't have to take care of me. I really thought she'd let me come back. I thought she loved me, but ..." Curtis hung his head.

"What did she say when you begged her to stay?" Vanessa asked.

Curtis didn't reply for several seconds. "She told me that she was sixteen when she had me, and her parents wanted her to abort me." Tears slipped down his face. He didn't bother to wipe them. "She said she could've gone to college, and she asked me if I thought she liked doing what she was doing." Curtis shook his head. "I told her that I didn't understand. She said, that it was simple, that her life—" His voice caught. "That her life would've been better if she'd never had me."

CHAPTER 154

Sara Resurrected

Curtis's phone chimed incessantly with numbers he didn't know. He listened to one of the messages.

"This is Amy Garfield from NBC News. We'd like your comment on your involvement with the incident from 2016 at the Sigma Chi fraternity house—"

Curtis ended the message and dropped his phone on his bedside table, like it was on fire. *They're telling everyone I raped Tania. It's five against one. Can they send me back to prison?* Curtis searched the internet for "statute of limitations rape Virginia." *Twenty-years.* Curtis screamed in rage and frustration. He paced back and forth. *They're trying to ruin me, just like before.* He went to his window, his body shaking. Several news vans were parked out front. *I'm not going back. Fuck these people.*

He left his apartment and took the stairs to the top floor of the building. Curtis climbed the metal ladder to the hatch, but it was locked this time. *Shit.* He descended the ladder then the stairs to the ground floor. He exited his apartment building out the back.

Curtis walked along the city streets to the light rail station, his hood covering his head. Curtis climbed the steps to the elevated train platform. The outdoor rail station was mildly busy just after rush hour. Despite his raised hood, he thought he heard someone say, "That's him."

He walked to the southernmost end of the platform, away from everyone. He guessed it was around 7:30 p.m. He had left his phone at home, and he couldn't see the time on the digital schedule from his spot on the platform.

Curtis waited for what felt like several hours for the station to empty. He didn't want a scene. He didn't want any intervention. Only a handful of people were left at the station. One couple stared at Curtis from afar. He figured they must've recognized him, but they kept their distance. *Stop stalling. It's time. The next train.*

He thought about Mr. H. Curtis tried to rationalize the aftereffects of his suicide. *He'll be ... He'll be better off. He'll have more time to help the group home kids. He won't have to bother with me anymore.* Curtis thought about Mr. H.'s dead son, the one who died in his crib for no reason. Curtis knew Mr. H. thought of him as his own flesh and blood. *He'll have to deal with losing another son. He'll be devastated.* Curtis pushed the thought from his mind. He needed to concentrate on the task at hand. It wasn't about anyone else. It was *his* life, and, if he wanted to end it, it was *his* choice.

Curtis heard his mother's voice in his head. *My parents wanted me to abort you. I could've gone to college. My life would've been so much better if I never had you.*

The train appeared in the distance, barreling toward the station. He inched to the platform edge. His muscles were taut, ready to jump at the last possible split second, giving the conductor no time to stop or slow the train.

Curtis figured he had about fifteen seconds left on Earth. His entire body trembled. His mouth was like cotton. His mother's voice came once again. *My life would've been so much better if I never had you.*

The train was a few seconds away from impact.

His mother's voice came again. "Curtis, don't do it. Curtis Duffy."

The voice wasn't in his head. He gaped at a woman running his way, her red hair wild in the breeze and her bright white skin shimmering in the moonlight. It was like his mother had been resurrected.

"Don't!" she shouted, still running his way.

Curtis stepped back reflexively, as the train blasted past, bringing a gust of wind. A man ran behind her. It was the same couple who had been staring, two people he had never met. But she had said his name. *The news.* Curtis brushed past the redhead and her boyfriend, headed for the station exit.

"Don't do it," the woman said to his back. "You have too much to live for."

Curtis pivoted to the couple. They stood together now. "You don't know me."

"Everyone knows you," the woman replied, her blue eyes glassy. "It wasn't right what they did to you, but you have too much to live for."

Curtis furrowed his brow.

"It's all over the internet," the man said. "Taylor Wilde said what you did."

CHAPTER 155

No Way Back

Curtis returned to his apartment, his head spinning. *What did she say? Did she finally tell the truth? Why would she? She has everything to lose.* When he neared his apartment building, he spotted several news vans parked on the street and reporters and cameramen milling about. He covered his head with his hood and fast-walked toward his apartment building. They didn't notice him until he was very close to the front door of his building. Then they lobbed a barrage of questions, the cameras now pointed in his direction.

"Curtis Duffy. What did you think of Taylor Wilde's press conference?" one reporter asked.

"Do you have anything to say to Justin Love?" asked another reporter.

"Have you had any contact with Taylor Wilde?" a third reporter asked.

Curtis pushed through the crowd and entered his building without a word. Two reporters followed him inside.

One of them asked, "Do you have any comments on the sexual assault allegations from 2016?"

Curtis ran to the stairwell, leaving the reporters behind. He ran up the stairs to the seventh floor. He stepped into the hallway tentatively, half-expecting more reporters at his apartment door, but the hallway was empty. Curtis went to his door, put his key in the dead bolt and turned, noticing there wasn't any resistance. *Did I lock it before I left?*

He entered his apartment, shutting the door behind him.

Gabriella stood from the couch, ran to him, and hugged him tight. "I'm so sorry," she said.

His body stiffened. He removed her hands from his lower back and stepped back from her. "What do you want?"

"I've been texting you and calling you. I was worried. I'm sorry. I used the key …" She trailed off.

Curtis glared at her. "I texted and called you too. I begged you. I *needed* you. But I was just a fucking *rapist* to you."

Gabriella blanched. "I'm so sorry—"

"*No.* You left me. You threw me away like trash, like I was nothing to you." Curtis held out his hand. "I want my key, and I want you to leave."

Tears welled in her eyes. "Please, Curtis. We can work it out—"

"*No.* We can't. Gimme my key and get out."

Tears slipped down her cheeks. She reached into her purse, handed Curtis his extra apartment key, and left without a word.

CHAPTER 156

The Press Conference

Curtis sat on his couch, his laptop on his thighs. He typed *Taylor Wilde* into the search bar. The top result was a YouTube video titled "Taylor Wilde Press Conference." Curtis clicked the video with over eight million views, his stomach in knots, wondering if she really had told the truth.

Tania aka Taylor Wilde was still beautiful and petite, with long dark hair. She stood behind a podium filled with microphones, an audience of reporters before her.

She looked down for a time. Then she gazed into the camera. "Have you ever hurt someone so badly that you just wanted to forget about it? Have you ever been hurt so badly that you just wanted to forget about it? I've been in both of those situations at the same time." She took a deep breath. "When I was a first year at Central Virginia University, I used to sing on the quad. Nobody really noticed at first. I didn't think I was any good. Then a young man stopped and put a five-dollar bill in my guitar case. It was the first dollar I'd ever made singing. He told me that I had a beautiful voice and said that I would have a crowd of fans in no time. He suggested I put some dollar bills in my guitar case because it made people more likely to give money."

Taylor paused for a beat. "His name was Curtis Duffy. Yes, the same Curtis Duffy who punched Carolina quarterback Justin Love." She cleared her throat. "Anyway, Curtis was right. Over the next week or two, I got more money by adding some cash to my guitar case, and

I had a small crowd of fans. The next time I saw Curtis, he asked me to go to a fraternity party with him. I was hesitant because I didn't like him like that."

Curtis frowned and thought, *No shit. The world's seen my mug shot. They know too.*

"He assured me that we'd be going as friends, and he mentioned that I could try to get some stage time at the fraternity," Taylor said. "It sounded like a good opportunity, so I agreed. We went to the frat party, and we talked to some of the fraternity brothers, and they agreed to let me sing. I was so nervous. It was the biggest crowd I'd ever performed for. It started out really bad with a bunch of guys demanding that I take off my clothes, but I won them over.

"After my set, I met Justin Love, and we hit it off. I was enamored with him right from the start. He was the superstar quarterback, the big man on campus. When I left the frat, Justin offered to walk me home. Curtis was outside waiting for me. He was obviously disappointed that Justin was walking me home."

Curtis glowered at the screen, thinking, *I wasn't stupid. I was well aware that you didn't like me.*

"I didn't see Curtis for like two weeks," Taylor said. "Then I saw him on the quad. I went up to him to thank him. I was booking tons of gigs at fraternity houses. He was a big reason why. But he seemed mad at me, so I asked him about it. He denied being mad. I thought he was mad because of Justin, so I said something like, 'You know that wasn't a date, right?' He said that he knew I wasn't interested, but he said it kind of angry. I said something like, 'I thought you were different.'"

Taylor let out a heavy breath. "I remember very clearly what he said next. He said, 'If I'm not different, I don't know who is.' But I went on this mean rant. Said he was like every other guy, that he was pretending to be nice to get with me. He told me that I wouldn't be saying this to Justin Love. He was right. Ironically, Justin and I never dated.

"I didn't see Curtis for a year after that. Not until the night of September 11, 2016. I sang at Sigma Chi. Then I partied with Justin Love. I was the *it girl* at CVU. Everyone knew who I was." Taylor gripped the podium. "I drank a lot that night. Too much. Justin prepared several shots for me. I could do three shots and feel okay in the morning, but I didn't realize they were double shots, so I was in bad shape when Justin took me up to his room."

Taylor dropped her gaze for several seconds, as if praying. She looked at the camera again. "I liked Justin. If he had been nice to me, I might've agreed to sleep with him. We went to his bed, and we were making out. Then the door opened, and I sat upright, startled. Four big football players came into the room. Kavon Drake, Andre Willis, Preston Waylon, and Thomas Creese. All of them are currently in the NFL."

Curtis's neck vein pulsed, Taylor's words transporting him back to the scene of the crime.

"I thought Justin would tell them to leave, but he didn't. I tried to leave—" Her voice caught. Her face contorted with emotion. When it passed, she said, "I tried to leave, but Justin grabbed me and threw me on the bed face down. He hiked up my skirt, removed my underwear, and raped me. I tried to get away, but he was too strong and too heavy." She wiped her eyes. "Someone knocked on the door, and I screamed for help. They told the person to go away, but then Curtis busted into the room, breaking the door. They tried to push him out, but he fought for me. Curtis ..." Tears slipped down her face. "Curtis pulled Justin off of me. That's when I ran." She stared at the podium. "They beat him up pretty badly."

Curtis blinked, tears sliding along his nose.

Taylor sniffled and wiped her eyes again. "But that wasn't even the worst part. I just wanted it to be over. Justin's family gave me a settlement in return for my silence. I took the money and ran. I used it to build my singing career. I didn't know they were going to do what they did to Curtis. Had I known, I never would've signed the nondisclosure agreement. They kicked Curtis off the football team. Police officers showed up at his dorm and arrested him for marijuana possession. His roommate Ben Davidson confirmed that it was his marijuana and that Curtis only pleaded guilty because they let him off with a fine. But Curtis didn't know that the conviction meant an automatic expulsion from CVU."

Taylor stood straighter. "In light of what recently happened between Curtis and Justin, I couldn't stay silent. To Justin, I would like to say, go ahead and sue me for breaking the NDA. I would love the opportunity to tell the world what you did to me in open court. To Curtis." Taylor paused for a long moment. "I don't deserve forgiveness, but I'm so sorry for what I did to you."

Taylor walked off screen, as the room erupted with questions.

CHAPTER 157

The Twitter Mob

Curtis watched ESPN, thankful to no longer be the NFL supervillain. That mantle had been passed to Justin Love. Gabriella had called and texted several times, but Curtis ignored her messages. Curtis gaped at the screen. ESPN showed a live press conference. A balding man with a crescent of gray hair stood behind the podium. Eric Weiner, Owner, Carolina Panthers, was scrawled at the bottom of the screen.

"I understand that Ms. Wilde told a story, but I have to make decisions based on facts, not stories. None of her story has been affirmed by the police or the courts. This is America, and, in America, we're innocent until proven guilty, not the other way around. On the other hand, Mr. Duffy assaulted Justin Love. That's a fact. Mr. Duffy's lucky Justin Love chose not to press charges or to file a lawsuit.

"Furthermore, Justin Love has never been convicted of a crime or arrested. By all official accounts, he's a model citizen. Curtis Duffy, on the other hand, has been arrested and convicted of aggravated assault *and* drug possession. The Carolina Panthers stand by Justin Love, as he seeks to clear his name from these heinous and unfounded accusations. I hope you people in the press will refrain from printing rumors and innuendo from attention-seeking individuals. Thank you."

Eric Weiner left the podium, ignoring the questions from reporters.

During the commercial break, Curtis scrolled through his Twitter feed. He had 37,421 notifications. He checked the most recent posts he had been tagged on. One was an article about Garrett Woodson aka Coach Woody resigning, as the Special Teams Coordinator for the Carolina Panthers.

Another was an article about Jodie Hauser, a former athletic trainer at Central Virginia University, who claimed to have been fired after making a complaint about Justin Love. In the article, she claimed that Justin Love had purposely exposed himself to her in the training room and had whispered in her ear, *You know you wanna suck it.* Curtis believed he had witnessed the event, although he doubted his testimony would help at this point, as he would be viewed as someone with an ax to grind.

Another article cited three other women with sexual assault complaints against Justin Love. Curtis didn't know these women, but he found Jodie Hauser's Twitter account. He sent her a direct message, letting her know he had witnessed the sexual harassment, and, if she needed his testimony, he would be happy to give it.

Another article was entitled "How Head Coach Frank Goodman Sold his Soul for the National Championship." The article speculated on Taylor Wilde's accusation that five CVU football stars were in that bedroom. It was easier to sacrifice one walk-on nobody for five offensive starters, two of them being All-ACC selections, and Justin Love being the Heisman Trophy winner.

CHAPTER 158

Facing the Press

Over the weekend, Curtis had stayed in his apartment, avoiding contact with the press and everyone, except for Mr. H. They had talked twice over the phone. Curtis had an open invitation to stay at the group home, but Curtis was uncertain what he wanted to do next, so he decided to stay put, until his lease was up in October.

On Monday afternoon, Curtis was going stir-crazy, so he left his apartment, wearing his running gear. He exited his apartment building into the attached parking garage. Two reporters spotted him and ran toward him. The reporters with accompanying cameramen surrounded Curtis as he walked toward his SUV, peppering him with questions.

Curtis stopped at his SUV and faced the reporters. He thought about the NDA he had signed.

"Is Taylor Wilde telling the truth about what happened with Justin Love?" the female reporter asked.

"I can't talk about it," Curtis replied.

"Do you believe Taylor Wilde is an honest person?"

Curtis nodded. "Yes. She's a very honest person."

"Have you talked to Taylor Wilde since the press conference?" the male reporter asked.

"No. I haven't talked to her since 2016."

"Did you see Justin Love raping Taylor Wilde?" the female reporter asked.

"I can't talk about that," Curtis replied. "I'm sorry. I have to go."

"One more question," the male reporter said.

Curtis frowned, then nodded.

"In a recent press conference, Carolina Panthers owner, Eric Weiner defended Justin Love, stating that Taylor Wilde's story has never been affirmed by the police or the courts. Do you have any comment about Eric Weiner's statement?"

"I imagine Mr. Weiner would rather believe that Taylor Wilde's a liar, than his 260-million-dollar quarterback is a rapist." Curtis turned from the reporters, opened the driver's side door of his SUV, and climbed inside. He backed out of his space slowly, mindful of the newspeople.

Curtis drove to Frazier Park. Along the way, he listened to sports talk radio, *The Joe and Jane Show*.

Joe said, "Justin Love's never been arrested or convicted of any crime. We're innocent until proven guilty in this country."

"As of a few hours ago, there are now eight women accusing Justin Love of sexual assault," Jane replied.

"Gold diggers often target rich and famous athletes."

"Rich and powerful people often step on people like Curtis Duffy."

"Curtis Duffy is a convicted felon who should go back to prison for punching Justin Love."

"I think Taylor Wilde's telling the truth. She had nothing to gain and everything to lose by telling her story. It makes perfect sense that Duffy would do what he did. I also think it's telling that Coach Woodson quit immediately after Eric Weiner's statement of support for Love. My sources tell me it was Woodson's endorsement that helped Curtis Duffy make the practice squad. Apparently, he loved Duffy's attitude and work ethic. I think Coach Woodson quit because he didn't like what the organization did."

"That's a lot of speculation."

Curtis parked his SUV in the Frazier Park lot.

"There needs to be more speculation," Jane said. "I think the NFL should investigate all the guys who were in that bedroom. Kavon Drake, Andre Willis, Preston Waylon, and Thomas Creese. They all need to be investigated. They should also look at Coach Frank Goodman. I think he sacrificed Curtis Duffy for two National Championships."

"That's ridiculous," Joe replied. "You have no evidence of that. You sound like the rest of these internet conspiracy theorists."

"That's why I said they need to be *investigated*."

Curtis cut the engine and the radio. He ran along the creek, enjoying the sun on his face. Thoughts of Gabriella seeped into his mind. He ran faster, trying to vanquish the thoughts, his breathing elevated, and his legs burning. He sprinted until he couldn't go any farther, until his legs were filled with lactic acid, and he wheezed for breath.

Curtis doubled over and vomited in the grass. He spit, his throat burning from his stomach bile. Despite the pain, he couldn't get Gabriella out of his mind.

CHAPTER 159

Taylor Wilde

Curtis dressed in his running gear, intending to return to Frazier Park. A knock came at his door. Curtis padded to his apartment door. He peered into the peephole, expecting a reporter, but seeing Taylor Wilde, accompanied by two large men with crewcuts. In some ways she was still Tania from college. She still had her long dark hair parted down the middle. Her face was still perfectly symmetrical. But her eyes were bloodshot and dim. Her cheekbones were too prominent. She wasn't just petite; she was gaunt.

Curtis thought about retreating to his room, waiting for her to leave, but he opened the door instead.

Taylor forced a smile. "Hi, Curtis."

"Hi, Tania, … Taylor," Curtis replied, his voice monotone.

"Can we talk in private?"

Curtis hesitated, then stepped aside. "Come in."

Taylor stepped into his apartment, her purse over her shoulder, and her bodyguards right behind her. She pivoted to them. "Do you guys mind waiting in the hall?"

They did as they were told.

Curtis shut the door and faced Taylor.

She did a 360, scanning the apartment. "Your house is nice."

"None of this is mine. It comes furnished," Curtis replied.

She nodded. "Do you mind if I sit down?"

Curtis led her to the couch. Taylor sat on the end. Curtis remained standing, a safe distance away from her. She chewed on her lower lip. Curtis stared at her, refusing to be the first to speak.

"I'm really sorry for what I did, or more accurately what I didn't do," Taylor said.

Curtis rubbed the stubble on his chin. "I know it must've been hard for you back then, but you hung me out to dry, and … things didn't work out so well for me after that."

Taylor bowed her head. "I was so scared. I didn't have the strength to stick up for you, like you did for me." She raised her glassy eyes. "I'm so sorry, Curtis. If I could go back and fix it, I would." She reached into her purse, retrieved a check, and handed it to Curtis. "I know I got you kicked out of CVU. That's to finish your degree."

Curtis stared at the check for $250,000. He handed it back to Taylor.

"It's yours," she protested, refusing to take the check.

"It's not your fault I didn't finish college. It's theirs. If anyone should pay, it should be them, not you." He ripped the check several times, letting the tiny pieces rain down on the carpet.

Taylor stood from the couch and stepped closer to Curtis. "I'd like to make it right with you. Tell me how I can help you. What do you need?"

"I need a job."

Her face brightened. "I could give you a great job. I'm always looking for—"

"An *NFL* job."

Her mouth turned down. "Oh, right."

Curtis took a deep breath. "What I needed from you, you already did. You told the truth. I'm sure you have lawyers who told you not to do it, but you did it anyway. I … I forgive you."

Taylor lunged at Curtis, hugging him briefly, then stepping back. Curtis hadn't had time to decide whether to hug her back.

"Sorry," she said.

"It's okay. We should stick together with all this. It's you and me against a lot of them. I'll testify, if you plan on pressing charges."

Taylor shook her head. "That's my trump card. If Justin sues me over the NDA, I'll press charges and countersue, but I would rather let it all go."

"But you brought it all up for me."

"I was just trying to soothe my guilt."

Curtis shook his head. "You were trying to do the right thing."

CHAPTER 160

Trauma

"Gabriella called me a rapist," Curtis said, sitting on Vanessa's couch. "She left me when I needed her the most. I wanna forgive her, but I can't. What happens the next time something bad happens? She'll just leave me. I can't take that chance."

"Are you expecting something bad to happen?" Vanessa asked, sitting in the tweed chair across from Curtis.

Curtis peered through Vanessa. "Something bad always happens. Even when things are going good ... I can feel it coming."

"What did it feel like when your mother left you at the group home?"

Curtis hung his head and wrung his hands in his lap. "It was ... the worst pain I've ever felt."

"That's understandable. It's also understandable that you would be sensitive to putting yourself in that position again."

Curtis raised his gaze to Vanessa. "What position?"

"The position where someone you love could leave you again."

"You think I'm overreacting to Gabriella leaving me because of my mother?"

Vanessa shifted in her seat. "Do you think you're overreacting?"

"I don't know."

"Did you ever consider that *she's* overreacting?"

"How so?"

"Well, she has an abusive ex-boyfriend who held her at knifepoint.

It seems reasonable to me that a smart woman such as Gabriella would be sensitive to repeating the same mistake. Because of that history, she might overreact to the incident with Justin Love or to your arrest record."

Curtis crossed his arms over his chest. "Maybe it's for the best. I am a violent person. I could hurt her."

Vanessa tilted her head. "I will have to push back on that. As far as I know, you've never hit a woman. Is that true?"

Curtis nodded.

"I'm not saying you weren't justified, but I do worry that you are placing yourself in harm's way with men. I think we need to work on skills to handle disputes without descending into violence. Having said that, the altercations you described were largely unavoidable. Have you ever bullied a man? Hit someone for no reason?"

Curtis shook his head.

"I think Gabriella's attracted to you because you're the opposite of her abusive ex-boyfriend. The opposite of an abusive person isn't a passive person. It's a protective person. That's you. You protected your mother as a child. You protected Tania in college. You protected Destiny. You protected Gabriella. You have a track record of protecting the people you care about. Unfortunately, that protection hasn't always been reciprocal. But, from what you told me, Gabriella loves you and wants to be there for you. She made a mistake. She overreacted because of her trauma, just like you overreacted because of yours."

After his therapy session, Curtis sent Gabriella a text.

Curtis: I'd like to talk. Can I come over?

CHAPTER 161

Curtis and Gabriella

Curtis sat on one end of Gabriella's couch, and she sat at the other end. The television before them was black. Gabriella wore baggy pajama pants and a UNC sweatshirt. Her eyes were puffy.

"Tania—I mean, Taylor—showed up at my house yesterday," Curtis said.

Gabriella arched her eyebrows. "What did she want?"

"She apologized and gave me a check for $250,000."

Gabriella sat up straighter. "What did you say to her?"

"I accepted her apology but not her money."

Gabriella smiled. "Good for you."

An awkward silence passed between them.

"Why didn't you tell me that the girl in college was Taylor Wilde?" Gabriella asked.

Curtis shrugged. "I felt like it made my story less believable. I wanted you to believe me, so I left it out. I know I should've told you the whole truth."

"Is this what you wanted to talk about?"

Curtis shook his head. "My therapist said some things to me that really made me think."

Gabriella lifted one eyebrow. "You have a therapist?"

"You didn't know? Your mom recommended her."

"She didn't say anything to me, but I think it's really good that you're talking to someone. What did your therapist say?"

"She told me that I'm sensitive to people leaving me. When my mother left me, it hurt more than anything I've ever experienced. It made me never wanna repeat that feeling. When you left me, it felt like that …"

Gabriella stood and stepped to him, sitting next to him on the couch, their thighs touching. "I'm sorry, Curtis. I never should've left you. I feel so terrible for what I said to you. I didn't mean it. I was out of my mind, after what happened with Dylan."

"You don't need to apologize. I think you were worried about being hurt too. When you found out about me roughing up Dylan, punching Justin, and my aggravated assault, I think it was too much. I don't wanna speak for you, but I think you were worried that you were picking the wrong guy again, that I was like Dylan."

Gabriella nodded. "I was. But, after hearing Taylor's story, I know you're not like Dylan. You're not abusive. You're caring and self-sacrificing. I need to be that for you too."

"I want you to know that I would never hurt you. *Ever.* You mean the world to me."

Gabriella hugged Curtis. She said into his ear, "I love you."

CHAPTER 162

Options

Curtis parked in the driveway of the group home behind the old van, with Gabriella riding shotgun. The siding of the group home was dirty. Paint chipped off the window frames and the front door. The asphalt driveway was cracked and crumbling. Several brand-new bikes lay in the front yard, along with a kickball and a Nerf football.

The radio broadcaster said, "Philadelphia attorney, Omar Khan, claims to represent eleven women who are accusing Justin Love of sexual assault. Mr. Khan stated that he will be filing all eleven complaints in civil court on Monday."

Curtis cut the engine and the radio.

"Do you think they'll win?" Gabriella asked.

Curtis turned in his seat to face Gabriella. "I think they'll settle. I learned from my time in the justice system that almost everyone settles. I think Justin will pay them off, and it'll go away."

"He should be in prison."

"People with his money and power don't go to prison. His reputation will never be the same though."

Curtis exited the rental car. He waited for Gabriella, and they approached the front door, hand in hand. A cacophony of excited voices came from the backyard—the boys likely playing football. Curtis knocked on the front door of the group home with Gabriella at his side.

Bobo answered the door. He smiled from ear to ear and held up his hand. "Curtis, my man."

"Hey, Bobo." Curtis high-fived the undersized boy, then tried to keep up with his elaborate handshake.

Bobo winked at Gabriella. "You're still lookin' fine."

Curtis frowned. "Be respectful."

Gabriella squeezed his shoulder. "Good to see you, Bobo."

Bobo ushered them inside. "Mr. H. is in the kitchen." As they followed the boy into the kitchen, Bobo said, "Sorry about your football job. I knew Justin Love was a punk-ass bitch. I'm glad you busted him in the mouth."

Mr. H. turned from the stove and glared at Bobo. "Language."

Bobo grinned at Mr. H., no doubt testing his limits. "You know it's true." Then the boy ran outside to join his foster brothers.

Mr. H. hugged Gabriella and Curtis, beaming in their presence. Boys came and went, but Mr. H. was the constant. He was aging, but, in many ways, he was exactly the same as he was when Curtis came to the group home sixteen years ago. Mr. H. wore the same old clothes. He had the same old watch.

As Mr. H. and Gabriella exchanged niceties, Curtis thought about Mr. H. and his Spartan lifestyle. The last car Mr. H. had was the one he'd given to Curtis. Since then, Mr. H. had used the group-home van, which wasn't his. The group home itself wasn't his. He had no biological family of his own. He had been working for a long time. *What did he do with his money?*

After all these years, it hit Curtis like Brian Dawkins in his prime. Mr. H. had hundreds of kids. A thousand maybe. His money went to needy boys and young men, like Curtis. Those new bikes in the front yard probably came from Mr. H. Curtis stared at his father with reverence.

Mr. H. met Curtis's gaze, winked, and smiled, as if he had read Curtis's thoughts.

Mr. H. pivoted to the stovetop and set the pasta sauce to simmer. He gave them glasses of ice water, and they all sat around the kitchen table. They shared pleasantries about their trip and the latest happenings at the group home, before they discussed anything serious.

Once the chitchat had been exhausted, Curtis said, "We canceled the wedding."

Mr. H. raised his eyebrows.

"We didn't *cancel* the wedding," Gabriella clarified. "We're not going to have it in the Bahamas. We'll have it in Charlotte. It'll be small but nice." Gabriella nodded to Mr. H. "You're invited of course."

Curtis's phone chimed. He reached into his pocket and silenced his phone, without checking it.

"That's for the best," Mr. H. replied. "You don't need an extravagant wedding. It's the marriage that matters."

"We thought, with me losing my job, we should be more practical," Curtis said, then sipped his water.

"What are you planning to do?"

Curtis set down his glass and glanced at Gabriella. "She gave me a job in her office. I'm gonna be in charge of billing and collections. I figure all I need to do is threaten to break some jaws, and the money will come in right quick." Curtis laughed at his own joke.

Gabriella mock-frowned at Curtis.

"Too soon?"

"Way too soon."

Curtis turned his attention back to Mr. H. "I'm planning to finish my social work degree, while I help out Gabriella. I still wanna do what you do."

Mr. H. cocked his head. "You sure you wanna parent a houseful of Bobos?"

Curtis nodded. "I do."

Mr. H. smiled. "I think you'd be outstanding. You have a lot more patience than I do."

Curtis's phone chimed again.

"You need to get that?" Mr. H. asked.

Curtis reached into his pocket and checked the screen. "It's Coach Woody. I'll be right back." Curtis stood from the table, walked toward the sliding glass door, and answered his phone. "Hey, Coach."

"Curtis," Coach Woody said. "How are you?"

Curtis stepped onto the back patio. "I'm doing great. Thanks for asking. How are you? I saw that you resigned."

"Yeah. Between you and me, I didn't like the way they handled that mess with Justin Love. I got three daughters. I can't work for an organization that employs a rapist."

"I appreciate that, Coach." Curtis watched the boys playing football in the backyard. "I don't know what to say."

"You don't need to say nothin'. It was my choice. Anyway, I was callin' because I got a job with Atlanta, as a special teams consultant. I told the special teams coordinator about you, and they want you to come down for a tryout. If you run a halfway decent forty, you got a real good chance of makin' the roster. Worst-case scenario, they'll stash you on the practice squad. You interested?"

Curtis was stunned for a beat. "Yeah, I'm interested. Can I think about it and call you back?"

"Don't wait too long. They want you at the facility as soon as possible."

"I won't. Thanks, Coach." Curtis disconnected the call and returned to the kitchen.

"What did he say?" Mr. H. asked, standing from the table.

"He's working for Atlanta now. They want me to come down for a tryout. He said, if I run a decent forty, I have a good chance of making the roster."

"That's *great* news," Mr. H. said.

Gabriella stood and hugged Curtis. "I'm so proud of you."

When they separated, Mr. H. asked Curtis, "What are you gonna do?"

Curtis looked from Mr. H. to Gabriella and back. "I don't know. For the first time in my life, I feel like I can't lose."

If you enjoyed this novel, ... you'll love *Redemption*.

Do you really trust your husband?

That's what I had to decide. I had it all. At least that's what people told me. Beauty, brains, and a rich husband. I deserved it too. My fiancé had cheated on me with my best friend. But I won in the end, or at least I thought I had.

Until Christmas of 1999. My ex-fiancé, Danny, showed up at my parents' house, wanting to talk to my father. Danny's a police officer, and my father's a retired officer. A six-year-old girl had disappeared without a trace, resembling a case my father had worked on years earlier.

My parents still loved Danny. The gregarious local cop. A man's man with manners. What's not to love? My introverted and awkward husband, Jason, couldn't compete. My parents weren't impressed by his money. Jason's job in finance was too abstract. He made money from other people's money, like a banker or a loan shark.

I think this made it easier for my family to blame Jason. They were right to blame him. He was alone with her. It was his DNA. It was an impossible choice for me. My family or my husband. I suppose we all made our own choices. We were never the same after that. We all suffered from his terrible crime.

Twenty years later, I had a happy life and a happy family. I wanted to forget the past, but it all came back, forcing me to choose all over again. This time we couldn't bury the secrets. Jason. Danny. My parents. My daughter. All those missing girls.

Never in a million years could I have seen it coming.

Buy *Redemption* today if you enjoy page-turning domestic thrillers that will keep you reading late into the night.
A 2022 Finalist National Indie Excellence Award
Adult language and sexual content.

<u>What Readers Are Saying</u>

"Mr. Williams is an amazing author. His storylines are some of the best I've read, and I read a lot. I average about 135 books a year. His writing is like silky poetry. That may be an unusual way to describe someone's writing style, but that's the way it feels to me. He is very talented."

– AMB ★★★★★

"I am an avid reader and seldom come across a book this good. It was brilliant! Awesome plot, well-written, fantastic characters. This was the real deal."

– Mark ★★★★★

"This was my first book by this author, and all I can say is, WOW. Pick this one up early, unless you want to stay up all night with it. It's a page turner that can't be put down!"

– Kindle Reader ★★★★★

"This is one of the best books I have read in a long time. I was unable to put it down once I started to read it."

– L. Hayden ★★★★★

"Phil Williams is probably my favorite author right now. … I love his writing style, and he writes the type of books that I want to stay up all night to finish. I read several books a month and get excited every time I come across a new one by this author. *Redemption* drew me in from the first chapter, and I couldn't wait to finish reading it. You feel very much like you're in a movie in your mind, with his vivid and descriptive character development, and I get emotionally invested very quickly. I appreciate that he is not afraid to confront the hard issues either and does so in a tasteful and enlightening manner. Finished this book in day and look forward to my next Phil Williams read!"

– Jessica ★★★★★

For the Reader

Dear Reader,

I'm thrilled that you took precious time out of your life to read my novel. Thank you. I hope you found it entertaining, engaging, and thought-provoking. If so, please consider writing a positive review on your favorite retail site. Five-star reviews have a huge impact on future sales. The review doesn't need to be long and detailed if you're more of a reader than a writer. As an author and a small businessman, competing against the big publishers, I greatly appreciate every reader, every review, and every referral.

If you're interested in receiving two of my novels for free and/or reading my other titles for free or discounted, go to the following link: www.PhilWBooks.com. You're probably thinking, *What's the catch?* There is no catch.

If you want to contact me, don't be bashful. I can be found at Phil@PhilWBooks.com. I do my best to respond to all emails.

Sincerely,
Phil M. Williams

Gratitude

I'd like to thank my wife for being my first reader, sounding board, and cheerleader. Without her support and unwavering belief in my skill as an author, I'm not sure I would have embarked on this career. I love you, Denise.

I'd also like to thank my editors. My developmental editor, Gary Smailes, did a fantastic job finding the holes in my plot and suggesting remedies. As always, my line editor, Denise Barker (not to be confused with my wife, Denise Williams), did a fantastic job making sure the manuscript was error-free. I love her comments and feedback.

Thank you to my mother-in-law, Joy, one of the best nurses on this planet. She is always gracious with her time and extremely knowledgeable about all things medical.

Thank you to my beta readers, Ray and Ann. They're my last defense against the dreaded typo. And thank you to you, the reader. Without you, I wouldn't have a career. As long as you keep reading, I'll keep writing.

www.ingramcontent.com/pod-product-compliance
Lightning Source LLC
Chambersburg PA
CBHW020626020726
47494CB00001B/69